THE DEATH
OF
KING ARTHUR

THE DEATH OF KING ARTHUR

Thomas Mallory's
La morte d'Arthur

A retelling by
PETER ACKROYD

ISIS
LARGE PRINT
Oxford

First published in Great Britain 2010
by
Penguin Classics
A member of the Penguin Group

Published in Large Print 2012 by ISIS Publishing Ltd.,
7 Centremead, Osney Mead, Oxford OX2 0ES
by arrangement with
Penguin Books Ltd.

British Library Cataloguing in Publication Data
Ackroyd, Peter, 1949–
    The death of King Arthur.
    1. Arthur, King - - Fiction.
    2. Camelot (Legendary place) - - Fiction.
    3. Arthurian romances.
    4. Large type books.
    I. Title
    823.9'2–dc23

ISBN 978–0–7531–8900–9 (hb)
ISBN 978–0–7531–8901–6 (pb)

Printed and bound in Great Britain by
T. J. International Ltd., Padstow, Cornwall

Contents

Introduction

Sir Thomas Malory came from a family steeped in the values and traditions of the chivalric code. His ancestors were "gentlemen that bear old arms", and their blood relationship with both the Normans and the Vikings suggests that they were sufficiently robust to do so. They had settled at Newbold Revell, in Warwickshire, and had managed to acquire vast estates throughout that county. As the inheritor of a name and domain, Malory himself was ineluctably drawn into the contests of the wider world.

He was born, in the first decade of the fifteenth century, at a time of great violence and uncertainty. Richard II had been deposed and murdered in 1400; his successor, Henry IV, was continually beset by all the confusion that surrounds any successful rebel. So the realm was disordered. This context of suspicion and almost continual violence can be glimpsed in the pages of *Le Morte d'Arthur*, most particularly in the conflict between Arthur and Mordred.

In this period of battles, and rumours of battles, there can be little doubt that Malory would have been acquainted with the great chivalric tales of the age. They were part of any gentleman's education. He would have heard readings of *Brut* and the alliterative *Morte Arthur*, those great clarion calls to the knightly spirit. He would also have attended jousts and tournaments, where the words of the ballads and epics took on a formidable and glamorous life. We may apply to the young Malory his own words, "This child will always be shooting or casting darts, and is glad to see battles and prancing knights."

He was also trained in all the feudal arts of chivalry — arts that included hunting, riding, hawking and archery. His earliest biographer, writing in the sixteenth century, described him as "outstanding from youth for his heroic spirit and for many remarkable gifts". At the age of fourteen, in fact, he went to war against France in the retinue of the Earl of Warwick. He served as a "lance" at Calais and four years later he was mentioned at a muster roll in Normandy. In that capacity he may have participated in the siege of Rouen, and was part of the army under the command of Henry V. It is perhaps not coincidental that Henry V was often compared to the legendary Arthur.

In 1433 or 1434, while he was in his early twenties, Malory inherited the familial estate; eight years later he became a knight, the goal of all chivalric ambition. He also became Justice of the Peace, Member of Parliament, and Sheriff of Warwickshire. These were all highly significant positions, emphasizing Malory's status at the very summit of the county hierarchy. To be sheriff was, indeed, to be the most important person of the shire. He was directly responsible to the king. The house at Newbold Revell was enlarged, no doubt because he was in the process of acquiring a wife and family. He had in any case a large household of servants, one of whom was a harpist whose task was to sing of love and chivalry as the wine was being passed around. He must also have owned a large collection of books, which in those days were locked and guarded as precious objects.

Yet he was in no sense the embodiment of literary or courtly virtue. At the beginning of the twentieth century an American scholar discovered a court record, partially burned, that accused Malory of rape, ambush, intent to kill, theft, extortion and gang violence. That is probably a good summary of the career of a fifteenth-century knight, even though it is not a model example of the ideal of medieval chivalry. In 1451 he was briefly imprisoned at Coleshill Manor, but escaped by swimming across the moat. It sounds a romantic feat, but at the time the moat was filled with sewage. Then he gathered up a motley army and attacked Coombe Abbey in his own county, from which place he stole money and valuables. He was taken into custody, and for the next eight years he was in and out of prison. He broke out of gaol in Colchester in 1454, while threatening his gaolers with an assortment of weapons. He was never formally put on trial, owing to the annoying inability of jurors to turn up on the appropriate occasions, and as a result he was often freed on bail. He spent a further period in Newgate, but the cause of his imprisonment is not known.

Life in prison was not necessarily as hard as it is in the twenty-first century. He had his own set of chambers, and was granted access to his family. He had enough money, too, to purchase the comforts of home. At the end of one of the Arthurian stories he refers to himself as "a knight presoner", so we know that he wrote at least part of *Le Morte d'Arthur* while incarcerated; this great epic may therefore be seen as a towering example of prison literature, to be compared to Bunyan's *The Pilgrim's Progress* and *The Consolations of Philosophy* by Boethius. The setting may also help to explain the tone of melancholy that seems to invade the narrative, a wistfulness combined with a dour sense of fate. The story of Arthur is accompanied by sensations of loss and transitoriness, as well as a note of stoic resignation, which may reflect the author's own experience.

The judicial pardon of Sir Thomas Malory was inscribed on an official roll in the autumn of 1462. He is mentioned in a list of knights about to march into Northumberland. He was by now an old, as well as an experienced, warrior. Then once more he disappears from the record until his death in the spring of 1471. It is not known how or where he died. He was buried in the Greyfriars Church by Newgate, however, and the proximity to that famous gaol suggests that he was once more a prisoner. The church and graveyard are now no more than ruins. But of course he left behind a greater monument. *Le Morte d'Arthur* was published by Caxton's press in the summer of 1485, and has been continually in print since that time.

Malory's work is suffused with the imperatives and rituals of the chivalric code, the important testament of military virtue that had first emerged in the twelfth century. King Arthur was supposed to fight, for example, and a warlike ruler was considered to be a good ruler. If God looked kindly upon a monarch, He would bequeath him success in battle. It was the law of life. It was one of the essential prerogatives, or duties, of sovereignty, reflecting a period in which warfare was endemic. Throughout Malory's narrative kings are constantly engaged in sieges and in battles. No land goes uncontested, and no crown is necessarily safe. So military valour was crucially important.

The medieval nobleman was trained in courage and prowess. The young squire, so noticeable a feature of Malory's adventures, was always a boy of noble birth. He was educated in a great household, where he served his master and was also taught the use of arms. His highest ideal was that of knighthood, preferably gained on the battlefield but acquired, as a rule, on reaching the age of twenty-one. It was, in one sense, another form of baptism. Before the honour was conferred upon him he took part in a ritual bath and repeated a vow of chastity; he fasted until nightfall, and then spent the night in prayer. At dawn he confessed his sins, attended mass and took Holy Communion. He then kneeled before his godfather and promised to obey the rules of knighthood and to protect the virtue of all women; he also declared that he "would speak the truth, succour the helpless and oppressed, and never turn back from an enemy". There were material, as well as spiritual, benefits to be gained from his new status. Henry II ordered that a knight arrested for debt should not be consigned to a common prison; his property could be sold to pay his debts, but his horse was protected from confiscation.

Chivalry can on one level be understood as the practice whereby the laws of honour supersede those of right or justice. There were elaborate laws of warfare, for example, that governed the conduct of sieges. There were also principles concerning the treatment of hostages, the respect for envoys, and the terms of truces. In warfare knights would spare the lives and privileges of other knights, while happily massacring the women and children among the local population. There are no tears shed in Malory's account for the fate of peasants or of shepherds. He is a frankly aristocratic writer without the sensibility of Chaucer or Langland.

That is also the context in which Malory's lavish description of jousts and tournaments is best understood. These were rituals of battle with their own codes and values. Originally they had been real conflicts, staged over a large area of ground, between trained bands of knights. They closely resembled actual battle, with the proviso that a dismounted knight had to retire from the field and give horse and armour to his combatant. By the fifteenth century they had become stage-managed jousts in which the principles of combat were demonstrated and in which ambitious young men could advertise their skills.

As the quest for the Holy Grail demonstrates, chivalry was closely bound with the ideals and aspirations of Christianity; it might be said to spring from the first crusades, in fact, when knights fought under the banner of the Cross against the heathen. The crusading knight would be expected to prepare himself with vigils, fasts and prayers. The forces of Christ were meant to be pilgrims as much as soldiers. There grew up cults of military saints, such as Saint George and Saint Victor, and the roles of knight and monk were combined in the religious orders of Templars and Hospitallers. A knight was meant to be chaste and pious; the model of knighthood was of course Sir Galahad, whose apotheosis is admirably described in Malory's account.

But chivalry was also associated with the code of courtly love that celebrated the female as the source of all virtue and honour. A knight fought for his lady; his love for her rendered him stronger and more courageous. Lancelot and Guinevere, Tristram and Isolde, are among the most famous lovers in literature; much of Malory's narrative is therefore devoted to them. Like the Platonic love of an earlier civilization — then generally between male and male — courtly love was a shadow or echo of heavenly harmony.

The two creeds of chivalry and courtly love are alike in being quite remote from the experience of life, especially for the period in which Malory was writing. In the fifteenth century the knights of England no longer played their old military role; they were now more likely to serve as members of parliament than as leaders in the field. Some of the sadness of Malory's account, therefore, may spring from the fact that he is celebrating a code of chivalry and courtly love at the very time they were being diminished.

In Malory's own account this great epic was composed from sundry "old books". These "old books" were made up of the *roman courtois* and the *roman d'aventures* that were so popular among the French nobility. In fact he had thoroughly digested the French prose romances concerning the adventures of Arthur, and had reworked them as a series of self-contained stories following the path of one knight or group of knights. He cut the theology, and generally curbed the excesses of the French originals. He is practical rather than theoretical or spiritual. Malory's brevity is in fact the essential engine of the plot, which turns upon sudden crises and arbitrary adventures; there are moments of dramatic speech rather than rambling interior monologues; there are incidents rather than well-formed characters. He then introduced these stories one after the other as if they were the organic elements of some total design, in the same fashion as the architecture of the English cathedrals.

As a result of Malory's plangent and often elaborate prose, the song of Arthur has never ended. *Le Morte d'Arthur* inspired both Milton and Dryden with dreams of Arthurian epic, and in the nineteenth century Tennyson revived the themes of Malory in *Idylls of the King.* William Morris wrote *The Defence of Guenevere,* and Algernon Swinburne composed *Tristram of Liones.* The Round Table was reconstituted in the libraries of nineteenth-century England.

Malory created for posterity the images of Lancelot and Guinevere, of Galahad and Gawain, of Tristram and Isolde, of Merlin the wily magician and of Arthur the once and future king. Indeed it was through the agency of *Le Morte d'Arthur* that Arthur took on a posthumous life in medieval histories. There is no evidence that such a monarch ever existed. There may have been a British warrior king who flourished in the late fifth century, and who won a victory against the English invaders at a place known only as Mons Badonicus, but there is no certainty on the matter. King Arthur may simply be a figment of the national imagination. Yet it is still a remarkable tribute to Malory's inventive genius that Arthur, and the Round Table, have found a secure and permanent place in the affections of the English-speaking people.

A Note on the Text

In my translation I have changed the name of the text from *Le Morte d'Arthur* to *The Death of King Arthur*; this gives a more accurate summary of its contents. I have tried my best to convert Malory's sonorous and exhilarating prose into a more contemporary idiom; this is a loose, rather than punctilious, translation. I have also chosen to abbreviate the narrative in pursuit of clarity and simplicity. I hope that by these means the essential story of Arthur and his knights emerges more clearly, and that the characters of Camelot are drawn more convincingly. Malory is often rambling and repetitive; much that would have amused and interested a medieval audience will not appeal to a modern readership. I have also quietly amended Malory's inconsistencies. Despite these alterations, I hope that I have been able to convey the majesty and pathos of the great original.

THE TALE OF
KING ARTHUR

Merlin

In the old wild days of the world there was a king of England known as Uther Pendragon; he was a dragon in wrath as well as in power. There were various regions in his kingdom, many of them warring one against another, and so it came about that one day he summoned a mighty duke to his court at Winchester. This nobleman was of Cornwall, and he was called Duke of Tintagel; he reigned over a western tribe from the fastness of his castle on the rocks, where he looked down upon the violent sea. Uther Pendragon asked the duke to bring with him to court his wife, Igraine, who had the reputation of being a great beauty. She was wise as well as beautiful, and it was said that she could read the secrets of any man's heart on the instant she looked at him.

When the duke and his wife were presented to the king, he rose from his throne and invited them forward with open arms. "Come," he said, "embrace me. This dragon will not bite." They were treated with all possible courtesy and honour by the whole court, but the lady Igraine had seen into the king's dark heart. She knew well enough that he wanted to violate her. He looked at her with lust and cunning. The moment came when he took her by the shoulders and whispered something in her ear. She shook her head, disgusted, and broke away from him. She went to her husband at once, and told him what had occurred. He was enraged, so angry that he smashed his fist against one of the tapestries that lined the wall of the great palace. "We were summoned here to be dishonoured," he said. "I will never submit to that. Pride is the essence of knighthood."

"We should take our horses," Igraine told him, "and ride out of here as soon as we can. I would be willing to ride all night." Even though night is an evil time they fled, turning their faces towards Tintagel. As soon as Pendragon knew of their departure he grew very angry. And, as the people of England knew well enough, the wrath of the king is death. He called together his council of nobles, and explained to them that he had been dishonoured by "that little duke who rules the little people of Cornwall".

One of his council suggested to him that he should call back the duke and his wife, under pain of his severe displeasure. Yet the duke's answer to the summons was swift. He would never allow his wife into the presence of the tyrant. Pendragon then grew more violent still. He sent him a sword that had been bent in the middle, as a sign of contempt. "Prepare yourself for war," he wrote. "Summon your servants. Protect your castles. Uther Pendragon is coming to destroy you. I will grind you to dust. I will split your wife with my spear."

Once the duke had received the broken sword and the letter, he wasted no time in calling for arms and reinforcements. He left his wife in the Castle of Tintagel, where the rocks and the waves might protect her, while he rode out to command the castle known as Terrible. It was truly mighty to behold, made of black granite and black marble, filled with many cunning passageways and secret doors where death and treachery were waiting for the unwary.

Pendragon marched out from his palace at Winchester and, with his great army, advanced into Cornwall. It was a desolate region, largely unknown to the rest of the country, where witches and warlocks were reported to have the mastery. Eventually he came to Castle Terrible, situated beside the confluence of two rivers, and proceeded to lay siege to it for fifty days and fifty nights. Much blood was shed, and many brave men lost their lives, in the skirmishes and sallies that sustained the siege.

But then Pendragon grew sick. His face was pale, and his eyes large. He could hardly draw breath, his heart was so weak. One of his lords, Ulfius, approached him as he lay sighing upon a bed of silk wrought with jewels in the form of stars. "Ah, king," he whispered, "you are suffering from some great distemper. Do you know anything that might have caused it?"

"The two greatest enemies of man, wrath and love, are now fighting over me. My wrath for the Duke of Cornwall consumes me. My love for his wife, Igraine, is destroying me. Where can I turn? To whom should I

5

pray? I know that I will die far from my family in this bitter land of Cornwall."

"There is one person who can save you, sire."

"Who is that?"

"Merlin. The great magician. He is the man who made the abbey church of Derby disappear into the earth. He will know how to heal you. He will find a cure."

"Bring him before me. Let him work his magic on my poor bones."

So Ulfius rode out, whispering the name of "Merlin" under his breath many times; he knew that the magician was aware of the secret life of all things, and would know that his name was being murmured in the wind. The birds, or the singing grasses, would tell him. As Ulfius rode on he suddenly encountered a beggar standing in the high road; the beggar wore a hood, and his back was turned to the knight. He seemed to be peering at something lying on the ground. "Move," Ulfius told him. "Get out of my way."

"Do you begrudge a poor man the space of a dusty road?" the beggar replied.

"Move on, or I will cut you with my sword. It is not right for a knight to argue with one such as you."

"Even if I know for whom you seek? Even if I know that your name is Ulfius?"

"Who are you?"

"I am the one you wish for. I am Merlin." He put out his hands, palms outward, and his beggar's clothes were transformed into robes of white satin. "I am the man of magic."

"Well met then."

"Tell Uther Pendragon that I will cure him of his sickness. There is one condition. He must grant me whatever I wish, without reluctance or hesitation. If he agrees, then I will fulfil all of his desires."

"I will tell him this as soon as I return to him. I am sure that he will keep any promise he makes to you."

"Good. The king will gain the object of his desire. I guarantee that. Now ride back to him. I will not be far behind you. I will never be far away."

In good spirits Ulfius galloped off and made his way to the king's pavilion, which had been erected in the field in front of Castle Terrible. He walked in and made reverence to Pendragon, who was still lying in his bed sick at heart. "I have found Merlin, lord king."

"Where is he?"

"He said that he will not be long, sir."

Here we will tell of the birth of King Arthur

There was a sound as of bird wings beating, and at that moment Merlin appeared at the entrance of the pavilion. Suddenly the magus was standing at the king's bedside. "Sir," Merlin said, "I know what is in your heart. I know your secrets. If you will swear to me on the honour of a true and anointed king that you will fulfil my desire, then you will have your wish."

"Bring me the Holy Book," Pendragon asked a courtier. Then he swore his oath upon it.

"This is my desire," Merlin said. "On the first night that you lie beside Igraine, you will conceive a child. I wish that child to be delivered to me the next day. I will raise it so that it will bring great worship and renown to you."

"I swear to do this," the king replied. "The child is yours."

"Then prepare yourself, sir king. This night you will lie with Igraine in the Castle of Tintagel. You will appear there in the shape of her husband, the duke; Sir Ulfius here will be changed into Sir Brastias, a knight of the duke's retinue, and I will become Sir Jordanus. Do not speak much to her but say you are sick. Then take her to bed. Do not stir from her side until I come to you on the following morning. Let us go now. We will ride out. Tintagel is only ten miles off." So the three of them mounted their horses and rode away.

The Duke of Cornwall, standing on the battlements, had seen them leaving; he had no idea where they were going, but he decided to take advantage of the king's absence. He issued with his warriors from the postern gate of the castle and attacked the besieging army. In the ensuing struggle he was slain. He was brought down by an arrow in his left eye, like a later king. He fell dead to the ground even before Pendragon had reached the Castle of Tintagel.

The scheme devised by Merlin worked. Uther Pendragon, in the shape of the Duke of Cornwall, lay that night with Igraine; three hours after the death of the duke, Pendragon begat upon her the babe that became known as Arthur. At the break of day Merlin came to the bedside and advised the king to depart; so the king kissed Igraine, and took his leave of her. When she learned later that her husband had died in battle, hours before the arrival of the one who had assumed his form, she wondered who had lain beside her in the likeness of her lord. But she mourned in private, and kept silent. She was discreet.

The barons of the kingdom now agreed one with another that the king should reach an accord with the noble lady Igraine. Sir Ulfius was chosen to make a treaty between them. "This is a pact that will please all of us," Ulfius said. "She is a fair lady and our king is a fine warrior. Happiness and prosperity will spring from the union between them."

So they approached their sovereign with the plan, and of course he gave his assent at once. Secretly he was delighted. On a bright morning later that month, Uther Pendragon and Igraine were married with much mirth and rejoicing. They were conveyed in a chariot to the great stone circle on the plain of Salisbury, where the kings of England were always wed, and the people gathered around them with sprigs of laurel newly cut.

At the same time the king ordained that the new queen's daughters should also be wed. King Lot of Lowthean and Orkney married Morgause, and from their union came Gawain. King Nentres of the land of Garlot wed Elaine. Igraine's third daughter, Morgan le Fay, was put into a nunnery where she learned the mysteries of the magic stone as well as other secret arts. In later years Morgan le Fay was married to King Uriens of the land of Gore; they bore a son who became known as Sir Uwain of the White Hands. Much trouble was being stored for the future of the kingdom.

Day by day Igraine grew greater with child. Uther lay with her one night and asked her, on the faith she owed to him, whose offspring it was. She was too ashamed to answer. "Do not be dismayed," he told her. "Tell me the truth. I shall love you all the more for your honesty."

"I will speak the truth to you, my lord. On the night that my husband died a stranger came to Tintagel in his shape; he had the same speech, and the same countenance, as the duke. There were two companions with him, whom I thought to be Sir Brastias and Sir Jordanus. So I was deceived. I did my duty, and lay beside him in our bed. I swear to God that, on the same night, this child was conceived."

"I know, sweet wife, that you are speaking the truth. It was I who came to the castle. I entered your bed. I am the father of this child." Then he told her of the magic of Merlin, and she marvelled at it. But she was overjoyed, too, that Uther Pendragon was the sire of her offspring.

Merlin came to the king a little while later. "Sire," he said, "you must keep your promise. You must hand the child to me."

"If that is your wish, then so be it."

"I know a lord in your land who is true and faithful. His name is Sir Hector, and he holds territories in England and in Wales. I have chosen him to take care of your child. He will guard it well. Send for this lord, sir, and ask him to bring up your child in love and honour; let his wife nourish your baby as her own. When the child is born, bring it to me unbaptized at the postern gate here."

All was done as Merlin had ordained. Sir Hector came to court and, having pledged faith to the king, consented to raise Uther Pendragon's child as his own. The king rewarded him with many gifts. When Igraine was delivered of her baby it was wrapped in cloth of gold; the king then ordered two lords and two ladies to take it to "whatever poor man you find at the postern gate of the castle. Ask no questions of him." So the child was carried to Merlin, who with his finger traced the secret sign on the baby's forehead. Then he took the boy to Sir Hector's castle, where he was baptized by a priest and given the name of Arthur. And Arthur was nourished by Hector's wife.

Here we will tell of the sword in the stone

Two years later, Uther Pendragon suffered a severe illness. Even as he lay upon his sickbed, sighing, his enemies attacked his kingdom and devastated his armies. "Sir king," Merlin said to him, "you must not lie here. You must advance into battle, even if you are carried in a litter. The king is the strength of the land. You will never get the better of your enemies unless you go against them in person. Only then will you gain the victory."

"I will do as you wish," the king replied. "I know that your spells will surround me."

The king's men carried him in a litter, at the head of a great host, and at Saint Alban's he won a great victory over his enemies from the North. His armies slew many people, and put the rest to flight. Uther Pendragon returned to Winchester in triumph, the banners of battle raised high.

But the sickness of the king returned, worse than before, and he lay for three days and three nights without speaking. The barons of the realm were greatly alarmed, and asked Merlin for his advice. "There is no remedy," the magician said, "God's will be done. But I tell you this. Assemble before the king tomorrow. I will make sure that he speaks to you."

So the barons came together on the following morning, in the presence of their king, and Merlin spoke aloud to Uther Pendragon. "Sir," he said to him, "is it your will that your son, Arthur, be anointed as king after your death?"

The king turned to him and, in hearing of them all, responded, "I give him the blessing of Almighty God, and I grant him mine. May he be crowned king in my place, and I entreat him to pray for my soul when I have been laid to rest." And, with those words, he died. He was buried soon after, with all the ceremony of state, within the great circle of stone. One thousand men and one thousand women grieved aloud, sending many shrieks and laments into the sky; beacons were lit throughout the land, to mark his passing.

There then followed a period of disturbance and danger. There were many lords in this land who longed to be king, and who were prepared to do battle for the crown of England. So Merlin visited the Archbishop of Canterbury. "Call together all the nobles and knights of the realm to London, reverend sir," he said to him. "Tell them to assemble in the city by Christmas Day, on pain of excommunication. They will witness a miracle, I assure you of that. The king of the universe will on that day declare who is to be king of the realm." So the archbishop sent his summons, and the magnates set out for the city in the hope that they might see their new sovereign. They prayed and confessed themselves on their journey, so that they might be all the more pure.

In the great church of London — whether it was the Abbey or Saint Paul's, I do not know — all the estates of the realm were gathered on Christmas Day. They assembled here before dawn, and heard matins as well as the first mass. When they walked out into the churchyard, however, they witnessed a wonder. There was a sound as of thunder and a great slab of stone, some four feet square, hovered above their heads before landing against the wall of the church; it was made of marble and, in the middle of it, was a steel anvil which held a sword. There were letters written upon the side of the sword, stating that WHOEVER PULLS OUT THIS SWORD FROM THE STONE AND ANVIL WILL RIGHTLY BE KING OF ALL ENGLAND. There was much astonishment, and the excited noise of the crowd could be heard inside the church.

The archbishop came outside to find the cause of the commotion. When he saw the sword and the stone, he bowed his head and whispered some words. "I command you all," he said, "to return to the church and pray. No man may touch this sword until the end of the high mass."

When the service was over, the great ones of the land hurried into the churchyard. They saw the stone, and the writing inscribed upon it. Those who wished to be king tried to lift the sword from the anvil, but they could by no means move it.

"The man is not here who can lift the sword," the archbishop said. "Yet it is my belief that God will make him known to us. In the meantime let ten knights guard the stone. Then send out a proclamation that all who seek to rule this realm should travel to this place and try their fortune."

Here we will tell of Arthur and the stone

On New Year's Day a great joust was held on the smooth plain of Smithfield, just outside of the walls of the city. It so happened that Sir Hector and his son, Sir Kay, came forth to take part in the tournament; with them, too, was Arthur, who had become Hector's adopted child. As they rode towards Smithfield, Kay realized that he had left his sword at his father's lodgings. So he asked Arthur to ride back and retrieve it for him.

"Of course, brother. I will be back in a moment." When he arrived at the house he found that all the servants had gone to the joust, and that the doors were locked. In great annoyance he said to himself, "I will ride into the churchyard, and take the sword that is sticking in the stone. My brother must not be

14

without his weapon on this day." He came into the churchyard, tied his horse to the stile, and walked into the tent where the ten knights were supposed to watch over the stone. But they, too, had gone to the joust.

So he went over to the stone and, taking the hilt with both hands, lightly and easily took out the sword. Then he galloped back to Smithfield and gave the sword to Sir Kay.

As soon as Sir Kay saw it, he knew what it was and from where it had come. So he rode over to Sir Hector. "Father," he said, "I have here the sacred sword. I am meant to be sovereign."

Hector looked at the sword, and then at his son. "Come with me," he told him. With Arthur beside them they rode back to the church and Hector, taking his son up to the altar, made him swear on oath where he had obtained the sword.

"Sir," Kay said, "Arthur gave it to me."

Hector turned to Arthur. "Where did you get this sword?"

"I will tell you, sir. I went back to our lodgings to find Sir Kay's sword, but there was no one there. So I came to the churchyard here, and pulled the sword from the stone. It was easy."

"There were no knights here?"

"None."

"Arthur," Hector said, "I understand now that you must become king of this land."

"Me? Why?"

"It has been ordained by God that the one who takes up this sword will reign over us. Let me see whether you can replace the sword and then remove it again."

"That will not be hard."

So Arthur put the sword back in the stone. Then Sir Hector tried to take out the weapon, but it would not be moved. Sir Kay tried, too, but the sword could not be dislodged from the stone. "Now you try," Hector said to Arthur.

Arthur stepped forward and with the greatest ease withdrew the sword. At once Sir Hector and Sir Kay kneeled down before him. "What is the matter?" he asked them. "Why are you kneeling before me? You are my father and brother."

"My lord Arthur," Sir Hector replied, "it is not so. I never was your father. I am not of your blood. But I did not know till now the height of your lineage." Then he told Arthur the story of Merlin's commission to him. The young man wept when he understood that he was not Hector's real son.

"Sir," Hector said to him, "will you be my good and gracious lord when you become king?"

"Of course. Otherwise I would be greatly to blame. You are the man in the world to whom I owe the most. Your wife — my good mother, or so I thought — has nourished me and kept me from my earliest days. If it is true that I am destined to be king, as you say, then you may ask of me anything you wish. I will not fail you, so help me God."

"Sir," Hector replied, "I will ask only one thing of you. Will you make your foster-brother, Sir Kay, the steward of all your lands?"

"Gladly. It shall be done. And I swear to you that no other man shall hold that office as long as Sir Kay lives."

The three men then visited the archbishop, and told him the story of the sword. The barons assembled in the churchyard some days later, but none of them could remove the sword from the stone; then, in front of them all, Arthur achieved this easily. Many lords grew angry with him then, and declared that they would not be ruled by one who could boast no high birth. "This boy is more slender than my sword," one of them said. "How can he govern us?" So the decision was deferred until the day of Candlemas, at the beginning of February, and the archbishop ordered that the sword be watched and defended by the same ten knights as before.

At Candlemas the lords gathered together again, yet not one of them could gain the sword. Arthur stepped forward, and raised the weapon in his hand. But the lords wished to delay their decision once more, and put off the day until Easter; then they moved it again to Pentecost. Meanwhile the archbishop guarded Arthur from all harm, and placed around him such gallant knights as Sir Baudwin and Sir Ulfius. At Pentecost the magnates met again and all essayed the sword, but none of them could remove it. Only Arthur could perform the feat.

So the people of London set up a great cry. "We will have Arthur to be sovereign over us. There must be no more delay! The day has come. God's will be done!"

All the people, rich and poor, then kneeled before him, denouncing their own delay in doing homage to him. Arthur declared that he had forgiven them and, taking the sword in both hands, he placed it upon the altar. Then he was dubbed the first knight of the kingdom.

The coronation followed soon after. He was anointed to the sound of drums and trumpets, and the crown was raised three times above his head. The nobles cried out their allegiance to him, brandishing their swords and their spears. Arthur rose from the throne with his sceptre in his hand; he swore to be a true king, and to do justice to them all the days of his life. Then many came forward with complaints of the wrongs done to them since the death of Uther Pendragon, and Arthur promised to correct these wrongs. The king made Sir Kay steward of all England, as he had promised, and distributed the offices of state to his household knights. He made Sir Brastias warden of the North, for example, where the enemies of the realm wandered in the wild lands beyond the River Trent.

Here we will tell of the first use of the sword

After the coronation Arthur removed from London to Wales, and summoned a host to meet him at Caerleon-upon-Usk on the first anniversary of his coronation. Here was held a great feast to which he

18

invited many kings with their warriors. King Lot of Orkney came with five hundred knights, while King Uriens of Gore arrived with four hundred; the King of Scotland, although still a young man, rode to Wales with six hundred horsemen.

Arthur was pleased by their arrival, since he believed that they had come to greet and to honour him. So he sent them many rich gifts. But they rejected them, and rebuked the messengers who had brought them. "We do not hold him in worship," they said. "We will not accept gifts from a beardless boy of low blood. We have come with our swords, and will give him fierce strokes in return. We have come to drive him out. It is past all sadness that such an illustrious realm should be ruled by a boy."

So the messengers returned, and repeated these words to Arthur. On the advice of his barons the king then called for five hundred knights, and withdrew to a high tower that was well defended. The other kings then laid siege to it. The tower became known as Arthur's Tower, and can still be visited. There are some who say that, on moonlit nights, they can see the ghosts of warriors defending it.

Within fifteen days the magician, Merlin, came to Caerleon-upon-Usk, He was well known to the kings who besieged Arthur, and they gathered around him. "Tell us this, Merlin," King Lot asked him. "For what reason has that boy, Arthur, been made your king?"

"I shall tell you the reason, sir. He is the son of Uther Pendragon, begotten on Igraine."

"Then he is a bastard," Uriens replied.

"Not so, sir. He was begotten three hours after the death of Igraine's first husband, and within thirteen days she was married to Uther Pendragon. So by the laws of the realm Arthur is no bastard. Say what you will. He does not yet know of his high birth. I have kept this secret from him for now. But this boy will be king. He will overcome all of his enemies and rule over the whole realm. He will conquer Ireland, and even more distant regions."

Some of the kings marvelled at Merlin's words, and judged that he had spoken the truth. Others laughed at him, and called him "warlock" or worse. But they agreed among themselves that Arthur should be given safe passage to leave the tower and to speak with them. So Merlin climbed the high tower and told him that he might leave without harm. "Fear nothing," he said. "They cannot hurt you. Address them as their lord and leader. You will overcome them all, whether they like it or not. The force of the world is with you."

Arthur went out to them, with a garment of chain mail under his tunic, and among his companions were the Archbishop of Canterbury, Sir Baudwin of Britain, Sir Kay and Sir Brastias. These were all good and gallant men. There was no peace between the opposing parties, and the kings burst out in pride and anger. Arthur answered their taunts, and told them that one day they would bow down before him. So they left in rage, bidding him good day.

"And good day," he replied, "to you."

He returned to the tower, where he and his knights waited with weapons drawn.

Then Merlin went up to the kings. "Why do you carry on this siege?" he asked them. "You will not be successful. Not even if you had ten times as many men."

"Why should we listen to the words of a magician, a reader of dreams?" King Lot responded.

Merlin gave him no answer but made his way to King Arthur. "Sire," he said, "fight with good spirit."

"My spirits are high," Arthur replied. "Three hundred of the kings' men have come over to my side."

"I will give you one piece of advice. Use your old sword in battle. Do not use the sword you lifted from the stone, until you believe that you may be losing the fight. Only then may you draw it."

So Arthur and his knights rode out and descended upon the kings. They went among them with their spears and lances, wreaking havoc upon them. Arthur was always at the front of the battle, beating back the foe. But then King Lot galloped up from the rear with his five hundred knights and fell upon Arthur. Arthur turned and twisted his sword this way and that way, cutting down the knights who attacked him, but then his horse was killed beneath him. King Lot knocked him to the ground, but four of his knights rescued him and remounted him on a fresh horse. Arthur knew it was time. He drew out the sword that he had lifted from the stone. It was so bright that it gave out a light like thirty burning brands, and its rays seemed to pierce the sky. Once he had borne it aloft, he carved it through the ranks of the kings. The common people of Caerleon were much comforted by this, and taking up clubs and staves they ran among the ranks of the enemy. The knights formed a defensive circle, with their kings in the centre, but then they broke and fled from the field. Arthur had won his first battle.

Here we will tell of Arthur's doleful dream

While Arthur resided at Caerlon, King Lot of Orkney, convinced of his true royalty, sent his wife, Morgause, to pay homage; a large retinue travelled with her, including her four sons, who were named Gawain, Gaheris, Agravain and Gareth. She was a beautiful woman still, and Arthur bore great love and desire for her. She consented to share his bed, and he begat upon her a child who was named Mordred. He did not realize that he had in fact slept with his half-sister. From this much woe would spring.

After the lady and her sons had left his court, he was disturbed by a dreadful dream. He dreamed that dragons and serpents had invaded his land; they killed and devoured all of his people before pursuing him. He fought with them and was badly wounded, but after a bitter battle he got the better of them.

Arthur awoke from this dream in much fear and, to ease his mind, he arranged that he and his chosen knights should go hunting. When he came into the forest, the king saw a great hart in front of him. "I will chase you down!" he cried out and at once rode off in pursuit. There were times when he might have come close to the beast and killed it, but the hart always managed to flee to another part of the wood. Arthur rode so long and so hard that his horse failed beneath him, and a yeoman was obliged to fetch another for him.

In his dismay at the change of his horse Arthur sat down beside a natural spring. Then all at once he thought that he heard a great noise, as of thirty hounds barking, and to his horror he saw a hideous beast coming towards him. It seemed to be part dog and part lion, part horse and part serpent. The beast did not seem to notice the king, but instead went to the spring and drank from it. The noise of the hounds came from his belly and the barking ceased only when he drank. Whereupon the beast made its way into the bushes, the noise of barking all about him, and vanished from sight. Arthur marvelled at this; he grew thoughtful, and then he fell asleep by the spring.

He was roused by the approach of a knight. "Knight full of thought and sleep," the man said, "have you seen a strong and strange beast pass this way?"

"Such a one I have seen. It must have gone more than two miles by now. What do you want with it?"

"I have followed it for a long time. I have lost my horse. I wish to God I could find another steed to finish my quest."

At that moment the yeoman came up with Arthur's fresh horse. The knight then pleaded with the king to give it up to him. "I am King Pellinor, and it is my fate to follow this beast or be stripped of my strength. I have been in pursuit of it for this past year."

"Leave your pursuit," Arthur urged him. "Let me take on the quest. I will ride after the beast for another twelve months."

23

"You are a fool to speak so. Only I, or my next of kin, can catch and kill this creature. If I should die, Sir Palomides will follow me." With that he leaped into the saddle of Arthur's horse. "Thank you for your help," he said. "I must make haste. By the way, this horse is now mine."

"You may take the horse by force," Arthur replied. "But I wish that I had the chance to prove who is most worthy of the chase."

King Pellinor laughed. "When you want to find me," he said, "look for me here beside the spring. I will not be long in coming." Then he rode off.

Arthur was startled at this sudden turn of events, and ordered his men to bring him another horse. Then Merlin approached him, in the guise of a fourteen-year-old boy, and asked him why he was so pensive.

"I have good reason," the king told him. "I have just seen the greatest wonder."

"I know that," Merlin replied, "just as I know all of your secret thoughts. Brooding will do you no good, Arthur. I know who you are, you see. You are the child of Uther Pendragon and Igraine."

"You are lying to me, boy. You are too young to have known of these things."

"I understand the truth better than you or any other man."

"I do not believe you." Arthur was angry with the boy but, before he could berate him, the child ran off into the wood.

Then came Merlin again in the guise of an old man. "Why are you looking so stern?" he asked the king.

"I have every reason. I have just spoken to a child who told me of things that he could not have known. He never knew my father."

"The boy spoke the truth to you," Merlin said. "He would have told you other things, if you had not scared him away. He would have told you that God is displeased with you for sleeping with your half-sister Morgause. On her you have begotten a child who will one day destroy you and all of your knights."

"What is his name?"

"I cannot tell you. It lies in a dark place."

"Who are you? Why do you tell me this?"

"I am Merlin, my lord. I came to you in the likeness of the child."

"You amaze me once more, Merlin. But why do you tell me of my death?"

"It is God's will. You must be punished for your wicked deeds in this world. Yet it is I who should be downcast. You will have an honourable funeral. As for me, I will be buried alive."

The king's attendants then brought up two horses, upon which Arthur and Merlin rode back to Caerleon. When they reached the court the king asked Hector and Ulfius how he was begotten. They told him that he was the child of Uther and Igraine.

"So Merlin has told me. But now summon my mother. If she tells me the same story, I will believe it."

So in all haste the queen was sent for. She brought with her Morgan le Fay, her daughter, and a great banquet was held for them. But then Sir Ulfius rose and, in the hearing of all the guests, he rebuked Igraine. "You are false," he said to her. "You are a foul traitor."

"Beware!" Arthur cried out. "These are dangerous words!"

"Sir," Ulfius replied, "I am well aware of what I say and what I know. If she had told the court of your birth, and your upbringing, you would have been hailed as king. You would never have been forced to go to war. If the lords of this land had known whose son you were, they would have submitted to you without a struggle. But this lady kept her silence and so led you into great perils. That is why I accuse her of treason. If anyone dares to disagree with me, I am ready for trial by combat."

Igraine rose to reply. "I am a woman, and therefore I cannot fight you. But is there no one here ready to defend me and save me from dishonour? I can only tell you all the truth. Merlin knows well enough that Uther Pendragon came to me at the Castle of Tintagel, and there lay with me in the guise of my lord the duke, who had died in battle three hours before. Merlin also knows that I married Uther after thirteen days and that, when the child was born, it was given up to the magician himself. I never knew where the child had gone, or what name had been granted to him."

Then Sir Ulfius turned to Merlin. "You are more to blame than the queen," he said.

Arthur took Merlin by the hand. "Is this lady truly my mother?" he asked.

"Yes, sire, she is."

26

Then Sir Hector stepped forward, and explained how he had fostered the child.

Arthur then embraced Igraine; mother and son wept. The king ordered a great feast, in celebration, that lasted eight days.

Here we will tell of Arthur's battle
in the enchanted wood

One day there came into court a young squire, leading a knight on horseback who had been mortally wounded. He hung down from his saddle in the last agony of death. The squire told the king and his courtiers that his master, whose name was Sir Miles, had been attacked by King Pellinor, who had raised his pavilion beside a spring in the forest. It was Pellinor who pursued the beast of strange sounds. "I beseech you, sire," the squire said to Arthur, "please bury my master. And I beg you, also, to send out a knight to avenge his death."

The news of the death led to great clamour, and all the knights gave their advice. One young squire then came forward. His name was Griflet, and he was the same age as Arthur. "I ask you, sir," he said to the king, "for the sake of the service I have done you, raise me to the order of knighthood. Let me ride out to the spring and meet King Pellinor."

"It would be a pity," Merlin murmured to the king, "to lose this young man. He will make a good knight one day, and he will be loyal to you. Pellinor is one of the strongest and bravest of all warriors. Griflet will be in great peril."

But Arthur ignored him. "Very well," he said, "I will make you a knight, if you so wish it." So he dubbed him there and then with his sword. "Now, you must pledge me your word on one thing."

"What is it, sire?"

"You must promise me that, after one joust, you will join in no more contest. Whether you be on foot or on horseback, you will return here without more fighting."

"I promise you, my lord king."

So Griflet took up his shield and spear, and galloped into the wood. When he came up to the spring he saw a richly painted pavilion; beside it was a horse, well saddled and bridled, and on a tree was hanging a shield decorated with all manner of devices. Griflet struck the shield with his spear, and knocked it to the ground.

The king came out at once from the pavilion. "Fair knight," he said, "why did you strike down my shield?"

"I wish to joust with you."

"You had better not do that," the king replied. "You are still young. Your might will be no match for mine."

"No matter. I wish to joust with you."

"Since you are so sure of yourself, I have no alternative but to fight. From where do you come?"

"From the court of King Arthur."

So the two warriors fought against each other. Their battle was hard and fierce; King Pellinor broke the shield of Griflet and, smashing the spear, laid Griflet low upon the ground with a wide wound in his side.

28

When the king saw him fall to the earth, he dismounted and ran over to him. He feared that the young man was dead, but saw with relief that he was slowly beginning to recover. He placed him on his horse, invoking God's blessing. "He has a mighty heart," he said to himself. "If he lives, he will prove to be a great warrior." So Griflet went back to Arthur's court, where he was tended by doctors and was healed.

Then there came into the court twelve wise and aged knights, sent to England by the Emperor of Rome. As soon as they came into Arthur's presence they asked that tribute be paid to their master. "Or else," one of them said, "he will lay waste to you and all of your land."

"Well," the king replied, "you may speak with impunity as ambassadors. But I tell you this. Under other circumstances your words would have meant death. I owe your emperor no tribute. The only thing I will offer him is a sharp sword or a sharp spear in the field of battle. May that day come soon!"

So the twelve knights left in a rage. Arthur was angry at their presumption. But he was still more angered at King Pellinor for wounding Sir Griflet. "Get my horse and armour ready," he told his chamberlain. "I have work to do in the wood."

On the following day he was armed and mounted outside the city, for the sake of secrecy, and then rode off alone towards the spring. As he made his way he saw Merlin being chased by three ruffians along a woodland path. So he raised his sword and, charging them, called out, "Flee, churls!" Which is, of course, what they did.

"Ah, Merlin," Arthur said. "If I had not chanced upon you here, you would have been killed."

"Not so, sire. I could have saved myself at any moment. You are in fact nearer to death than I am. You are about to meet a mortal foe. And God is not your friend."

They went on their way, talking, until they came up to the spring and the bright pavilion where King Pellinor sat fully armed in a chair of gold. "Sir knight," Arthur asked him, "why do you sit here challenging every knight that passes this way? That is not a good custom."

"I have followed this custom for a long time. If you wish to amend it, then you must fight me to the finish."

"I will amend it."

"I will defend it."

They prepared themselves for battle. They both brought out their spears and rode against each other so hard that their weapons were shattered in their hands. Then Arthur raised his sword.

"No swords," King Pellinor said. "We should fight only with spears."

"I have none left," Arthur told him.

"My squire will bring one for both of us." The squire brought out two sharp spears, and each warrior chose between them. Once again they were so furious in fighting that these spears were shattered. Arthur put his hand on his sword.

30

"Not so!" Pellinor called out to him. "You are the finest jouster I have ever known. For the sake of the high Order of Knighthood, we must still ride against each other with spears." So his squire brought them two more, and they resumed their battle. In the course of it, King Pellinor proved so strong that Arthur fell to the ground. But he was still eager to continue the contest and now, on foot, he was able to use his sword. "I will test you now," he said to King Pellinor.

Pellinor dismounted, and pulled out his own sword. They fell upon each other like rams in conflict, and by dint of hard blows much blood was spilled. The part of the forest in which they fought was covered in gore. When their strength ebbed they rested, and then they clashed swords again. Pellinor struck hard, after many hours of fighting, and dashed Arthur's sword to pieces. "Now," he said, "you are in my power. I can slay you or save you. So yield to me now, or else face certain death."

"As to that," Arthur replied, "death is welcome to me. I will never surrender." The king then leaped at Pellinor and caught him by the waist, throwing him to the ground and taking off his helmet. They wrestled briefly, but Pellinor was a man of great might. He pinned Arthur down, and was about to smite off his head when Merlin rushed over.

"Knight," he said, "hold your hand. If you slay this man you will endanger the whole kingdom. He is of more worship than you know."

"What? Who is he?"

"He is Arthur."

Pellinor was still ready to kill him, and raised his sword. But Merlin cast an enchantment on him, and the warrior fell to the ground in a great sleep. Then the magician took up his king and rode away with him on Pellinor's horse. "What have you done?" Arthur asked him. "Have you killed this man with your craft? He was a noble knight. I would rather have lost my land than that he should lose his life."

"Have no fear," Merlin replied. "He is in better health than you. He will awake within the hour. I told you of his fearlessness and strength. If I had not come to your aid, you would now be lying dead. But in time to come he will do you good service. His name is King Pellinor. He will sire two sons, Percival and Lamorak, who will surpass all other knights living. He will also tell you the name of the child your half-sister will bear, and who will be the bane of your kingdom."

Here we will tell of the Lady of the Lake

The king and Merlin made their way to a hermitage, where there dwelled a skilful doctor. This man tended Arthur's wounds with herbs that grew around the hermitage, and within three days they were healed.

Then Arthur and Merlin rode off. "I am the shadow of myself," the king said. "I have no sword."

"Do not concern yourself. A sword will be found for you soon enough."

So they rode until they came to a fair lake with placid waters. "Look," Merlin said. "There is your sword." And, at that moment, from the surface of the water there emerged an arm clothed in white that in its hand held a shining sword. The air was filled with sweet sounds, and the light from the sword suffused the whole lake. Then Arthur saw a lady sailing towards him in a dark boat; she was wearing a black cape, and her hair was covered with a hood. "This is the Lady of the Lake," Merlin told him. "She lives in a great palace within a cavern. Speak graciously to her, and she will give you the sword."

The lady came up to the shore and greeted the king with a deep bow. He saluted her in turn. "Fair lady," he said, "whose sword is that, being held above the water? I wish that it were mine."

"Arthur," she replied, "the sword is mine. But if you will present me with a gift, for which I will ask you soon, then I will give the sword to you."

"What is this gift you desire? It will be yours."

"Go into the barge over there. Row yourself to the sword, and take it with its scabbard out of the water. I will ask you for my gift when the time comes."

Arthur and Merlin dismounted from their horses, tied them to two trees, and then climbed aboard the barge. When they came up to the sword the king took it by its handle and lifted it from the water. Then the arm and the hand disappeared into the lake.

So they came back to the shore, and rode off. "Which is finer," Merlin asked him, "the sword or the scabbard?"

"The sword."

"Now there you are wrong. The scabbard is worth ten times more than the sword. I will tell you the reason. While you have the scabbard about you, you will never lose a drop of blood. Keep it beside you. Even when badly wounded, you will be safe."

They returned to Caerleon, where the knights welcomed them with great joy. When the men heard of the adventures of Arthur, they wondered why he had put himself in such jeopardy. But the wiser among them realized that it was good to serve such a king, who put himself at the same risk as his warriors.

Here we will tell of a dark deed

Soon after this adventure Arthur called for the gathering of all noble children born on the first day of May; that was the day, according to Merlin, when the future destroyer of the king and of his kingdom had been born to his half-sister. The king was determined to act on this prophecy. So the children of lords and knights were yielded up to him, on pain of death, among them the child named Mordred, who was sent by the wife of King Lot.

Then Arthur ordered that all these infants should be embarked on a ship and left to the mercy of the sea; but by the fortune of the winds and the waves this sad ship was wrecked on the cliffs near a castle. Most of the children were drowned but Mordred himself was saved; he was fostered by a good man of the country, and was brought to Arthur's court at the age of fourteen. This story is yet to be told.

Many of the lords of the realm were angry at the loss of their children, but for the most part they blamed Merlin rather than Arthur. Yet, for fear and dread of their sovereign, they said and did nothing. An evil world had been born.

The Knight with the Two Swords

After the death of Uther Pendragon, as we have written, Arthur became sovereign of England. Yet this was not accomplished without a struggle, because there were many kings residing upon the land who fought one with another and aspired to become leader of the whole country. One day, when the court was at Winchester, Arthur was told that King Rience of North Wales had invaded the kingdom; he was laying waste the realm, and killing the people.

"If this report is true," Arthur said, "we must launch our power against him and lay him waste."

"It is true," one of his knights told him. "I have seen his army."

"Then the moment has come to destroy him before he reaches further."

So Arthur called all of his warriors, and lords, and knights, to a general council at the castle called Camelot. In those far-off days Winchester itself was known as Camelot. It was a blessed city.

Wherein Sir Balin wins a sword

When the king was comfortably lodged there, in the company of all his kin, there came to him a lady who had been sent by the great Lady Lile of the enchanted island of Avalon. She said that she bore with her a message from that lady. Then she let her mantle fall, and revealed a noble sword strapped to her side.

"Fair lady," the king said to her, "why do you wear such a weapon? It is not fit for a female to carry a sword."

"I carry this sword to my shame, sire," she replied. "It brings me sorrow. But it can be taken only by a knight of absolute truth and valour. Only he will be able to lift it from its sheath. If a knight of these virtues stands before me, I will be saved. I travelled to the court of King Rience, where I was told by report that many good knights were gathered, but not one of them could take out this sword."

"This is a marvel," the king said. "I will try myself to take it. I may not be the greatest and most valiant of all knights, but I will set an example to everyone else here."

He put his hand around the hilt of the sword, but however hard he tried he could not lift it. "Sire," the lady said, "there is no need to struggle with it. He that is destined to take it needs to use little strength."

"You speak the truth," Arthur told her. "Now come up, all the rest of you. Try your skill."

The lady then turned to them. "But take care that you are not tainted by treachery or any other fault. The knight who removes this sword must be free of all sin." So most of the knights of the Round Table tried to lift the sword, but none of them succeeded. At that point the lady wailed in sorrow. "I had hoped," she said, "that at this court I would find a faithful knight filled with virtue."

"I swear in God's name," Arthur told her, "that the knights of my court are as good as any others in the world. But it is not in their destiny to help you. I am sorry. I beg your forgiveness."

It so happened that in Arthur's company that day was a poor knight who had been held prisoner in London for half a year after he had killed a cousin of the king in open combat. His name was Sir Balin. He had been released from prison, and had travelled secretly to the court to restore his fortunes. He had seen the failure of the other knights to remove the sword from its sheath, and he believed that he could succeed in the task. But he was so poor and so piteously arrayed that he dared not put himself forward. Yet he knew in his heart that he could do it. So, just as the lady was departing, Balin called to her, "Good lady, I beg you to let me try to lift the sword. I may seem poor to you, but I will prove that I can assist you."

The lady saw that he was a good-looking man, but she believed that his outward show of poverty meant that he had committed some villainy in the past. "Do not put yourself to any trouble," she told him. "What makes you believe that you can succeed where the

38

others have proved unable to do so? You do not look like a fortunate knight."

"Ah, lady, fine clothes do not make an honest man. I have within me that which passes show. I have strength and sincerity. Many good knights go through the world unknown."

"You speak the truth, sir. So. Try your strength."

Sir Balin took the hilt, and drew out the sword without any difficulty. The king and the court looked on in astonishment, but the bitter envy of other knights was thereby aroused by his triumph.

"You have succeeded," the lady said. "You are the most virtuous of all knights, free of the vices of felony or treason. You will achieve many wonderful feats in the course of your life. Now, gentle and courteous knight, give me back the sword."

"Oh no, dear lady. I have earned the right to keep it. I will fight anyone who tries to take it from me."

"Well," she said, "this is not wise of you. I tell you this. With this sword you will slay your best friend. With its blade you will cut down the man whom you most love in the world. This sword will bring your ruin."

"I will take the chance. I will abide by God's will. But I shall not surrender it to any man."

"You will repent of this very shortly," she replied. "I am sorrowful for your sake, not for mine. It is a great pity that you will not be persuaded." With that she left the court, weeping, while Balin called for his horse and armour.

"Why are you leaving us?" Arthur asked him. "I suppose that you are displeased with me for showing you some unkindness before. But lay no blame at my door. I was not told the truth about you. I did not know that you are a knight of valour and virtue. So stay with us. If you remain at court, I will advance you through the ranks of the knights."

"God thank you, sire, for your goodwill towards me. I cannot praise you highly enough. But I must go on alone."

"I am sorry to lose you," the king replied. "But do not be absent for too long. Come back in good time. We will all be here to welcome you. And I will be able to remedy the mistakes I have made against you."

"Thank you again," Sir Balin said. "And God save you." So he prepared to ride away from the court. He had hardly put on his stirrups when some knights started to whisper that he had seized the sword by witchcraft.

Wherein the Lady of the Lake meets her destiny

But then there came to the court the lady known as the Lady of the Lake. She rode on a horse richly caparisoned, and her robes were of the finest silk. She saluted the king, and then spoke to him. "I claim," she said, "the gift that you promised me when I gave you the sword."

"I was not told the name of the sword."

"It is called Excalibur. That is to say, it is Cutter of Steel."

"A good name for a noble weapon. Please ask me what you wish for it, and I will keep my promise if I can."

"Well," the lady said, "I want the head of the knight who won the sword today. If I cannot have it, then I demand the head of the lady who wore that sword. I would in fact prefer to have both of their heads. He killed my brother, a true and good knight, and she was the cause of my father's death."

"Alas, fair lady," the king replied, "I cannot grant these requests. It would bring great shame upon me. Ask me for another gift, which I will gladly grant you."

"I want nothing else."

At that moment Sir Balin rode up, ready to depart, and saw the Lady of the Lake. He blamed this woman for the death of his mother three years before, and for all that time he had sought her. Now he learned that she had asked for his own death. So he acted. "This is an evil hour for you," he said. "You wanted my head, but instead you will lose yours!" And with his sword he struck off her head.

Arthur cried out. "What have you done? You have shamed me and my court by killing a guest. I owed much to her, and she came here under my pledge of safe conduct. I can never forgive your crime."

"Sire," Sir Balin replied, "I am sure that I deserve your displeasure. But consider this. This lady was the most wicked woman in the world. By enchantment and sorcery she has destroyed many good knights. And she caused my mother to be burned alive by reason of her false witness."

"Whatever cause you had," the king replied, "you should have held back in my presence. Do not doubt my word. You have committed the greatest crime against courtesy, and therefore you must renounce my court for ever. Leave now with all possible speed."

Sir Balin took up the severed head of the lady, and rode off to his lodging. There he met his squire, and together they rode away from Winchester. "You must take this head," he told the squire, "and bear it to my friends in Northumberland. Tell them that I have destroyed my worst enemy. Tell them, also, that I have been allowed to leave prison. And please relate to them the adventure that brought me this sword."

"Ah, sir," the squire replied to him, "you are greatly to blame for displeasing the king."

"As for that," Balin said, "I have a plan. I will strive with all speed to meet King Rience and challenge him to combat. If I die, I die with honour. If I kill him, then Arthur will once more be my friend."

"Where shall I see you again, sir?"

"At the court of King Arthur. At Camelot. Where else?" So he and his squire left each other on the road.

Meanwhile Arthur had mourned the death of the Lady of the Lake, and had buried her body in splendid state. She lay in a white tomb on a hillside, and upon the sides of her sepulchre were carved images of flowing water. Then there came to the court a young knight, Sir Launceot, who was the son of the King of Ireland. He was an envious and overweening man who resented the fact that Sir Balin had won the sword. So he came up to Arthur, and asked permission to challenge and kill him for the shame he had inflicted on them all.

"I wish you well," the king told him. "He has done me a great wrong." So Sir Launceot prepared himself for the fight.

Merlin came back to the court at this time, and was told about the lady and the enchanted sword. He also heard about the death of the Lady of the Lake. "I will tell you something," he said. "The lady who brought the sword to court is false and unfaithful. She has a brother who, by the strange chance of battle, captured and killed her very own lover. She was enraged by this, and so she went to the Lady of the Lake for revenge. The Lady of the Lake gave her that sword, and told her that the knight who took it from its sheath was destined to kill her brother before himself being destroyed. That was the reason she came here. I wish to God that she had not come, because in the company of good people she always tries to do harm. The knight that gained the sword will die from it."

Wherein two die from one stroke

Meanwhile Sir Launceot had armed himself and ridden after his foe at a furious speed. He had travelled into the mountainous region, where the stone is weathered into strange shapes of men and beasts, and there he caught sight of Sir Balin ahead of him. "Stay, knight!" he called out. "You must make a stand here, whether you like it or not. Your shield will not help you now! I have come here to cut you down!"

"It would have been better for you to have remained at home," Sir Balin replied. "It often happens that a man who means harm is himself badly hurt. From what court do you come?"

"From the court of King Arthur. I am here to avenge the crime you committed by killing the Lady of the Lake. It was against all the rules and customs of courtesy."

"I see, then, that I must fight you. But know this, knight. That lady did great damage to myself and my family. Do you think that I would slay a female for no cause?"

Sir Launceot was very proud. "Prepare yourself. Couch your spear. Only one of us will survive."

Then they put their spears in their supports, by the saddles, and rode against each other at great speed. Sir Launceot broke Sir Balin's shield, but Balin put his own spear through Launceot's shield and sundered his chain mail. Launceot, fatally wounded, was thrown from his horse by the force of the blow. Sir Balin turned and took out his sword, but then he saw that his opponent was dead. At that moment he heard the sound of another horse, galloping towards him, and he looked around. A young woman was riding in his direction and, when she saw Launceot lying on the ground, she let out a loud wail. "Ah, Balin," she cried, "you have slain two bodies with one heart, two hearts with one body. You have sacrificed two souls." She made such grievous sounds of sorrow that he wished to comfort her; she took out a sword, and Balin tried to seize it from her. But she held it tightly and then with a sigh turned it upon herself. She died at once.

When Sir Balin saw her dead, he despised himself and his deeds that had brought doom to a valiant knight and a fair lady. "I repent for breaking the bond of true love between them," he said. But he could not stay in that place. He could not bear to see the two bodies lying upon the ground. In his sorrow he stirred his horse and rode on for miles and miles until at last he came to a fair forest; under the boughs of the trees it seemed that time itself was suspended. No wind stirred the leaves, and there was no sound of life. And then who should ride towards him but his own brother, Balan.

When they met they took off their helmets, wept, and kissed one another copiously. "Brother," Balan said, "I had no notion of meeting you so soon. When I left I presumed that you were still a prisoner, but I met a knight on the way who told me that you had been seen at the court of King Arthur. That is why I rode into this realm."

Sir Balin then told him of his adventures at court, of his freeing the sword and of the fate of the Lady of the Lake. "The king," he said, "is angry with me. And the wrath of the king can mean death. That is why he sent a knight to kill me. Now he lies sprawled upon the ground with his young lover. I am truly sorry for that."

"It is right to be rueful when mortals are slain. But be of good cheer. You must face whatever God has prepared for you."

"That is why I am riding to Castle Terrible, besieged by King Rience. If I do battle against Arthur's most bitter enemy, I will prove my prowess in his cause."

"I will ride with you," Balan replied. "Brother, we are well met!"

Wherein Merlin makes a prophecy

As they were talking here, under the ancient trees, a dwarf from the castle of Camelot came riding up on a donkey. In truth it was Merlin, the magician. "Ah, Balin," he said to him, "you have done yourself great harm. You should have saved that lady from self-slaughter. It was in your power to help her."

"That is not so," Balin replied. "She took up the sword so suddenly that I could do nothing."

"Repentance is ripe for you. Because of her death you will deliver the most dolorous stroke since that which Christ Our Saviour suffered. You will strike down the truest knight in the world, and for twelve years three kingdoms will endure endless poverty and pain."

He turned away, but Sir Balin took him by the shoulder. "Say it is not so. If I believed that you spoke the truth, I would kill myself here to make you a liar."

But Merlin vanished from sight. Balin and his brother then made their way through the forest, but when they moved they made no sound. All was still and silent. After a while Merlin once more appeared before them, but in disguise. "Where are you going, young men?" he asked them.

"Why should we tell you?" Balan replied.

"And what is your name?" Balin asked him.

"At this time, I cannot tell you."

"That is an evil sign. A good man will always give his name."

"That may be. But I know where you are riding. You are ready to challenge King Rience. You will not succeed until you receive my counsel."

"Ah," Balin said, "you are Merlin. Speak. We will be ruled by your advice."

"Then follow me." The magician led them into a glade beside the track, where they rested their horses and waited. Then just before midnight Merlin roused them. "Come," he said. "Make ready. King Rience is riding this way. He has come with sixty of his knights to visit the Lady de Vaunce. He wishes to sleep with her. So you may surprise him."

"Which one is the king?" Balan whispered to him.

"There. Coming towards you."

So they rushed down upon him, and knocked him from his horse. Then they put to the sword most of his retinue, to right and left, while the rest of them fled into the forest. King Rience lay wounded on the ground, and the two warriors would have killed him if he had not surrendered. "Stay your hand, brave knights!" he called to them. "You will win nothing by my death, but by my life you may win much." So they took up the king and laid him on a litter.

Merlin vanished, and then reappeared beside Arthur at Camelot. "Your enemy has been taken," he told him. "King Rience is captured."

"By whom?"

"By two knights, who would dearly love to serve you. You will know their names soon."

On the next day Balin and Balan rode into court with King Rience as their captive. They left him in the charge of constables before riding back to their lodging. On hearing of the arrival of Rience, Arthur came up to his adversary. "Sir king," he said, "you are welcome. How did you come this way?"

"By hard necessity. I was beaten in combat."

"By whom?"

Merlin answered for him. "By Balin, known as the Knight of the Two Swords, and by his brother, Balan. He is a knight of great virtue but, alas, he will not live long. But this is not yet a time for mourning. He will still do you more service very soon. Look abroad, sire. King Nero, the brother of Rience, is fast approaching with eleven kings in his retinue. Tomorrow morning they and their armies will advance against you. Prepare yourself."

So Arthur mustered his troops. Although he was outnumbered by Nero's men, he was not outmatched by them. The king himself killed twenty enemy knights, and wounded forty more. He killed six of the kings. Balin and Balan were at the forefront of the fighting, slashing furiously on all sides; they killed six kings between them, including King Nero. Those who saw them believed that they were either angels come down from heaven, or devils sent from hell. No one admired them more than Arthur.

So Arthur caused to be made statues of copper, overlaid with gold, in the image of the twelve kings who had fallen in the field. Each one of them held a taper in his hands that burned night and day. A statue of Arthur himself was set up in gold, with a sword drawn in his hand, and the twelve kings were given gestures of submission. Merlin completed this wondrous work, as a sign of Arthur's success.

Then Merlin told Arthur that, after the king's death, the twelve candles would burn no longer; he also prophesied the adventures of the Holy Grail, and the dolorous stroke that would come from the sword of Sir Balin.

Wherein a virgin gives up a dish of her blood

Within a day or so, Arthur fell sick. He pitched his pavilion in a meadow, filled with sweet medicinal herbs, and laid himself down on a pallet to sleep. It was hoped that the sight and the smell of the herbs might cure him. But he could find no rest. As he lay there he heard the sound of a horse galloping towards the pavilion; he looked out and saw a knight going past him with the sound of great mourning. "Stop," he shouted to him. "Why are you in such great sorrow? I may be able to help you."

"Nothing now can do me any good," the sad knight replied before riding on his way.

Then there came up behind him Sir Balin. When he saw Arthur he dismounted and saluted him with due reverence. "You are welcome, Balin," the king said. "There just came this way a knight in great distress, but I do not know the reason. Can you please ride after him and bring him before me? You may use force, if necessary."

"I am at your command," Balin replied. He was astride his horse in a moment, and rode after the mournful knight. He found him in a forest, by the side of a fair lady, and he greeted him gallantly enough. "Sir knight," he said, "you must come with me to the king and explain the causes of your sorrow."

"That I cannot do. It will bring down evil on my head, and be of no help to you."

"Then make ready, sir. I must capture you in battle and bring you by force to the king. But I am unwilling to make a fight of it."

"Will you be my warrant, if I go with you?"

"Indeed. I will protect you even at the cost of my own life."

So the knight named Sir Harleus rode out with Balin, leaving the lady in the forest. Just as they came up to the king's pavilion, however, Harleus was pierced by a spear from an invisible rider. As he lay dying he whispered to Balin, "This is the work of a knight called Garlon. Take my horse. It is better than yours. Ride back to the forest and rescue the fair lady. She will lead you on the quest that I have pursued. Avenge my death."

"I will follow the road you have taken. In the name of God I will complete your quest." So Balin went to Arthur, and told him what had occurred. Then he returned the way he had come. After a while he rode into the forest and found the fair lady. He gave her the shaft of the spear that had killed Harleus, and she greeted his death with sorrow and dismay. Then together they rode from the forest, until they came up to the gates of a great castle. Balin had just passed through the portcullis when it was closed behind him, leaving the lady separated from him. At this point some knights surrounded her with their swords and would have killed her. But Balin mounted the stone steps of the gatepost and flung himself down into the moat, where he drew his sword and challenged them to combat. They refused to fight, saying that they were only following the custom of the castle. They told Balin that their mistress had lain sick for many years; she had been told that she must have a silver dish brimming with the blood of a noble lady, a virgin and a king's daughter, in order to be healed. So they drew blood from any damsel who came close to the castle. "Well," Balin told them, "bleed her if you must, but do not endanger her life." She gave up her blood willingly enough, and filled the silver dish, but it did not bring health to the lady.

Wherein the dolorous stroke deals death

They rested that night at the castle, and in the morning went on their way. They rode for four days without meeting any adventure, but then by chance on the fifth day they lodged in the manor house of a rich gentleman. As they sat at supper with their host, Balin heard cries and complaints coming from another room. "What is that noise?" he asked.

"It is my son," the host told him. "I will tell you what happened. I contended at a joust, where twice I managed to defeat the brother of King Pellam. In retaliation he swore to revenge himself on my best friend. That friend is my son. He is now so sick that he can be cured only by the blood of the man who has injured him. But I do not know his name. And he rides invisible."

"I know him," Balin replied. "His name is Garlon. He has killed a knight who was in my safe keeping. I would rather meet him in combat than acquire all the gold of this land."

"I will tell you how you can achieve that. King Pellam of Listenoise has proclaimed a great feast, to be held within a fortnight, but no knight may come there unless he is accompanied by his wife or paramour. You will be able to see him on that day."

"Then I promise to bring you some part of his blood in order to heal your son."

"We will leave in the morning."

At the dawn of the next day they rode out to the court of King Pellam, where they were received with great reverence and ceremony. Balin was taken to a chamber, and clean robes were brought for him. The servant then asked him for his sword. "I cannot part with it," he said. "It is the custom in my country for the knight to keep his weapon." So they allowed him to wear it, and with the fair lady he went down into the hall of the castle where the other knights were gathered. Balin glanced around. "Is there a knight in this court," he asked one of the guests, "who goes by the name of Garlon?"

"Indeed there is. He is over there, the knight with the necklace of black jet. He has performed marvellous deeds."

"Well," Balin said to himself, "so that is the man. If I were to kill him here, I would not escape this castle with my life. But if I leave him, I may never meet him again. And what mischief might he then make?"

Sir Garlon had seen that Balin was staring at him, so he went up to him and slapped his face with the back of his hand. "Knight," he said, "why do you look at me for so long? Eat your meat and leave me in peace. Do what you have come for."

"Sir, this is not the first time you have slighted me," Balin replied. "So now I will do what I have come for." He rose to his feet and, with his sword, he cut off the head of Garlon. As the knight lay dead on the floor, Balin called out to the lady, "Give me the shaft of the spear that killed Harleus!" he cried. She carried the shaft everywhere with her, and handed it to him. With this weapon he opened a wide wound in Garlon's side. "You used this against a good knight," he said. "I am glad to use it against you."

Then Balin shouted to his old host, "Now we will fetch enough blood to heal your son!"

The knights at the other tables arose at once and drew their swords. King Pellam himself was fierce. "Why have you slain my brother? Prepare yourself to die."

"If I am to die," Balin replied, "let it be at your hand."

"Precisely so. Brother must avenge brother."

So the king thrust at him with his sword; Balin tried to parry the stroke, but his own sword was cut asunder. Now he had no weapon. He ran from room to room of the castle, looking for some form of blade, while all the way Pellam followed him roaring. At last he entered a costly and secluded chamber. Balin could see that a corpse lay here, covered in cloth of gold; beside this bier stood a table of pure gold, supported by silver legs, and upon it lay a strangely wrought spear.

Balin took up the spear and turned upon Pellam. At the first stroke the king fell down in a swoon. At that moment the roof and the walls of the castle collapsed in ruin. There was a sound as of thunder, and the air became dark as pitch. A large groan issued from the depths of the earth, and the whole land trembled. The dolorous stroke had been delivered and could never be undone. The two men lay beneath the remains of the broken stone for three days, caught in a trance until Merlin came to their rescue. He took up Balin and gave him a new horse. "I cannot leave," the knight said, "without the fair lady."

"Look at her lying there," Merlin replied. "She is dead. All the others are dead, too."

Pellam lay, wounded and wasted, for many years. He could not be cured until the high prince, Galahad, healed him in his quest for the Holy Grail. Do you wish to know the secret of the spear? It was that which entered the side of Christ as he lay upon the Cross. It had drawn out the Holy Blood that Joseph of Arimathea later brought to England. It was Joseph himself who had lain upon the bed, covered in cloth of gold, and Pellam was his kinsman. So the dolorous stroke inflicted death and dismay upon the world.

Wherein two brothers fight and die

Balin left Merlin in much fear. "I will never see you again," he said to the wizard. He wandered from land to land, and from city to city, where he found the people dead or dying. "What have you done?" those still alive cried out. "You have caused havoc and harm to all of us. The dolorous stroke you gave Pellam will destroy us all. For that deed, you yourself will suffer!"

He rode onward, away from the lands of desolation, until one day he found himself within a fair forest.

He travelled for five days through unknown countries until he came upon a stone cross set at the mouth of a valley. It was inscribed with letters of gold and read: IT IS NOT FOR NO KNIGHT ALONE TO RIDE TOWARDS THIS CASTLE. "This is a riddle," Balin said, "that I cannot unravel."

An old man was suddenly walking towards him. "Balin the Savage," he called out to him. "This is no place for you. Turn back before it is too late." The old man then disappeared, and at that moment a horn blew as at the death of a hart.

"That blast," Balin said, "has been blown for me. I am the prize. Yet I am still alive." There appeared before him a hundred ladies who with music and dancing led him into a castle, at the other end of the valley, where he was greeted by many good knights. The mistress of the castle came up to him, smiling. "Sir Balin with the Two Swords," she said to him. "It is time for you to joust with the knight who holds this place. No man may pass this way without meeting him. It is the custom."

"An unhappy custom," Balin replied.

"It is only one knight."

"If I must joust, then I will," he said, "even though I have travelled many miles. My horse is weary, but my heart is still fresh."

"Sir," one knight said to him, "your shield is not good. I will lend you a bigger and better one, if you wish."

So Balin exchanged his shield for another, and rode out for battle. Before he could prepare himself a lady appeared and advanced towards him. "Oh, Balin!" she cried. "What have you done? By your shield you would have been known. It would have protected you from any peril."

"I am sorry," he said, "that I ever came into this country. But I cannot turn back. That would bring shame upon me. I will face my fate, come what may. Life or death will be mine at the end of this day."

He blessed himself, and rode forward. He saw before him, riding out of the castle, a knight dressed in red; the warrior's horse was harnessed in the same colour. He did not know that it was his own brother, Balan, who was preparing to charge him. Balan did not recognize the shield of Balin, borrowed for the occasion, and so the two brothers fought one another unawares. They clashed spears and shields so sharply that both men fell to the earth. Balan was the first to rise to his feet, and went after Balin with his drawn sword; Balin parried the thrust with his shield, and rose up for battle. They fought long and bitterly, until the ground was covered in their blood. Both of them by now were badly wounded and close to death. Balan, the younger brother, now withdrew himself a little and lay upon the earth.

"What knight are you?" Balin called to him. "I have never known any other man to match me as you have."

"I am Balan. I am brother to the mighty knight Balin."

"Oh God!" Balin cried out. "Why have I lived to see this day?" He fell backward in a faint. Balan crawled over to him and took off his helmet. But Balin's face was so bloody and disfigured that he could not make out his features. But then Balin recovered from his faint, and cried out, "Oh, Balan, my brother! You have killed me, and I have killed you. All the wide world shall speak of us both!"

"I did not know you, brother," Balan replied. "You were carrying the wrong shield, so I mistook you for another knight."

"Someone in this castle was plotting against us. I was given this shield. I wish I could destroy this place, and put down its evil customs."

"When I rode to this castle," his brother told him, "I was forced to confront a knight dressed in red. After I had defeated him I was doomed to remain here to challenge all newcomers. It would have happened to you."

The mistress of the castle then came out to them, and heard them moaning in their grief. "We came out of the same womb," Balan said to her. "We spring from the same mother's belly. So bury us together here, where we fought in battle." Graciously she granted them their wish. She sent for a priest who anointed them and read the last rites to them.

"When we are buried in the same tomb," Balin said, "make mention of the fact that we were two brothers who fought and slew one another by sorrowful mischance. No worthy knight or good man will see this sepulchre without praying for our souls." Then Balin died, and his brother breathed his last at midnight. The lady set up the tomb, and recorded there the fact that Balan had been killed by his brother. But she did not know the name of Balin.

Then Merlin came to this tomb, and inscribed his own message in letters of gold: HERE LIES BALIN THE SAVAGE. HE WAS KNOWN AS THE KNIGHT WITH TWO SWORDS. IT WAS HE WHO DELIVERED THE DOLOROUS STROKE. Merlin also made a bed out of magical wood, so that any man who lay in it would go out of his wits. Only Lancelot, in later years, was able to break the spell.

By his sorcery Merlin also buried the tip of the sword in a stone of marble that, in years to come, would float down the river to the city of Camelot that is in English called Winchester. Here it would come under the gaze of the high prince, Galahad. This story is to be told in the Book of the Holy Grail, the holiest book in the world.

Arthur and Guinevere

In these first far-off days of Arthur's reign, the king relied very much on Merlin's counsel. So there came a time when he came to him and spoke thus: "My barons will let me have no rest, Merlin, until I take a wife. But I will not choose a lady without your wisdom and advice."

Merlin's warning

"They are right, sire," he replied, "to press you so. A king should always have a consort. Is there anyone you love more than another?"

"There is indeed. Guinevere is the daughter of King Lodegreaunce, the lord of the land of Camelerd. She is the fairest and most fearless woman I have ever met in my life."

"I grant you that she is the loveliest. But if you waited a little, I could find you another lady of beauty and of wisdom. But once a man's heart is set, there he will abide."

"True in my case."

Then Merlin warned Arthur that Guinevere in time would cause him great anguish — that Sir Lancelot would fall in love with her and that she would return his love. All this turned out as he predicted. Then he told the king certain secret matters concerning the Holy Grail, about which the old books are silent.

The magician then travelled to the court of King Lodegreaunce, and informed him of Arthur's proposal of marriage. "That is the best news I have ever heard," Lodegreaunce told him. "I cannot think of a better husband for her. I would give all my lands as a dowry, but I know that he has territory enough. I will send him a gift that will please him even more. I will dispatch to him the Round Table that his father, Uther Pendragon, granted to me. It can seat one hundred and fifty good knights. I have one hundred of my own, but the other fifty have been killed during the course of my reign."

So King Lodegreaunce, with his daughter and one hundred knights, made their way to the court of Arthur at Winchester. When they arrived at the city, they were royally greeted. Arthur was filled with joy at their coming. "This is the fairest lady in the land," he said, "and most worthy to be my wife. And this Round Table pleases me more than gold and riches. The knights that sit here will surpass all others in the world. It will be the source and spring of great adventures. I am sure of it."

A feast was then prepared and, on the next day, Arthur and Guinevere were married with great solemnity in the abbey church of the city. They were taken in chairs of state along the nave of the great church to the sound of sacring bells ringing all around them; a cross of gold, six feet in height, was carried before them, and at the end of the ceremony they kissed it five times in token of the five wounds of Christ.

The doom of Merlin

It so happened that Merlin also fell madly in love with a young woman, once a companion of the Lady of the Lake; her name was Nineve. He would never let her rest, but followed her everywhere; she flattered him, and pretended to welcome his favours, until she had learned all she needed from him. Still he was besotted by her, and could not be brought from her side.

Merlin also told Arthur many secrets. He said that he himself would not live for much longer, and that he would be buried alive in the earth. He informed the king of many ills that would beset him, too, and warned him to keep safe his sword and scabbard. "Yet this also is true," he told him. "Your sword and scabbard will be stolen from you by a woman whom you trust most in the world. She wishes to take Excalibur from you. Then you will miss me, sir. Then you would rather have my wisdom than all of your wealth."

"To be buried alive is a terrible thing," the king replied. "But if you see your fate so clearly, why can you not avert it by the force of your magic?"

"It cannot be. This is my destiny. But I do not know the day when it will come."

At this time Nineve left the court and Merlin rode beside her. Wherever she went, he was with her. He tried to seduce her with the wiles of his sorcery, but he did not succeed. Then she made him swear an oath that he would not try to take her by force of enchantment or any spell. Together they went overseas to the court of King Ban in the region of Benwick, in the land of France, where Merlin spoke with the wife of the king. Her name was Elaine. There also he saw young Lancelot. When Elaine told Merlin that her lands were being ravaged by King Claudas of the Desert, he pointed to the boy. "Be comforted, madam," he said, "within twenty years this child will pursue your cause against Claudas. He will overcome that wicked king. All Christendom will marvel at his bravery. The boy will be the foremost warrior in the world. His baptismal name was Galahad. But you have since confirmed him as Lancelot."

"That is correct. His name was indeed once Galahad. How did you know that?" The magician smiled, and said nothing. "Ah, Merlin, can it be true that I will live to see my son a man of prowess?"

"Yes, madam, you will see it. The name of Lancelot will ring around the world. And you will live for many years."

Merlin and Nineve went on their way soon after, and he showed her many marvels. He taught her how to talk to the animals of the forest, and how to still a tempest. All the while he schemed to take her, by fair means or foul, but she had grown tired of him. She longed to be rid of him. He was the son of the devil, however, and could not be escaped so easily. One day he was showing her a great wonder concealed within a rock, and she persuaded him to work his way beneath it; but he was caught there by a spell he had taught her, in a cavern beneath the rock, and no manner of magic could release him. So she went on her way rejoicing, while Merlin was buried alive.

Arthur's battle with the five kings

Meanwhile King Arthur had moved with his court from Winchester to Carlisle, where came to him unwelcome news. A messenger told him that five kings had invaded his land, and were intent upon burning all the castles and cities they could find. They were the King of Ireland, the King of Denmark, the King of the Vale, the King of Sorleyse and the King of the Island of Longtains.

"Ah," Arthur cried out, "I have never known one month of repose since I took up the crown. I have lost the key to contentment. I shall not be able to rest until I have met these five kings on the fair field of battle. I cannot allow my subjects to be slaughtered. Come with me who will, and the others abide here."

Arthur then wrote to King Pellinor asking him to come to his aid, with as many men as he could muster. He also summoned his lords, and tenants-in-chief, and ordered them to gather their forces for the fight. Then the king came into the chamber of his queen, Guinevere, and gathered her up in his arms. "Madam," he said, "make yourself ready to ride alongside me. I cannot leave you here. I would miss you too much.

Besides you will instil bravery in me. I will defend you at all costs."

"Sir," she replied, "I am yours to command."

So the king and queen, with all the company they could muster, travelled south-east through the moors and the marshes; they eventually couched themselves in a forest beside the River Humber. When news of their arrival reached the five kings they were counselled by one of their kinsmen. "You know well enough," he said to them, "that Arthur's knights are praised the world over for their might and their valour. So make your way to them as quickly as you can; if you delay, the king will only grow the stronger. Supporters will join him, and his army will gather more force."

The five kings considered this advice and, after some argument, accepted it. So with their armies they left North Wales and travelled across the country towards him. They reached Arthur by the onset of night, when the king and his knights were resting in their pavilions. Sir Kay had just told him that it was unwise to sleep unarmed, but Sir Gawain had replied that there was no need. Yet then there came a great cry and calls of "Treason!"

"Alas!" Arthur shouted. "We have been caught unawares! To arms! To arms!"

A wounded knight entered the pavilion and came up to the king. "Sire," he said, "save yourself and the queen. Our army is surrounded, and many of our men have been slain."

So Arthur, Guinevere and three knights took horse and rode towards the Humber. The waters were so high and so rough, however, that they hesitated on the shore. "It is your choice," the king said to his wife. "Do you wish to tempt the waves, or stay on this side of the river where the enemy might find you?"

"I would rather drown," Guinevere said, "than fall into the hands of those men."

Even as they stood talking Sir Kay saw the five kings approaching on horseback with spears in their hands. "They have come alone," he said. "Let us ride out and force them to combat."

"That would be foolish," Sir Gawain told him. "They are five. We are only four."

"So? I will take care of two of them myself, leaving only three."

He charged forward and caught one of the kings with his spear, killing him instantly. Gawain galloped out and gave the second king such a stroke that he fell dead to the ground. Arthur dispatched a third, and Sir Griflet gave the fourth king a blow that broke his neck. Sir Kay, true to his word, dispatched the fifth king with his sword.

"Well done, Sir Kay," Arthur told him. "You have kept your promise. You are a man of worship."

Then they placed the queen in a barge so that she might cross the river. Before she was borne away from the bank she addressed Sir Kay. "If any lady were to reject your love and loyalty," she said, "she would be greatly to blame. I shall report your noble fame to all whom I meet. You spoke a great word and performed a great deed."

The king and the three knights then rode back to the forest to find the remnants of their army, and they told the survivors that the five kings were dead. "So let us rest here till daylight," Arthur declared to them. "When the enemy learn that their leaders have been killed, there will be sorrow and suffering out of measure." And so it was. When they were told of the fate of their kings, the armies were lost in loud lament. Arthur took advantage of their grief, and rode out against them. With a few hundred of his companions he led a charge, slashing on all sides; his forces killed some thirty thousand men, and after the fight not one of the enemy was left alive. Of his own men, two hundred were dead, eight of them being knights of the Round Table. So the king kneeled down upon the field of battle and thanked God for his great victory. On the site of the battle he raised and endowed an abbey in memory of his triumph, and he called it the Abbey of Good Adventure. Yet it was not good for his enemies; they were all heavy of heart. The kings of the North, and of Wales, were mournful that Arthur had grown so great in their midst.

The king returned to Camelot soon after, and called to him King Pellinor. "You have heard," he said, "that eight of my best knights have been killed. There are empty seats at the Round Table. Whom shall I choose to take their place?"

"Sir, I will give you the best counsel I can. At your court there are old knights and young knights. Choose four of each."

"Which of the old do you prefer?"

"I would take King Uriens, who has married your sister Morgan le Fay, and then the King of the Lake. Finally I would choose Sir Hervis de Revel, a noble knight, and Sir Galagars."

"All good men," the king replied. "And what of the young?"

"The first among them must be Sir Gawain, your nephew, who is as good a knight as any in this kingdom. Then I would select Sir Griflet and Sir Kay as worthy warriors. As for the fourth, you may choose between Sir Bagdemagus and my son, Sir Tor. I cannot speak for my son, of course, except to say that there is no better knight of his age in the land. He has done no wrong, and has deserved much praise."

"You are telling the truth," Arthur replied. "I have seen the proof of your son's prowess. He says little, but he does much. I will take him at this time, and leave Sir Bagdemagus for another occasion."

So the knights were all chosen and, after the barons had assented, they were led to their seats at the Round Table with much acclamation. Sir Bagdemagus was angry at having been excluded, with Sir Tor advanced before him. So he left the court with his squire and went in search of adventure.

They had been riding all day in a dark wood when they came upon a stone cross in a secluded grove. Sir Bagdemagus and his squire dismounted and kneeled down in prayer. Then the squire noted some words inscribed upon the stone. "Do you see these words, sir? They say that Bagdemagus should not return to court until he has seen a wonder."

"That is the way to win worship," Bagdemagus said. "I will become worthy of the Round Table."

They went on their way, and Bagdemagus found beside a little path a herb so holy that it was a sign or token of the Holy Grail itself. "This is the wonder," Bagdemagus said. "This herb cannot be seen in the ordinary light of day. It is visible only in the light of holiness. No man could find it if he were not blessed."

It so happened that on this same journey he came upon the great rock where Merlin had been consigned by Nineve. As soon as he heard the magician wailing and sighing, he dismounted and strode over to the rock. He tried to lift it, but it would have taken the strength of a hundred men to move it one inch. Merlin told him to leave off his labour, since only the lady herself could release him. "I am doomed to lie here," he said, "until she relents." So the knight departed and, after many adventures, returned to the court of King Arthur where he was made one of the order of the Round Table.

The Wickedness of Morgan le Fay

It happened one day that Arthur, with many of his knights, went hunting in a great forest. The king caught sight of a white hart slipping between the trees and, in the company of King Uriens and Sir Accolon of Gaul, went in pursuit of it. The three of them were well horsed and they rode so hard that they were soon separated from the rest of the hunt; they had not gone ten miles before their horses fell exhausted to the ground. They continued on foot, but the hart still fled before them.

"What shall we do?" Arthur asked them. "We are weary and hard pressed."

"Let us walk on," King Uriens said. "We will find some lodging."

They made their way through the forest until they came on to the shore of a lake, where they saw the hart being killed by a pack of hounds. Arthur blew his horn as a symbol of his reward and then quartered the hart.

The enchanted boat sails upon the lake

Now Arthur saw a boat coming towards them across the lake. Its sails were of white and purple silk, and silently it came up to the shore. The wind that filled its sails smelled of violets. The king went over to it, curious to see who sailed it. But there was no earthly creature within. "Come, sirs," he said. "Let us explore this ship."

The three of them went aboard, and found it richly furnished with cloths of silk. By this time twilight had fallen, but the boat was suddenly lit by a hundred torches; they shined so brightly that the entire lake glowed with the light. The trees that encircled it cast enormous shadows. Thereupon appeared twelve fair ladies who fell to their knees and greeted the king by name. Then they led him and his companions into another room where a table was laid out with all manner of meats and wines, marvellous to behold. After the meal was over the three men were taken to their bedchambers, richly furnished, where they fell into a sound sleep.

When King Uriens awoke, on the following morning, he was in the arms of his wife, Morgan le Fay; to his amazement he was returned to Camelot.

When King Arthur awoke he found himself in a foul prison, while all around him rose the complaints of fearful knights. "Why are you so woeful?" he asked them.

"We are all prisoners here. Some of us have been lying here for eight years or more."

"For what reason?"

One of them then began to speak. "The lord of this castle, Sir Damas by name, is the most false and treacherous knight in the world. He is a coward as well. He has a younger brother, Sir Oughtlake, who is loved by all as a man of worship and of courage. But he has no lands. His older brother holds them all. So Oughtlake has challenged his brother to combat, whereby the victor will win the whole estate. But Damas does not dare to fight him. Instead he has tried to find a knight who will take his place in the contest. But he is so hated that no knight will fight for him. He has captured us all, as we rode out on various adventures, and when we refused to comply with his requests he condemned us to perpetual imprisonment. That is why we sit here in sorrow. We have so little food and drink that we can barely live."

"God save you," Arthur said to them.

Then a fair lady came into the cell, and asked the king how he was.

"I cannot say," he replied.

"I will tell you this, sir. You have a choice. You can either fight for the master of the castle and be delivered from this place. Or you can die in prison. Which will it be?"

"This is hard for me. I would rather fight with a knight than lie here festering. If all the other prisoners here are released with me, then I will accept the challenge."

"I promise you."

"Then I am ready. All I need is a horse and armour."

"You shall have them soon enough."

"I believe, lady," he said, "that I have seen you at the court of King Arthur."

"No," she replied. "I was never there. I am the daughter of Damas, who is the lord of this castle." Yet she was lying. She was one of the retinue of Morgan le Fay, the sister of the king.

So she went to Sir Damas and informed him that there was a knight in his custody who was ready to fight for him. He sent for Arthur, and at once saw that he was strong and sturdy. "It would be a pity," he said, "for such a knight to die in prison. Are you prepared to do battle on my behalf?"

"If you free the others, I will serve you."

So the other knights were released from their cells, and rejoiced when they saw the light.

We turn now to Sir Accolon of Gaul. When he awoke, after his sleep in the enchanted boat, he found himself hanging over the edge of a deep well in peril of falling to his death. From this well there came a fountain; the water flowed through a silver pipe before splashing on to a slab of marble. When he saw this wonder he quickly made the sign of the Cross to ward off harm. "Jesus save us all," he whispered. "The ladies of the ship have betrayed us. They were fiends, not women. If I escape from this place I will destroy them all and put an end to their enchantments."

There came up to him a dwarf, with a great mouth and a flat nose. He greeted Sir Accolon and told him that he had been sent by Morgan le Fay. "She bids you welcome, and asks you to be of bold heart. You will do battle this morning with a brave knight. So she has sent you the sword Excalibur, together with its enchanted scabbard. She commands you to fight to the uttermost, showing no mercy. You must cut off the king's head — for he is a king — and Morgan le Fay promises that the lady who brings her that head will be made a queen."

The old books tell us that Morgan le Fay had stolen the sword from her brother by magic art; she had made herself invisible, and crept into the chamber where he kept Excalibur. As soon as she touched the sword, it also vanished from men's sight.

"Now that I have this sword," Accolon said, "I will do as she desires. When did you last see Morgan le Fay?"

"Just now."

The knight clasped the dwarf in his arms. "Send my greetings to the lady," he told him. "I will do her bidding or die for it. I suppose it was she who summoned up the lovely spirits on the boat?"

"You can believe it, sir."

The earth is soaked in blood

There now came up a knight with six squires in attendance. He saluted Accolon and asked him to rest himself in a manor house near by. So Accolon mounted the horse they had brought with them, and rode in their company.

Meanwhile Sir Damas had sent for his brother, Sir Oughtlake, and warned him to get ready. He had found a knight to fight in his service. Oughtlake was dismayed at this news. He had been wounded one week before by

74

a spear thrust in his side at a tournament, and he was in no condition to do battle with anyone. But the magic of Morgan le Fay now changed the course of his destiny. Accolon had in fact been taken to the manor house of Oughtlake. When the knight told his guest of his trouble, obliged to fight when he had no strength, Accolon offered to take his place. "I have Excalibur," he said, "and I fear no enemy." He did not know, of course, that he was about to fight Arthur.

Arthur was armed and ready. He and Sir Damas heard mass, and then the king mounted his horse. At that moment a messenger came from Morgan le Fay, bearing a sword that resembled Excalibur. "Your sister sends you this," she said, "for the sake of the love between you. She bitterly regrets stealing it from you. She was overcome by madness." But the sword was a counterfeit, false and brittle.

Sir Oughtlake rode over and announced that his champion was ready. So Arthur proceeded to the field of battle, where Accolon was waiting for him. Nineve, the companion of the Lady of the Lake, had also come to this place. She knew well enough that Morgan le Fay was intent on killing Arthur, and she had come to save him from his sister.

The two men rode against each other with such force that they were flung from their horses on to the ground; both of them got to their feet and, summoning up all their strength, drew their swords. They did battle, stroke for stroke. As soon as he felt the first wound Arthur knew that his sword was a false one; he could not injure his opponent, whereas he was losing blood all the time. The earth was soaked with it. He soon realized that the other knight held Excalibur in his hand, and in his heart he suspected treason by Morgan le Fay.

"Now, knight," Accolon shouted to Arthur, "keep well away from me!"

Arthur did not answer him, but gave him such a blow that he almost fell to the ground. Then Accolon raised Excalibur into the air, and struck him with such force that the king reeled backwards. Still they fought on. At one point Arthur withdrew to rest himself but Accolon pressed forward. "This is no time for retreat," he said. He swung Excalibur and with one stroke broke Arthur's sword, which fell into the grass. Arthur was fearful of death, but he held up his shield and parried the heavy blows as best he could.

"Sir knight," Accolon called to him, "you are overcome. You cannot continue. You have no weapon, and you have lost much blood. So surrender to me before it is too late."

"No, sir. I cannot. I have given an oath that I will fight to the end. I would rather die with honour than live in shame. If I could die a hundred deaths I would choose such a fate rather than yield to you. I am without a weapon, as you say, and if you kill me you yourself will be shamed."

"So be it. Stay away from me now, or you are a dead man." Accolon attacked him again with his sword, but Arthur pushed him back with his shield. When Nineve saw that Arthur was about to fall, she made use of the sorcery she had learned from Merlin. She made a sign, and Excalibur fell from the hands of Accolon. Arthur leaped upon it and took it up.

"Ah," he said, "you have been away from me too long. Look how much damage you have done!" Then he saw the enchanted scabbard by Accolon's side. In one bound he snatched it from him and threw it as far as he could. "Sir knight," he shouted, "you have done great deeds with my sword today! Now you are about to die. I will repay you for my blood in kind." He ran towards Accolon and struck him so furiously that his helmet broke and he fell to the ground. Then Arthur gave him a beating; the blood burst from his mouth, his ears and his nose. "Now I will kill you!" he screamed.

"Kill me, sir, if you must. I have never seen a knight fight so courageously. I know that God is with you. I have made a pledge to do battle until the end, and I will never perjure myself. God may do with my body what He will."

Arthur thought that he recognized the man, bloody and disfigured though he was. "Tell me," he said, "what country do you come from? What court?"

"I come from the court of King Arthur. My name is Accolon of Gaul."

Arthur was angry to the point of fury. He recalled the sorcery used against them on the boat, and he was overwhelmed with suspicion. "Tell me, sir, who gave you this sword?"

"I wish that I had never seen it. It has caused me much grief."

"But who gave it to you?"

"It was the gift of Morgan le Fay. It was sent to me yesterday, by a dwarf, with the intention of killing King Arthur. I must tell you this. He is the man she most hates in the world. She once promised to place me on his throne. We would have ruled together. That is all past now. I am prepared for nothing but death."

"It would have been dishonourable to have destroyed your lord," Arthur said to him.

"True enough. My love for Morgan le Fay led me astray. But who are you, sir?"

The king took off his helmet. "I am Arthur."

The king condemns his sister

Sir Accolon looked at him aghast. "Oh my God! Have mercy on me, your grace. I did not know you."

"I will be merciful. Your words assure me that you did not recognize me here. But by your own witness you are guilty of planning my death. You are a traitor. Yet still I am inclined to forgive you. My sister has woven her spells around you, and by her sorcery she has brought you to ruin. I shall be avenged upon her. I will do to her such things as will resound through Christendom. Once I loved and honoured her. Now she will reap the fruit of my hatred."

Arthur then called for the keepers of the field, and told them that two good knights had come close to killing each other. "If I had known who he was," he said, "I would never have raised my sword against him."

Then Accolon called to all the spectators. "Kneel down. This is your king. This is Arthur."

They all fell to their knees and cried out for forgiveness.

"I grant you mercy," the king said. "You see what happens when two knights are led astray. I have fought here with one of my own men. We are both badly hurt. I crave rest. But, before that, I must pass judgement on the two brothers." So he called before him Sir Damas and Sir Oughtlake. "Damas, you have brought dishonour upon yourself. I convict you of cowardice and villainy. Therefore I order you to give all your lands to your brother. In return he will give you a palfrey each year on which to ride. Only good knights can be carried by a proper horse. I charge you to compensate these knights for their long time in your prison, and to promise on your life that you will never keep captives again. If any word of complaint is heard against you in my court, you will die for it. Do you hear me?" Sir Damas bowed his head in silence. "As for you, Sir Oughtlake, you have proved your prowess and your valour. I charge you to come to my court as soon as you can, where I will make you one of my own knights."

"God thank you," Sir Oughtlake replied, "for your goodness and generosity. From this time forward I am yours to command. If I had not been wounded, I would have been the one to do battle with you today."

"I wish you had been my opponent, for I would not have been hurt so badly. My own sword was used against me, and I was almost killed by sorcery."

"It is distressing," Sir Oughtlake said, "that so great a king as you should be threatened by traitors."

"They will get their reward. And she will also be punished. Be sure of it. Now tell me this. How far are we from Camelot?"

"Two days' ride, sir."

"I would like to go to some religious house, where I might rest and where my wounds can be healed."

"There is a rich abbey of nuns close by, founded by your father."

So Arthur and Accolon took horse and journeyed to the abbey. They were tended there by good doctors, but Accolon died of his wounds four days later. He had lost too much blood. The king recovered his strength, however. He placed the body of Accolon on a horse-bier and ordered six knights to accompany it back to Camelot. "Bear it to my sister Morgan le Fay," he told them. "Tell her that it is my gift to her. And inform her, too, that I have recovered my sword and my scabbard."

Morgan le Fay wishes to kill her husband

Meanwhile Morgan le Fay, believing that the king was dead, made plans to murder her husband. She wished to govern the realm with her lover, Accolon, and gain all glory. She saw King Uriens asleep on his bed, and called for one of her maidens. "Fetch my lord's sword," she said. "There is no better time to kill him."

"Madam," the girl said, "if you murder your husband, there will be no escape for you."

"Hush. This is the time. Bring me the sword."

So the girl left the chamber, and went straight to the queen's son. She roused Sir Uwain from sleep. "Get up, sir," she told him. "My lady, your mother, is intent upon killing your father. She has asked me to bring his sword to her."

"Go on your way," Sir Uwain replied. "I will deal with her."

With quaking hands the girl brought the sword to the queen. Morgan le Fay took it with a smile and approached the bed. Just as she lifted the weapon, to smite her husband, Sir Uwain caught her hand and forced it down. "What kind of fiend are you!" he shouted at her. "If you were not my mother, I would take this sword and cut off your head! It is said that Merlin is the offspring of the devil, but I am sure that I am the son of an earthly demon."

"Have mercy on me, fair son. I have been tempted by a fiend, and have been led astray. I will never do anything like this again. Have pity on me. Do not denounce me to the court."

"As long as you keep your promise, I will not betray you."

"I give you my promise."

Then the report reached her that Sir Accolon was dead, and that the king had gained his sword again. At this news she almost swooned with grief. But she did not want her sorrow to be known, and so kept her countenance. She realized well enough, however, that when Arthur returned her life would be in peril. "No gold will I get from him," she said to herself. So she went quickly to the queen, Guinevere, and asked permission to leave the court on urgent business in her own country.

"But you will wait for the return of your brother?" Guinevere asked her.

"I cannot stay, my lady. The summons is too urgent."

"Then of course you must leave."

So at dawn, on the next day, Morgan le Fay mounted her horse and rode day and night from Arthur's court. On the second day she arrived at the abbey where Arthur was resting from his wounds. When she knew that he was there, she asked how he was. "He is asleep now," the abbess told her. "He slept little for the last three nights."

"Well then," she replied, "I order you not to awake him before I do."

She was scheming to steal his sword and scabbard once more. She went straight to the chamber where her brother lay, and there saw him asleep with his drawn sword in his hand. "I cannot take Excalibur from him without waking him," she whispered. "What am I to do?" Then she saw the enchanted scabbard and, in a moment, snatched it up. She left the chamber and called for her horse.

When Arthur awoke he saw that his scabbard was missing. "Who has come in here while I slept?" he asked the abbess.

"Only your sister, sire. Queen Morgan le Fay."

"You have failed me. You have not watched me carefully."

"What could I say to the queen? I did not dare to disobey her."

"Obey me now. Fetch me the best horse that can be found. Arouse Sir Oughtlake. Tell him to meet me, well armed and well horsed, within the hour."

The two of them galloped off in pursuit of Morgan le Fay. After many miles they came up to a stone cross, where they found a poor cowherd. They asked him if any lady had come riding that way.

"Sirs," he said, "there was a lady. She was with an escort of forty men. They entered the forest. Over there."

They sped off into the forest and, after finding a path, they caught sight of Arthur's sister riding ahead of them. So they chased her through the trees. When she saw them in pursuit she spurred on her horse. She came to a lake, and stopped for a moment. "I do not care what may happen to me," she said. "But Arthur will never have this scabbard." She threw it with all her strength into the middle of the lake, where it sank in a moment. It was weighed down by gold and precious stones.

Then she rode into a valley of rocks, from which there was no escape. So by sorcery she changed herself, and her men, into great marble stones that lay cold and silent. Arthur and Oughtlake came into the valley soon after. "They have not come this way," the king said. "Let us turn back to the abbey."

As soon as they had gone Morgan le Fay undid the spell, and returned them all to their human shapes. "Sirs," she said, "now we may go where we will." Soon after this they came upon a knight on horseback, leading another knight bundled upon a horse; he was blindfolded, and his hands and feet were bound. Morgan le Fay stopped him. "What are you going to do with this knight?" she asked.

"I am going to drown him in the fountain ahead of you."

"For what cause?"

"What cause? I found him with my wife. She will die in the same way soon enough."

"That would be a pity," she replied. Then she addressed the knight who was bound. "What do you say? Is he speaking the truth."

"No, lady. He lies."

"From where do you come? What country?"

"I am from the court of King Arthur. My name is Manessen. I am cousin to Sir Accolon of Gaul."

"You have spoken well. For the love of Accolon, I will free you. You may treat your foe in the same way as he treated you."

So Manessen was set free, and the other knight was tied and thrown into the fountain where he drowned. Then Manessen took horse and prepared to ride off. "Is there anything you wish me to tell Arthur?" he asked her.

"Tell him that I rescued you for love of Accolon, not for love of him. Tell him this, too. I do not fear him as long as I can turn myself and my men into stones. He will know what I mean. And whisper this to him. I will do more, when the time comes."

So she departed into the country of Gore, where she was richly received and welcomed. She made sure to strengthen her towns and castles. From this time forward she dreaded the wrath of her brother.

THE ADVENTURES OF
SIR LANCELOT DU LAKE

Soon after King Arthur had returned to his court, all the knights of the Round Table came together and fought many jousts and tournaments. Some proved themselves to be strong and valiant, but none more so than Sir Lancelot du Lake. He was the victor in all of his contests. He was only ever overcome by spells and enchantment. He so increased in fame that he is the first knight that the French books mention in their accounts of Arthur. He also became the favourite of the queen, Guinevere, for whose sake he fought many battles. He himself so loved the queen that, as we shall see, he saved her from false men and even from fire.

The pursuit across the plain

After Sir Lancelot had grown tired of tournaments he summoned his nephew, Sir Lionel. "We have spent too much time in games," he said. "Now we must ride into the world and seek out strange adventures." So they armed themselves and mounted their horses. Soon after they rode on to a wide plain, dotted with rocks and trees. It was noon, and the sun was beating strongly upon them. Sir Lancelot said that he felt a great desire to sleep. "There is an apple tree," Sir Lionel told him. "By the hedge there. Why not rest in its shade?"

"So I will. It has a fair shadow. And I have not felt so drowsy for seven years."

They dismounted and tied their horses to the trees. Sir Lancelot laid himself down beneath the apple tree, and put his helmet beneath his head. As he slept Sir Lionel kept watch. As he watched, three knights came galloping across the plain as if in fear of their lives. They were pursued by one man alone, but he was the best proportioned and most powerful knight Lionel had ever seen. This mighty knight rode down each of the three knights in turn and struck them to the earth, senseless; then he tied them to the backs of their horses with the reins of their bridles.

Sir Lionel decided to test his own strength and, even while Sir Lancelot still slept, he mounted his horse and challenged the powerful knight. The man turned and, with his sword drawn, he charged Sir Lionel and thrust him on to the ground. Then he bound Lionel's wrists and bundled him on to his own horse. The man rode for a little way, with the other three knights helpless on their horses, and then threw all of them into a dark prison where other men lay dead or dying.

Meanwhile Sir Ector de Maris had learned that Lancelot had left the court in search of noble adventures. Thoroughly ashamed of being left behind, he set off on a similar quest. He had been riding a long time in a deep wood when he met a man who resembled a forester. "Fair fellow," he called to him, "do you know where I might find an adventure?"

"I know this country well," the man replied. "If you ride for a mile or two you will find a large manor house with a moat around it; to the side of it there is a ford where your horse might drink its fill. Over this ford there grows a tree, from the branches of which hang the shields of many good knights dead or defeated in combat. There is also a basin, made of silver, hanging there. Strike that basin with the butt of your spear three times. You will see what you will see."

"I thank you," Sir Ector replied and rode off at once. He came up to the manor house, a dwelling of thick stone; its windows were small and inset, as if the place were a castle. He stopped before it, and then saw the tree by the ford. But what was this? He was surprised to see the shields of many knights of the Round Table hanging from its branches. He took it hard that among them was that of his brother, Sir Lionel, and he promised to himself that he would avenge him. Then he beat furiously upon the silver basin, as if he had gone out of his wits, and led his horse to the side of the ford. Before long he heard the voice of someone calling out to him. He turned, and faced a knight, strong and serious. This was the knight who had pursued and captured the three men upon the plain. His name was Sir Tarquin. "Take your horse from the water," Tarquin said to him, "and prepare to fight me."

So Ector galloped towards him and gave the warrior such a buffet with his spear that he spun around with his horse. "That was well done," the man said. "But see what I shall do to you." He went for him with sword and spear, bearing Ector out of his saddle and seizing him before he had a chance to escape. Then Tarquin took him into his castle and threw him down upon the floor. "You have fought me better than any other knight in these last twelve years," he told him. "So I will spare your life, on condition that you become my prisoner."

"I will never agree to that," Ector replied.

"All the worse for you." He stripped him of his armour, and then beat him with thorns before throwing him into the same deep prison where Lionel lay.

Ector recognized Lionel at once. "Dear brother, what are you doing here? And where is Sir Lancelot?"

"I left him sleeping beneath an apple tree. I do not know what has become of him."

"We need his help to deliver us from this place. Only Lancelot will be able to defeat the knight who has imprisoned us."

The four wicked queens

Now we will leave these knights and return to Lancelot sleeping beneath the tree. As he lay there, four queens of great estate approached him. One of them was Morgan le Fay, the wicked sister of Arthur. They were riding on four white mules, and four knights in white armour carried a canopy of green silk above them to shield them from the heat of the sun. As they came up they recognized Sir Lancelot at once, and each of them declared that they would strive with the others to win his love.

"There is no need for us to fight each other," Morgan le Fay said to them. "I will cast a spell on him that will last seven hours. In that time we will take him to my castle. When he awakes from the enchantment, he will choose one of us for himself." So they led him to Castle Chariot, where they placed him in a cold chamber. After the seven hours were past a young lady brought him supper. She greeted him and asked him how he was.

"I cannot tell you, lady," he replied. "I do not know how I come to be in this place. Perhaps I was taken here by magic."

"Be cheerful, sir," she replied. "I will tell you in the morning."

So he lay there all that night, confused and restless. At dawn the four queens came into his chamber and greeted him. He looked up at them in surprise. "Good morning, fair ladies. Can you tell me what I am doing here?"

Morgan le Fay spoke out. "You must be aware, sir, that you are our prisoner. We know you. You are Sir Lancelot du Lake, son of King Ban. We also know that you are the noblest knight in the world. You love Guinevere above all others, but she is married now to my brother, Arthur. So you must choose one of us to be your paramour. I am Morgan le Fay, queen of the land of Gore. Here are the queens of North Wales, of East Land and of the Outer Isles. Which of us will it be? If you refuse us, then you will remain here as my prisoner until your death."

"I see that I am hard pressed," Lancelot replied, "either to die here or marry one of you. But I would rather spend the rest of my life in prison than take one of you as my wife. You are all witches and false enchanters."

"Is that your answer?" Morgan le Fay asked him.

"Yes it is. I will have none of you."

So they left him alone in his cell, lamenting his fate. When the same young lady brought him his dinner, later that day, she asked him how he was. "I have never been so ill used," he replied.

"Sir," she said, "I am prepared to help you. But you must make me a promise."

"Willingly. I am determined to escape from these four queens who have destroyed so many good knights."

"I will tell you what you must do. Next Tuesday my father must meet the King of North Wales in combat. If you help him to win, I will arrange your escape tomorrow."

"Tell me your father's name before I give you my answer."

"He is King Bagdemagus."

"I know him well. He is a noble knight indeed. I will be happy to serve him. And you."

"Thank you for that. Be ready at dawn tomorrow. I will bring your horse and armour to you. Ride for ten miles until you come to an abbey of white monks. Wait for me there. I will bring my father with me."

So on the following morning she knocked at his door, and found him ready. She had the keys to the twelve doors that held him fast. She unlocked each one in turn, and led him out into the courtyard of the castle. His horse and armour were there, together with his sword and spear. Lancelot leaped into the saddle. "For this relief," he said to her, "much thanks. I will not fail you, lady." Then he rode off.

The wrong bedfellow

He came into a great forest where there was no track or path; at nightfall he found himself in a glade where there was pitched a tent of fine red silk. "I will rest here," he said, "until the morning." So he tied his horse to the tent, took off his armour, and lay down upon a soft bed that he found there. Soon he was sound asleep.

The knight who owned the tent came back an hour later. He believed that his lover slept in the bed, so he lay down and kissed the sleeping body. As soon as Lancelot felt the rough beard of a man he leaped from the bed, swiftly followed by the unfortunate knight. They took up their swords, and Lancelot wounded him so badly that he was forced to concede the fight.

"Why did you come into the bed?" Lancelot asked him.

"This tent is my own. I was expecting my lady to be here. But now I am likely to die."

"I regret your wound, sir. But I was afraid of treachery. I have lately been beguiled. Let us go into your tent, and I will help you staunch the flow of blood. What is your name?"

"Belleus."

"Come, Belleus."

Sir Lancelot was binding the wounds when the lover of Belleus arrived. When she saw the blood she cried out in alarm, and almost fainted in her distress. "Be calm," Belleus told her. "This knight is a good man. He has helped me." Then he told her the story of their meeting.

She turned to Lancelot. "Sir knight, from whose court have you come? Who are you?"

"I am Lancelot du Lake."

"I thought so. I have often seen you at Arthur's court, and I know you better than you imagine. But now I ask you this. For all the dangers Sir Belleus has passed through, and for the wounds he has suffered at your hands, will you make a request to the king? Will you recommend that Belleus join the Round Table? He is worthy of it."

"Fair lady, let him come with you to the court at the time of the next high feast. There I will put him forward. If he triumphs in arms, he will be selected."

The tournament

When dawn broke Belleus showed Lancelot the direction to the abbey of the white monks. As soon as he arrived there, the daughter of King Bagdemagus came to a window and welcomed him. She led Lancelot into a comfortable chamber, where she urged him to rest. Then she sent word to her father, and the king rode to the abbey with many of his knights. He strode into the chamber and clasped Lancelot in his arms, greeting him with warm words.

Sir Lancelot explained how he had been beguiled by Morgan le Fay. "Your daughter saved me, sir," he said, "so I have pledged my service to her and all her kindred."

"So you will help me on Tuesday?"

"Willingly. I will not fail you. I am told that the tournament will take place two miles from this abbey. Let me have three of your best knights. Give them shields painted white. Provide me with one, too. We will wait in a small wood close to the field of battle. When I see your followers fighting those of the King of North Wales, I will come out in open combat against the king. Then you will see what kind of knight I am." Bagdemagus embraced him again.

On the following day he sent Lancelot the three knights he had requested, and their shields were painted white. They took themselves off to the wood close to the tournament and there waited their turn. First on the field came the King of North Wales; he had with him one hundred and eighty warriors, together with three knights of the Round Table. They were Sir Mordred, Sir Marhalt and Sir Gahalantine. Lancelot knew them well. You may recall that Sir Mordred was the son of King Arthur himself, fruit of the incestuous union between the king and his half-sister. King Bagdemagus entered the field with only eighty knights, and at the first challenge they were pushed back; twelve of them were killed, with only slight casualties on the side of the King of North Wales.

So Lancelot gave his men the signal to advance; they rode out together into the thickest of the press. Lancelot thrust his spear into five knights, and broke the backs of six more. Then he bore down upon the

97

King of North Wales, who fell from his horse and broke his thigh. The three knights of the Round Table witnessed the deeds of this knight with the white shield, and wondered who he might be. "This is a valiant man," Sir Marhalt said. "I will advance against him." So he charged but Lancelot caught him with his sword; Marhalt fell and injured his shoulder.

"I will bring vengeance on him," Sir Mordred called out. He galloped forward but Lancelot forestalled him; he struck at him with his shield so forcefully that Mordred fell into a swoon.

It was now the turn of Gahalantine. He fell upon Lancelot, and they fought long and hard. But Lancelot proved the stronger. Gahalantine bowed his head in surrender, and his horse bore him away. Then Lancelot turned to the other knights, but none of them would joust against him. So King Bagdemagus was awarded the victory. He took Lancelot back to his castle, where they revelled into the night. Lancelot himself was rewarded with rich gifts.

The release of the prisoners

On the following morning he said farewell to his hosts. "I must find my brother, Sir Lionel," he told them, "who disappeared as I slept beneath an apple tree. When I woke he was gone, I do not know where." He turned to the king's daughter. "Fair lady," he said, "if at any time you need my service, let me know. I will not fail you. Now God be with you all."

So Lancelot left them, and before long, he found himself upon the wide plain close to the apple tree where he had slumbered. A young woman was coming towards him on a white palfrey. "Can you tell me this, lady," he called out to her, "where in this land will I find adventures?"

"They are closer than you think, sir. Are you a valiant knight?"

"Why else would I be here?"

"I can take you to the castle of the fiercest and most powerful knight that ever lived. But first you must tell me your name."

"I am Lancelot du Lake."

"Well, Lancelot du Lake, your chance has come. Close to us here dwells Sir Tarquin, who boasts that he can beat any knight in battle. I believe that he holds many of Arthur's knights in prison, where they are tightly bound. But if you succeed, sir, you must promise me this. You will help me, and other young women, who are in daily distress from the actions of a false knight."

"I swear to assist you, lady."

"Then come with me."

She led him to the ford and to the tree from which hung the silver basin; there he also saw the shields of Sir Lionel and the others. He beat the basin with his spear for some time, but no knight came. So Lancelot galloped with the lady around the moat and, on the other side, he saw coming towards him Sir Tarquin with another knight bound to his horse. He recognized the captured man at once: it was Sir Gaheris, a knight of the Round Table and brother of Sir Gawain.

"I know that knight," he told the lady. "By God's grace I will rescue him. And if I can wreak vengeance on his captor, I will deliver all the prisoners in the dungeon here."

Having caught sight of Lancelot, Sir Tarquin raised his spear in defiance.

"Put down the man you have bound," Lancelot called to him, "and match your might with mine! I will avenge the knights of the Round Table!"

"If you are of that fellowship, sir, then I defy you. Do your worst."

So they rode against each other, exchanging many strong blows. Finding no sure victory, they leaped down from their saddles and raised their swords against each other. For two hours they fought, hot and furious, and there was no end in sight. Sir Tarquin stopped for a moment. "Hold your hand for a while," he told Lancelot. "Listen to what I have to say."

"Speak."

"You are the strongest and most powerful knight I have ever fought. You are very like one I hate above all others. If you are not he, I make you this promise. I will release all the knights in my prison, if you tell me your name. Then the two of us will live in fellowship. I will never fail you while I have life."

"You speak fair words, sir. But tell me this. Who is the knight you hate above all others?"

"His name is Sir Lancelot du Lake. He killed my brother, Sir Carados, at the Dolorous Tower. I have

100

sworn to seek him out and slay him. I have already slaughtered a hundred knights, and wounded a hundred more, so that they could not help Lancelot. I have thrown others of his fellowship into a foul prison. Now, sir, tell me your name."

"I could go in peace now, or I could fight you. Prepare yourself. I am Lancelot du Lake, son of King Ban and knight of the Round Table. I killed your brother beside the Dolorous Tower. I defy you. Do your worst."

"Ah, Sir Lancelot. I have longed for this day. Welcome indeed. You will not depart from this place until one of us is dead."

So they fought long and hard for more than two hours; they were like wild bulls in battle for their lives, the ground soaked with their blood. Sir Tarquin seemed to tire first; he stepped back and let down the guard of his shield. Lancelot seized the moment and slashed at his helmet with his sword; the helmet broke, and then with one blow Lancelot took off his head. Tarquin was dead.

When Sir Lancelot saw this, he went over to the lady who had led him here. "Fair lady, I am ready now to go wherever you wish."

The wounded knight, Sir Gaheris, now saluted him. "Sir," he said, "you have this day defeated the strongest and most ferocious knight in the world. Will you tell me your name?"

"I am Lancelot du Lake. I have defended you for the sake of King Arthur, and for the sake of your brother, Gawain. When you enter this manor house, you will find many knights of the Round Table confined there. I believe that among them are my two brothers, Sir Lionel and Sir Ector, who rode this way and were never seen afterwards. When you free them, give them all my greetings. Tell Ector and Lionel to ride to the king's court and wait for me there. I will return by Pentecost, after I have fulfilled my promise to this lady."

Then he and the lady rode off. Gaheris returned to the manor house, and went down into the dungeons. He released the knights from their cells and, seeing him wounded, they all believed that it was he who had slain Sir Tarquin. "Not so," he told them. "Sir Lancelot du Lake is your saviour. He sends you his greetings. Are Sir Lionel and Sir Ector among you?"

"Here!" Ector called out. "Still alive and now rejoicing."

"Sir Lancelot asks you to meet him at the court of King Arthur. He requests you to wait for him there."

"Oh no. We will not wait without purpose," Sir Lionel replied. "While we have life and breath, we will make haste to find him."

So after a fine supper of venison, and a night of rest, the two brothers rode out in quest of Lancelot.

Lancelot's love for Guinevere

Now we return to Lancelot, and the lady riding beside him. They had come to a path that led into a dark wood. "This is the place," she said, "where a knight of ill fame attacks all women that pass. He robs them, and then he ravishes them."

"Robs them? And rapes them? Such a knight shames his order and dishonours his oath. He should not live. Ride on a little way, lady, and I will hide myself in the bracken here. If he comes to trouble you, I will break cover and rescue you."

So the lady went on at a slow, ambling pace and, within a short time, a rider came out of the wood and confronted her. She cried out in fear and at once Lancelot rode from his hiding place. "False knight and traitor," he called out, "who taught you to trouble maidens and gentlewomen?" The man pulled out his sword and charged Lancelot. But the knight hurled a spear that caught the man in the throat and instantly killed him. "You have suffered the punishment," he said, "you have long deserved."

"That is the truth," the lady told him. "Just as Sir Tarquin injured good knights, so this man harmed good women. His name was Sir Peris of the Savage Forest."

"Is there anything else I can do for you, madam?"

"Not at this time, sir. May Almighty Jesus protect and preserve you, for you are the meekest and most gentle knight I have ever met. You lack only one thing, sir. You must find a wife. It is rumoured that you love Queen Guinevere, and that she has put an enchantment upon you; it is said that you can love no woman but her. For that reason, the great lords of the land are in deep distress."

"I cannot help what others say," he told her. "But I will never marry. I am wedded to a life of battles and adventures. Nor will I take a lover. A good knight must be chaste and virtuous. If I lay with a woman I would lose half my strength. I might be undone by a lesser knight. No. I would rather be unwed than unhappy."

The two giants

So they took their leave of each other. Sir Lancelot rode for three days through a thick forest until he came to a long bridge that crossed a deep and swiftly running river. He was about to ride upon it when he was accosted by a churlish porter who struck his horse on the nose. "Who are you," the man asked him, "to ride across this bridge without a licence?"

"Why should I not come this way? I cannot ride beside it. I cannot ride on water."

"You have no choice in the matter." The porter raised a great club of iron and was about to bring it down on Lancelot's back when the knight raised his sword and, with one blow, cut the man in two.

He rode on to the end of the bridge, and came to a village. The people gathered around him. "Fair knight, what have you done?" they cried. "You have killed the chief porter of our castle." Sir Lancelot listened to them in silence, and then made his way to the castle itself.

He rode into the courtyard, and tied his horse to a great iron ring set in the stone. He looked around, and saw that there were many people standing at the doors and the windows. They called out to him. "Sir knight, what are you doing here? This is not the place for you."

Then all at once two giants came out, wielding clubs of great size, and advanced upon him. Sir Lancelot put

104

his shield before him and struck the club from the hands of one of them; he raised his sword and smashed the giant's head. The second giant then ran in fear, but Lancelot followed him. He flung himself upon him and finished him with a thrust through the neck.

He went back into the castle, and there came before him sixty ladies; they kneeled before him, and called out with one voice, "Welcome, gentle knight. You have rescued us from seven years' imprisonment. We were forced to make silk tapestries to earn our food, even though we are all gentlewomen. So we rejoice at our deliverance and bless the day that you were born. Will you tell us your name?"

"Good ladies, I am Lancelot du Lake."

"We have hoped and prayed for your coming," one of the women said to him. "No other knight has been able to conquer the giants. They were afraid only of you."

"I am glad of it. If I come this way again, I hope you will make me welcome. In recompense for your labour take all the treasure that the giants have amassed. And then restore the castle to its rightful owner. To whom does it belong?"

"This place is called Tintagel. It was the property of Igraine who bore a son, Arthur, to Uther Pendragon. Do you know the story?"

"Yes. I have heard it."

The wanderings of Lancelot

Lancelot mounted his horse, and rode off. He journeyed through many strange countries, through waters and woods, along dark paths and evil ways. He crossed desolate heaths and marshes where the wild things dwell. Then at last by good fortune he found a castle in the keeping of an old lady; she welcomed him and lodged him with good will. After a delightful dinner she took him to a chamber, above the gatehouse, where he laid himself down to sleep.

He was roused by the sound of someone knocking at the gate. He went over to the window and saw one knight pursued by three others; they were threatening him with their swords. Lancelot recognized the man under attack as Sir Kay, son of Ector. "It would be a great dishonour," Lancelot said, "to suffer one man to defend himself against three. I will not be a sharer in his death." So with the help of a twisted sheet he let himself down from the window. "Turn, knights, upon me!" he shouted. "Leave your unequal fight."

So they turned to Lancelot, and the three of them alighted from their horses. Then they charged him with drawn swords. Sir Kay advanced to help him, but Lancelot waved him away. "I will not need your assistance," he said. "Leave me alone with them." With seven strokes he laid all three of them at his feet.

"Sir knight," they said, "we surrender. Your sword is too strong for us."

"Surrender to this man," he told them. "Then I will spare your lives."

"Surely we may yield to you? We would have overcome Kay."

"There is some justice in what you say. So this is what you will do. On next Whit Sunday you will go to the court of King Arthur, and there you will surrender yourselves to Guinevere, the queen. Say that Sir Kay sent you there as prisoners."

The three knights swore on their swords that they would do so, and Sir Lancelot let them depart in peace.

Then Lancelot knocked on the gate with the pommel of his sword, and his host came out. "I had thought," she said, "that you were asleep in your bed."

"So I was, but I was obliged to come to the rescue of an old comrade of mine." They had come into the torchlight, and Sir Kay at once saw that his saviour was Lancelot. He fell to his knees, and thanked him for his service. "It was the least I could do," Lancelot said. "Now rest yourself. Eat and sleep."

Lancelot left him the next morning. Before he departed, however, he took the trouble of taking Sir Kay's armour and saddling Sir Kay's horse. He left his own armour and horse behind. "I know why he has done this," Sir Kay said, when he discovered it. "He has left me his armour so that I might ride safely and in peace. He has taken mine to provoke more knights into battle with him."

Sir Lancelot, meanwhile, had been travelling for a long time through a great forest filled with the sound of birdsong. At last he came into a country of fair rivers and meadows. He saw before him a long bridge, with three tents of silk raised upon it. The first of the tents was covered in blue silk, the second in purple silk and the third in green silk. There was a white shield before each tent, together with a spear, and at the entrance to each of the three tents stood a knight in armour. Sir

Lancelot rode past them, and said nothing. When he had galloped into the distance, one of them, Sir Gawter, spoke out. "That was Sir Kay," he said. "He considers himself the finest knight in the world. I will ride after him and test his pride. You will see how I fare."

So Sir Gawter mounted a great horse, took his spear in his hand, and pursued Sir Lancelot. "Slow down!" he called out to him. "You shall not pass this way unscathed!" So Lancelot turned, took his sword, and came after Sir Gawter; he knocked him and his horse to the ground with one blow.

Another of the knights, Sir Gilmer, was astonished. "That was not Sir Kay. This man is far stronger. This man must have killed Sir Kay and taken his armour."

The third knight, Sir Raynolde, prepared to mount his horse. "Whether it is Kay or not," he told Gilmer, "let us ride out and rescue our brother. We will be hard pressed to match this knight, so be prepared to die."

Gilmer was the first to reach him, but Lancelot took his spear and thrust him from his horse. Raynolde reined in his horse. "Sir knight, you are a strong man. But my anger makes me stronger. I believe that you have killed two of my brothers. Prepare yourself for my revenge."

They fell upon each other. Their spears broke, and so they took out their swords and slashed furiously. Gawter and Gilmer had risen to their feet. They were weakened but they were not badly wounded. "Come, brother," Gawter said. "Let us go to the aid of Raynolde, who is fighting so well against this unknown

108

knight." So they went for Lancelot, brandishing their swords. He made short work of all three of them. He cut down Raynolde before bringing Gawter and Gilmer to the ground once again.

Raynolde, his head all bloody and bruised, advanced on Lancelot, but the noble knight put up his sword. "Let it be," he said. "I was not far from you when you were made a knight, Sir Raynolde, and I know you to be valiant. I do not wish to kill you."

"Thank God for your goodness," Raynolde replied. "If I may speak for my brothers, we are willing to submit. But tell us your name. You are not Sir Kay."

"That is a matter for another day. Go to the court on Whit Sunday and there surrender yourselves to Queen Guinevere. Say that Sir Kay sent you."

They swore that this should be done and, after Sir Lancelot had departed, they helped each other on to their horses. On their journey back they wondered aloud who this noble knight might be.

The path to the Perilous Chapel

Lancelot himself had ridden into a dark wood, where the boughs of all the trees were bent into strange shapes, when he came upon a black hunting dog sniffing the air; she was on the trail of a wounded deer, so it seemed to Lancelot, and he followed her. The dog looked back at him from time to time, as if she were leading him forward. In the course of this journey, Lancelot passed a track of blood. They crossed marshland and streams until they came to an ancient castle. The dog ran over the bridge that crossed the moat, waiting for Lancelot on the other side. The knight then followed her into a great hall, where he saw a knight lying dead upon the floor; the dog had begun licking the knight's bloody wounds when a young lady came out, weeping.

"Sir knight," she said to Lancelot, "you have brought me too much sorrow."

"Why do you say that? I did no harm to the dead man lying here. The dog brought me to this place. Do not be displeased with me. I grieve for you."

"I believe that you are speaking the truth. I was testing you. But it was not you who killed my husband. He who performed that deed will himself be badly wounded. And I shall make sure that he never recovers."

"What was your husband's name?"

"Sir Gilbert the Bastard. No better knight rode in the world."

"God send you comfort."

With these words he left her and went back into the dark wood. Within a short time he was hailed by a lady who seemed to know him. "You are well found," she called out to him. "On the vows of your knighthood I request you to help my brother, who lies helpless and bleeding close by. He fought Sir Gilbert the Bastard in plain battle, and was badly wounded. The dead man's wife is a witch. She told me that my brother's wounds would never be healed until I could find a knight that was willing to ride to the Perilous Chapel; in that sacred place he will find a sword and a cloth smeared in blood. A piece of that cloth, together with the sword, will restore my brother to health."

"This is a marvellous thing," Lancelot replied. "What is your brother's name?"

"Sir Meliot de Logris."

"I know him well. He is a knight of the Round Table. Of course I will help him."

"Then follow this path. It will bring you to the Perilous Chapel. I will remain here until by God's grace you return. If you cannot succeed in this quest, I know of no other knight that can save him."

So Lancelot rode off. When he came up to the Perilous Chapel he tied his horse to a little gate and entered the churchyard. It was a small chapel made of stone, and on the stones themselves were carved many curious signs and devices; some were in the shape of an "S" and others had images of the Holy Cross. As he came towards the door of the chapel, itself wondrously carved, thirty giant warriors rose up from the ground of the churchyard; they wore black armour and carried black shields before them, as if they were the guardians of this sacred place. When Lancelot saw their faces he was a little afraid, so fierce and formidable they seemed, but he put his shield before him and walked forward. They made way for him, scattering to either side, and so emboldened he entered the chapel. It was suffused with the dim light of candles, and the air was sweet with incense. A corpse was lying before the altar, covered by a cloth of silk. There was a sword beside the bier. And the cloth was all bloody.

Sir Lancelot stooped down and cut out a piece of that cloth; as he did so he felt the ground shaking beneath him. The chapel trembled. He picked up the sword and strode out. The knights in the churchyard now menaced him. "Knight," they said, "lay down that sword or you shall die!"

"No words of yours will sway me," he replied. "Whether I live or die, you must fight me to win the sword." So they moved aside, and he went on his way.

Beyond the churchyard he came across a fair lady. "Sir Lancelot," she said. "Abandon this sword, or you will die for it."

"I take no heed of threats, lady."

"You have answered well," she replied. "If you had laid down that sword, you would never have seen Guinevere again."

"I would have made a mistake then."

"Now, gentle knight, I must ask you to kiss me. Just once."

"God forbid."

"You have saved yourself, sir. If you had decided to kiss me, you would have fallen dead at my feet. All my labour has been lost. Shall I tell you the truth? I have loved you for the last seven years, but I know that no woman can embrace you except Guinevere. I had decided that if I could not have you alive, I would have you dead. I would have embalmed your corpse, and kissed it night and day."

"Thank you for telling me, lady. And Jesus save me from your subtle crafts!" With that, he rode away. The books say that, on his departure, this woman pined away and died within a fortnight. Her name was Hallewes the Sorceress.

So Lancelot rode on and, in the course of his travels, he came upon the sister of Sir Meliot once more. When she saw him she clapped her hands and wept for joy. "Now at last," she said, "I can take you to my brother." She led him into a castle where Sir Meliot lay bleeding.

When the wounded man saw Lancelot he got to his knees. "Lord," he said, "help me in my distress." Lancelot leaped from his horse and touched Meliot with the sword he had taken from the Perilous Chapel, and then wiped his wounds with the cloth he had found there. The wounded knight was healed at once. There was much joy and feasting but, before Lancelot took his leave, he told Meliot to appear at the court of Arthur on the next Whit Sunday.

Deeds of shame

Lancelot rode along many rough paths and wild ways, always in search of adventures. One morning he came up to a fair castle, when suddenly he heard the bells of a falcon ringing in the air. He looked up and saw the bird flying towards a tall elm tree, where the long tassels about the bird's feet became entangled with the branches. A lady came running out of the castle. "Ah, Lancelot!" she cried. "As you are the flower of all knights, save my falcon. If my husband knows that I have lost her, he will kill me. I am sure of it."

"What is your lord's name?"

"He is Sir Phelot, and comes from the court of the King of North Wales."

"Well, lady, since you know my name and call upon my knighthood, I can do nothing other than help you. Will you help me to take off my armour?" So he undressed himself, down to his shirt and hose, and then began to climb the tree. He reached the falcon, unravelled its tassels and then came down with the bird. As soon as he had reached the ground, and returned the falcon, he found himself confronting Sir Phelot.

"Ah, Lancelot," the knight said. "Now I have you at my mercy."

Lancelot looked at the lady. "Why, madam, did you betray me?"

"Do not blame her," Phelot said. "She acted on my orders. Now your hour has come to die."

"Do you not feel shame," Lancelot asked him, "to attack an unarmed man?"

"Be that as it may, you must fight as best you can."

"Put my sword over there, at least. Hang it from the bough so that I might have the chance to reach it."

"Oh no. I know you better than you think, Lancelot. I will grant you no weapon."

"I must devise my own remedy then." He looked around, and saw above him a great branch with no leaves upon it; it was as thick as a man's neck and, with one leap, Lancelot reached at it and broke it from the tree. Bearing this in his hand he charged Phelot, who slashed at him eagerly. But Lancelot was too strong for

Phelot, and knocked him from his horse; then he took Phelot's sword, and sliced off his head.

"You have killed my husband!" the woman called out.

"You were willing to betray me with a trick," he replied. "Now I have repaid both of you."

He took up his armour and, mounting his horse, rode away from the castle, thanking God that he had escaped a hard reckoning. After many days' journey he came to a valley where, to his dismay, he saw a knight pursuing a lady with drawn sword. The knight was about to slay her when the lady, seeing Lancelot, cried out for assistance. So he rode quickly between them. "Knight, for shame!" he shouted. "Why do you hunt down a woman?"

"You have no right to come between me and my wife," he replied. "I will kill her despite your warning."

"No. You will not. You must fight me first."

"You do not know what you are doing, Lancelot. This woman has betrayed me."

"It is not true!" she cried out. "Just because I love and cherish my cousin, Germaine, he believes that there is something between us. He has become jealous. But I have done nothing wrong. I implore you, Lancelot. You are known to be the most honourable knight in the world. Please rescue me. This man is merciless."

"He will not harm you, lady. I am here now."

"So be it," the man said. "I will do as you wish, sir."

The three of them went on together, Lancelot riding between man and wife. After a while the knight looked

115

around. "Do you see, sir, these men of arms riding towards us?" Lancelot turned and, at that moment, the man took up his sword and cut off his wife's head.

"Traitor!" Lancelot cried. "You have shamed me for ever. You have slain a woman in my safe keeping." He dismounted, and drew out his sword. But the man came off his horse and fell to his knees, calling on Lancelot for mercy.

"You can have no mercy," Lancelot replied. "Get up. Prepare yourself to do battle."

"I will not fight you."

"Listen. I will take off my armour, and strip down to my shirt. I will carry only a sword."

"No, sir. You will still win."

"Then I charge you with this. You will take up the corpse and the head of your wife, and carry them with you everywhere until you come to the court of my lady Guinevere. Do you agree to my terms?"

"I swear that I will obey you, Lancelot."

"What is your name?"

"Sir Pedivere."

"You were born in a shameful hour, Sir Pedivere. Go on your way."

So Pedivere mounted his horse with his terrible burden, and rode to Arthur's court at Winchester where he found Queen Guinevere. "This is a dreadful deed," she told him after listening to his story. "You have shamed Lancelot as well as yourself. You must do penance. So I order you to travel with the body of your dead wife to Rome, where you must seek an audience with the pope. Only he can absolve you. You must not rest. If you do sleep, your dead wife must lie beside you."

He obeyed the queen in all things, and the old books tell us how he obtained the pope's pardon and how his wife was buried in Rome. From that time forward he lived as a holy man and became a hermit.

Now we turn again to Lancelot, who came back to court two days before Whit Sunday. All those he had summoned had arrived in good time. The three knights, who had come as the prisoners of Sir Kay, told the king how Lancelot had overcome them. Sir Gawter and his two comrades told a similar story. Meliot explained to the court how Lancelot had healed his wounds. Never was so much honour shown to any knight. The world rang with praise of Sir Lancelot.

TRISTRAM AND ISOLDE

Isolde the Fair

Once upon a time, during the reign of King Arthur so many centuries ago, there was a king called Melodias; he was lord of the country of Liones, a land now lost beneath the waves off the coast of Cornwall. It was his good fortune to marry Elizabeth — the sister of King Mark of Cornwall — who was acknowledged to be both good and beautiful. When Elizabeth knew herself to be with child, she and her husband were overjoyed.

Yet there was a lady in that country who also loved King Melodias, but without achieving her desire. So when the king rode out one day to hunt she set before him an enchanted deer, which led him deep into a forest; the king pursued the deer to the door of an old castle, where he was taken prisoner by the sorceress.

When Elizabeth realized that her husband was missing, she almost went out of her mind. She was already big with child, but insisted on riding with a gentlewoman to seek her husband. When they had travelled far into the forest, she fell into labour. By the grace of heaven, and with the help of the gentlewoman, the baby was born safely. But Elizabeth could not survive the ordeal, and the gates of death opened for her. That was her destiny. When she knew that she must die, she addressed the lady: "When you see my lord," she told her, "greet him for me. Let him know what I have suffered for his sake. Tell him that I am sorry to leave this world without seeing him again." Then she asked to see the new-born infant. "Ah, sweet child," she whispered, "you have murdered your mother. Let my lord name you Tristram, that means 'sorrowful birth'." Thereupon the queen gave up her ghost and died. The gentlewoman laid her beneath an ancient oak, and comforted the child as much as she could. Some of the lords of Liones had been riding in search of the queen and, when they found her dead, there was much sorrow. They took the child back to court, where he was wrapped in cloth of gold.

Read of the early life of Tristram

It so happened that Merlin, hearing of the plight of Melodias, had by means of magic rescued him from the sorceress. Merlin had travelled through the air and, at the sound of a certain word, the locks of all the dungeons were opened. When the king had returned to Liones, his lords greeted him with joy. But Melodias was distraught at the death of his wife. He buried her in a rich tomb, and christened his son Tristram as she had wished. He lived without a wife for seven years but then, at the end of this time, he married the daughter of the King of Brittany. She bore him several sons, and her resentment of Tristram grew ever greater. Why should the boy inherit the kingdom? So she decided to give him poison. She put the potion in a silver goblet, mixed with some sweet drink, and conveyed it to the chamber where he and her sons played; but one of her own sons took up the cup, and drained its contents. He fell down dead on the spot.

The queen was mortified by this accident, but she had made up her mind to kill the king's oldest son. So she put more of the poison in a goblet, and gave it to him. But the king, coming by, reached for the goblet to quench his thirst. He was about to swallow the draught when she ran over and knocked it from his hand. The king marvelled at her actions, but then recalled the death of her son.

"You false traitor!" he shouted at her. "Tell me what is in this cup, or else I will kill you!" He pulled out his sword, and demanded the truth from her.

"Have mercy on me," she said. "I will tell you all." So she confessed her plot to kill Tristram for the sake of her sons.

"You have spoken," the king told her. "Now you shall receive justice." She was brought before the barons, who condemned her to death by burning. Before the sentence was carried out, however, young Tristram kneeled before his father and asked for a gift.

"Of course," the king told him. "On my oath."

"Spare the life of my stepmother."

"That is not a good request. She would have killed you, and you would be right to hate her. That is why she must die."

"I forgive her, father. And I beseech you to pardon her. You made me a promise."

"Very well then. Unbind her. Lead her from the fire, and do as you like with her. I give her to you."

So the queen was rescued from death, but Melodias refused to have anything to do with her. He banned her from his bed and his table. But then, sometime later, Tristram brought them together again.

It was time for Tristram himself to leave court. With a gentleman scholar, Gouvernail, he travelled to the court of France in order to be tutored in the arts of chivalry. He stayed there for seven years, learning the language and culture of that most civilized of courts. He was taught the rules of music, and became an expert harper. He learned how to hunt and to hawk. He even wrote down all the terms of these sports, so that the book of hunting is still called *Sir Tristram's Book*. It is a volume used by all gentlemen, and it will be read until the day of doom.

Tristram returned to his father's court at the age of eighteen. King Melodias was delighted to find him grown so strong and handsome, and his wife welcomed him back all the more warmly for saving her from the fire. She gave him many gifts, and in truth all the people of the realm celebrated his return.

There came a time when King Angwish of Ireland demanded tribute from King Mark of Cornwall, complaining that it had not been paid for seven years. The King of Cornwall sent back a defiant message, saying that he would pay no tribute. "If Angwish wishes to insist upon this," he said, "let him send a knight into my realm that will fight for it. I trust that I will find a defender."

When the King of Ireland received this message, he grew terrible in his anger. He sent for Sir Marhalt, knight of the Round Table and his brother-in-law. "Marhalt," he said to him, "fair brother, I must ask you to sail to Cornwall and do battle on my behalf."

"Willingly. I will fight any knight of the Round Table for your sake. It can only increase my fame."

So without more ado Marhalt was armed and prepared for the combat to come. He sailed to Cornwall within the week. When King Mark was told that Sir Marhalt had come to the coast, by Tintagel, he was greatly disturbed. Marhalt had a reputation as one of the best knights in the world, and the king doubted that he had a worthy opponent to put against him. Marhalt remained at sea, in sight of the battlements and towers of Tintagel, demanding that the tribute be paid or that battle be joined. Some of the lords of Cornwall counselled the king to send word to the court of King Arthur and ask for the help of Lancelot. But others dismissed the idea, saying that Lancelot would not wish to travel so far.

Meanwhile the cry had gone through all Cornwall, asking for the aid of a brave knight. Not one had come forward. When word of this reached Tristram he was enraged at the cowardice of the Cornish men. He went to the king and sought his advice. "We are bound by treaty to the land of Cornwall, Father," he told him. "It is our duty to release it from bondage to Ireland. There would be shame upon us all if Sir Marhalt should sail away from here without being challenged."

"Do you not know," the king asked him, "that he is considered to be one of the best knights in the world? Who here could match him?"

"Then I will be made knight. If you give me permission, I will ride to the court of King Mark."

"I am content," his father said, "if your courage rules you."

So Tristram made himself ready and rode to the court. He came into the presence of the king, and there pressed his case. "Sire," he said, "I ask you to enrol me in the order of knighthood. I will do battle on your behalf against Marhalt."

The king saw that this boy was well made and powerful. "From where have you come?" he asked him.

"I come from King Melodias. I assure you that I am a gentleman."

"What is your name and where were you born?"

"I am called Tristram. And I was born in Liones."

"You are welcome, Tristram. I will make you a knight, as long as you fight Marhalt."

"That is why I came, sire."

So Tristram was made a knight, and a message was sent to Marhalt that a knight was ready to meet him in battle. "Very good," he said. "But tell King Mark that I will fight only with a knight of royal blood. He must be the son of a king or a queen."

Sir Tristram was sent for, and told the conditions of this battle. "Very well," he told the king, "you may inform Marhalt that I am of blood as noble as his own. I am the son of King Melodias. My mother was your own sister, sir, who died in the forest on the day of my birth."

"Jesus save us!" the king exclaimed. "You are more welcome than ever, fair nephew."

So Tristram was armed and mounted in earnest, with trappings of gold and silver. When Sir Marhalt was told that his opponent was the son of a king, he was delighted to be matched against him. It was agreed that they would fight upon an island close to Marhalt's ships, and so Tristram boarded a great vessel with his arms and horse. When King Mark and the court saw him depart, they wept with mingled joy and sorrow at the thought that he might suffer on their behalf.

So Tristram sailed towards the island where Marhalt was waiting for him; he saw six ships at anchor, and he ordered his men to land at this spot. His companion, Gouvernail, was with him. "Where," Tristram asked him, "is the man I am supposed to fight?"

"He is there. In the shadow of the ships. Just there."

"Ah. Now I see him. I see the spear in his hand, and his shield upon his shoulder."

So, with his own spear and shield, he prepared himself for combat. "Go back to King Mark," he told Gouvernail, "and give him this message. If I am slain in battle, ask him to bury me as he deems best. Tell him this, too. I will never be accused of cowardice. If I die with honour, he must pay no tribute to Ireland. But if I should flee, then let him flay my corpse and deny me Christian burial. Do not return to this island until you have seen the outcome of the battle."

When Marhalt saw that his opponent had landed, he rode over to Tristram. "Young knight," he asked, "what are you doing here? I feel sorry for you. Truly. Do you not know that I have fought many noble knights and that I have never fallen? I have defeated the best knights in the world. Take my advice. Return to your ship."

"You must realize, fair knight, that I will not avoid battle with you. I was made a knight precisely in order to fight you. I am the son of a king. I have sworn an oath to assail you with all my strength, and to save Cornwall from the exaction of tribute. That is my cause. That is why I come against you here. I have never yet proved myself in combat. Now is my chance. If I am able to defeat you, my renown will ring around the world."

"So you wish to win fame, do you? If you can withstand just three strokes of my sword, you will have done well. Are you ready?"

So they levelled their spears and rode against each other. They both fell to the ground but, in their struggle, Marhalt had given Tristram a bad wound in his side. They pulled out their swords, put up their shields, and attacked each other like wild men. They gave no quarter but clashed again and again. They fought for the whole of the morning, until the ground beneath them was soaked in their blood. Tristram battled harder than ever, even as the strength of Marhalt ebbed; with a mighty stroke he severed Marhalt's helmet in two, and his sword broke open his head. The sword was so firmly lodged in his skull that Tristram had to wrench at it three times in order to free it. Marhalt fell to his knees, moaning; when he saw how things stood he threw his sword and shield from him, and fled to his ships. Tristram picked up the man's weapons, and taunted him as he ran. "Ah, sir knight," he called out, "why are you leaving? You do yourself and your king great shame. I am young and untested. But I would rather be torn to pieces than surrender to you." Sir Marhalt made no reply, but went on his way still groaning. "Well, sir," Tristram continued, "I promise that I will keep safe your sword and your shield. I will take them with me when I ride on my adventures."

So Marhalt and his companions sailed back to Ireland in disgrace. When he came to the court of King Angwish the doctors examined his wounds. They found a piece of Tristram's sword lodged in Marhalt's skull, but by no means could they extract it. He died in agony. But his sister kept the fragment with her, with the aim of being revenged whenever she could.

Read of the meeting of Tristram with Isolde

We turn again to Sir Tristram, who was so badly wounded and bloodied that he could now hardly stand. He fell into a fever, shivering, and laid himself down upon a little hill, where he lost more blood. Yet King Mark soon came across the water to the island, and with his lords walked in procession to honour his knight. He carried Tristram back in his ship to Tintagel, where the young knight was laid in a soft bed. When the king inspected his wounds, he wept. "So God help me," he said, "I would give up my lands to save my nephew."

Tristram lay for more than a month. He had been wounded by Marhalt's first stroke, but he did not know that the sword had been poisoned. The king and court were in dismay, because they believed that he would die. All manner of doctors and surgeons were called, but none could cure him.

One day a wise woman came to court, and learned of his plight. She said plainly to the king, and to Tristram himself, that he would be cured of his wound only if he went to the country where the poison had been refined. He would be helped there, and nowhere else. So King Mark ordered a vessel to be prepared, and Tristram set off for Ireland; that country had been the source of his sorrow. He took his harp with him.

By fortune, good or ill, he landed close to the place where King Angwish and his queen had a castle. On his arrival he played such a marvellous lay upon his harp that no one in Ireland had ever heard anything like it. The report of a sick knight, able to play wonderfully upon the harp, reached the king. He asked for the man to be sent to him. "Make sure that his wounds are examined," he said to his courtiers.

On Tristram's arrival the king asked for his name. So Tristram was careful. "I am called," he said, "Sir Tramtrist. I am from the land of Liones. I received these wounds in combat for a lady's hand."

"I promise you, sir," the king replied, "that you will have all the help that I can give you. I know how you feel. I have just endured pain of my own. I have lost the best knight in the world. His name was Marhalt. Have you heard of him? I will tell you what happened."

Sir Tristram dissembled. He listened to the story, and said that he was sorry for the dead knight; he knew the truth better than the king. But Angwish looked favourably on the young man, and gave him into the care of his daughter. Her name was La Belle Isolde, and she was at this time the fairest lady in the world. She was a skilful doctor, too, and she discovered where the poison lay within his wound. As the wise woman had predicted, Isolde healed him. Tristram fell in love with her, and taught her the secrets of the harp. She in turn loved him.

There was another knight, Sir Palomides the Saracen, who had always loved Isolde and gave her many gifts. Tristram saw this, and was envious. When Isolde told him that Palomides was to be baptized a Christian for her sake, Tristram grew more jealous still.

It so happened that King Angwish declared a tournament for all worthy combatants; his messengers went into Wales, Scotland, England, France and Brittany proclaiming the news. When Isolde heard of it, she went to Tristram and urged him to take part in the combat. "Fair lady," he told her. "I am still weak. If it had not been for your help, I would now be dead. What can I do? You know well enough that I should not joust."

"Oh, Sir Tramtrist," she replied, "what are you saying? I have been assured that Sir Palomides will ride there. I ask you to reconsider. Otherwise he will win the prize."

"That may be so, lady. But I am a young knight. In the very first battle I fought, I was almost killed. Yet I bow to your will. I will go to the joust on one condition. You must reveal to no one that I am taking part. I shall pledge my poor person for your sake. Perhaps Sir Palomides will feel the force of my spear."

"Do the best you can," she said. "I will procure horse and armour for you."

"As you will. I am yours to command."

So on the day of the joust Sir Palomides, armed with a black shield, overthrew many knights. Yet Sir Tristram held back. When King Angwish asked him the reason, he gave the same reply as before. "I was recently wounded. As yet, I dare not ride against him."

A warrior from the court of King Melodias, the father of Tristram, had come to the tournament. His name was Hebes le Renownys. As soon as he saw Tristram, he bowed deeply to him. Isolde saw this, but said nothing. She was convinced that Tristram was a man of some renown, and she loved him all the more because of it.

Tristram took the young man to one side and asked him not to reveal his name. "I will not disclose it, sir," Hebes said, "unless you wish it."

"Now tell me this. Why have you come to Ireland?"

"I have come with Sir Gawain to be dubbed a knight. I would like to receive that honour from your hands, if I may."

"Come to me secretly tomorrow morning. I will make you a knight in the field of tournament."

132

On the following morning Sir Palomides rode on to the field, as he had done on the first day, and defeated the King of Scots as well as the King of the Hundred Knights. But then Sir Tristram came forth, wearing white armour and riding on a white horse. He looked like a bright angel sent down upon the earth. Sir Palomides saw him, and aimed straight for him. But Tristram lowered his spear, and caught him squarely in the middle. When Palomides fell to the earth, a great shout went up from the spectators. "Look," some said, "the knight with the black shield has fallen!" Others shouted, "It is Sir Palomides!" Isolde was delighted that her unsought suitor had been beaten. Sir Gawain and his nine companions wondered who this white knight might be, but none of them dared to fight with him.

In the glow of this victory Sir Tristram made Hebes a true knight, and the young man followed him ever after.

After Palomides had risen to his feet, he was bitterly ashamed of his defeat and tried to leave the field unseen. But Tristram spotted him, and rode after the retreating warrior. "Turn around," he told him. "I challenge you once more." So both men drew their swords and cut at one another. Tristram disarmed his opponent with a great blow, so that Palomides was bowed down upon the earth. "Surrender," Tristram said. "Obey me now or I will kill you."

"I yield to you."

"This is my charge to you. First, upon pain of your life you must leave off your pursuit of Isolde. You will never more come near her. Second, I command you to bear no arms for a year and a day. Promise me these things, or I will slay you."

"This is the greatest shame I have ever endured."

"Nevertheless, swear."

So Palomides was forced to swear an oath. In anger and distress he cut off his armour and flung it as far as he could.

Sir Tristram rode back to the castle where Isolde was waiting for him. On his way, however, he met a fair lady who greeted him. "Who are you?" she inquired of him.

"I am he who has just defeated Sir Palomides in combat."

"What is your name? Are you by any chance Sir Lancelot du Lake? I am sure no one else could have performed such a feat."

"No, lady. I cannot claim to be so great a knight. I must trust to God to give me strength of that kind."

"Fair knight, put up your visor."

When he lifted his visor she almost fainted. She had never seen such a fair-looking knight. Then she took her leave of him. He went on to the castle, where he was welcomed by Isolde.

When the king and queen knew that Sir Tramtrist had defeated Palomides, they rejoiced; he was entertained even more royally than before.

Read of the discovery of Tristram's identity

There came a day when the queen and her daughter prepared a bath for Tristram. While Gouvernail and Sir Hebes were attending to him, the queen and Isolde

134

were sitting in the chamber where Tristram was lodged. The queen saw his sword lying upon the bed, and on an impulse drew it from its scabbard. She saw that a large piece was missing from its point, and she recalled the piece of metal found in the skull of her brother, Marhalt; they seemed to match exactly.

"Alas!" she cried out to Isolde. "This is the sword of the traitor who killed your uncle. I will prove it." So she rushed into her own chamber and opened the wooden coffer she kept there; she took out the piece of metal and came back to Tristram's room. She put it against the sword, and it fitted exactly. "Do you see this?" she asked Isolde.

Isolde was now distraught. She loved Tristram still, and she knew how cruel her mother could be. The queen now took up the sword and ran to the bath where Tristram lay; she was about to pierce him to the heart but Sir Hebes held her arm and pulled the sword from her. Thwarted in her plan, she hurried to the king.

She fell to her knees. "Oh, my lord," she said, "you have under your roof the traitor that killed my brother. You have welcomed here the knight who dispatched your dutiful servant!"

"What do you mean? Who are you talking about?"

"I am talking about Tramtrist. The man my daughter healed of his wounds."

"This is a dark day for me," the king replied. "I have seen Tramtrist in the field, and he is a worthy knight." He raised the queen from her knees. "I charge you, lady," he said, "not to meddle with this man. Leave him to me."

So he went to Tristram's chamber. He found him fully armed, and ready to depart; he knew that his identity had been discovered. His horse was waiting for him in the courtyard. "It will do you no good, sir," the king told him, "to thwart my anger by trying to escape. Out of love and respect for you, I promise you this. I will allow you to leave this court in safety if you tell me who you really are. And if you tell me the truth about the killing of Marhalt."

"I will not lie to you, sir," Tristram replied. "The name of my father is Melodias, King of Liones, and my mother is Queen Elizabeth, who is the sister of King Mark of Cornwall. My mother died at the time of my birth, which is why I am named Tristram, or 'sorrowful coming'. I called myself Tramtrist here because I did not wish to be known. Yet I must tell you, sir, that I fought your knight on behalf of King Mark of Cornwall. I wished to be called a true knight who fought for those he loved."

"As God is my judge," King Angwish told him, "I hold no grudge against you. You were behaving according to the proper forms of knighthood. But I cannot let you stay here. My barons, and my family, would be very displeased."

"I thank you, sir, for your kindness to me. You have been a good lord to me. And I thank your daughter, too, for all the benefits she has given me. She healed me when my life was in danger. I believe that I will be able to help you more in life than in death, because I will always be at your service. Whenever you come to England, I will be happy to ride at your side. And I also promise you this. I will be devoted to your daughter, Isolde, and I will never fail her. Will you allow me now to say farewell to her?"

"With all my heart."

Read of Tristram's farewell to Isolde

So Tristram went to Isolde's chamber. She began weeping when he told her of his departure. "Ah, gentle knight," she said, "I am so filled with sorrow that I scarcely know what to say."

"Madam," he replied, "my real name is Sir Tristram de Liones. I am of royal blood. Rest assured that I will be your knight for the remainder of my life."

"Is that your promise? Thank you. I will make a pledge to you in turn. For the next seven years I will not marry except with your assent. You may pick my husband for me."

Then they exchanged rings.

Tristram now came into the court of King Angwish and addressed the lords assembled there. "Good lords," he said, "the time has come for me to leave you all. If I have offended any man here, let him tell me now. I will make amends, if I can. And if there is any man who bears ill will to me, let him declare it now. I will prove myself by force of arms."

Yet they all stood still. Not one of them said a word. There were some of Sir Marhalt's kin among them, but even they would not meddle with him. So Tristram departed and, taking to sea, was brought by a fair wind to Tintagel on the coast of Cornwall. When King Mark learned that he had returned, completely healed, he rejoiced. Tristram then rode to the domain of his father, where the king and queen were so pleased by his return that they granted him many lands. After that, with their permission, he went back to the court of King Mark.

Read of the enmity between Tristram and King Mark

Tristram lived at the Cornish court for a long time until, in an evil season, strife rose up between him and the king. They both loved the same lady, the wife of Earl Segwarides, but the lady loved only Tristram. King Mark grew jealous. It so happened that one day the lady sent a dwarf to Tristram, entreating him to visit her on the following night. "Also," the dwarf told him, "she urges you to come well armed. Her husband is a tough fighter."

"Send my respects to the lady, fellow, and tell her that I will not fail her. I will be with her tomorrow night."

The king received news that the lady's dwarf had visited Tristram, and so he sent for the dwarf. Under threat of torture, the dwarf revealed the message he had brought. "Very well then," the king said to him, "now go on your way. But tell nobody that you have spoken to me. Do you understand?" The dwarf nodded, and left hurriedly.

Secretly King Mark arranged a plan to ambush Tristram on his way to the lady. He chose two of his best knights, and rode ahead along the path he knew Tristram would take. As soon as Tristram came into sight, the king rushed for him with his spear aloft; his two companions followed, swords drawn, and cut at him. Tristram was badly wounded in the breast, but not before he had beaten down the two knights. Then he launched his spear against King Mark, and brought him down to the ground, where he lay unconscious.

Tristram then made his way to his lady, who took him in her arms and led him to her bed. They made love so madly that he paid no heed to his wound; but his blood was all over the sheets and pillows. Then there came word that her husband, Sir Segwarides, was on his way. She urged Sir Tristram to leave her bed, arm himself, and ride off as fast as he could. When Segwarides entered the chamber, he saw that the bed had been disturbed. He came closer and, by the light of a lantern, saw that the sheets were covered in blood. "You have been false to me," he told her. "Why have you betrayed me?" He took out his sword. "I will slay you on the spot if you do not tell me who has been here with you."

"Mercy, my lord!" she cried out. "I will tell you his name!"

"Who is it?"

"Tristram. He was wounded while on his way to me."

"Traitors, both of you! Where is he now?"

"He left on his horse a few minutes ago. He cannot have gone far."

"Then I will find him." Segwarides leaped on his horse, and rode straight for Tintagel. He overtook

Tristram, and turned on him with his spear and sword. "Defend yourself," he called out. "False traitor knight!"

"I advise you to desist," Tristram told him. "I know that I have done wrong to you, and I do not want to fight you."

"That may not be," he replied. "Either you or I must die."

He charged him, but Tristram parried his blows with his sword before knocking him from his horse; he fell to the earth in a swoon.

So Tristram left him, and rode on to Tintagel. He took secret lodgings because he did not want the world to know that he had been wounded. Segwarides's men found him and carried him home on his shield. It was a long time before he recovered, but in the end he was well again.

Here is the knot. King Mark did not want to reveal that he had waited in ambush for Tristram, and in turn Tristram did not know that the king was involved in the attack. So Mark, when he discovered that his knight lay wounded in bed, came to visit him under cover of goodwill and compassion. He muttered fair words, but there was no love in his heart.

Many weeks passed. All was forgiven and forgotten. Segwarides did not want to challenge Tristram any further. Who would wish to add public shame to private hurt?

There came a time when a knight of the Round Table, Sir Bleoberis by name, arrived at the court of King Mark. He asked the king for a favour. "I believe," he said, "that I have the right."

The king wondered at his words but, since this knight was of great renown, he consented to his request.

"I wish to take as my lover the fairest lady to be found in your court."

"I cannot refuse you," King Mark told him. "You may choose as you wish."

So Bleoberis took the wife of Segwarides, and rode off with her on his horse. He made her sit behind his squire. When Segwarides heard of this, he set off in pursuit. The whole court was angered at the affair. Certain ladies knew of the love between Tristram and Segwarides's wife. One of them rebuked Tristram, in the most insulting terms, for failing to come to that lady's defence. "You are a coward," she said. "Shame on you for allowing a strange knight to carry her off."

"Fair lady," he answered, "it is not my part to defend her when her husband is here. If her lord had not been at court, of course I would have been her champion. If it happens that Segwarides does not succeed in rescuing her, then I may well ride in pursuit of Bleoberis."

The squire of Segwarides soon came back to the court, with the message that he had been badly wounded by Bleoberis and was now close to death.

141

King Mark was disconsolate. So Tristram, moved and saddened by this news, prepared himself to do battle with Bleoberis. Gouvernail, his companion, went with him, carrying his sword and spear. They rode a long way until they came to a valley, where they saw ahead of them Bleoberis, his squire and the lady herself.

Sir Tristram galloped hard after them. "Knight of Arthur's court," he called out. "Stay! Return this lady or surrender her to me."

"I will do neither. I have no fear of any Cornish knight."

"No fear? Then fight."

So they rode down upon each other and clashed with a sound like thunder. They jumped from their saddles, and lashed at each other with their swords. They fought for more than two hours, and were sometimes so weary that they lay gasping on the ground. Eventually Sir Bleoberis stood back. "Gentle knight, rest your arm a little. Let us speak together."

"Say what you will. I am listening."

"I would like to know, sir, your name and your descent."

"I will tell you. I am the son of King Melodias, and my mother was the sister of King Mark. I am called Sir Tristram de Liones."

"I am very glad to meet you. You are the knight who defeated Marhalt in hand-to-hand combat over the tribute due to Cornwall. You are the knight who overcame Sir Palomides at the tournament."

"I am the man. Now I have told you my name, you must tell me yours."

"I am Bleoberis de Ganis, brother of Blamoure and cousin of Sir Lancelot du Lake."

"Cousin of Lancelot? I will fight you no longer. I have too great a love for that peerless knight."

"I will return the compliment. Since you have come this way to rescue the lady, I will leave her free to decide her own fate. I will place her midway between us. She may choose whomever she pleases."

"I believe, sir, that she will come to me."

"Well, sir, we will see."

So the lady dismounted and stood between them. Then she spoke to Sir Tristram. "You know well enough that you were the knight I trusted and honoured most in the world. I supposed that you loved me above all others. But when you saw this knight ride off with me, you made no attempt to rescue me. You left it to my husband. I had thought you had more concern for me than that. So now I forsake you, and renounce my faith in you." With that, she went over to Bleoberis. Tristram was incensed with her. How could he return to court without her?

"I believe you are to blame," Bleoberis said to him. "I hear that this lady loved you but in the end, as she says, you deceived her. But I am not eager to keep her. A bolter is always a bolter. What will happen when she becomes tired of me? Here. Take her back."

"Oh no, my lord," she said, "I will never go with him. He forsook me in my hour of need. Ride off, Sir Tristram. Even if you had defeated this knight, I would still not have been yours." She turned to Sir Bleoberis. "Before you leave this land," she pleaded with him, "I ask you to take me to the abbey where my husband lies wounded."

"Do you hear her, Sir Tristram?" Bleoberis asked him. "She does not want you. As for me, I have completed my quest. But for your sake, sir, I will now escort her to her husband."

"Thank you," Tristram replied. "I will be more wary in future where I put my affections. Had her husband been absent from the court, I would have been the first to ride to her rescue. But now — farewell."

Tristram rode back to Tintagel, heavy of heart, while Bleoberis took the lady to her husband. Segwarides was greatly comforted by the sight of her, and was grateful to Tristram for fighting to save her. When she came back to court, she told the story of the battle to King Mark. When she praised Tristram for ensuring that she was returned to her husband, the king was secretly enraged. He resolved to kill Tristram, and pondered on the means of doing this. He decided to send him to Ireland, where he might be dispatched by his enemies. Tristram had often told him of the beauty and grace of Isolde, so now he asked the knight to bring her back to Cornwall; the king told him that he wished to marry her. Tristram was aware of the danger in returning there, but he could not refuse his uncle's request. He made himself ready for the journey, and took with him some worthy knights.

They had just set sail when a storm at sea sent them eastward along the coast of England, not far from Arthur's court at Camelot. They came to land, sick and weary, at the place now known as Portsmouth. They scrambled for the shore and, when they reached dry land, Tristram set up a pavilion from which he suspended his shield as a token of his willingness to fight. He had not reached Ireland, after all, but the King of Ireland was closer than he thought. It so happened that Sir Bleoberis and Sir Blamoure had summoned King Angwish to the court of King Arthur, the King of Ireland's overlord; they accused him of killing their cousin. In those far-off days, murder was considered to be a form of treason; so King Angwish had to fight the charge in his own person or find a champion. There was no other remedy. The judges granted him three days to give his answer. Gouvernail came to Tristram's pavilion and told him of the plight of the king. "God save me," Tristram said, "this is the best news I have heard in seven years. The King of Ireland now has need of my help. I dare say that there is no knight in the kingdom, outside Arthur's court, that would dare to do battle with Sir Blamoure. I will take it upon myself to be the king's champion, so that he will gladly give me Isolde."

Gouvernail went at once to King Angwish. "I know a knight who wishes to speak to you, sire. He desires to serve you."

"What is his name?"

"Sir Tristram de Liones. For the favours you showed him in your own country, he wishes to fight on your behalf."

"Come with me," the king replied. "We will call upon Sir Tristram."

With a few friends they took horse and rode to the pavilion. When Tristram saw the king coming, he would have taken his stirrup. But the king dismounted lightly and held Tristram in his arms.

"My gracious lord," Tristram said, "of your great goodness to me, I cannot speak enough. So instead I will serve you to the full extent of my power."

"Gentle knight, I have never had more need of you than now. You know that I have been challenged by Sir Bleoberis and Sir Blamoure. These are hard men to beat. You have come upon Sir Bleoberis before, I believe."

"I will do battle for you, as long as you swear on oath that you had nothing to do with the death of their cousin."

"I do so swear."

"There is one other thing. If I win this battle for you, will you give me any reward that I believe to be reasonable?"

"God help me, you will have whatever you wish."

"Well said, sir. You may proclaim that your champion is ready. I would rather die in this combat than be considered a coward."

"I have no doubts about you," the king replied. Then he returned to court, and informed the judges that a knight had come forward to do battle on his behalf. Sir

Tristram was called before them, to hear the charge against King Angwish. When the knights of the court saw Tristram they spoke much of him, extolling his exploits against several great warriors.

Sir Bleoberis came over to Sir Blamoure. "Brother," he said, "remember what stock we come from. Sir Lancelot is our cousin. None of our kin has ever been defeated in battle. Suffer death rather than be shamed!"

"Have no doubt about me, brother. I shall never shame one of our blood. I have heard that this knight here is as valiant as any other in the world, but I will never surrender to him. That vile word will not pass my lips. I would rather that he killed me."

"God be with you then. But be careful of him."

"I put my trust in God."

So Blamoure and Tristram rode out to either end of the lists, and then galloped against each other with their spears thrust out. They came together with the noise of thunder, and Blamoure was dislodged from his horse. He took out his sword at once, telling Tristram to alight and face him on the field. "My horse has failed," he cried, "but I trust to God that the earth is on my side!"

So Tristram leaped off his horse, and the two of them fell upon each other with their swords. The battle went this way and that, now favouring one and now inclining towards the other, as the blood of both men spread over the ground. Then Tristram delivered one astounding blow, and Blamoure fell to his knees before sinking down. Sir Tristram stood still and watched him.

When Blamoure could speak, he said this: "Sir Tristram de Liones, I require you, as a noble knight, and the best I have ever fought, to kill me now. I would rather die here with honour than live in shame. I will never surrender, not even if I were offered all the world. So come. Deliver the final blow."

When Sir Tristram heard him speak so nobly, he was not sure what to do. For the sake of Sir Lancelot he was unwilling to slay Blamoure. Yet if he did not surrender, Tristram was duty bound to kill him.

Tristram went over to the judges and kneeled down before them. "I beg you, sirs," he said, "to decide this matter. It would be, for me, shame and pity if this knight were to die. I know well enough that there will be no shame for him in living. He has discharged himself with honour. And I will ask the king, in whose cause I have fought, to take mercy on this man."

King Angwish then stepped forward. "So help me God, Sir Tristram, I will be ruled by you. Let the judges here make their decision."

The judges then called for Sir Bleoberis to speak with them. "My lords," he said, "the body of my brother has been beaten this day. But his heart is as noble as ever. Let Sir Tristram now finish his task. Better to die than be dishonoured."

"That cannot be," they cried out. "Both the king and his champion have taken pity upon him."

"As you will then," Bleoberis replied. With that the judges came together and cleared King Angwish of the charges against him. Then they reconciled the parties of this combat. Tristram promised never to fight the two brothers again, and they in turn swore that they would always treat the noble knight with respect.

Read how Tristram and Isolde drink a magic potion

King Angwish and Tristram then returned to Ireland, where the king proclaimed the valour of his champion. No one was more joyful than Isolde herself, who loved Tristram more than any other man. Before long, the king asked Tristram a question.

"Why, sir, have you not asked me for the boon I promised you?"

"Now, my lord, has come the time. I ask for the hand of your daughter. Not for myself, but for my uncle, King Mark of Cornwall."

"Alas, Tristram, I would give all my lands if you would wed her yourself!"

"That cannot be. I will not be false to my lord. Therefore, sir, I beg you to keep the promise that you made me. Allow me to take her back to Cornwall."

"I place her entirely in your hands. You may do as you wish with her. If you decide to marry her yourself, that would please me most. If you must give her to King Mark, that is your choice."

So, to cut matters short, La Belle Isolde was made ready for her journey together with her lady-in-waiting Dame Bragwaine. Before they left for Cornwall, Bragwaine and Gouvernail, Tristram's companion, had an audience with the queen. "Take this, both of you," she told them. It was a flask of liquor, amber of hue. "On the wedding night, make sure that King Mark and my daughter drink this. When they have done so, they will love each other all the days of their lives."

So they took the drink, and departed for the boat. They were not long at sea when Tristram and Isolde both grew thirsty. They saw the flask, on a table close to them, and Tristram took it up. He thought that it contained good wine, and he held it in his hands. "Madam Isolde," he said, "we have been denied a blessing. Here is wine that our servants, Bragwaine and Gouvernail, were going to keep for themselves!" They both laughed and drank to each other; they had never tasted sweeter liquor in all their lives. And in that moment they fell so deeply in love that their hearts would never be divided. So the destiny of Tristram and Isolde was ordained.

They sailed on until they came close to the coast of Cornwall, and by chance landed near Castle Pleure, which in English means Castle of Weeping. It was an unhappy place to visit. They rode up, looking for welcome, but instead they were taken prisoner by six armed knights. They were led to a prison in the depths of the castle where they could see no light and hear no voices. While Tristram and Isolde languished in confinement, a knight and lady came to cheer them. "What is the reason for this treatment of us?" Tristram asked them. "I have never heard before of guests being taken and cast into prison."

"The master of this place," the knight replied, "is Sir Brewnour. It is his custom. If a knight comes here, he must fight with him. And the weaker must lose his head. There is something else. If the lady he brings with him is less beautiful than Brewnour's wife, then his lady must also be beheaded."

"God knows that is a shameful custom. I have one consolation. The lady I bring with me is fair beyond any mortal creature. She will not lose her head. I know that well enough. So inform Sir Brewnour I will be ready to meet him in battle whenever he wishes."

On the following morning he was led to the field, where he was furnished with his own horse and armour. Sir Brewnour came out, holding the hand of his wife, whose face was covered with a scarf. "Sir Tristram," he said, "now comes the moment of truth. If your lady is fairer than mine, then I give you permission to take off my lady's head. If mine is more beautiful than yours, then I will behead your lady."

"This is a foul course you have chosen," Tristram told him. "I would rather lose my own head than put any lady at risk."

"No. It cannot be. The ladies must be shown together."

So Tristram brought forth Isolde, and with his sword turned her three times so that all might see her. Then Sir Brewnour took off the scarf, and presented his lady. As soon as Brewnour saw Isolde, however, he knew that she would be awarded the victory. And so it was. All the people that were present agreed that Isolde took the palm for beauty.

"There we have it," Tristram said. "It seems that my lady will not lose her head. As for yours, well, her case is a hard one. You and she have continued a barbaric custom here in this castle, and it would be no sin to behead you both."

"If you slay her, doubt not that I will slay you and keep your Isolde."

"We shall see." And, with that, Tristram strode over to Sir Brewnour's wife and with one stroke of his sword took off her head.

"Well, knight," Brewnour said, "you have brought great dishonour to me. Mount your horse and let us fight it out."

So they rode against each other, and Tristram knocked Brewnour to the ground. But he got up and thrust his spear between the sides of Tristram's horse, so that it fell dead. Tristram dismounted lightly, and they both traded blow for blow. They fought for two hours, until Tristram took Brewnour in his arms and threw him grovelling to the earth. He grabbed Brewnour's helmet, and his vizor, and tore them off before beheading him.

Then all the company of the castle came out, praising Tristram for breaking the power of evil company and evil custom. It so happened that one of the knights then galloped to the castle of Sir Galahalt, son of Brewnour, and told him the news. So Galahalt took off in the company of the King of the Hundred Knights, and sent out a challenge to Tristram. It was accepted, of course, and the weapons of the two warriors soon clashed. When Galahalt stumbled, and was likely to be slain, the King of the Hundred Knights rode out with all his companions.

Tristram turned to Galahalt. "This is great shame to you," he said, "to send all your fellowship against me."

"There is no other way. Either you must yield to me or die."

"So. I surrender. But not to you. To the might of these men massed against me." And, with that, he put the pommel of his sword in his opponent's hands. At that moment the king and his company charged Tristram.

"Hold back!" Galahalt cried out. "I have promised this man his life."

"More shame on you," the king replied. "He has killed your father and your mother."

"As for that, I cannot blame him. My father obliged him to do battle." Then he told the king of his father's shameful custom of beheading the ladies who came to the castle. "That is why," Sir Galahalt said, "I would never fight on his behalf."

"You were right," the king said. "It was a wicked practice."

Then Galahalt turned to Tristram. "Tell me, sir, what is your name?"

"I am Sir Tristram de Liones. I have been sent by King Mark of Cornwall to bring back this lady here. She is Isolde, daughter of the King of Ireland."

"Well met! I give you leave to ride wherever you wish, on condition that you look out for Sir Lancelot and join his fellowship."

"I promise you. As soon as I see him, I will ask to become one of his company. Of all the knights in the world, I most desire to serve him." Then Tristram took his leave of Galahalt and, with Isolde, put out to sea again. The two lovers sailed to the court of King Mark at Tintagel, where they were greeted by all the lords and ladies waiting on the shore. As the ship came in sight the courtiers waved to them, and called out blessings upon them. Isolde was then given to King Mark in matrimony, and there was much feasting. Yet, as the old books tell us, Tristram and Isolde were steadfast in their love.

Read of Isolde's rash promise

It so happened that two of the ladies of the court had conceived a great hatred for Dame Bragwaine, Isolde's chief companion, and plotted to destroy her. She was sent into a nearby wood, in search of some rare herbs, where she was then attacked and tied to a tree for three days. Quite by chance Sir Palomides was hunting in the same wood, and came upon the lady in distress. He released her and took her to a nunnery, where she could recover in peace.

As soon as Isolde missed her companion, she grew melancholy. They had come from Ireland together, as we have seen, and Bragwaine was the lady whom she loved and trusted most. In her grief Isolde wandered in the gardens of the Castle of Tintagel, where she encountered Sir Palomides. He knew the reason for her woe. "Dear madam," he said, "if you grant me a promise, I will return Dame Bragwaine to you."

"Gladly," she replied. "I cannot refuse you."

"Well, madam, I will bring her to you within an hour."

"I shall wait here for you, sir."

154

So Palomides rode to the nunnery, and persuaded Bragwaine to go back with him — even though she was still fearful for her life. When Queen Isolde saw her, she wept with happiness. "Now madam," Palomides said, "remember your promise to me. I have fulfilled my part."

"I do not know what you will ask of me, sir," she replied. "I will do whatever is in my power. But I tell you this. I will do nothing to my dishonour."

"You will learn in due course, lady."

"Come before my husband, the king. Then let me know what you wish."

So they walked into the presence chamber, and Sir Palomides bowed before the king. "Sire," he said, "I ask you to give me justice."

"Tell me your cause."

"I promised your lady, Queen Isolde, that I would return Dame Bragwaine to her on condition that she granted me a wish."

King Mark turned to his wife. "What do you say, dear lady?"

"He speaks the truth, so help me God. I was so eager to see Bragwaine again that I promised him whatever he wished."

"Well, madam," the king replied, "you may repent your haste. But you must perform your promise. What is it that you want, Sir Palomides?"

"I wish to take the queen into my charge, and govern her as I choose."

The king sat silent for a moment. "I grant your wish. Take her and care for her. I do not suppose that you will have her for long." He was already thinking of Tristram.

"As for that," Palomides replied, "we must wait and see." Then he took Isolde by the hand. "Madam, do not resent me. I require nothing but the performance of your promise."

"I do not resent you or fear you," the queen replied. "I will keep my promise. But I fully expect that I will be rescued." So she went into the courtyard of the castle, where she was given her favourite horse. Then they rode on their way.

King Mark at once sent for Sir Tristram, but he could not be found. He had gone hunting in the woods. "This is a grievous day," the king said. "I have lost my wife by my own assent. I will be shamed for ever."

Then a young knight, Lambegus, stepped forward. "My lord," he said, "I am one of Sir Tristram's affinity. Let me ride out for his sake, and rescue the queen. I will deserve your trust."

"God speed to you," the king replied. "When you come back with her, I will reward you."

So Lambegus galloped after Palomides, and caught up with him close to a waterfall whose waters fell with the sound of bells ringing. "Who are you?" Palomides asked him. "Are you Tristram?"

"I am one of his companions. My name is Lambegus."

"I would rather fight with Tristram."

"You would repent that, sir. When you meet that knight, you will surely have your hands full."

156

So they dashed against each other with swords and spears until Palomides caught Lambegus with such a great blow that the young man fell to the ground. Palomides had no time to exult in his victory, however. When he looked around, he groaned aloud. Isolde had gone.

Read of Isolde's rescue

Isolde had run into a wood close by, where she came upon a well. She looked into its darkness, and meditated on her fate. Would it not be better to plunge down into the depths of the earth? Then she heard the sound of a horse coming into the clearing behind her. Sir Adtherpe was the lord of this region. He had been riding through the wood in search of game, but now he came to the aid of the lady in distress. He persuaded her to go with him and take refuge in his castle. There he learned that she was Isolde, Queen of Cornwall; she told him, with many tears, all the details of her capture. "I will ride after Palomides, madam," he said, "and avenge you. This is insupportable. This is evil." He rode out that same day and, following Isolde's description of the place where Lambegus had mounted his challenge, he soon found Sir Palomides. The two knights rode against each other at once, but Adtherpe was so badly wounded that he was forced to surrender. "Tell me now where the queen is," Palomides demanded of him. "Otherwise you will die here."

"She lies in my castle."

"Where is it?"

"I am too wounded to take you there. But if you ride down this path, you will find it."

So Palomides followed the narrow road. When Isolde saw him riding towards the castle, she ordered that all the gates be barred and bolted. When he realized that he could not force his way to her, he leaped from his saddle and sat down on the ground beside the main gate. He seemed mad with anger and disappointment.

Let us turn back to Sir Tristram, who has just returned from hunting. When he learned that Palomides had taken Isolde, he burst out in his wrath. "This day I am shamed!" he shouted. Then he called for Gouvernail. "Come. Bring me my arms. Lambegus will not have been strong enough to withstand the assaults of Palomides. If only I had been there instead! I would have prevented all this grief."

As soon as he was well armed, he rode into the forest. He found Sir Lambegus quickly enough, lying wounded on the forest floor. He took him up in his arms, and carried him to a forester's cottage. He rode on and found Sir Adtherpe by the side of the path, also suffering from his wounds. "What has happened here?" Tristram asked him.

"I saved the queen from drowning herself. And for her sake I did battle against Sir Palomides. But I was not strong enough."

He was about to say more, but Tristram held up his hand. "Where is she now?"

"She is safe in my castle."

"God thank you for your goodness." Then he galloped off with his squire in attendance.

158

He soon came up to the castle, where he saw Sir Palomides sitting by the gate like a man out of his wits. "Go up to him," he told Gouvernail, "and tell him to prepare for combat. I am thirsty for him."

Gouvernail rode over to him. "Arise, Sir Palomides," he said. "Sir Tristram wishes to make a venture against you." But Palomides did not reply; he appeared to be in a stupor. Gouvernail went back to Tristram. "He is asleep, sir, or he has lost his reason."

"Go to him again. Tell him that his mortal enemy is close by."

Gouvernail rode over, and nudged Palomides with his spear. "Come on, sir, wake up. Get yourself ready. Tristram, your mortal enemy, waits for you."

Without speaking, Palomides rose and went over to his horse. As soon as he was in the saddle he made a dash for Tristram with his spear in his hand. Tristram parried the blow and knocked his opponent from his horse. Then they both took out their swords and began a bloody combat. They fought for two hours, both of them fired by love of the same lady.

Isolde watched them from one of the tall windows of the castle. "I love Tristram more than life itself. But I cannot allow him to kill Palomides. That man is still a Saracen, and has never yet been baptized. If he dies, he will be damned for ever." So she ran out from the castle on to the field of battle, and begged both men to desist. "For the love I bear you," she said to Tristram, "put up your sword."

"What do you mean, madam?" Tristram asked her. "Do you wish to bring shame upon me? You know well enough that I will obey you in all things."

"Oh, my lord," she replied, "you know that I do not mean to dishonour you. But for my sake spare this Saracen. Let him be baptized as a Christian before he dies."

"I will obey your command," Tristram said. "For your sake I will save his soul."

Then Isolde turned to Palomides. "This is my charge to you. You must leave this country, and never return while I remain here. You will go to the court of King Arthur, and there send my greetings to Lady Guinevere. Tell her from me that there are only four lovers in the world — Guinevere and Lancelot, Isolde and Tristram."

So with heavy heart Palomides departed, and Tristram took Isolde back to the court of King Mark, where he was met with great rejoicing. He then returned to the house of the forester and took up Sir Lambegus to be treated by skilful surgeons.

Read of Tristram's further adventures

All passed fairly and favourably at the court of King Mark but there was one who looked with hatred and suspicion on Sir Tristram. This man was his cousin, Sir Andred, who schemed against him secretly. One day he saw Tristram and Isolde talking together in the embrace of a bay window; they were standing close to one another, and their hands were clasped. He went at once

160

to the king with his suspicions of treachery. The king hastily took up his sword, and ran to the chamber where Andred had seen them. "False traitor!" he called out to Tristram. He would have struck him with his sword, but Tristram rushed over and took the weapon from him. The king cried out, "Where are my knights and my men? I charge you all to kill this traitor!"

Not one of them obeyed him.

When Tristram saw that no one opposed him, he shook his sword at King Mark and snarled at him. Whereupon the king ran away in fear and trembling. Tristram followed him, and laid the flat of his sword on his neck so that with a groan the king fell to the floor.

Tristram, knowing his danger, then armed himself and rode into the forest with his men. The king's knights followed him, but Tristram easily defeated them all. He killed one brother and wounded another, charging the survivor to carry the head of his dead brother back to the king. "Tell him," he said, "that I defy him."

King Mark called his advisers together. "What shall we do with this foe?" he asked them.

"I think, sire," one of them replied, "that you must make your peace with him. He has many supporters in the land, and he is supposed to be the most valiant and pious knight in the world. Only Sir Lancelot can rival him in virtue. What if Sir Tristram were to travel to the court of King Arthur? You would then be at a disadvantage. The two best knights in the world would be in the retinue of your rival. So I counsel you, my lord, to seek a truce with him."

"Very well," King Mark replied. "We will send for him, and secure his friendship once more."

So this was done. Tristram returned to court, and was welcomed by the king. Their confrontation was forgiven, if not forgotten. All was, for a while, good cheer.

It so happened that King Mark and Queen Isolde went out on an expedition with Sir Tristram. They pitched their pavilions in a great meadow beside a river, where all the knights rode out in joust and tournament. Among them was Sir Lamorak de Galis, who boldly ventured against all the king's warriors, one by one, and defeated them all. "I marvel," the king said, "at the strength of this man. What is his name?"

"I know him well," Sir Tristram told him. "He is Sir Lamorak. Few knights are his equal."

"It would be a shame and a disgrace for him to leave here without being beaten by one of my own knights."

"My lord," Tristram replied, "this man has already done enough, and more than enough, to prove his valour. He has done as much as Lancelot ever dared. It would dishonour me to take the field against him now, when he is tired."

"As for that, I charge you — as you love me and my queen — to test him once more in combat."

"Sir, you order me to set a challenge against the laws of knighthood. If I give him a fall, there is no glory for me. Every good knight is disinclined to take advantage of another. But since you order me to do so, I can only obey."

So, taking up his spear and his sword, he mounted his horse. He and Sir Lamorak met each other with great force of arms, and Tristram slew the horse of his opponent with his spear. Sir Lamorak leaped to his feet, and drew his sword. "Alight, sir knight," he called out. "If you dare!"

"No, sir, I will not. I have already done too much, to my dishonour."

"I cannot thank you for that. Since you have defeated me on horseback I ask you, Sir Tristram de Liones, to fight with me on foot."

"You know my name, and I know yours. I can fight you no more, Sir Lamorak de Galis. I took the field against my will, but I was ordered to do so by my lord. I will not bring more shame upon my head. I know that you have courage enough for a company of men, but I cannot raise my sword against a tired warrior."

"So be it," Sir Lamorak replied. "There will come a day of reckoning."

Read of the magic goblet

Sir Lamorak had ridden for many miles, and was about to rest for the night when he encountered a knight who was on his way to the court of King Arthur, sent by Morgan le Fay. This knight carried with him an enchanted goblet, ornamented with gold, which revealed the secrets of a woman's heart. If a lady loved her husband, she could drink from the goblet freely; but, if she was unfaithful to him, she would spill its contents on the ground. Morgan le Fay was sending it to King Arthur, to show him that Guinevere really loved Lancelot. The goblet was meant to sow discord at Arthur's court. The knight readily described the magical properties of the goblet; he was a gabbler, and loved marvels. When he had heard everything, Sir Lamorak went up close to him and whispered in his ear. "You have a choice," he said. "You can die now. Or you can take this goblet to the court of the King of Cornwall. Tell him that I have sent it for Queen Isolde, in order to prove her true love for her husband." He wanted to be revenged against Tristram.

The knight took the goblet to King Mark, and told him of its power. The king immediately called Isolde, and a hundred of her ladies, into his presence. He ordered them to drink. The queen, and most of her company, failed the test. Only four of them drank from the goblet without spilling the liquid. "Ah," said the king, "this is a great shame and sorrow to me. The queen and the others must all be burned at the stake. They have all committed adultery in their hearts." In those days the penalty for adultery was death by fire.

But his lords and barons remonstrated with him. "Why do you trust this piece of black magic," one of them asked him, "come from the hands of the most evil witch in the world?"

"If ever I see her," another said, "Morgan le Fay will get short courtesy from me."

Tristram himself was angry, because he knew that Sir Lamorak had sent the goblet to test him. He knew, too, that Morgan le Fay was ever an enemy against true love.

164

Tristram continued to see Isolde whenever he could, day and night, and all the time his cousin Andred watched him. His waiting was over when, one night, he took twelve knights and surprised Tristram naked in bed with the queen. Tristram was bound, hand and foot, and imprisoned in the bedchamber until day. Then, at the command of the king and some of the barons, he was taken to a chapel of black stone that stood upon a rocky shore. It was a seat of judgement by the swirling water. It was an ancient place of doom. When he saw the soldiers of the king gathered there, he knew that they had come to witness his death.

"Fair lords," he said to the assembled crowd. "Remember everything I have done for Cornwall, at the risk of my own life. All of you refused to do battle against Marhalt. Only I took up the challenge. Is this my reward? You bring shame upon knighthood itself to treat me in this way."

"Say no more, false traitor!" Sir Andred called out. "This is your last day on earth."

"Ah, Andred," Tristram replied, "you are my kinsman, but you are ready to kill me. Is that so? I tell you this. If we were alone together, you would not dare to raise your sword against me."

"No?" Andred drew his sword, and advanced upon him. Tristram was tied by the hands to two knights, but with one great effort he hauled his guards together and managed to wrench himself free from the ropes. Then he sprang upon Andred and wrestled his sword from

165

him. He fought wildly, as others came for him, and killed ten of his enemies. Then he fled into the chapel. The cry went up against him, and a hundred men flocked to Andred. Tristram knew that he might be trapped. He bolted the door of the chapel, and then unbarred a window at the back. From there he leaped on to the rocks below, and hid from sight in a small cave. He placed a great stone against the entrance, so that he would not be found. Andred and his men departed at last after a long search, in the belief that Tristram had dived into the sea and perhaps been drowned. Then he came out of hiding, in the knowledge that his companions would search for him along the coast. And so it proved. By good fortune they found him safe between the crags and the sea, from which rough place they pulled him up by means of a strong rope. As soon as he was on dry ground, he asked them about Queen Isolde.

"Sir," Gouvernail said, "the king agreed that it would be wrong to burn her. Instead he has consigned her to a house of lepers."

"A lady among lepers? She will not be left there for long."

So he took his men and rescued her from the leper house. The poor lepers were so terrified of the knights that they willingly led them to the chamber in which she lay. The knights themselves took the precaution of sowing magic spells into their clothing to ward off the disease; each one of them also carried a crucifix as a sure defence. Tristram then took her to a fair manor house in a forest, where he lived with her in bliss. That manor house exists still, and is known as Isolde's Bower.

Read of Tristram's wound

Tristram went out into the forest on a bright day, happy to wander, when he fell asleep beneath a plum tree. It so happened that a knight came upon him there, whose brother had been killed by Tristram. So the man promptly took up his bow, and wounded Tristram in the shoulder with an arrow. Tristram started up, with a shriek, and killed the man with his sword.

The report of this slaying reached the court of King Mark, and it was not long before the king discovered the location of the manor house. With many of his men in attendance, he rode out to kill Tristram. The knight had in fact gone hunting — no one knew where — and so the king had to be content with recapturing Isolde. He led her back to his court, and imprisoned her in a closed room where she was served by certain chosen attendants. When Tristram returned he noticed the tracks of many horses, and soon realized that his lady had been taken. His sorrow was aggravated by the pain he now felt, for the arrow that had pierced his shoulder had been filled with poison.

Isolde heard of his wound from one of the ladies who served her, and by secret means she sent this lady to Tristram. "You will not easily be healed," she told him. "Your lady, Isolde, cannot come to you. She bids you to travel to Brittany, and there visit the court of King

167

Howell. His daughter, Isolde of the White Hands, will be able to cure you."

Tristram and Gouvernail decided then to set sail for Brittany, where they were greeted warmly at the court of King Howell. "Your fame precedes you, Sir Tristram," the king said. "I will do anything to assist you."

"I have come here, sir, to seek help from your daughter. I have been told that only she can heal my wound." So the king sent for Isolde of the White Hands, and indeed she was able to cure Tristram's wound. She had learned her skills from a priestess who had once worshipped one of the pagan goddesses.

There was a war in Brittany at this time between King Howell and an earl named Grip; the earl had already won a great battle against the king and was likely to besiege his castle. The king's son had issued forth against Grip, but had been badly wounded. So Gouvernail sought an audience with Howell. "Sire," he told him, "I advise you to summon Tristram to help you."

"Good advice," the king replied. "Call him here."

Sir Tristram took up the king's cause and sallying forth from the castle with a few companions-in-arms, he inflicted a great defeat on Grip. He killed the earl with his own hands, and slew or captured all of his knights. Howell was of course entirely happy at the outcome. "I will give you my kingdom," he said to Tristram.

"Oh no, sir. It was the least I could do. Your daughter saved me from a lingering death. I am indebted to her."

The king and his son then tried by every means at their disposal to bring together Tristram and Isolde of the White Hands. She was wise, and she was beautiful. She was of royal blood. What else is there to say? Sir Tristram had such welcome and fair words from her that he almost forgot Queen Isolde. There came a time, in fact, when he agreed to marry Howell's daughter. After the ceremony was over, and they were brought to bed, he recalled his old love for Isolde and was overwhelmed with sorrow. He would only embrace, and kiss, his new bride. He would not take her virginity. According to the old books, these were the limits of his lovemaking.

One day a knight from Brittany came to the court of King Arthur. He met Sir Lancelot du Lake at Camelot, and told him of Tristram's marriage to the king's daughter. "Shame on him," Lancelot said. "How could he be untrue to the lady he loves? How could he desert Isolde, the Queen of Cornwall? Tell him this. Once I loved and admired him beyond all other knights. I applauded all of his noble deeds. But now I am turned into his deadly enemy. The love between us has gone for ever."

The knight went back to Brittany, and told Tristram what had taken place. "Lancelot," he said, "will be your mortal foe."

"I am sad and sick at heart for this," Tristram replied. "I am shamed for deserting my lady."

At the same time Isolde wrote a grieving letter to Guinevere, in which she berated Tristram for betraying her and taking the king's daughter as his bride.

Guinevere replied with words of comfort. "Do not despair," she told her. "There will come joy after sorrow. Tristram has been undone by craft and sorcery. In the end, all will be well. He will come to hate her, and to love you better than he ever did."

Tristram's Madness and Exile

After a few months had passed, Isolde ceased to weep, but she was still sorrowful. She sent a sad letter to Tristram, in which she invited him and his wife to her court in Cornwall. "You will both be made welcome," she said. But Tristram had other plans.

Here we tell of the Perilous Forest

In the first days of spring, the time of awakening, Tristram called for one of his faithful knights; his name was Sir Kehadius, son of the King of Brittany. Tristram asked if he would be his companion on a secret journey to Cornwall. "I am ready to serve you at all times," Kehadius answered. So Tristram ordered a small vessel to be made ready, and there embarked with Kehadius and with his squire, Gouvernail. While they were at sea, however, a contrary wind drove them on to the shore of North Wales near the borders of the Perilous Forest. This was a wild and desolate place, close to a great mountain that is always covered in snow.

"There are many stories about this forest," Tristram told Kehadius. Then he turned to Gouvernail. "Wait for us here for ten days," he said to him. "If we have not returned by then, take the road to Cornwall. I have been told that this forest holds many strange adventures, and I have a desire to experience them for myself. Have no fear. When we can, we will follow you."

So the two companions rode into the forest for a mile or so, until they came upon a knight sitting armed beside a well. His horse was tethered to an oak tree, and his squire was busy with some spears. He was deep in thought, however, and seemed to be dismayed. "Why are you looking so mournful?" Tristram asked him. "You are a worthy knight, I can tell. So prepare your arms and joust with me!"

The knight did not speak but stood up and asked his squire for sword and spear. He mounted his horse, and rode a little way off, where he waited. Sir Kehadius asked leave of Tristram to joust first.

"If you wish," he replied. "Just do your best."

Kehadius then rode against the knight, but received a wound in the chest that disabled him. Then Tristram took over. "Knight, you have jousted well!" he called out. "Now prepare yourself."

"I am ready, sir, whoever you may be."

So he took up his spear and forced Tristram from his horse. Tristram was shamed by this, and with a look of scorn he brandished his sword. "Dismount," he said, "and do me the honour of fighting on foot with me."

"By all means." He leaped lightly from his horse, and they began a battle that lasted for more than two hours.

"Fair knight," Tristram said, "stay your hand a little. Let me know who you are."

"If you give me your name."

"Tristram de Liones."

"And I am Sir Lamorak de Galis."

"Well met, Lamorak. We have encountered each other in combat before, when I unhorsed you. It was you who sent the magic goblet to King Mark in revenge."

"No more words. Prepare to fight." Then Tristram lashed at him, but Lamorak dodged the blow. They fought long and hard, until both were exhausted. "I never fought with a knight," Tristram said, "who is so strong. It would be a shame to injure one another."

"Sir Tristram, for the sake of your great renown I will surrender to you."

"No. You are acting out of fairness, and not for any fear of me." Tristram offered him his sword. "Sir Lamorak. I yield to you. You are the bravest knight in the world."

"Shall we make a pledge never to fight one another again?"

"Willingly."

So they swore an oath that they would always maintain their friendship.

Then they took up Tristram's wounded comrade, Sir Kehadius, and carried him on a shield to the cottage of a forester. They cared for him there for three days. They left him to recover and made their own way. When they came to a stone cross, they parted company.

Sir Lamorak took the left path along a dusty road, choked with brambles and wild grasses. He rode on until he came to a chapel, where he put his horse out to pasture. While he rested there Sir Meliagaunt, the son of King Bagdemagus, dismounted. He did not see Lamorak, but laid himself down in the chapel, where he lamented his hopeless love for Queen Guinevere.

Lamorak heard all of this lament. When Meliagaunt left the chapel in sorrow, Lamorak went up to him. "You did not see me," he said, "but I was close by when you made your lament. Tell me this. Why do you love Queen Guinevere so fervently?"

"Why? That is my fate. She is the fairest woman in the world. I will challenge anyone to deny it."

"I for one do deny it. The loveliest lady in the world is Queen Morgause of Orkney, the mother of Sir Gawain."

"Not so. I will prove it with my spear."

"Oh? Prepare yourself then. This will be a proper fight."

So they descended upon one another in great wrath, and their spears clashed like thunder in a storm. They fell from their horses and then began a deadly battle with their swords. Wild boars could not have been more ferocious.

In the Perilous Forest there were always strange chances and meetings, magical encounters and mysterious vanishings. So it happened that Lancelot and his cousin Bleoberis then rode up, and recognized

174

the two warring knights. Lancelot came between them. "What is the cause of this?" he asked them. "You are both knights at the court of King Arthur. Why do you fight one another so fiercely?"

"I will tell you the reason," Meliagaunt said. "I praised my lady Guinevere as the fairest in the world. But Lamorak denied it. He declared that Queen Morgause of Orkney was more lovely."

"Ah, Lamorak," Lancelot said, "it is not right that you should dispraise your own queen. Make yourself ready. I am prepared to challenge you myself."

"My lord," Lamorak replied, "I am reluctant to quarrel with you. Every knight thinks his own lady is the fairest. That is human nature. If I praise the lady I love, there is no reason to be angry with me. Of all the men in the world, with the exception of Sir Tristram, you are the one I most fear in battle. But, if you want to fight, then I will be forced to defend myself."

Sir Bleoberis then spoke out. "My lord Sir Lancelot, Lamorak speaks the truth. I have a lady, too, and I believe her to be the most beautiful on earth. Will you then fight me? You know well enough that Lamorak is one of the most valiant knights living. Put down your sword, I pray you. Be friends."

Sir Lancelot was abashed. "Sir," he said to Lamorak, "I have done you wrong. Forgive me. If I was too hasty, I will make amends." So they embraced in friendship and left one another.

Here we tell of Tristram's new adventure

Sir Tristram had taken the other path through the Perilous Forest, where he saw strange shapes slipping between the trees and heard unaccustomed sounds as of bells and hammer blows. He was still searching for adventures. On his way he met Sir Kay, who hailed him.

"What country are you from?" he asked Tristram.

"I am of Cornwall."

"Is that so? I have never known any good knight to come from Cornwall."

"So you say. And who are you, sir?"

"Sir Kay."

"Oh. I know of you. You are believed to be the most ribald and evil-tongued of all knights. You are valiant enough, but you have enough venom to kill a viper."

They rode together until they came to a bridge, where was stationed a knight who would not let them pass until one of them jousted with him. Sir Kay responded to the challenge, but he took a fall. The knight's name, by the way, was Sir Tor.

The two men then made their way to a lodging; Sir Tor followed them, and joined them for supper. Sir Kay and Sir Tor, drinking deeply, then began to curse and scorn the knights of Cornwall. "They are boasters," Kay said, "foolish beyond all measure." Tristram listened to them in silence, revolving many thoughts in his head.

The next morning he rode with them. He took pleasure in jousting with them both, defeating them

176

easily. "That blow," he said to himself, "was for Cornwall."

Tor went up to Kay. "What is this knight's name?" he asked him.

"I do not know as yet. Come with me. We will ask him."

So they rode after him, and found him sitting by a well; he had taken off his helmet, and was using it to scoop up water. As soon as he saw them he put on his helmet, and offered to fight. "No," Sir Kay said, "we have already jousted with you. We have come to ask your name. On your honour as a knight, you must tell us."

"Since you have asked, my fair lords, I will answer. My name is Sir Tristram de Liones. I am the nephew of the King of Cornwall."

"We are fortunate to have met you," Sir Tor said. "I apologize for our harsh words last night. If we had known you were in our company, we would not have insulted you. But enough of that. Let me give you an invitation. We belong to a fellowship that would be pleased to greet you. You are the one knight in the world whom the Round Table would welcome."

"God thank you all," Tristram replied. "But I feel as yet that I am not ready for your fellowship. I have not performed deeds that would make me worthy of membership."

"If you are really Sir Tristram," Sir Kay said, "then you are too modest. Your reputation precedes you. You are a man of renown." They spoke a little more, and then went their separate ways.

Here we tell of King Arthur's escape from death

King Arthur himself had come to Wales in order to assert his rule over that country. He took his court to a great castle in Cardiff, where the citizens did him homage. But there arrived a less welcome visitor. A sorceress, by the name of Aunowre, had come to the castle with the intention of luring the king into her bed. This sorceress had loved him for a long time, and now wished to lie with him. "Let me greet you in my own dwelling," she said to Arthur. "I live in a high tower that was built by giants many hundreds of years ago."

"Where is this ancient tower, lady?"

"In the Perilous Forest, sire."

"The Perilous Forest? I have heard of that place. I have always wished to visit it."

So he took up her invitation. When the king was gone, many of his knights rode after him in case of mischief. Among them were Sir Lancelot and Sir Braundiles. The lady took Arthur to her tower and entreated him to make love to her; but Arthur, remembering the grace of his lady, Guinevere, refused. None of the sorceress's tricks or spells could persuade him. So she took him out riding every day with her own knights within the forest, and waited for an opportunity to slay him secretly. Now that he had rejected her, her love had turned to thoughts of revenge.

Nineve, once the servant of the Lady of the Lake, had become by means of her power and wisdom the new Lady; there must always be a Lady of the Lake, ever fresh and ever renewed, or the waters will leave the land to dust and weariness. The Lady, always a good friend to Arthur, understood by means of sorcery that he was likely to be destroyed by Aunowre. So she made her way to the Perilous Forest in order to warn Sir Lancelot or Sir Tristram of the danger to their king. She could see in her enchanted mirror that they were riding in that place. Only these two knights might save him. She rode into a field, close by the forest, where she saw Sir Tristram emerging from the trees. "Ah, good knight," she said, "we are well met. You must seize the moment. On this day, two hours from now, there will be committed the most destructive deed that has ever been done in this land."

"Fair lady, how can I help?"

"Come with me. I will show you the most noble man in the world in great peril of his life."

"Willingly. Who is this noble man?"

"None other than your sovereign, Arthur."

"God defend him from any distress!"

They galloped into the forest, until they came to a castle made entirely of granite stone. Under the walls of this stronghold two knights were attacking a third. They had forced him to the ground and, when they unlaced his helmet, Tristram saw that King Arthur himself was at their mercy. The sorceress was standing beside them; she quickly took up Arthur's sword and was about to behead him.

"Traitors!" Tristram screamed out. "Stay away from the king!" He rode over and broke the backs of both knights with his spear. The sorceress uttered a scream and ran for cover among the trees.

The Lady of the Lake then cried out to Arthur, "Do not let that wicked woman escape!"

The king chased after Aunowre, and beheaded her with the sword he snatched from her. The Lady of the Lake took the head and tied it to the strings of her saddle. It was a fine trophy.

Sir Tristram now went over to the king, and helped him to mount his horse. When the king thanked him and asked for his name, Tristram replied that he was a poor knight adventurer. Nothing more. He accompanied Arthur through the forest, until the king found one of the knights who had been searching for him.

"Will you not tell me your name?" he asked Tristram as he was about to depart.

"Not at this time," Sir Tristram replied.

Here we tell of Tristram's quarrel with Isolde

The valiant knight now made his way back to the forester's cottage, where he had left Kehadius wounded, and to his delight found his companion restored to health. "Let us find our boat," Tristram told him. "We will make our way over the waves to Cornwall."

When a message was brought to the court of King Mark that Tristram had landed, Isolde fainted for joy. "Bring him to me," she asked the seneschal, Sir Dinas. "I must speak to him or my heart will break." So as soon as they arrived Dinas led Tristram and Kehadius to the private chambers of Isolde. No tongue can tell, no pen define, no heart reveal, the joy between Tristram and Isolde. No book can begin to describe the love between them.

This was the first time that Kehadius had seen the queen, and he was so enamoured of her that he could find no rest or relief. From that time forward he sent her poems and songs. She pitied him and, out of a misplaced sense of compassion, she sent a letter of comfort to him. But you will see that, in the end, Kehadius died for love of her.

Tristram himself was lodged at the queen's command in a turret of finely dressed stone, where she visited him as often as she could. One day he came into her private chamber with Sir Kehadius, when by chance he found the letters of Kehadius and the pitying reply of the queen. He approached her in a rage. "Madam," he said, "here is a letter that has been sent to you. And here is the letter you sent in reply. Alas, lady, did you not know how much I loved you? Did you not think of the lands and treasures that I have forsaken for you? I am heartbroken that you have betrayed me."

Then he turned to Kehadius. "As for you, sir, I have brought you out of Brittany. I saved the lands of your father, the king. I married your sister, Isolde of the White Hands, for the goodness she showed to me. By my faith as a knight, she is still pure and untouched. And this is how you repay me! But know this, Sir Kehadius. For all your falsehood and treason, I will have my revenge." He drew out his sword. "Prepare yourself."

At the sight of his sword, Isolde swooned. When Sir Kehadius saw Tristram come for him, he had no choice.

He jumped out of the bay window of the chamber, and landed on the earth not far from a garden seat where King Mark was playing chess. The king was surprised. "Fellow, who are you? And why have you fallen from your window?"

"My lord king," Kehadius replied, "I fell asleep in the window above your head. I slipped and fell as I slumbered."

Tristram would have followed him, but he did not want to be caught in the queen's chamber. It would compromise her too badly. He waited to see if anyone would discover him but, when he found himself safe, he took horse and rode through the gates of Tintagel towards the forest. On the way he met one of his fellows, Sir Fergus, who agreed to accompany him. Now that he was beyond Tintagel, he fell a victim to his sorrow. He was bowed down with violent grief, and for three days could not be comforted. He sent Sir Fergus to the court, in an effort to find out news of Isolde. On his way there, Fergus encountered a lady of the court who had been sent to find Tristram and plead with him to return. "How is he?" she asked him.

"Almost out of his mind."

"That is bad news. Where shall I find him?"

"Take that path. You will soon hear him sighing." Fergus went on his way and, when he arrived at the court of King Mark, he learned that Isolde was confined to her bed. She was sick with a great sorrow.

When the lady found Tristram she wept with pity at his plight, but there was no way of helping him. The more she tried, the more he resented her. He wished to be alone with his sorrow. After three days, he rode away. But she followed him, bearing meat and drink. He would not eat. He left her again, and rode on weeping. By chance he came to a castle. The lady of the castle came out and recognized him. He had once come to this place and, in sheer joy of spirit, had begun playing his harp among the trees. She had been entranced by the music, and begged Tristram to give her the instrument. He gave it to her willingly enough for, as he said, music reveals the harmonies of the world. Now she offered him wine, food and rest. "I still have the harp you gave me," she said. "Will you play it for me? You bear the palm for music in all the world."

Gently he put the harp aside. He ate very little. But that night he took up the harp and, through his tears, he played one or two songs. On that same night he took off his armour and untied his horse. He went out into the wilderness, wailing, and broke through the branches and bushes. There were some days when he took up the harp. There were other days when he wandered into the wood. When the lady of the castle could not find him, she sat beneath a tree and played the harp herself. He would come to her, and listen to the music.

Here we tell of Tristram's madness

So passed three months. At the end of this period he ran off, and the lady did not know what had become of him. He was now all but naked, and he was wretchedly thin. He joined the company of some shepherds and herdsmen, who clipped his hair with their shears so that he looked like a fool. They shared their meat and drink with him but, if he displeased them, they beat him with their staffs.

It so happened that, one day, Sir Dagonet — the fool of King Mark — rode out with two of his squires for company. They took a path into the forest and after a while came upon a well where Tristram was accustomed to sit. The weather was hot, and they dismounted so that they might drink the water of the well. Their horses wandered off. By chance Tristram came upon them and, quick as a flash, he ducked Sir Dagonet and his men in the well. The shepherds were delighted.

Dagonet was furious and vowed to be revenged upon the shepherds who, as he believed, had set a poor wretch upon him and his companions. So they searched for the shepherds in the wood and, once they had found them, they beat them soundly with their swords. Tristram saw all this, and rushed out of the undergrowth. He seized Dagonet and hurled him to the ground. He snatched up the fallen man's sword, and with it beheaded one of the squires. The other squire escaped. Then Tristram, with the sword in his hand, ran howling through the trees like a man possessed.

Sir Dagonet, on recovering his senses, went back to King Mark and told him that a wild man was dwelling in the wood. "Do not go near the well," he warned him. "That is where he came for me. I am your fool, but the greater fool gained the mastery over me."

"That will be Sir Matto le Breune," the king replied. "He lost his mind when he lost his lady. There is much to pity in this world."

But pity does not run in the hardened heart. Sir Tristram's cousin Sir Andred wished to take over Tristram's lands. So he persuaded his lover to spread it abroad that she was with Tristram at the time of his death. She told King Mark that she had buried him beside the well, and that before his death he had begged the king to award all of his lands to Andred. When the king heard that Tristram was dead he wept with shame and grief. When Isolde was told the news, she cried out. She came close to madness. She decided to kill herself, as she could not live without Tristram.

Secretly she procured a sword and took it into her garden. There she fastened it to an apple tree, at breast height, with the blade pointing outward. It was her intention to run against it, and thereby end her life. Yet King Mark was watching her. He walked softly towards her as she kneeled in prayer.

"Sweet Lord Jesus," she whispered, "have mercy on me, a poor sinner. Sir Tristram was my first love, and he will be my last. I cannot exist without him."

The king then came up to her, and took her in his arms. He placed her in a high tower, under strict supervision, where she remained for many months close to death.

Here we tell of Tristram's battle with a giant

After his encounter with Sir Dagonet, Tristram ran naked through the wood screaming strange words into the air. Eventually he came to a hermitage, where he laid himself down and slept. The hermit took away his sword, and left meat in its place. Tristram was served with food for ten days, until he had recovered his strength. After that time he went back to the shepherds.

There was a giant in this region by the name of Tauleas, who, in terror of the reputation of Tristram, had not dared to leave his castle for seven years. But then he heard tidings that Tristram was dead. He felt able to roam at large once again. It so happened that one day he came upon the shepherds, and set himself down to rest among them. As he lay at his ease a Cornish knight called Sir Dinaunt, accompanied by a lady, rode up and alighted by the well. As soon as the giant saw the knight he went to hide himself behind a tree. When the horse ambled off the giant seized it and, mounting on its back, went after Sir Dinaunt. He took him by the scruff of the neck, and seemed about to behead him.

"Help this man!" the shepherds called out to Tristram.

"You help him."

"We do not dare."

So Tristram, seeing Dinaunt's sword by the ground, took it up and cut off the head of the giant with the first stroke. Then he made his way back to the shepherds, who rejoiced at his easy victory.

186

Sir Dinaunt picked up the giant's head and carried it back with him to the court of King Mark. He told the king how he had been rescued from a fierce giant by a naked man.

"Where did all this happen?" the king asked.

"It was by the well, sir, in the dark wood. That is where the madman lives."

"I have heard of him," said the king. "I would like to see this fellow."

Here we tell of the reunion of Tristram and Isolde

King Mark commanded his huntsmen to prepare themselves for some sport on the following morning. When dawn broke, he led them into the wood. He made straight for the well, where he found a naked man sleeping with a sword by his side. He called to his knights. "Take up this man," he told them. "Treat him with care. Do not provoke him. When he is calm, bring him to my castle."

They covered the man's body with their mantles and, very tenderly, led him to the Castle of Tintagel. Tristram seemed to be in a daze, and followed them like a child. They bathed him and dressed him. They gave him soup and hot stews. Despite all this, not one of them recognized Sir Tristram. He was so altered in countenance and behaviour.

Isolde heard news of this man, who had run naked in the wood, and of his rescue by King Mark. So she called her companion to her. "Bragwaine," she said, "come with me. We will visit this wild man from the wood."

They walked through the grounds of the castle, and asked a passing squire where the sick man was being kept. "He is in the garden," he said. "He is resting in the sun."

Isolde and Bragwaine went into the garden, and saw the man lying on the grass. Isolde did not recognize him, but whispered, "I believe that I have met this man before. There is something familiar about him."

Tristram turned towards them, and he knew Isolde at once. He hid his face, and wept.

There was a dog with the two ladies, a little spaniel that Tristram had given to Isolde as a present when she first came to Cornwall. The dog would never leave her side unless Tristram was close by, in which case it would follow him faithfully. Now, in the garden, the dog caught Tristram's scent and bounded over to him; it jumped upon him, licking his ears and nose, whining and whimpering with joy.

"Oh, my lady," Bragwaine exclaimed. "Here is Tristram!"

At that, Isolde fainted away. When she had recovered, she saw Tristram standing above her. "Oh, my lord," she murmured. "Thank God that you are still alive. Yet now your identity will be discovered. This little dog will never leave you. When King Mark finds you, he will either force you into exile or kill you. I beg you, leave this place. Go to the court of King Arthur, where you are beloved. When I need you, I will send for you. I will

188

always be at your command, your most obedient servant."

"Ah, fair queen," he replied. "Your great love has saved me from madness. As soon as I saw you, I felt whole again. But listen. Leave me for now. It is not safe for you to be seen with me."

Isolde left him, in tears, but the little spaniel would not move from his side. When Sir Mark and his courtiers came into the garden, the dog sat upon Tristram's lap and barked at them.

"Well, well." It was Sir Andred who spoke out. "I believe that we have Tristram among us."

"Oh no," the king replied. "I cannot believe that." He went up to Tristram, and asked him his name.

"Sir Tristram de Liones," he replied. "Do with me what you will."

Here we read of Tristram's exile

"I am sorry that I rescued you," the king told him. "Now you must die." He brought Tristram before his barons, but they refused to pronounce the sentence of death upon him. Instead they advised the king that Tristram should be banished for ten years. Tristram swore an oath that he would depart and not return for that length of time; then the lords escorted him to a ship waiting to take him away.

Just at the moment he was about to embark, Tristram was challenged by a knight from the court of King Arthur. "Fair knight," he called out, "you must joust

189

with me before you leave this land. My name is Dinadan. My seat is at the Round Table."

"Willingly," Tristram replied, "if these lords will let me." The barons of Cornwall granted the contest, and Tristram easily defeated Dinadan.

"You have got the better of me," the knight said, "in a fair fight. I have never seen a more valiant knight. So I ask you this. May I accompany you, wherever you are going?"

"You are welcome, sir. We will ride on the waves together." They both took their horses and embarked. Before he left, Tristram turned to his escort. "My lords, greet King Mark and all of my other enemies. Tell them I will return when the time has come. Do you see how the king rewards me for saving his country? Thank him on my behalf. Thank him, too, for his gratitude that I brought Isolde to him from Ireland. I shall not mention all the other battles I have fought at his request. He has recompensed me enough, I am sure. Banishment is his gift to me."

Then he and Sir Dinadan took to the sea. They sailed along the coast until they found safe haven in a small harbour known as the place of lime trees. On first landing they rode into a forest where they were met by a young lady. She was distraught and anxious. She was in search of knights, from the court of King Arthur, who could rescue Sir Lancelot. Morgan le Fay had ordered thirty knights to lie in wait for him and kill him. This young lady knew the place where he was to be ambushed, and she begged Tristram and Dinadan to make their way there. "Tell me where it is," Tristram said to her. "I will ride there at once."

"What are you saying?" Dinadan was very indignant. "How can two knights beat off thirty? I would be a match for two, or three, but I can hardly defeat fifteen."

"Shame on you, sir. But do as you wish."

"I will come with you on one condition. Lend me your shield. With the arms of Cornwall upon it, the knights will consider me to be a coward and refuse to fight with me."

"Oh no. I will not give up my shield. I bear it in honour of the lady who gave it to me. I will make one promise to you. If you stay here, I will slay you. So come with me. I expect you to kill only one knight. And if you are too scared to take part, then simply look on."

"Sir," Dinadan replied, "I will stand by and watch. And I will do whatever necessary to defend myself. I will tell you this also. I wish I had never met you."

So, with the lady as their guide, they came upon the thirty knights waiting in ambush. Sir Tristram rode towards them, crying out, "Here comes one who loves Lancelot!" He killed two of them with his spear, and another ten with his sword. Sir Dinadan also fought well, so that in the end only ten knights remained. They saw the way the battle had gone, and fled.

The two companions now continued on their way until they came upon a group of herdsmen. "Tell me," Tristram asked them, "do you know of any lodging near by?"

"Indeed, sir," one of them answered. "There is a castle here where you may rest, but it is the custom there that any guest must first joust with two knights."

"Just what I need now," Sir Dinadan said. "I have no intention of taking lodging there."

"Shame on you," Tristram replied. "You are a knight of the Round Table, are you not? You cannot refuse to fight."

"If you are beaten," the herdsman told them, "you will not be allowed to stay. But if you are victorious, then you will be well cared for."

"Let us hope then," Sir Dinadan said, "that they are not too strong for us."

So they rode to the castle and, to be short, they duly defeated the two guardians of the castle. They took off their armour, and were about to enjoy a well-earned repast when Sir Palomides and Sir Gaheris arrived at the gates. "What is going on?" Sir Dinadan said. "I was about to relax."

"Not yet," Tristram told him. "We must carry out the custom of the castle. We now must joust with the two knights. So put on your armour. Prepare yourself."

"It was an evil day," Dinadan replied, "when I came into your company. God help me."

So he resumed his armour, and rode out with Tristram. He was not so fortunate as before, and received a fall at the hands of Palomides. Tristram got the better of Gaheris, so it was fall for fall. They now had to stand their ground and fight with their swords. Sir Tristram went over to Dinadan, who was still lying badly bruised beside his horse. "Get up, man," he said. "We have to fight."

"Oh no," Dinadan replied, "I will do no such thing. I was injured by some of those thirty knights, and now I am wounded again. I can fight no more. A man would be out of his mind to risk another battle. I curse the day I met you. You and Lancelot are two of the maddest knights in the world. I know that well enough. I once sought the company of Lancelot, and it cost me three months in bed. I was in such pain. God save me from both of you. Especially you."

"All right," Tristram replied, "I will fight both of them."

The outcome of the battle was never in doubt.

Here we tell of Morgan le Fay's evil

Tristram heard news that there was going to be a great tournament, between the kings of Scotland and of North Wales, at the Castle of Maidens. The King of Scotland called for Lancelot to be his champion, and the King of North Wales called upon Tristram. So Tristram was determined to ride there. On his way to the Castle of Maidens, he met a fair lady who asked him to pursue and challenge a knight who was doing great damage all over the land. Tristram was glad to comply with her request, and to win more worship. So he rode with her for six miles, until they met Sir Gawain. Gawain knew the lady to be at the court of the sorceress Morgan le Fay, and he realized that she was leading Tristram into great trouble. "Fair knight," he said, "where are you going with this lady?"

"I do not know," he replied. "She is leading me."

So Gawain drew his sword, and came close to her. "If you do not tell me what you intend, lady, you will die here. I know well enough the treachery of your mistress, Morgan le Fay."

"Have mercy," the young woman replied. "Spare my life, and I will tell you everything."

"So speak."

"Morgan le Fay has sent out thirty of her ladies in search of this man. I am one of them. He is to be lured to her castle, with the promise of winning renown, where secretly she has placed fifty knights to waylay and kill him in revenge for the thirty knights whom he defeated."

"Good God," Gawain said. "To think that a king's sister could be planning such treason." He turned to Tristram. "Sir, will you come with me? I have a plan to surprise these fifty knights."

"Willingly. I also wish to meet them. I have fought against Morgan le Fay's men before."

So the two men rode towards the castle of Morgan le Fay and, as they approached it, Gawain called out. "Queen Morgan, send out the knights that lie in wait for Sir Lancelot and Sir Tristram. I know your false treason, and will proclaim it to all the world."

The queen called back from the battlements. "I know you well, Sir Gawain. And I know that you speak so proudly because you have one beside you who is full of

194

prowess. I know the knight who bears the arms of Cornwall. I will not allow my men to do battle with both of you. Together you are too dangerous."

Tristram rode off, disappointed; he said his farewell to Gawain, at a turning of the path, and made his way to the Castle of Maidens. He had ventured into a grove, where he came upon a well; he dismounted there, and refreshed himself. He took off his helmet and, settling beneath a tree, he fell asleep. As he lay on the earth Dame Bragwaine, Isolde's servant and companion, came close to him. She had been looking for him for a long time, and had followed reports that he was in this region. Now she had found him. She withdrew herself a little, and waited until he had awoken. "Greetings to you, Sir Tristram," she said. "I have been searching for you."

"Salutations to you, Lady Bragwaine. Why have you come for me?"

"I have letters here from Queen Isolde."

He read them, and was moved by the queen's complaints. "Come with me now to the Castle of Maidens," he said. "There I will give you a letter of comfort for the queen."

Here we tell of the tournament

She rode with him willingly enough and, in the course of their journey, they met an ancient knight by the name of Pellownes. He lived in a manor close to the fields of the tournament; he told them that the preparations at the Castle of Maidens were almost complete, and that Lancelot was to sport the shield of Cornwall. He invited them to lodge at the manor, to which his son had returned after an absence of two years. "We will be merry," he said, "now that Persides has come back."

"I know your son," Tristram told him. "Sir Persides is a worthy knight." He had in fact jousted with him once, and had flirted with his lady.

The three of them rode back to the castle, where Tristram was welcomed by young Persides. "You are from Cornwall, are you not?" he asked him. "I was once in that country. I jousted before King Mark, and was fortunate enough to overthrow ten knights. But then Sir Tristram came against me. Do you know him, by any chance? He tried to take my beloved from me. I will never forget it, or forgive him."

"Ah," Tristram said, "I can quite understand why you hate him. Do you think that he will be able to prevail against you?"

"I know that Sir Tristram is a good knight, and perhaps a far better knight than I will ever be. But he will never be able to win my goodwill."

They stood talking at a bay window, from which they could see the various knights preparing to take part in the tournament. Tristram observed a knight dressed all in black, riding upon a black charger. "What knight is that?" he asked Persides.

"One of the best knights in the world."

"Lancelot?"

"No. Palomides. The knight who has not yet been christened." They heard many squires and others salute the man with "God save you, Sir Palomides!" and "Jesus keep you safe!" A servant came over to Persides, and told him that Palomides had already defeated thirteen challengers.

"No wonder," Tristram said, "that he is greeted on all sides. Come, sir. Let us put on our light cloaks, and watch the great play."

"No," Sir Persides answered. "We should not dress like knaves. We must be arrayed like knights, armed and ready for combat." So they prepared for the tournament.

When they rode out Palomides recognized Persides, and sent a squire over to him. "Go to that knight with the green shield, embossed with a lion of gold, and tell him that I, Palomides, wish to joust with him." Persides took up the challenge, but was defeated and thrown.

Then Tristram determined upon revenge. But he was not yet ready, and Palomides tossed him from his horse. Tristram recovered quickly, and leaped back on to the horse. He was angry with himself for the fall, and immediately challenged Palomides to further combat.

"Not at this time," Palomides replied. "If you are still full of anger, you may prove yourself tomorrow at the Castle of Maidens. I will be there, with many other knights."

"Then I will have my revenge," Tristram said to him.

Persides came over to him. "You have learned one thing, sir. There is no good knight that does not take a fall. No knight is ever so brave that he may not be beaten."

Here we tell of Tristram's good and bad fortune

Palomides rode to the house of a friend, where he lodged that night. He was too exhausted by his efforts on the field to take his place on the first day of the tournament. Instead he sat with his lord, King Arthur, on a dais and helped to judge the combatants. On that first day, it was Sir Tristram who received the prize for his valour. He fared among his opponents like a greyhound among hares. No one knew who he was. The field of combat was filled with praise for him. The wind carried the voices of the lords and ladies for two miles around, calling out, "The knight with the black shield has won the field!"

Yet Tristram had already gone, no man knew where. King Arthur sent ten of his best knights to find him, saying that he was worthy to be part of the Round Table.

But then fortune turned for Sir Tristram. At the tournament that day he had killed two brothers, the sons of Sir Darras. When Darras was told that they had been slain by the knight with the black shield, he went in search of him. He found him in a forest and, with the help of a hundred followers, he caught him and bound him. Then he dispatched him to his prison. In that dark place Tristram fell into sickness. He endured great pain. When a prisoner enjoys good health, he may endure all in hope of release. But when sickness touches his body, he lies bereft of everything. He can only wail and weep. So did Tristram, who suffered so much that he wished to kill himself. Here we must leave him for a while.

Tristram and the Round Table

The knights, riding on Arthur's order to seek out Tristram, travelled to diverse parts of the land. Sir Kay went westward. Sir Gaheris, the nephew of the king, rode straight into Cornwall. He was entertained there at the court of King Mark, and he explained to his host all the events of the tournament. "It was the greatest event ever seen in the kingdom," he said. "The noblest knights in the world attended. But there was one knight that excelled over all others. He bore a black shield."

"That will be Sir Lancelot," the king told him. "Or else Sir Palomides the Saracen."

"Oh no. Both of them were challenged by this knight."

"Then it must have been Sir Tristram de Liones." The king was secretly angered, even as he spoke the name, because he feared that Tristram would become so powerful that he would not be able to withstand him. But the king ordered a royal feast, and among those who attended was Sir Uwain, known as Uwain with the Red Hair. After the feast was over, Uwain challenged all of the knights of Cornwall. No one accepted the challenge until Sir Andred, nephew of the king, stood up. "I will meet you in the field," he said. So he put on his armour and rode out on his horse. Uwain defeated him immediately and left him, half-conscious, on the ground.

King Mark was ashamed that he had no knight to take revenge for Andred. He went over to Sir Gaheris and asked him to fight on his behalf. "I am unwilling, sire," Gaheris replied. "I do not want to go out against a knight of the Round Table. But for your sake I will joust with Uwain."

He rode into the field but Uwain, on seeing Gaheris's shield, rode over to him. "You are not permitted to do this," Uwain told him. "When you became a member of the Round Table you swore that you would never raise a spear or sword against any other. You see my shield. You know me, just as I know you. You may be inclined to break your oath, but I will not do so. I do not care if others think that I am afraid of you. I prefer my honour. And you have forgotten something else. Our mothers are sisters."

And, at that, Gaheris was ashamed and threw down his spear. Uwain rode away but King Mark, still full of wrath, followed him secretly. Before Uwain was aware of it, the king broke through a hedge and fell upon him with his sword. Fortunately Sir Kay was riding by, and saw the injured man.

"Who has done this to you?" he asked him.

"I have no notion. A knight came upon me suddenly. That is all I know."

At this moment Sir Andred rode past, looking for the king. "You false knight!" Kay shouted at him. "Have you done this? If you are the villain, you will never survive this day!"

"I did not hurt him, sir," Andred replied. "On my honour."

"Honour? You knights of Cornwall are all the same."

Kay then carried Uwain to the Abbey of the Black Cross, where his wounds were healed.

Learn of King Mark's deceit

Meanwhile Sir Gaheris took his leave of King Mark. But before he departed, he gave the king some advice. "You should never have sent Sir Tristram into exile," he said. "Had he been here, no knight would have withstood him." Sir Kay entered the chamber at this moment, and the king made a semblance of welcoming him. Then he turned, and bit his lip. "My lords," he said, "I wonder which of you is willing to take on an adventure in the forest of Morris?"

"I will take up the challenge," Sir Kay said.

"I will wait," Sir Gaheris replied. He did not trust the king, suspecting that he was a treacherous friend. He left the court, but took care to travel on the road that Sir Kay would use. Then he stopped to rest, and stayed there until he saw Sir Kay riding up. He hailed him. "You are not wise," he said, "to obey the request of the king. He is deceitful. I know him."

"If that is the case," Sir Kay told him, "then I must ask you to accompany me."

"I will not fail you."

They rode for a while until they came to the water known as the Perilous Lake. They made a halt there in a small wood by the shore. Meanwhile King Mark remained at his castle with a few companions who were closest to him. At midnight he called for his nephew, Sir Andred, to arm and prepare himself. When he was ready the two men rode out together, dressed all in black, and made their way to the lake.

Sir Kay saw them first. He took his spear in his hand and issued a challenge. King Mark rode against him, and his spear gleamed in the moonlight. The king had a more powerful horse, and Sir Kay's mount stumbled, throwing him from the saddle.

Sir Gaheris was ready. "Knight!" he shouted to the king. "Sit fast in your saddle. I am here to avenge my companion."

King Mark readied his spear, but Gaheris was too strong for him and smote him down. Then Gaheris went for Sir Andred, and unhorsed him. He fell so badly that he might have broken his neck. Gaheris then helped Kay to stand. The two knights took up their swords and confronted their enemy. "Get up," Gaheris said, "and surrender. Tell us your names, or you will die."

Sir Andred spoke first, although he was still in great pain. "This man is King Mark of Cornwall," he said. "And I am his nephew Andred."

"Treacherous men, both of you. You would do harm to us under the guise of hospitality. It would be a pity if you lived any longer."

"Spare me," the king said, "and I will make amends to you. Remember that I am an anointed king."

"The more shame to you. When you were anointed with chrism you swore an oath that you would protect all men of worship. You are worthy to die."

He lashed out with his sword, while the king tried to cover himself with his shield. But it was not enough to save him. The king kneeled down and surrendered; he then swore an oath on the cross of his sword that never again would he ride against any knights. He also promised to be a good and true friend of Tristram, if that knight should ever return to Cornwall. By this time Sir Kay had pinned Sir Andred to the ground, and was about to kill him.

"Let him be!" Gaheris called out. "Spare his life."

"Sir, there is no reason to spare him. He betrayed Sir Tristram. He was responsible for sending him into exile."

"I have given the king his life. I ask you to do the same for Andred."

Sir Kay reluctantly let Andred go. Sir Gaheris went over to Kay. "Well," he said, "you have learned this, Kay. It is hard to root out from the flesh what is bred in the bone." By which he meant that a bad king cannot change.

Learn of Tristram in the dark prison

They could not find Tristram, however hard they rode, because he was still closely kept in the prison to which he had been consigned by Sir Darras. Among his fellow prisoners were two knights of the Round Table, Sir Dinadan and Sir Griflet. The prisoners argued among themselves, and often Griflet offended Tristram with his words. "I wonder at you, Griflet," Dinadan said, "for stirring up bad feeling. If a wolf and a sheep were in prison together, the wolf would leave the sheep in peace."

Then Tristram turned to Griflet. "I have heard all your bad feelings towards me. But I will not defend myself at this time. I will wait and see what the lord of this place chooses to do with us."

Griflet was silent, and peace descended upon them. But then a lady entered the place where they lay. "My lords," she said, "be of good cheer. I have heard Sir Darras say that your lives are safe." So they were comforted.

It was at this time that Tristram fell sick, and seemed ready to die. Griflet and Dinadan wept for his plight. When the same lady came to see them, she found them mourning. So she went back to Sir Darras. "My lord," she told him, "the knight with the black shield is likely to die."

"That cannot be," he said. "I will not allow any good knight to lose his life in my castle. Call the three of them to me."

When Tristram stood before him, Sir Darras went up to him. "Sir knight," he said, "I am sorry for your sickness. I know that you are called a noble knight, and I can see from your countenance that is correct. You have killed two of my sons. That grieved, and still grieves, me. But I will never let it be said that I allowed the death of a knight in my care. So go with your companions. Take your horse and armour. Ride wherever you choose. But I release you on one condition. That you will be a good friend to the two sons who are left to me. And tell me this. What is your name?"

"I am Tristram of Liones. I was born in Cornwall, and I am nephew of the king there. As for the death of your sons, I could have done nothing other. If they had been my own kin, I could have treated them no differently. If I had killed them out of malice or treachery, I would be worthy of death."

"Yes. What you did was according to the code and custom of chivalry. I know that. That is why I could not put you to death. But I beseech you, Sir Tristram, to be a good friend to my surviving sons."

"On my oath as a knight," he said, "I will do you faithful service."

Tristram remained at the castle until he had recovered from his sickness. When he had regained his strength, he and his companions rode out until they came to a crossroad. "Now, sirs," Tristram said, "we must separate. Each of us must seek his own destiny."

Learn of Tristram's capture by Morgan le Fay

He rode on, delighted by his freedom and still eager for adventure. He had the misfortune, however, of entering a castle where Morgan le Fay was lodged. He was shown fine hospitality all that day and night but, on the following morning when he wished to depart, Morgan le Fay stopped him. "You must know," she said, "that it will not be easy to depart. You are here as my prisoner."

"Jesus defend me! I have just been released from a prison."

"Nevertheless you will stay with me until I know who you are and from what court you come." So Tristram, maintaining his silence for the moment, was forced to remain with Morgan le Fay. She had with her a lover, Sir Hemison, who grew more and more resentful of the favour she showed to Tristram. Hemison would have liked to run Tristram through with his sword, but shame prevented him. Then one day the queen said to Tristram, "I will relent a little. If you tell me your name, I will allow you to leave."

Tristram, tired of his imprisonment, spoke out. "Well, lady, I am Sir Tristram de Liones."

"Is it really you? If I had known that, you would not be allowed to leave so soon. Nevertheless I have made my promise. I must keep it to save my honour. But you must perform one task for me. I will give you a shield. You must carry it to the tournament that King Arthur has called at the Castle of the Hard Rock. You must perform as many deeds of arms in my name as you did at the Castle of Maidens."

"May I see the shield you wish me to bear?" She showed it to him. The device showed three figures on a field of gold — a king and a queen, with a knight standing above them with one foot on the head of each. "This is a superb shield," he said. "But what do these three figures signify?"

"I shall tell you. Here are depicted King Arthur and Queen Guinevere, with a knight who holds them in his power."

"And who is that knight?"

"I cannot tell you at this time."

But the old books tell us that Morgan le Fay was in love with Lancelot, and resented the devotion of that knight towards the queen. She had designed the shield to shame Guinevere, and to provoke the king.

Sir Tristram took the shield and promised to bear it at the Castle of the Hard Rock. He did not realize that it was painted as a rebuke to Lancelot and Guinevere. He would discover this later.

As Tristram rode out, Sir Hemison prepared to follow him. "Fair knight," Morgan le Fay said, "do not ride after that knight. You will not defeat him."

"Him? He looks to me like a coward. No good knight came out of Cornwall except Sir Tristram de Liones."

"And what if that is his name?"

"Oh no. Tristram is with Isolde of the White Hands. This man is a mere toy in comparison."

"Ah, my friend. You will find him more fearless than you think. I know him better than you do."

"Madam, for your sake, I will kill him."

"If you go, you are very unlikely to return. Consider."

Hemison was not to be prevented. He pursued Tristram as quickly as he could and, when he caught up with him, he called out, "Knight, prepare yourself for combat!"

They clashed, but Hemison was no match for Tristram. The knight from Cornwall cut him in so many places that he seemed likely to bleed to death. So Tristram left him, and found lodgings with an old knight who lived near by.

Hemison's squire came up to his lord, took off his helmet, and asked him gently if he was fit to travel. "There is very little life left in me," Hemison replied. "Climb up behind me and hold me fast to the saddle so that I do not fall. Bring me to my queen, Morgan le Fay. The deep draughts of death are about to engulf me. I must speak to her before I die."

They returned to her castle but, before Hemison could talk to her, he fell dead at her feet. She was distraught and, taking off the armour of her knight, she laid him on a bier. She caused a tomb to be built, bearing the words: HERE LIES SIR HEMISON, SLAIN BY SIR TRISTRAM DE LIONES. LORD HAVE MERCY.

Learn of Tristram's victory over Arthur

The next morning Tristram took leave of his host, and rode to the Castle of the Hard Rock. When he reached it, he saw five hundred tents pitched before it. The jousts began soon after, with the King of Scotland and the King of Ireland battling against the knights of King Arthur. Tristram took part, also, and carried the shield that Morgan le Fay had given to him. He performed many marvellous deeds of arms, so that the eyes of everyone were upon him. King Arthur saw the shield, and wondered what its device meant. He could not

guess. But Guinevere knew at once, and was downcast.
A female servant of Morgan le Fay was present, in the
same pavilion, and came up to Arthur quietly. "You ask
about the shield, sir? It is a reminder of the shame and
dishonour due to you and the queen." And, with that,
she disappeared no one knew where. Morgan le Fay
had cast a spell so that she vanished.

Guinevere called one of her ladies to her. "I fear,"
she told her, "that Morgan le Fay has made this shield
to spite me and Lancelot. I am afraid that I may lose
my life."

Arthur was still watching Tristram, and wondering
who he was. He knew well enough that he was not
Lancelot. He had been told that Tristram was in
Brittany with Isolde of the White Hands. He did not
know who this brave knight might be. He scrutinized
the shield again and again. And the queen grew ever
more fearful. Tristram was by now beating all others
back. The King of Scotland and the King of Ireland
retreated. When he saw that, Arthur decided that he
himself would challenge the unknown knight. He called
Sir Uwain to him, and asked him to arm himself. Then
the two of them rode out, and called to Tristram,
"Stranger knight, where did you get that shield?"

"I received it from the king's sister Queen Morgan le
Fay."

"If you are a worthy knight," the king replied, "you
should be able to explain its meaning to me."

"I will answer you as best I can. Morgan le Fay gave
me the shield. I did not ask for it. I do not understand

209

the meaning of it. I am expected to bear it with honour. That is all."

"Surely every knight should know what arms he bears? Well, at least tell me your name."

"Why?"

"I want to know."

"Not for the time being."

"In which case, you must do battle with me."

"Is it good to do battle for the sake of a name?" Tristram asked him. "Is it important? If you were a valiant man, you would not challenge me. You have seen how much I have laboured already. Never mind. I will take you on. I do not fear you. You may think you have me at an advantage, but I will prevail."

They rode against one another. Arthur's spear was broken to pieces against the shield of Tristram, and Tristram then gave the king such a blow that he fell to the earth with a bad wound on his left side. Sir Uwain saw the plight of his sovereign, and rushed out against Tristram. But he was easily defeated, thrown out of his saddle at the first strike.

Tristram then turned his horse about and addressed them. "Fair knights," he said, "I have done enough for one day. I must leave you."

Then Arthur rose to his feet. "We have deserved this," he told Tristram. "Our pride tempted us into battle. And still we do not know your name."

"This man is as strong as any knight living," Sir Uwain said. "I will swear upon the Cross that I have not seen his like."

Learn of the knight with the covered shield

Sir Tristram departed, and continued his quest for adventure. One day he was riding by a forest, when he came upon a fine castle. On one side of it was a marsh, and on the other side lay a meadow. He saw ten knights fighting in the meadow but, as he rode closer, he saw that they were in fact nine knights attacking a tenth. But the tenth was getting the better of them. He had unhorsed all of them, and the horses themselves wandered off into the fields or forest. Tristram saw by the knight's shield that he was Sir Palomides and he reckoned that he might need help. Palomides was his enemy but Tristram prized fairness and justice above all things. He rode into the meadow and called on the knights to stop their attack. "There is no worship," he said, "in nine of you defeating one opponent. Stop now."

One of them turned to him. "Sir knight, what has this quarrel to do with you? Go your way. This man will not escape us."

"It would be a great pity," replied Tristram, "if so good a knight should be killed by such cowards. I will do what I can to rescue him."

He leaped down from his horse to meet them on foot. He unleashed his sword and fell upon them like a storm, slashing right and left until most of them were struck down. Seeing his force, they fled for their lives. He followed them, but they escaped into the castle and shut the great gates. Tristram then returned to

Palomides, and found him sitting underneath a tree. "Ah, fair knight," he said, "I am glad to see you alive."

"Thanks to you."

"What is your name, sir?"

"Palomides."

"I thought as much. You have been rescued today by the man in the world who most hates you. Prepare yourself for another battle."

"And what shall I call you?"

"I am your mortal enemy. I am Tristram."

"Is it you?" Tristram nodded. "You have done too much for me today. I cannot fight you. Besides you are fresh and I am wounded. Assign another day. Name a place. I will be there without fail."

"Well said. I ask you to meet me, then, in the meadow by the river of Camelot. Where stands Merlin's Stone. Two weeks from today. For the time being I will stay with you until you are out of danger. You have too many enemies." They mounted their horses, and rode together into the forest. They continued on their way until they came upon a well filled with cool, clear water. "Let us stop and drink," Tristram said. "This sweet water will refresh us."

After they had dismounted and drunk, they saw a great horse tied to a nearby tree. They looked closer, and they saw a knight asleep under the same tree with his head resting on his helmet. Tristram noticed that his shield, lying beside him on the ground, was covered with a cloth. "This knight looks strong," Tristram said. "Why is his shield covered? What shall we do?"

"Wake him up."

Tristram prodded him with the butt of his spear. The knight started up and looked at them wildly. He put on his helmet, got on to his horse, and took a great spear into his hand. Without more ado he charged Tristram and brought him to the ground. Then he turned on Palomides and, with another blow, knocked him from his horse. He said nothing, but turned away into the forest.

Tristram and Palomides regained their horses, with some difficulty, and asked each other what should be done. "I am going to follow him," Tristram said. "He has put me to shame."

"Very well," Palomides replied. "But I am going to stay here."

"As you wish. But don't forget that we are meeting in the meadow at Camelot in two weeks' time."

"I have not forgotten. I will be ready for you. If you return, that is, from your pursuit of this brave knight."

The two men went their separate ways. After a while Tristram came upon a lady, lying on the body of a dead knight and weeping. "Lady," he asked her, "who has killed your lord?"

"A knight came riding in our path," she told him, "and asked my husband the name of the court from which he came. When he learned that he came from Arthur's court at Camelot, he challenged my husband to a joust. He said that he hated all of Arthur's knights. They fought. My husband was killed with a spear. That is all there is to say. The rest is lamentation."

"I am sorry for it. Do you know anything of this knight?"

"His shield was covered."

Tristram then left her, and for three days rode through the forest without finding a place to rest. On the third day he came upon a lodge, where Sir Gawain and Sir Bleoberis were recovering from wounds they had just received. He asked them what had happened. "We met a knight," Gawain told him. "He got the better of us. First he struck down my friend here. He heard Bleoberis say that he was too strong for us. But he thought he was just being scornful and making fun of him. So he rode against him and, as you can see, did him great damage. Then he turned to me, and on the first charge he utterly unseated me. He might have killed me. But he rode away through the forest. It was an evil day when we met him."

"What was the device on his shield?" Tristram asked him.

"It was covered."

Tristram realized that this was the same knight whom he was pursuing. "It happened to me, too," he told them. "This knight has put us all down."

"Do not pursue him now," Sir Gawain said to him. "Leave him be. I am convinced that he will come to us at the next feast of the Round Table. He will not miss the occasion."

"By God," Tristram declared, "I cannot wait to be revenged upon him." Sir Gawain asked his name. "I am Tristram." Then he departed. On that same day he met Sir Kay and Sir Dinadan. "Greetings," he said. "What news?"

"None good," Sir Kay told him.

"Tell me. I am seeking a knight. You may be able to help."

"What is depicted on his shield?" Sir Kay asked him.

"His shield is covered."

"That's him!" Dinadan cried out. "That's the one! It is the knight who met us. We were lodging in a widow's house near by, and he was also one of the company. When he discovered that we were from the court of King Arthur, he called us villains and cowards. He hurled abuse at the king, and at Guinevere also. So we challenged him to battle. I rode against him first, and he flung me to the ground. Kay here refused to defend me, and retired from the field. Then this knight with the covered shield departed."

"I will find him," Tristram told them. "I promise you." He went on his way and, in the company of his squire, Gouvernail, rode from the forest on to a wide plain. After he had gone a little way he found a priory, where he stayed for the next eight days and recovered his strength.

Learn of Lancelot du Lake

It was time then for Tristram to travel on to Camelot, to fulfil his engagement with Palomides. He took horse and rode up to Merlin's Stone. This was the stone where judgement was delivered. This was the stone where sacrifice was made. At one time Merlin had prophesied that two of the best knights, who were also two of the greatest lovers, would fight beside the stone. And so it came to pass.

Tristram waited by the stone for Sir Palomides, but that knight was not to be seen. Instead the knight with the covered shield rode into the field; he called out to Tristram, "I see that you have kept your promise to your enemy. But now you must come against me instead. Prepare yourself." They lowered their shields and spears, and rode down upon each other; they met with such force that both of them were thrown to the ground. They sprang to their feet and began to trade blow for blow with their bright swords. They fought for four hours, slashing and cutting, until the grass beneath their feet was bathed in blood.

The knight with the covered shield at last spoke out. "Sir," he said, "you fight better than any knight I have ever known. What is your name?"

"I am reluctant to tell you, sir."

"Really? I will not hesitate to tell you mine."

"Then speak."

"Fair knight, my name is Sir Lancelot du Lake."

Tristram was astounded. "Sir Lancelot? Is it really you? You are the knight I love and admire most in the world."

"Now tell me your name."

"I am Tristram de Liones."

Lancelot fell to his knees. "Jesus, why are we fighting?" Then he offered Tristram his sword. But Tristram also kneeled on the ground, and gave his sword to him. They yielded equally. Then they went over to Merlin's Stone, took off their helmets, and kissed each other on the cheek. Merlin had prophesied rightly. These were the greatest lovers — Lancelot for

Guinevere, Tristram for Isolde — and the finest knights in the world.

Then they took their horses and rode on to the castle at Camelot. On their way they met Sir Gawain and Sir Gaheris, who had promised Arthur that they would never return to court without Tristram. "Your quest is ended here," Lancelot told them. "This is Sir Tristram de Liones."

"Greetings," Gawain said. "You are more than welcome. You have taken a great burden from me. But tell me. Why have you ridden into this country?"

"I came here to challenge Sir Palomides. He was meant to meet me by Merlin's Stone. I marvel that he has not arrived. It was by chance that Lancelot and I met."

King Arthur now came up in the company of Sir Kay and, when he was told that it was Sir Tristram before him, he took him by the hand. "Sir Tristram," he said, "I greet you. You are as welcome as any knight that ever came into my court."

When the king heard how Tristram and Lancelot had fought, giving each other fierce blows, he was greatly moved. Then Tristram told him of his adventures, especially the occasion when he and Palomides came across the most powerful of all knights. "His shield, sire," he said, "was covered with a cloth. We challenged him, and he defeated us. There is no more to say. Then I followed him, and in many places I found knights who had been beaten by him. He had left a trail of havoc."

"It is the same man," Sir Gawain told them, "who successfully challenged me. Then he got the better of Sir Bleoberis."

"It is the same in my case," Sir Kay called out. "That knight wounded me badly."

"Jesus have mercy on us," Sir Gaheris said. "Who do you think this mysterious knight can be?"

"I will tell you who he is." Arthur was smiling at Tristram, who already knew the truth. "He is Sir Lancelot du Lake. Is that not so, Lancelot?"

They all looked at Lancelot in amazement. "My lord," he said, "you have found me out. I am indeed the knight with the covered shield. I did not wish it to be known that I came from your court. If I had been defeated, I might have brought shame upon you. So I dissembled. I pretended to have a hatred for your knights."

"That is true," Sir Kay said. "We heard him."

Then King Arthur took Sir Tristram by the hand, and led him to the Round Table. Guinevere and her ladies were already waiting there, and welcomed him warmly.

"You see before you," the king declared, "one of the best and most chivalrous knights in the world. You bear the palm for hunting and for blowing of the horn; you are skilled in hawking; and you are the best of musicians. So welcome to this place. But before you sit at the Round Table, I require one thing from you."

"I promise it before you put it to me."

"You must remain at my court. This is where you belong."

"But, sir, I have many responsibilities in other lands."

"You have made me a promise, Sir Tristram. You cannot renounce it."

"Very well. I will stay by your side."

Then the king studied all the seats of the Round Table, looking for one that lacked a knight. Then he saw one with the legend, inscribed in letters of gold: THIS IS THE SEAT OF THE NOBLE KNIGHT SIR TRISTRAM. The king was filled with wonder, and made Tristram a knight of the Round Table. And there was more rejoicing than you can ever imagine.

The Reunion of Tristram and Isolde

In the following years Sir Tristram won the most renown for his exploits and adventures. Isolde had managed to escape from her confinement at the court of her husband, King Mark, and by secret means had travelled across the borders of Cornwall; she had fled to the North, out of the reach of her husband, and had found refuge in a castle owned by Sir Lancelot. It was known as Joyous Garde. When Tristram knew that she was safe there, he rode swiftly to Joyous Garde to be with her. Soon after his arrival Isolde told him that there was to be a great feast at the time of Pentecost to which he was invited as guest of honour. "We must go," he said, gathering her up in his arms.

"Sir, I do not want to displease you. You are marked down by many knights for challenge because of me. If I am present, I may place you in danger. I would rather stay here."

"If you stay," Tristram told her, "then I stay also."

"God forbid. Then I shall be spoken of as shameful among queens and ladies of estate. You are known to be one of the noblest knights in the world, a worthy member of the Round Table. You must be present at the feast. What will the northern knights say otherwise? 'Oh, Tristram is happy to go hunting and hawking. He cowers in a castle, with his lady, and forsakes us. It is a pity that he was ever made a knight and that he ever loved a lady.' And what will the ladies say of me? 'It is a pity Isolde is alive. How can she bear to hold back her knight from winning worship?' That is what they will say." And Isolde sighed.

"God help me, I will go. You have spoken well, and given me good advice. I understand now how much you love me. I will do as you suggest. On Tuesday next I will go to the feast alone and unafraid. I will wear no armour. I will bear no arms except my spear and sword."

When the day came he departed from Joyous Garde. Isolde sent with him four knights, but he ordered them to return to the castle. Within an hour he met Palomides, who had just struck down a knight. Tristram then repented the fact that he had only sword and spear. As soon as Palomides saw him, he cried out, "Tristram, we are well met! Before we leave this place, we will have settled our old scores!"

"Ah, pagan Palomides," Tristram called to him. "No Christian knight has ever been able to boast that I fled from him. No Saracen knight, such as you, will do any better!" Then he made a charge at him, and broke his spear into a hundred pieces on Palomides' shield. Palomides sat on his horse, quietly watching Tristram's madness and folly. He said to himself, "If I attack

Tristram, without his arms and armour, I will be rewarded with nothing but shame and contempt. What am I to do?"

Then Tristram cried out to him again, "Coward knight, why do you hesitate? Come forward and fight. I can withstand you and all your malice!"

"Sir Tristram," Palomides replied, "you know very well my reasons. If I fight you, naked and unarmed as you are, I will deserve only dishonour. You have nothing to prove. I know your strength and courage. You have displayed them many times."

"I accept what you say," Tristram told him.

"May I ask you a question?"

"I will give you a true answer."

"If I was in your place, with no arms or armour, would you wish to fight me?"

"I understand you perfectly. As God is my saviour, I will now withdraw from the fight. Not for any fear of you, Sir Palomides, but for fear of the shame it will bring to you. Let us now go our separate ways. But before you leave, tell me this. Why has so good a knight as yourself not yet been baptized?"

"I made a vow many years ago. In my heart I know that Christ is my Saviour, but I swore an oath that I would not be baptized until I had fought fifteen battles. I have one left to fight."

"As for that, I will help you," Tristram replied. "Let it not be on my head that you remain a Saracen for a moment longer. I will fight you for your last battle. There is a knight lying there whom you overthrew. I will ask him for his armour, and then advance against you. Does that satisfy you?"

"Yes indeed."

So they both rode over to the knight, sitting disconsolate by the side of a stream. Tristram greeted him, and the knight feebly replied. "Sir knight," Tristram said. "I require you to tell me your right name."

"I am Sir Galleron of Galloway. I am a knight of the Round Table, although I now sit here in disgrace."

"I am sorry for your wounds," Tristram replied. "But may I beg a favour from you? May I borrow your armour? I must fight this knight here."

"Take it. I give it to you with my good will. But I warn you. This knight is as brave and as strong as any knight I have met before. What is your name, sir? And what is the name of the man who defeated me?"

"I am Sir Tristram. This knight is Sir Palomides. He is a Saracen."

"It is a pity that so noble a knight should still be unbaptized," Sir Galleron said.

"By the end of this day, if God wills, he will be baptized."

"I am glad to hear it. I know of you, sir. Your name and your deeds are renowned through many kingdoms. God give you strength."

So Tristram took off the knight's armour, and noticed a great bruise on his back where he had been buffeted by a spear. Tristram put on the armour and then, taking spear and shield, mounted his horse. Sir Palomides was waiting for him. They flew on each other like furies. The spear of Palomides was splintered, and he fell on to the ground. He quickly got up, and raised his sword and shield. Tristram alighted from his horse, and tied it to a tree, before advancing on him. They were ferocious in their attacks. Sir Tristram landed so many strokes that Sir Palomides was forced to kneel, but then a moment later Tristram himself was wounded. So it went on, blow exchanged for blow. These were men of war, ferocious combatants who were fast and fearless. After much fighting the sword of Palomides slipped from his hand. He was dismayed, but Tristram paused. "I have you at an advantage," he told him, "but never let it be said that Sir Tristram killed a knight who had no weapon. Pick up your sword, sir, so that we can swiftly make an end of this battle."

"I am willing to continue," Palomides said. "But I have no real heart for it. I never did mean you any harm. Surely we should be friends? My only crime was to love Isolde. You know well enough that I never dishonoured her, but sought only to serve her. If I offended you in any way, you have wreaked vengeance upon me with your sword. Look at my wounds. So it is time to forgive and to forget. If you agree, will you lead me to a church where I can be confessed and baptized? Then together we will ride south to Camelot and rejoin our king."

"I assent to that," Sir Tristram told him. "This is the time for forgiveness. Within a mile of here resides the Bishop of Carlisle. He will baptize you."

Together with Sir Galleron they rode to the palace of the bishop, where they requested that Sir Palomides be baptized. The bishop placed some holy water in a vessel of gold, blessed it, and then performed the rite of baptism. Sir Galleron and Sir Tristram were the godfathers.

The three knights rode back to Camelot, where the court of Arthur and Guinevere was assembled. The journey took many days. On their arrival the king and queen applauded the fact that Sir Palomides had been baptized. This was the occasion when Sir Galahad, son of Sir Lancelot du Lake, first came to court and sat in the Perilous Seat. You will soon learn that Galahad was the one who went in search of the Holy Grail. After a few days of feasting, Tristram returned to Isolde in the castle of Joyous Garde. Their fate was not a fortunate one.

THE ADVENTURE OF THE HOLY GRAIL

*Briefly drawn out of French,
which is a tale chronicled for one of the
truest and one of the holiest
that is in this world*

The Miracle of the Holy Grail

It was the vigil of Pentecost, when the entire fellowship of the Round Table returned to Camelot. On that day they heard mass before sitting down to a great feast in the hall. As they took their seats for dinner, a beautiful lady entered the hall on horseback; she must have ridden fast and furiously, for her horse was covered in sweat. She dismounted before the king, and saluted him. "Lady," Arthur said, "God bless you on this solemn day."

"Sir," she replied, "I thank you. But I must be brief. Tell me where I can find Sir Lancelot."

"Here. You can see him."

She went over to him. "Sir Lancelot," she said, "I greet you in the name of King Pelles. And I require you to come with me now." Lancelot then asked her where she lived. "I live with King Pelles," she replied.

"What do you want from me?"

"I will make that clear once you have accompanied me."

"Well," he said, "I will gladly go with you."

Lancelot ordered his squire to saddle his horse and to bring his armour. Then Guinevere came over to him. "Will you leave us, sir, at the time of our high feast?"

The lady answered for him. "Madam," she said, "Lancelot will have returned here by the time of tomorrow's dinner."

"If I thought that you were misleading me," the queen said, "I would not allow him to leave with you."

"You have my word, good queen."

Wherein Galahad is revealed

Lancelot left the court, and rode with the lady until they came to a great forest. Within this forest there was a valley. On the side of this valley there was a convent of nuns. They rode into its forecourt, and were greeted by many who flocked around Lancelot. He was led into the chamber of the abbess, and there he disarmed. Then he became aware of two knights sleeping upon a bed; they were his cousins, Sir Bors and Sir Lionel, and he roused them with the handle of his sword. They were delighted to see him, and jumped down from the bed. "Sir," Bors said to him, "what adventure has brought you here? We were expecting to see you at Camelot tomorrow."

"A gentlewoman has brought me here," Lancelot replied. "I do not know the reason yet."

As they talked there came into the chamber twelve nuns, leading with them a young man of great beauty and noble bearing. This was Galahad. "Sir," they said to Lancelot, "we bring you here this young man whom

230

we have nourished and brought up." All of them were now in tears. "We request that you make him a knight. No one is worthier of that honour."

Sir Lancelot gazed upon him, and recognized at once that he was a man of grace and goodness. He was as demure and as seemly as a dove. The knight had never seen a fairer form or a finer face. "Is this what he also desires?" he asked the nuns.

"He does so desire."

"Then shall he receive the Order of Knighthood on the feast of Pentecost."

On the following morning, then, at the hour of prime, Galahad was dubbed a knight. "God make you a good man," Lancelot said to him, "for He has given you a good face. Now, fair sir, will you come with me to the court of King Arthur?"

"Not at this time," he replied. "I am not ready."

Lancelot left the convent with his two cousins, and they rode back to Camelot. The king and queen were delighted to see Sir Bors and Sir Lionel again, and the whole fellowship of the Round Table proceeded to the minster, where they heard mass. When they returned from the service, the knights noticed at once that there were letters of gold written on some of the seats of the Round Table. One of them stated that HERE OUGHT TO SIT HE, while another had the words HE OUGHT TO SIT HERE. On the Perilous Seat was written: THIS SEAT WILL BE FILLED FOUR HUNDRED WINTERS AND FOUR AND FIFTY ACCOMPLISHED AFTER THE PASSION OF OUR LORD JESUS CHRIST.

The knights looked at the writing in wonder, at first not understanding its meaning; but they all agreed that it was a marvel. "In the name of God," Lancelot said, "this is the four hundred and fifty-fourth year after the Passion. These letters tell us that this seat is to be filled today. It is best to cover them until the chosen knight comes to us." So a cloth of silk was draped over the Perilous Seat to conceal the golden sentence.

The king then invited them to the feast. "Sir," Kay said to him, "if you go to your meat now, you will be breaking your own tradition. In the old days you never used to dine until you had seen an adventure."

"True enough," Arthur replied. "I was so cheered by the arrival of Lancelot and his cousins that I quite forgot the old custom."

At that moment a squire came into the hall and addressed the king. "Sire, I bring you marvellous news."

"What is it?"

"In the river below the castle, a great stone is being swept along with a sword embedded in it."

"I must see this marvel," the king said. "It is what we awaited." The king and all his knights went down to the riverside. There was the stone, floating on the waters, pierced by a sword that was richly decorated with rare jewels. Letters of gold were also engraved upon it. NO MAN BUT ONE SHALL REMOVE ME. HE WILL BE THE ONE THAT IS MOST WORTHY TO BEAR ME. FOR HE SHALL BE THE BEST KNIGHT IN THE WORLD.

When the king read these sentences, he turned to Lancelot. "Fair sir, surely you are the one to take up this sword? You are the best knight in the world."

Lancelot answered him solemnly. "This sword is not mine, sir. It does not belong to me. Anyone who tries, and fails, to remove it will regret the attempt. He will receive a wound from this sword that will never heal. I know the signs. On this day the adventure of the Holy Grail will begin."

"Now, good nephew," the king said to Sir Gawain, "will you try to remove it?"

"Sir," he replied, "I would rather not."

"For the love of me, attempt the task."

Gawain took hold of the sword, but by no means could he release it from the stone.

"I thank you," the king said.

Then Lancelot went up to Gawain. "You should know this. This sword will touch you so sorely that you would rather have given up the best castle in the kingdom than to have tested it."

"Sir," Gawain replied, "I could not withstand my uncle's will."

Then Arthur approached Sir Percival. "Sir," he said to him, "will you test your strength?"

"Gladly, my king." Sir Percival was happy to be given the chance. But he could not move the sword. After that, no other knight dared to set his hands upon it.

"Now we may all go into dinner," Sir Kay said. "We have seen our adventure."

They settled down to eat, and were served by the younger knights. All the seats were taken, except for the Perilous Seat. After the meal was over, there was a further marvel. The doors and windows of the palace shut of their own accord. Yet the hall was still filled with light. They fell silent, and the king was first to speak. "We have seen wonders, my lords, and I am sure that before night we will see further miracles."

An old man, dressed all in white, walked into the hall. No one knew from where he had come. With him was a young knight clad in red armour, with an empty scabbard hanging by his side. He had no sword or shield. The old man called out, "Peace be with you all, fair lords!" Then he spoke to King Arthur. "Sire, I bring with me a young knight of royal blood. He springs from the lineage of Joseph of Arimathea. He will accomplish such marvels that he will win undying fame for you and for your court." He took off the young knight's armour, and gave him a tunic of red silk; over his shoulders he placed a mantle that was trimmed with ermine. He led him to the Perilous Seat, and took off the silk cloth. The inscription had changed. The words now were THIS IS THE SEAT OF SIR GALAHAD, THE HIGH PRINCE. "This is your place," the old man told him.

So Galahad sat down. "You may go your way now, sir," he said to the old man. "You have fulfilled your vow. Commend me to my grandfather, King Pelles, and to my good lord, King Pecherre. Tell them on my behalf that I will visit them as soon as I can."

After the old man had left the hall the knights looked on Sir Galahad with wonder. He was so young. And yet he sat in the Perilous Seat without fear or shame. Had he come from God? Sir Kay turned to Sir Percival. "This is the one," he whispered, "who will win the Holy Grail. Who else could sit there without harm?"

Sir Bors called to the others across the Round Table. "I swear on my life that this knight will be honoured with fame and worship!"

Lancelot looked on Galahad with great joy, since now he knew him to be his son.

The clamour grew so loud that it reached the ears of Queen Guinevere. She went into the hall, wondering who it could be that had dared to place himself at the Perilous Seat. She saw at once the resemblance between Lancelot and Galahad. "I believe," she said to one of her ladies, "that this is the offspring of Sir Lancelot and the daughter of King Pelles. She made him lie with her by means of magic. His name is Galahad, I believe. He will be a noble knight, like his father before him." Then she went over to him, and read the inscription on his seat. She turned to Sir Gawain, sitting close by. "Fair nephew," she said, "now we have among us Sir Galahad. He will be a garland to this court. As Sir Lancelot once prophesied, this young man will win the Holy Grail."

The king himself then went up to Galahad. "You are most welcome here. You will inspire many knights to the quest for the Holy Grail. But only you will accomplish it. You will finish what others have begun." The king took him by the hand and led him down to the riverside where he could see the sword in the stone. The queen, and her company of ladies, came with them. "The sword," Arthur said, "is bound fast to the stone. Two of my best knights could not lift it."

"That is not surprising, sir. The sword is for me, not for them. See. I have brought with me an empty scabbard." He put his hand on the sword, and drew it out with the utmost ease. He put it in his scabbard. "At last it is where it belongs."

"God willing," the king told him, "you may also acquire a shield."

At that moment a lady rode up on a white palfrey. "Is Sir Lancelot here?" she cried out. Lancelot came forward and saluted her. "Ah, Lancelot, how altered are you from the morning!"

"Why do you say so?"

"This morning you were known to be the greatest knight in the world. But that is no longer true. There is one now greater than you. He took out the sword that you refused to touch. You are suddenly changed."

"As for that, lady, I always knew that I was not the best."

"Once you were the best. Of all sinful knights, too, you are still the greatest." Then she turned to the king. "Sir, the hermit Nacien sends you word that you will be blessed beyond any other king. On this day the Holy Grail will come within your court. It will feed you and the knights of the Round Table." And, with that, she departed.

"I know now," the king said, "that you will all soon begin your quest. From that adventure, some of you will never return. So this is the last time we will all be together. We must hold a tournament, which we will forever keep in our memory."

They all assented, and began to prepare themselves for the joust. The king had a secret reason for assembling them. He believed that Sir Galahad would never return to the court, and he wished to see how the young knight bore his arms. The contestants rode into the meadow, among them Sir Galahad. He was wearing a helmet and a light coat of armour. The king asked him to take a shield, but he refused. Then Sir Gawain told him that he must take a spear, as well as the sword, and he consented.

Guinevere and her ladies had decided to watch the tournament from a high tower. They looked down on Galahad as he galloped into the middle of the meadow, where he overcame all those who rode against him. He was a wonder-worker. Only two of Arthur's knights remained on the field, namely Sir Percival and Sir Lancelot.

On the queen's advice, Arthur now asked him to dismount and take off his helmet. Guinevere gazed at him for a long time. "I am sure now that Lancelot is his father," she said to the lady beside her. "Two men never resembled each other more fully. It is no wonder, then, that Galahad has proved to be so brave."

"Madam," the lady replied, "can he really be so great a knight?"

"Of course. Consider from what lineage he comes. Sir Lancelot du Lake is only eight generations distant from Lord Jesus Our Saviour. Galahad is of blessed birth."

Wherein appears the Holy Grail

The king and court now made their way back to Camelot, where they attended evensong in the minster there. After the ceremony they went to supper in the hall, with all the knights of the Round Table in attendance. As they sat in their places they heard a great murmuring in the air and the breaking of thunder, with a crash so loud that it seemed the palace might collapse. In the middle of the blast there came a sunbeam, seven times brighter than the light of day, and the company were lit with the grace of the Holy Ghost. They looked upon one another in wonder, because they seemed fairer and more radiant than they ever did before. They were unable to speak. They gazed, and were silent. Then the Holy Grail was carried into the hall, covered in a cloth of white samite, yet none could see who held it. The hall itself was filled with the odour of sweet spices, and before each knight appeared whatever food and drink he most wished for. When the Holy Grail had gone through the hall it vanished, as suddenly as it had appeared, in a cloud of light.

They all now could speak once more, and the king gave thanks to God for His great mercy in showing them the Grail. "We have seen," he said, "the cup that holds Christ's blood shed at the crucifixion. It has the power to heal all wounds. Now we know the meaning of grace."

238

"We have been given precious meat and drink," Gawain said, "but we did not see the Grail itself. It was covered with a cloth. So I make all of you a vow. I will follow the path of the Holy Grail for a year or more. I will start on my quest tomorrow. And I promise you this. I will not return to court until I have seen the Grail more clearly than was vouchsafed to me today. If that sight is denied to me, then I will bow to the will of God."

When the knights heard him, they rose and swore the same oath to follow the Grail. The king himself was greatly distressed at the thought of losing them. "Sir Gawain," he said, "you have come close to killing me. By making that vow you are taking from me the best and fairest knights in the world. After they leave here, few will ever return. Many will die on their quest of the Grail. We will never be together again. Why should I not grieve?" He began to weep.

"Be of good cheer," Lancelot said to him. "Take comfort from the fact that we go on a great and noble cause. All men must die, sire, but we will die in glory."

"Lancelot, I have loved you all the days of my life. Do you understand why I weep? No Christian king has been lord of so many brave and loyal knights. Now the Round Table will be empty for ever."

When the queen and the ladies of the court heard the news of their departing, they were distraught. No tongue can tell of their grief. They were losing part of their life. The most sorrowful of them all was Queen Guinevere. "I do not understand," she said, "why the king allows them to leave."

Many of the ladies wished to accompany their lovers on the quest, but they soon learned that it was forbidden. The hermit Nacien entered the hall dressed in robes of penitence. "Fair lords," he said, "who have sworn to pursue the Holy Grail, hear this. You must take no female with you on your quest. I warn you plainly that he who does not forsake all sin will not be permitted to see the mysteries of Our Lord Jesus Christ." This was the reason why the knights left alone.

When the hermit had gone Queen Guinevere came up to Galahad. "Am I right in thinking," she asked him, "that Sir Lancelot is your father?" He did not answer. "As God is my witness," she told him, "there is no shame in admitting it. Lancelot is the best knight in the world, and has royal blood. You also resemble him very closely."

"Why do you ask me," he said, "if you already know it to be true? I will reveal my parentage at the right time."

They all went to rest, but King Arthur could not sleep that night for sorrow at their departure. He rose at dawn, and met Gawain and Lancelot on their way to mass.

"Ah, Gawain, Gawain!" he cried. "You have betrayed me. My court will never be assembled again. But I tell you one thing. You will never be as sorry for me as I am for you." With that, he wept and turned to Lancelot. "Courteous knight, my own Lancelot, I need your counsel. I wish that this quest could end now."

"It may not be, sire," Sir Lancelot replied. "You saw yesterday how many worthy knights swore an oath."

240

"I saw it. No joy will ever alleviate my woe."

Then the king and queen went into the minster, followed by the knights of the Round Table, who wore their full armour except for their shields and helmets. After the service was over the king asked Lancelot how many men were ready to go on the quest. "One hundred and fifty, sire. All of our fellowship."

Guinevere went to her chamber, where she grieved alone. But when Lancelot could not see the queen, he went straight to the same chamber. "Ah, Lancelot!" she cried. "You have betrayed me. You have sentenced me to death by your absence."

"Do not be distressed, good lady. I will return to you as soon as I can."

"I curse the day I first saw you." Then she recovered herself. "May Christ, who saved the world by His death on the cross, be your protector and your guardian. Go safely."

Sir Lancelot left her and, with his company of knights, he rode through the broad street of Camelot. Rich and poor wept alike. The king turned away, and could not speak.

The knights rode out of Camelot together, and continued on their way until they came to a castle called Vagon. The lord of the castle, also known as Vagon, opened the gates and welcomed them all. They agreed, while dining there, that in the morning they would go their separate ways. When the time came to depart, they wept. But each knight took the way he thought best.

The Quest Begins

Galahad rode out of Vagon, still without a shield, and after four days he came to an abbey made of shining white marble. He was greeted with great reverence, and led to a quiet chamber. When he went down to supper, he saw that he was in the company of two knights of the Round Table, namely Sir Bagdemagus and Sir Uwain. They all greeted each other very warmly.

"Sirs," Galahad asked them, "what has brought you here?"

"Well," Bagdemagus replied, "we have been told that in this abbey is to be found a magic shield. It is said that no knight can carry this shield without dying or being maimed for ever. Within three days, he is overwhelmed by misfortune. I am going to test it. I am going to ride out with it tomorrow."

"In the name of God!" Galahad exclaimed.

"If I fail," Bagdemagus went on, "I urge you to take on the shield. I am sure you will prove stronger than its spell."

"Willingly," Galahad replied. "As you may know, I have no shield at present."

In the morning they rose and heard mass. Sir Bagdemagus then asked the monks where the shield was. One of them led him to a small alcove behind the altar where it was kept; it was snow-white, with a red cross. "Sir," the monk said, "this shield should be hung only around the neck of the noblest knight in the world. I counsel you, therefore, to be careful."

"Well," Bagdemagus said, "I do not believe that I am the best knight in the world. Nevertheless I will attempt to bear it." He turned to Galahad. "Will you stay until you hear how I have done?"

"Of course. I await your return with interest."

Bagdemagus set off with a squire who was told to bring news of the shield back to Galahad. The two men rode for a mile or so until they came to a valley with a hermitage on its southern slope. They saw a knight, dressed in white armour and riding a white horse, come furiously towards them with a spear ready in his hand. Sir Bagdemagus prepared himself for the contest, but the white knight was too strong for him. Bagdemagus was wounded in the right shoulder, where his shield did not cover him, and was thrown from his horse. The white knight then walked over to him. "You have committed a great folly," he said. "This shield should be carried by the noblest knight in the world. No one else." He turned to the squire. "Take this shield to the good knight Galahad, whom you left in the abbey. Greet him from me."

"Sir, will you give me your name?"

"That is not for you to know."

"But, sir, tell me this then. Why is this shield so fatal to all who bear it?"

"I can give you no answer. But I will say this to you. It belongs to Galahad alone."

The squire leaned over Bagdemagus and asked him if he was badly wounded. "God help me. I am so grievously wounded that I will barely escape death." The squire helped him on to his horse, and led him to the abbey. He was in great pain, and was taken down from the saddle very slowly. He was brought to bed, and lay there for many months. The old books tell us that he scarcely escaped with his life.

After the squire returned he told Galahad that an unknown knight had asked that the shield be given to him. "Sir," he said, "he told me that great deeds and adventures await you."

"Thanks be to God," Galahad replied. He mounted his horse and hung the shield around his neck. Sir Uwain asked if he might accompany him. "That may not be," Galahad said. "I must go on alone, save for this squire here."

Wherein the story of Joseph of Arimathea is told

Within a mile or two they encountered the white knight, waiting as before in the valley of the hermitage. The two knights greeted each other very courteously. "Sir," Galahad said, "I am sure that this shield has seen many marvels."

"Yes indeed," the white knight replied. "This is what happened. Thirty-two years after the death of Lord

244

Jesus, Our Saviour, Joseph of Arimathea — he who took down the body of Our Lord from the cross — left Jerusalem with a band of his kinsmen. They travelled to the island of Sarras where the king, Evelake, was about to make war upon his cousin. The warriors were both Saracens.

"Joseph went to Evelake and told him that he would be killed unless he converted to the true faith. He told him the doctrine of the Holy Trinity, and all the other mysteries of the faith, with such conviction and piety that Evelake became eager to be baptized. At that time a shield was made for the king, bearing the image of the Saviour upon the cross. He carried it into battle, covered with a cloth, but at a time of his own choosing he removed the cloth. When his enemies saw the body on the cross, they were thrown into confusion. So he had the better of the battle.

"It so happened that one of Evelake's soldiers had lost his hand in the fighting. He was carrying it with him, crying out for help. Joseph called him over, and asked him to place the severed hand against the image of the cross. All at once he was healed. There followed another marvel. The cross disappeared from the shield, and no one knew where it could have gone.

"It was time now for Joseph to leave the island of Sarras, but the king declared that he would accompany him — no matter where he chose to go. So they travelled on together until they arrived in this land. It was known at the time as Great Britain. One of the lords of this land, a pagan, was so hostile to the true faith that he flung Joseph into prison. Yet a worthy man, by the name of Mondrames, heard of Joseph's fate; he came with a great army across the seas and rescued him. Whereupon the people of Britain asked to be baptized.

"But Joseph was now growing old and weak. He lay on his deathbed and Evelake, weeping, kneeled down beside him. 'I left my country for love of you,' he said. 'If you are about to depart from this world, will you leave me some token or sign by which I will remember you?'

"Joseph looked upon him. 'Bring me your shield,' he said. 'The shield I gave you to carry in battle.'

"The king brought it to him. In his weakness, Joseph had a nosebleed that could not be staunched. So he smeared his finger in the blood, and with it made the sign of the cross upon the shield. 'I do this as a token of my love for you,' he said. 'Whenever you see this shield, you will think of me. The blood will always be as fresh as it is now, and no man will carry this shield without misfortune coming to him. The first knight who will bear it with honour will be Sir Galahad. He will be the last of my lineage, and he will perform many marvellous deeds.'

"Evelake then asked him where he should leave the shield. 'After your death,' Joseph told him, 'a hermit will take it to a secret place. It will then be given to Sir Galahad fifteen days after he has been made a knight.' All this, sir, has now been accomplished according to prophecy."

Saying that, the knight disappeared.

When the squire heard this tale he dismounted and kneeled at Galahad's feet. "I pray you, sir, to let me accompany you until you make me a knight."

"If I were to have a companion, I would certainly choose you."

"Will you make me a knight now, sir? I will be worthy of the honour, I promise you."

Galahad agreed to dub him as a knight, and both of them returned to the white abbey, where they were greeted with much good cheer and laughter. One of the monks then led Galahad to a tomb in the churchyard. "There comes from this grave so much noise of grief and torment," the monk told him, "that we believe a fiend dwells within it." Galahad walked towards it, fully armed except for his helmet. "Now," the monk said, "will you lift the lid of this tomb?"

There came a voice from the tomb, as if from the depths of hell itself. "Galahad, Galahad, servant of Christ, do not come near me."

But the knight was not afraid. He crossed himself, and then heaved up the stone. From the grave there arose a stinking smoke. There leaped out the fiend in the figure of a man, but the foulest that he had ever seen. Galahad crossed himself again.

"Galahad, Galahad," the fiend said, "I have no power to hurt you. I see you surrounded by angels." He fled, shrieking.

Galahad then looked into the tomb, and saw there the body of a knight with a sword lying by his side. "We must remove this body," he told the monk. "This man was a heretic and should not lie in holy ground."

They returned to the abbey, where Galahad took his armour. Then he was approached by another monk. "Shall I tell you the meaning of the body you saw? It is a token of the wicked world. There was once such wretchedness that father hated son, and son hated father. It was a world of woe. That was one of the reasons why Our Saviour came upon the earth, and was born of a virgin."

"I believe you," Galahad replied. "We are blessed."

He stayed that night in the abbey, and on the following morning he made his squire a knight. "Tell me this," he said. "What is your name?"

"I am Melias de Lile. Son of the King of Denmark."

"Since you come from a race of kings, you will prove yourself to be a noble knight. You will be the mirror of chivalry."

"That is my dearest wish," the squire replied. "But, sir, since you have made me a knight you must according to custom grant me one wish."

"If it be reasonable."

"I ask you, sir, to allow me to ride with you in quest of the Holy Grail unless and until some adventure parts us."

"I grant it willingly."

Sir Melias was given armour, sword and shield. Then he and Galahad rode out together, but they journeyed for a week without finding an adventure. Then, one morning, as they were leaving an abbey where they had rested, they came to a cross that stood at the parting of two roads. On the cross there was a parchment, inscribed with the following words: ALL OF YOU KNIGHTS, WHO RIDE OUT FOR ADVENTURES, CONSIDER YOUR CHOICE. THE ROAD ON THE RIGHT CAN BE RIDDEN ONLY BY GOOD AND WORTHY MEN. OTHERWISE YOU WILL COME TO GRIEF. THE ROAD ON THE LEFT IS DANGEROUS AND DEADLY. ALL WHO RIDE IT WILL SOON BE SORELY TRIED.

"Sir," Melias said, "let me take the left road. I hope then to prove my strength."

"It would be better if I went that way," Galahad replied.

"No, sir. I beg of you to let me have this adventure."

"Very well. Take it in God's name."

Wherein *Sir Melias is tested*

Sir Melias took the road and entered a great forest, in which he travelled for two days and two nights. He came out into a fair meadow, where he found a lodge of timber. When he entered this lodge he saw a chair upon which lay a crown of gold, richly and subtly wrought. On the floor was a white cloth, upon which had been heaped delicate and delicious meats. Melias was not hungry, but he had a great appetite for the crown. He went over and picked it up. As he did so a knight rode towards the lodge, calling out, "Put down that crown. It does not belong to you. You must fight for it."

Sir Melias crossed himself and murmured, "Fair lord of heaven, help this new-made knight!"

He mounted his horse, and the two men advanced against each other. The unknown knight was the stronger, and with his sword struck the left side of Melias with such force that Melias fell as if dead to the earth. The victor took the crown, and rode away. By great good fortune, Sir Galahad had decided to follow his squire and to protect him from harm. He saw Sir Melias lying still, badly wounded, and rushed over to him. "Who has wounded you? It would have been better if you had taken the other road."

"Lift me up, sir. Do not let me die in this forest. Carry me to an abbey where I can confess my sins."

"I will. But where is the knight that has hurt you so badly?"

At that moment Galahad heard someone calling from the forest. "Knight, protect yourself!"

"Ah, sir," Melias said, "that is the man."

Sir Galahad mounted his horse. "Sir knight!" he called out. "Come at your peril!"

The two clashed, and Galahad thrust his spear through the shoulder of his opponent; the man fell to the ground, and Galahad's spear was broken. Then a second knight rode from the forest, calling out a challenge, and lowered his spear against Galahad. Galahad turned and, taking out his sword, cut off the knight's left arm. The wounded knight fled back into the forest.

Sir Galahad then lifted Melias on to his horse; he had to be gentle, because the sword was still in him. Galahad took Melias in his arms, and together they went at a slow pace to the abbey. Melias was laid in a chamber, where he asked for Holy Communion. Once he had received it, he sighed. "Let death come to me when God wills it." He then extracted the sword from his own body, at which point he swooned.

An old monk, who had once been a knight, came into the chamber. He examined Melias very carefully, and turned to Galahad. "By the grace of God, I will heal him of his wound within seven weeks."

Galahad was overjoyed, and stayed a further three days to be near the wounded man. Melias then told him that he was getting better, and that he would recover. "Thanks be to God," Galahad said. "Now I can leave you with an easy conscience. I must return to my quest."

A good man came up to them both. "You speak of the quest, sir. That is why, for his sin, this young man was wounded. I marvel that you, Sir Melias, did not make your confession before setting out. Do you remember the two roads? The road on the right was the sign of the highway leading to Jesus Our Saviour, and it is the path for the virtuous man. The road on the left is a sign for the path of sinners and unbelievers. That is the one you took. The devil saw all your pride and presumption, in taking on the quest for the Holy Grail, and he paid you back in kind. Only a righteous and worthy knight may see the Grail. When you took up the crown of gold, you were guilty of greed and of theft. That is not the behaviour of a true knight. The two men you fought, Sir Galahad, were the emblems of these two mortal sins. They could not defeat you, because you are not spotted by deadly sin." Then the holy man went on his way.

Galahad now made ready for his departure. Melias saluted him. "As soon as I am able to ride," he said, "I will seek you."

"God send you health," Galahad replied.

Wherein Galahad meets further adventures

Galahad, mounting his horse, rode down many strange and rough paths. One morning he found himself by the side of a mountain, where there was a chapel of stone. It was old, and empty, except for an ancient altar. Galahad kneeled down before it and began to pray. Whereupon there came to him a voice. "Go now, good knight, and ride to the Castle of Sorrow. There is much wickedness there."

Galahad blessed his good fortune in being given such a summons. He mounted his horse, and before long he came to a valley beside the River Severn. Within the valley stood a strong castle, with a river encircling it. A labourer was working in a field close by. "What is this castle?" he asked him.

"Well, sir, that is the Castle of Sorrow. It is a cursed place, where all knights come to grief. There is no pity there, only evil and pain. I counsel you to turn away."

"No. I will not turn." He put his shield before him, and prepared himself.

Suddenly seven maidens appeared before him. "Sir knight," one of them said, "you are engaged in an act of folly. How can you pass over the river?"

"Why should I not pass the river?"

He rode on, through the swiftly running water, and on the opposite bank met a squire who spoke to him harshly. "My masters, the knights of this castle, forbid you to come any closer. They wish to know why you are here."

"Why? I am here to root out wicked men."

"You wish for too much. You will not succeed."

"Go on your way. Go quickly."

The squire rode back into the castle and then, a few moments later, seven knights came out of the gate. When they saw Galahad, they cried out in one voice, "Defend yourself! We are here to kill you!" They were all brothers.

"What?" called out Galahad. "Do you intend that seven of you should attack me at once?"

"So we do. Prepare for death."

Galahad lowered his spear and struck the first of them to the ground. He then set upon the other six with his sword, and scattered them; they rode off quickly, just as Galahad prepared to enter the castle. He was met by an old man in monk's habit. "Greetings," the old man said. "Here are the keys to the Castle of Sorrow."

Galahad rode through the gate, where he saw a concourse of ladies waiting for him. "Welcome," they cried, "welcome! We have long waited for our deliverance!"

A lady then came up to him. "The knights have fled the field, but they will return at nightfall. I am sure of it."

"What would you have me do?"

"You must blow upon this horn, and summon all the knights that owe service to this castle. You must persuade them to return to the ancient customs. They must swear to them. There is no other remedy." Galahad assented to this, and she brought to him a horn wrought richly with ivory and gold. "When you blow this," she said, "its sound will carry for two miles all around us."

Galahad did as he was bid, and then retired to a chamber in the castle. A priest came to him here. "Sir," he said, "the seven knights whom you saw came to this place seven years ago. They were welcomed by its lord, Duke Lianour, but they did not return his welcome. They killed him and his eldest son. Then they took over the castle, and raped the duke's daughter. She cried out in her agony that they had done great wrong to herself, to her father and to her brother. 'I prophesy this,' she said to them. 'You will not hold this castle for very long. There will come a knight who will conquer you.' They laughed at her, of course. 'Well,' said one of them, 'if that is the case then we will kill any knight who comes this way. We will also violate any virgin who falls into our power.' That is why this place became known as the Castle of Sorrow." And, at that, he sighed.

"Does the daughter of the duke still live?" Galahad asked him.

"Alas, sir, no. She died three nights after she was raped. But they kept her younger sister here, by force, as well as other maidens. They were the ones who greeted you in the courtyard."

254

The knights of the territory, summoned by the horn, now rode into the castle. Galahad made them swear fealty to the duke's younger daughter. A messenger then came to announce that the seven knights had been killed by Sir Gawain, Sir Gareth and Sir Uwain. "They have done well," Galahad said. "Now I can go on my way."

Wherein Lancelot is vouchsafed a vision

Galahad left the Castle of Sorrow and rode on until he came to a wild forest; in the dark depths of this place he came upon his father, Sir Lancelot, and Sir Percival. But they did not recognize him. The grace of God had covered his countenance. Sir Lancelot rode against him, but Galahad parried his blow and knocked him from his horse. Then he turned upon Sir Percival, and such was the force of his sword that Percival fell from his saddle.

This scene took place before a female recluse, who emerged from her hut and hailed Galahad. "God be with you, best knight in the world. If those two knights had known you as well as I know you, they would never have ridden against you." Galahad, fearful of being revealed to them, rode away swiftly. But Lancelot and Percival had heard the words of the recluse, and knew well enough that they had come against Galahad. They went in pursuit, but Galahad was already out of sight.

They parted, disconsolate, and Sir Lancelot entered a wild wood where there was no true path. He decided to wander wherever fate and fortune led him. He rode on until he came to a cross that, in the waning light, looked as if it had been made out of marble. Beside it was a small chapel of stone. He took off his shield, tied his horse to a tree, and walked towards the chapel. Its door was partly broken and, through the crack, he could see an altar covered by a rich cloth; upon it stood a silver candle-stick holding six great candles. When he saw the light from their flames, he wished to enter and perform his devotions; but the door could not be forced. In his dismay he returned to his horse, unharnessed it and let it graze on pasture. Then he took his shield and, placing it before the door of the chapel, laid down upon it and slept.

And as he slept he saw two white horses come beside him, bearing a litter in which lay a sick knight; as soon as they came up to the cross, they halted. Lancelot then heard the knight sigh and say aloud, "Sweet Lord and Saviour, when will this sorrow leave me? When will I see the Holy Grail and be cured? I have suffered so long for such a small sin!"

Sir Lancelot saw the candlestick, with the six candles, appear before the sick knight. Then there came a salver of silver, on which stood the Holy Grail itself. The knight then sat up, and held up his arms in adoration. "Fair Lord," he whispered, "I know that You are within this holy vessel. Take heed of my suffering." He touched the chalice, and then kissed it. All at once he was healed. "Lord God, I have been delivered," he said. "All praise to Your name." The Holy Grail, and the candlestick, were then returned to the chapel. But Sir Lancelot did not know how that had happened. He was in any case so overburdened with sin that he had no power to rise.

The sick knight walked over to the cross and kissed it; at this moment his squire came to him in wonder. "I am whole again, thanks be to Christ," the knight told him. "The holy vessel has healed me. Yet I am surprised that this knight here, before the chapel, slept. He was as still as any stone."

"I dare say," the squire replied, "that he dwells in some deadly sin for which he has not been confessed."

"Whoever he is, he is unhappy. I believe that he may be of the fellowship of the Round Table."

"Sir, I have brought you all of your armour, except for helmet and sword. Can you not take those from this man here?"

"Of course." The knight, miraculously healed, also took Lancelot's horse and, rejoicing, rode away from the cross.

Lancelot woke up a little while later; he sat up, and considered whether he had been dreaming or not. And, as he sat there, he heard a voice coming from the chapel. "Sir Lancelot, harder than a rock, more bitter than the leaf of a fig tree, listen to me. Leave this holy place. You do not belong here."

He did not know what to do. He listened and wept, as the words went to his heart. He believed that he had lost all his honour, and he cursed the day that he was born. He went over to the marble cross, and realized then that his horse, his sword and his helmet had been taken. It had been no dream.

"My sin and wickedness have brought me great shame and dishonour," he said. "When I rode out for worldly deeds I was always the victor. No one could defeat me. But now that I am on a sacred quest, I find that my sins hold me down. I could not stir or speak when the Holy Grail appeared before me. I am an unworthy wretch." So he lamented until dawn, when the song of the birds comforted him a little.

Wherein Lancelot learns from a hermit

He left the cross on foot, and went back into the wild wood without spear or helmet. After a few hours, he came to a high hill, on which stood a hermitage where a holy man was saying mass. Sir Lancelot kneeled down and called aloud on God to have mercy on him. When the mass was over he begged the hermit to hear his confession. "With a good will," the man said. "I believe that you are a knight of the Round Table. Am I correct?"

"Yes, sir. I am Lancelot du Lake. I was once of great renown, but all has changed. I am now the most wicked wretch in the world."

The hermit was astonished at this. "You ought to thank God, Sir Lancelot. You have been given great gifts. Of all knights you were the most beautiful. You were strong, and brave, beyond measure. But you have also committed great sins. That is why you sleep in the presence of Our Saviour, and why you are banished from the grace of the Holy Grail. If God is against you, your strength and courage will count for nothing."

Sir Lancelot wept. "I know the truth of it."

"Confess to me now," the holy man said.

"Father, I have sinned. I have been in mortal sin for the last fourteen years." Then he told the hermit all about his love for Guinevere. "I have fought for her, right or wrong, in all that time. I have tried to win her love and favour, and I never once considered the claims of God upon me. I pray you, sir, to counsel me."

"I can advise you, if you wish. You must no more come into the queen's company. You must forswear her for ever, as much as it lies within your power to do so."

"I do so swear."

"Make sure that your heart and mouth accord in this. If you are true to your word, I promise you that you will win more worship."

"Holy father, I must tell you of the words that came from the chapel." So he related all that had occurred.

"That is no marvel," the hermit told him. "It is proof that God still loves you. You are as hard as stone because you refused to leave your sinfulness. God's gifts did not soften you. A stone cannot be subdued by fire. In similar fashion the heat of the Holy Spirit cannot enter you. God gave you health and strength. He granted you wit and wisdom, to tell good from bad. You turned your face from Him. That is why you are more bitter than the leaf of a fig tree. You bear the weight of sin. When Our Lord preached in Jerusalem on Palm Sunday, he found the people there to be steeped in their iniquity. There was no one in that city who would welcome Him. He left the city, and found a fig tree growing outside the walls. It was flourishing there; it was full of leaves, but it had no fruit. Then Our Lord cursed the tree that bore no fruit, as a very token of Jerusalem itself. You are the fig tree, Lancelot. He found in you no fruit. He found neither good thought nor good will; he saw only lechery."

"All this is true," Lancelot replied, with bowed head. "I repent of my wickedness. And I vow to you to do penance for my sins."

The hermit pronounced his penance, and then absolved him. "Stay with me for this day," he said to him.

"Willingly. I have no helmet or horse."

"I will give them to you tomorrow evening."

And Lancelot kneeled down and prayed, in sorrow for his sins.

Wherein Lancelot speaks to a fiend

True to his word the hermit brought him a helmet, horse and sword on the following evening. Lancelot rode out, and soon found himself beside a small chapel; from the door of this place came an old man, dressed all in white. Lancelot saluted him, and gave him greeting. The old man smiled at him. "God keep you safe, sir, and make you a good knight."

Lancelot then dismounted and went inside the chapel. He saw there a dead man lying on a bier, clothed in white. "This monk," the old man told him, "was a man of faith for one hundred years. Then he broke his oath by wearing a garment of white wool." The man then placed a stole around his neck and, taking up an ancient book, murmured certain words. At that moment a fiend, more foul than words can tell, came among them.

"You have awoken me," the fiend said. "What is it that you want from me?"

"I wish to know how this man lying here died. Is he in heaven or in hell?"

Then in a horrible voice the devil replied to him, "He is not lost. He is saved."

"How can that be? He broke the oath of his order. He wore a white shirt when all clothes of that kind were forbidden to him."

"Not so. This man was of high lineage. His nephew came to him for help, in a war against Earl de Vale. So this hermit, lying here, left this place and fought against the earl, utterly defeating him. The earl decided to have his revenge. He sent two of his relations to the chapel here in order to waylay the holy man. They set upon him after he had finished saying mass. They drew out their swords, but no weapon could injure him. The Lord God was his protection. Then they tried to burn him by setting fire to his clothes. 'Do you try to destroy me with fire?' he said to them. 'Not one flame will affect me.' "

"Then they took him up, forced him to wear this white shirt, and thrust him into a fire. He lay there all day and all night, but he did not die. I arrived here on the following morning. He was then dead, but not one thread of his shirt nor one inch of his skin had been singed by the flames. I took him from the fire, in great fear of such saintliness, and laid him here. This is the truth. Now I must leave you."

Then, with a noise like a great tempest, the fiend vanished from sight. The holy man, and Sir Lancelot, both rejoiced that this dead man was not among the damned. Lancelot stayed with the holy man that night.

"Sir," the hermit asked him the next morning, "am I right in thinking that you are Sir Lancelot du Lake?"

"That is my name."

"What do you seek in this country?"

"I am in quest of the Holy Grail."

"You cannot catch sight of it, even if it were before you here. You can no more see it than a blind man can see a bright sword. Your sins come before you. Otherwise there would have been no knight more worthy." Lancelot bowed his head and wept. "Have you given your confession since you took on the quest?" the hermit asked him gently.

"Yes, father."

"I will say mass with you. And then we must bury this good man."

When they had put him in the ground, Lancelot kneeled down. "What shall I do to be saved?"

"Take this hair shirt that belonged to the holy man we have just buried. Place it next to your skin. It will be of great help to you. I also charge you, sir, to eat no meat and drink no wine while you remain on your quest. And, if it is possible, you must hear mass every day."

"I promise to obey you," the knight said.

At evensong Sir Lancelot left the chapel, and made his way into a forest. Among the trees he came upon a gentlewoman riding on a white palfrey.

"Sir knight," she asked him, "where are you travelling?"

"I go, lady, wherever fortune leads me."

"Ah, Lancelot," she replied, "I know well enough what you seek. You were nearer to it before than you are now. Yet soon you will see it more clearly than ever you did." Lancelot asked her where he might find lodging. "You will find none for a day and a night. But, after that time, you will find a good resting place."

So Lancelot rode on until he came to a cross. He dismounted and prayed, and before long he fell asleep beneath the cross. And as he slept he was vouchsafed a vision. A man came before him, adorned with bright stars and crowned with a circlet of gold. He led forward seven kings and two knights, who fell down on their knees before the cross and held up their hands in worship towards heaven. "Sweet Lord," they cried, "come to us here on earth. Bring us bliss or woe, according to our worth."

And in his vision Lancelot looked up at the heavens. It seemed to him that the clouds opened, and that an old man came down with a company of angels. This holy man blessed the kings and knights, and called them his servants — all except one knight, whom he approached with a look of warning. "You have wasted and profaned all the gifts I lavished on you," he told him. "You have fought in wars for the sake of your own glory. Pride, not truth, has been your tutor. Return those gifts to me or meet your ruin."

So ended Lancelot's vision. On the following morning he took horse and rode on until midday. Quite by chance he came across the knight who had stolen his helmet and horse, on the evening when the Holy Grail had appeared before the marble cross. "Prepare yourself!" Lancelot called out to him. "You have done me wrong."

They put their spears before them, and charged. Lancelot had the better of the contest, and soon enough the knight was upon the ground. Lancelot took back his old horse, and went on his way. He rode until nightfall, when he found a hermit praying in a small chapel by a stream. They greeted one another, and the hermit invited him to sleep that night beside the altar. "From where do you come?" he asked him.

"I am from the court of King Arthur, father, and my name is Sir Lancelot du Lake. I am in quest of the Holy Grail. So may I ask you this? What is the meaning of the vision I was granted last night?" He then recounted all that he had seen.

"This is a token of your high lineage," the hermit told him. "The seven kings and the two knights are the descendants of Joseph of Arimathea. The last of the seven kings, King Ban, was your father. The first knight, whom the holy man warned, is yourself. The second knight was your son, Sir Galahad, and he will be called the lion. He has the virtues of the lion."

"Is he, then, the most virtuous of all?"

"Did he not assume the Perilous Seat at the time of Pentecost? I entreat you to acknowledge him as your son. But do not attempt to challenge him. No knight will ever defeat him."

"No. I will beg him to pray for me instead. His virtue may help to vanquish my sins."

"You will fare all the better for his prayers. Yet you know that the father cannot bear the sins of the son, nor the son bear the sins of his father. Each man must carry his own burden."

They had supper together, and afterwards Lancelot lay down to rest. The hair shirt chafed and tore his skin, but he endured it for the love of God. The next morning he heard mass, and then rode out.

Wherein Lancelot joins a battle

He came on to a fair plain, where there stood a great castle. There were many tents beside it, of diverse hues, and on the plain paraded five hundred knights. Those from the castle were clad in black armour and rode on black horses; the strangers wore white armour, and had white horses. Lancelot watched as they rode against each other. It seemed to him that the white party had the better of it, and so he decided to go into battle on behalf of the weaker side. That is the sign of a good knight. He readied his spear and rode into the throng. He was successful at first, but the white knights surrounded him and so harried him that he hardly had the strength to stay on his horse. They took advantage of his weariness and led him and his horse from the field. "You are now out of the way," they told him, "thanks be to God." Then they defeated the fellowship of the castle, despondent at the absence of Lancelot.

Lancelot himself was left to his sorrow. "I am ashamed," he said aloud among his sighs. "I have never before been defeated. It is a sign that I am more sinful than ever."

He rode on, in despair, until he came to a deep valley. He could not descend its side and so he lay himself down to rest beneath an apple tree. He thought then that an old man appeared before him. "Sir Lancelot, Sir Lancelot," he said, "you are of little faith. Why is it that you are turned so easily to deadly sin?"

The old man then disappeared. Lancelot roused himself, and continued on his way. He rode along a path until he came to a chapel where lived a recluse; she had a small side room, with a window overlooking the altar. She called out to him as he rode past, and asked him several questions about his journey. He told her of his dreams and visions; he told her also of the tournament between the white knights and the black knights.

"Ah, Lancelot," she said, "that tournament was a token of Our Lord's grace. It was no enchantment. They were indeed earthly knights. The white knights were from the court of Eliazar, son of King Pelles, while the black knights came from Argustus, son of King Harlon. Yet they held another meaning. The black knights are a token of all those covered in sin, while the white knights are a sign of purity and chastity. You looked upon a battle between sinners and good men;

yet you were inclined to side with the sinners, were you not? You thought more of your pride and your standing in the world. Yet vainglory is not worth a turd. You must vanquish yourself before you will see the Holy Grail. That is why the old man, in a vision, accused you of little faith. If you do not mend your life, you will fall into the deepest pit of hell. Of all knights, I pity you the most. You have no peer among sinful men. Beware of everlasting pain."

Lancelot took his leave of her, and rode along the valley. He came to a river, overflowing with deep and terrible waters. It is known as Mortaise. He had to make his way through these black waves.

The Quest Goes On

After he had encountered Sir Lancelot and Sir Percival, Sir Galahad rode further and further into the wild wood, where the shadows faded in his presence, until at last he came out by the open sea. He went along the coast, until he arrived at a castle where a tournament was being held. He realized that the knights outside the walls were winning the battle against those who defended the castle from within. He went to the rescue of the defenders, and galloped into the midst of the attackers with his spear in front of him. He knocked the first man to the ground, and his spear broke. But he took out his sword, and made short work of those around him. It so happened that Sir Gawain and Sir Ector de Maris were among the knights assaulting the castle. When they saw him, with his white shield on which was painted the red cross, they knew at once that it was Galahad. "Only a fool," Ector said, "would ride against him. He is the high prince."

Yet at that moment Galahad rode past and, with his sword, slashed Gawain so severely that the blade gave the knight a great wound in the head and sliced into his horse. When Sir Ector saw Gawain fall to the ground, he went over and rescued him. "Now I understand the truth of what Lancelot said to me," Gawain told Ector. "The sword in the stone has given me such a stroke that I would have surrendered the best castle in the world to avoid it. Never have I felt such a blow."

"Sir," Ector said, "it seems to me that your quest is done. Mine is only beginning."

"You are right. I will seek no more."

See the Sword with the Strong Strokes

Gawain was taken into the castle, where he was laid in a fair chamber. A doctor was summoned to his side, and Ector would not leave him until his wound had healed.

Sir Galahad had left the field of battle, as soon as he was victorious, and rode so fast that before nightfall he reached the lands of the Castle of Corbenic. He found a hermitage there, where he lodged for the night; just as dawn broke, there was a knock at the door. The hermit rose to open it, and was greeted by a gentlewoman. "Father," she said, "will you awaken Sir Galahad? I must speak with him."

Galahad came to the door. "What is it you wish from me, lady?" he asked her.

"Sir Galahad, will you arm yourself and come with me? I promise you that, within three days, I will show you the most honourable adventure ever undertaken by a knight."

"If that is so, lady, I will follow you willingly." He said farewell to the hermit, and then mounted his horse. "Lead me forward," he told her. They travelled on until they came to the shore of the sea.

"Only a little further," she said.

There, in a small cove, a boat was waiting for them. As Galahad approached it, he saw Sir Bors and Sir Percival standing beneath the sails. "Welcome, Galahad," Sir Percival said. "We have been expecting you."

The lady and Sir Galahad took up their saddles and their bridles, but left their horses on the shore. They crossed themselves and boarded the boat. Galahad took off his helmet, and unbuckled his sword. "Where have you come from?" he asked the knights. "What are you doing here?"

"Truly," Sir Bors replied, "we came here by God's grace. We had no other guide."

"I never thought I would see you in this strange land."

"If only your father, Lancelot, was with us," Sir Percival told him. "Then we would be complete."

"That will not be," Galahad replied. "Not unless Our Lord wishes it."

The boat now travelled far from the land, driven by a blessed wind, and came to a whirlpool between two great rocks. They could not venture there without grave risk, but there was a second ship close by. "This ship is for us," the noblewoman said. "It has been sent to us by the Lord. Do you see the words carved upon its prow?"

And there was written: YOU WHO BOARD THIS SHIP MUST HAVE PERFECT BELIEF. I AM THE TOKEN OF FAITH ITSELF. IF YOU ARE NOT STEADFAST IN BELIEF I CANNOT SAVE YOU.

The noblewoman turned to Sir Percival. "Sir," she asked him, "do you know who I am?"

"I never saw you before in my life, lady."

"Then know this. I am your sister. I am the daughter of Pellinor, King of the Isles, and as such I love you more than any other man in the world. So I advise you of this. If you are not filled with faith, and a perfect believer, you must not come aboard this vessel. No sinner can sail in it."

When Sir Percival realized that this was indeed his sister, he was exultant. "Fair sister," he told her, "I will embark upon this ship; if I am guilty of sin, I will gladly perish."

Galahad crossed himself, and boarded the vessel; he was followed by the others, who marvelled at the furnishings they found there. In the middle of the ship was a bed, upon which had been placed a crown of silk. At the foot of this bed was a sword, pulled a little way out of its sheath. The sword itself was inlaid and decorated with rich devices. There were all manner of precious stones on the pommel itself, their colours a token of their particular virtues, and the hilt was made up of bone taken from two marvellous creatures. One was removed from the snake known as the serpent of the fiend; he who holds it in his hand will never weary or suffer a wound. The other bone came from the fish that lives in the Euphrates, and is known as Ertanax. This also protects the owner from weariness. Its other property is that it directs the mind forward, and prevents the remembrance of things past. On the hilt was inscribed the following words: ONLY ONE WARRIOR

WILL BE ABLE TO HOLD ME. HE WILL SURPASS ALL OTHERS.

"In the name of God," Sir Percival said, "I must try this sword." He put his hand to it, but he could not grip it. Sir Bors suffered the same fate.

Then Sir Galahad stepped forward, and suddenly on the sword there appeared letters as red as blood. LET US SEE WHO WILL DRAW ME OUT OF THIS SHEATH. HE MUST BE STRONGER THAN ANY OTHER. IF HE SUCCEEDS HE WILL NEVER BE SHAMED IN THIS LIFE NOR WILL HE EVER BE WOUNDED TO THE DEATH.

"I would willingly draw this sword," Sir Galahad said, "but I am sure that the penalty for any failure will be very hard."

"Only you, sir, can draw this sword," the noble lady said. "It is forbidden to all others. This is the sword with which King Hurlaine killed King Labor, father of the Maimed King. The death stroke caused great harm and dearth in the lands of both kings; there were famine and pestilence throughout the kingdoms. There was no fruit, nor grass, nor corn, nor fresh water. And so the two realms became known as the Waste Land, and the stroke was called the Dolorous Stroke. When King Hurlaine tried to place the sword back in the scabbard he fell to the earth dead. It has been proved that no man has drawn this sword without finding death or injury. King Hurlaine lay on the deck here, the same deck now beneath your feet, undefended. No man dared to board the vessel. Yet one day an innocent virgin came on to the ship and cast him into the waves."

272

The three knights now walked over to the scabbard, which seemed to be made out of serpent's skin. The belt, or girdle, was not so gaily wrought. On the scabbard itself were written letters of gold and silver. HE WHO SHALL WIELD ME MUST BE STRONGER THAN ANY OTHER. ONLY THEN WILL HE BEAR ME AS I OUGHT TO BE BORNE. THE ONE ON WHOSE SIDE I WILL HANG WILL NEVER BE SHAMED. YOU MUST NEVER REMOVE THE GIRDLE OF THIS SWORD. ONLY A MAID OF INCOMPARABLE VIRTUE MAY TOUCH IT. SHE MUST BE THE DAUGHTER OF A KING AND A QUEEN. SHE MUST BE INNOCENT IN WORD AND DEED. IF SHE BREAKS HER VIRGINITY SHE WILL DIE A WORSE DEATH THAN ANY OTHER WOMAN.

"Sir," Percival said to Galahad, "turn over the sword so that we can see what is on the other side."

They saw that the reverse side of the blade was blood red, with letters written as black as any coal. HE THAT PRAISES ME MOST WILL FIND ME MOST BLAMEWORTHY AT A TIME OF GREAT NEED. I WILL INJURE ONE TO WHOM I SHOULD BE MOST GRACIOUS. AND THAT WILL BE AT ONE TIME ONLY.

"What is the name of this sword?" Sir Bors asked her. "What shall we call it?"

"It will be known as the Sword with the Strong Strokes. The sheath will be known as the Mover of Blood."

Sir Percival and Sir Bors then turned to Sir Galahad. "Sir, in the name of Christ, we ask you to take up this sword and wear it by your side."

"I will hold it," he said, "to give you all courage. But it belongs to you as much as it belongs to me."

He took the sword out of its scabbard and held it aloft before Sir Percival's sister fastened it upon him. "Fair knight," she said to him, "there is a king known as the Maimed King who was once known as Dagdon. He was a good Christian who always supported Holy Mother Church. He was hunting one day, in one of his forests that reached down to the sea, when he lost all of his hounds and all but one of his knights. The king and the surviving knight came out by the shore, and found this ship. When Dagdon read the inscription upon its prow he was happy to go on board. But the knight, aware of his sins, was not ready to follow him. The king found this sword, and withdrew it from its sheath to the extent that you now can see. Thereupon a spear entered his body. That is why he is known as the Maimed King." She bowed to Galahad. "He is your grandfather. Maimed by his pride. You will meet him."

"In the name of God!" Galahad exclaimed.

"I am ready to die," she said. "I am now one of the most blessed maidens in the world, having served the worthiest knight in the world."

"Madam," Sir Galahad told her, "I will be your own especial knight for all the days of my life."

See a great slaughter

They left the holy ship and returned to the vessel in which they had first sailed. The wind drove them across the water. They had neither meat nor drink but they

274

trusted in the Lord. At last the waves brought them to the cliffs beneath a castle known as Carteloise, on the coast of Scotland, where they were greeted by a gentlewoman. She stood upon the rocks with her arms upraised. "There are men here," she told them, "that have no love for the knights of King Arthur's court."

"Do not be dismayed," Sir Galahad said. "He that saved us from the rocks and the whirlpools will deliver us from our enemies."

A squire then rode up to them, and asked them from where they came. "From King Arthur," Sir Bors told him.

"Is that so? Then you are in more trouble than I can tell you."

They walked on towards the castle, and from its battlements a horn blew. A noble lady approached them. "Turn back," she said. "For the love of God, return to your ship. Otherwise you will meet your death."

"We will not turn," Sir Bors said. "The Lord who has guided us here will be our guard. We work in His service." As they stood talking ten knights rode towards them, calling out to them to surrender or die.

"We shall not surrender," Sir Bors cried, "and you shall die!"

The ten knights attacked them, but Sir Galahad and his companions stood their ground. They knocked three of the knights from their horses and, taking the animals for themselves, rode into the hall of the castle. Here they caused such slaughter that all of the knights of that place lay dead or dying upon the ground. "If

God had not loved us," Sir Bors said, "we would not have had the strength to slay so many of them. They must have been great sinners."

"The vengeance is not ours," Sir Galahad replied. "It belongs to God. We can take no credit or worship for this feat of arms." At that moment a priest came out of a private chamber, holding the Holy Eucharist in a golden chalice. The three knights took off their helmets and kneeled before him. "Father," Sir Bors said, "have no fear of us. We come from the court of King Arthur."

The priest looked around him. "I see that these men have been suddenly and swiftly killed. God was with you. If you lived as long as the world, you could not achieve so much."

Sir Galahad bowed his head. "I repent that we have killed so many Christian men."

"They were not christened," the priest told him. "I will tell you all I know. The lord of this castle was known as Hernox. He had three sons, all of them knights, and a beautiful daughter. The three brothers were so besotted by their sister that one by one they raped her; when she cried out for help to her father, they killed her. Then they took their father, and consigned him to a cell in this castle. The three brothers then went on a rampage, slaughtering priests and monks; they destroyed churches and chapels, so that the Lord's service could not be said. I was called to the bedside of the father, the Earl Hernox, and I confessed him. He told me that three servants of the Lord would come to this castle, and destroy the beasts who were once his sons. So it has happened. You have done holy work."

"You are right, father," Galahad said. "We would not have slaughtered so many men today if God had not been on our side."

They were taken down to the depths of the castle, where they delivered Hernox from his prison. He had seen Sir Galahad in a vision, and he began to weep. "I have waited for you a long time," he said. "For God's sake hold me in your arms, so that I can depart this life in the embrace of a good man."

"Willingly, sir." And, as Galahad held him, Hernox died peacefully.

See a vision of holiness

A voice could be heard in the hall. "Sir Galahad, you have been well avenged on God's enemies. Now you must go into the presence of the Maimed King, who at your hands will receive the balm for his wounds."

So the three knights, together with the sister of Sir Percival, continued their journey. They came into a wild wood, where they found a white hart being led gently by four lions. They decided to follow the beasts, in search of a further adventure. They rode a long way until they came into a valley. There was a hermitage here, where a good man dwelled. The white hart and the four lions entered his cell and disappeared from sight. The three knights followed them, and found the hermit saying mass. As he raised the Eucharist the white hart was transformed into a man, while three of the lions were changed into the forms of a man, an eagle and an ox. The fourth lion retained its old form. Then these apparitions went through a narrow window, of which the glass remained unbroken.

And there came a voice saying, "In this manner did God enter the womb of Mary, whose virginity was neither hurt nor disturbed."

The four of them fell down, astonished, and saw around them a light brighter than the sun. When they recovered from their swoon, they asked the hermit to explain what they had seen.

"You are all welcome," he said. "I know that you are the knights who will accomplish the quest for the Holy Grail. You are the ones to whom Our Lord will show great secrets. The hart you saw is a token of Our Saviour himself, whose white skin is a sign of regeneration. So did Our Lord slough off earthly flesh, and take on the bright life of the spirit. The four that were with him — the lion, the ox, the eagle and the man — are symbols of the four evangelists who set down in writing some of the deeds of Jesus Christ. You have been privileged to see the white hart. I doubt that you will see it again."

See the death of a virgin

They heard mass, and left the hermitage on the following morning. Within a few hours they came up to the walls of a castle, where they were accosted by an armed knight. "Lords," he said to them, "tell me about this lady who accompanies you. Is she still a virgin?"

"Yes," she replied, "I am a maid."

He grabbed her bridle. "Then, my lady, you must obey the custom of this castle."

"Let her go!" Sir Percival shouted at him. "Do you not know that a virgin must remain inviolate?"

Then ten other knights rode from the castle, together with a noblewoman who carried a basin of silver carved into the shape of a mouth. They cried out in unison that "she must carry out the custom of this place".

"What is the custom?" Sir Galahad asked them.

"When a virgin comes by us, she must fill this dish with the blood from her right arm."

"That is barbarous," Sir Galahad said. "As long as I have breath within me, I will forbid it."

"God help me," Sir Bors added, "I would rather be killed than allow it."

"In that case," the knight of the castle said, "prepare to die. Even if you were the best knights in the world, you will not prevail against us."

The knights of King Arthur raised their swords against them, and of course beat them to the ground and killed them. But then sixty knights rode out from the castle. "Go back!" Galahad called to them. "You will not be able to defeat us."

"Is that so?" one of them said. "Our advice to you is to withdraw. We will permit you to leave, on condition that this lady carries out the custom and gives us her blood."

"That will not happen," Galahad told them.

"So you wish to die, do you?"

"I am not so sure that we will." The contest began, with Galahad and his companions maiming and killing all those whom they encountered. They seemed to be monsters rather than men. The fighting continued until nightfall, when a knight came out of the castle. "You have done much damage to us," he said. "But we offer you lodging and hospitality for the night. On our word of honour we promise to keep you from harm. And we hope that, once you have learned of our custom, you will choose to keep it."

"For the love of God," Sir Percival's sister said, "let us go in."

They entered the castle, and they were greeted with great admiration. Yet, more than anything, they were curious about the custom.

"We will let you know the truth," one of the keepers of the castle told them. "There lies within this place a noblewoman, who has been the lady of this castle for a long time. Some years ago she contracted a sickness that grew worse and worse until she fell into a coma. No doctor could cure her, or alleviate her condition, until a holy man came to see her and told us that she would be cured only with the blood of a virgin who was also a king's daughter. That is why we established the custom."

"In God's name," Sir Percival's sister said, "this lady is likely to die without my help. I must be bled for her sake."

"You might die," her brother told her.

"If I die to give her life, then I will acquire renown and worship. Better to lose my own life than to be

280

disgraced by cowardice. There need be no more battles. Tomorrow I will conform to the custom of the castle." The three knights accepted her decision, and on the following morning they heard mass. Sir Percival's sister was then brought before the sick woman. "Who will let my blood?" she asked.

One of the ladies took her right arm, and made the incision. She bled so easily that the dish was soon full. She blessed the sick woman, and said to her, "Madam, I have come to die here in order to save you. For the love of God, pray for my soul." And, at that, she fainted. Sir Galahad and Sir Percival lifted her up, but she had lost so much blood that she was unlikely to live. When she awoke from her faint, she whispered to Sir Percival, "Fair brother, I am dying. But do not bury my body in this country. Take my corpse into a barge you will find in the port, and then launch me over the waters. When you arrive at the island of Sarras, at the end of your quest for the Holy Grail, you will find the boat moored beneath a great tower. Bury me within the temple of that city. I must tell you the truth. You and Sir Galahad will be buried in the same place." Sir Percival wept, but promised to obey his sister.

There came a voice. "Lords, tomorrow at dawn, you three will leave this castle. You will not see one another again until you come before the Maimed King."

Sir Percival's sister asked for communion and, once she had received it, her soul left her body. On that same day the sick lady was anointed with Sir Percival's sister's blood and was healed. Sir Percival wrote a letter about the circumstances of his sister's death and placed it in her right hand; then her corpse was carried to a barge and covered with black silk. The wind arose and carried the barge over the waters, and the three knights watched until it had drifted out of sight. They parted on the following morning.

Lancelot and Galahad

It is said, in the old stories, that when Sir Lancelot came to the restless water of Mortaise he felt himself to be in deadly danger. The black waves oppressed his thoughts. He prayed for the guidance of God, and then laid himself down to sleep. And, as he slept, a man came in a vision before him. "Arise, Sir Lancelot. Put on your armour. You must embark on the first ship that you see." Lancelot awoke, and found himself surrounded by light. He made the sign of the cross, and took up his armour.

A ship came towards him across the water, without sail or oar, and as soon as he had boarded it he was filled with a sensation of sweetness and grace. "Good Jesus," he said, "this surpasses all other earthly joys."

He lay down on the deck, and slept until daybreak. When he awoke he found the body of Sir Percival's sister, lying upon a beautifully embroidered bed, and in her right hand was the letter that Sir Percival had written about her death. Lancelot travelled with this lady for a month or more. If you ask how he lived, then you must remember the ineffable grace of God who fed the people of Israel with manna when they wandered in the desert. So Lancelot was sustained by the Holy Ghost.

One night he came to a shore and, for weariness of the ship, he stepped on to the land. All at once he heard the sound of a horse coming towards him. He went back to the ship, and waited. Soon enough a knight rode up, and dismounted with saddle and bridle in his hand. The stranger asked leave to come on board the ship. "Sir," Lancelot said, "you are welcome."

"What is your name?" the strange knight asked him. "I feel a close sympathy with you."

"I am Sir Lancelot du Lake."

The knight took a step back. "You are my begetter in the world. You are my father."

"You are Galahad? My son?"

"Yes. I am."

So the son kneeled down and asked for his father's blessing. The father blessed the son and the son blessed the father. They kissed one another. They were so joyful that they could hardly speak. But then after a while they began to talk of their various adventures since they had left King Arthur's court. When Lancelot learned of the marvellous sword and sheath that Galahad had found on the ship, he expressed a great desire to see it. So Galahad drew it, and Lancelot kissed the pommel and scabbard. "Truly," he said, "you have witnessed some high adventures."

Lancelot and Galahad remained on that ship for half a year, praising and serving God with their prayers at all times. They ventured many times on deserted islands, far from the lands of men, where they found many strange beasts. Since they were not in quest of the Holy Grail, the old books make no mention of their adventures.

One day they sailed to land, and came up by the side of a forest. A knight rode before them, wearing white armour and leading a white horse. He saluted the two knights in the name of God, and then called out to Galahad. "Sir," he said, "you have been in the company of your father long enough. Come with me in quest of the Holy Grail."

Galahad knew that he must obey. He kissed his father gently on the cheek. "Fair sweet father," he said, "I do not know if I will see you before I see the body of Jesus Christ."

"For the love of God," Lancelot said, "pray for me in the course of your adventure."

Galahad left the ship and mounted the white horse, when a voice came from the sky. "Do well, father and son. You will not see each other again before the dreadful day of doom."

"Do you hear that, my son?" Lancelot was greatly moved. "I pray that we will both be saved."

"Sir," Galahad told him, "no prayer is more virtuous than yours. We will meet in paradise. Farewell."

Lancelot sees the Grail

Galahad left him and, with the white knight, entered the forest. Lancelot continued his life at sea; the wind took him wherever it wished, and he spent his days in prayer. There came a time when he arrived at the sea entrance of an ancient castle. There were no guards at the gate, except for two lions who lay beside it in the moonlight. Lancelot heard a voice calling his name. "Lancelot, Lancelot, leave this ship and enter the castle. There you will find what you most wish for."

He leaped from the ship, taking up his sword to ward off the lions. But a dwarf came from behind a rock and wounded him so badly that he was obliged to drop the sword. A voice came from far off. "O man of little faith and less belief. Why do you trust in your sword rather than in your Saviour? He will be of more service to you than any armour."

Lancelot fell to his knees. "Sweet Father Jesus. Out of Your great mercy You have reproved me for my sins. I hope and pray that I will become one of Your servants." He crossed himself, and rose. Putting his sword back into its sheath, he walked towards the lions. They looked threateningly at him, and growled, but he went past them without harm. Then he entered the courtyard of the castle.

All the doors and gates were open, but the hall was empty. He walked through the passageways, and at last found a chamber where the door was closed. He put his hand to it, but it would not move. He tried hard to undo the door, but stopped when he heard a voice that was not of this earth. It was part of the music of the spheres. And he heard the singing of "joy and honour to the Father of Heaven".

Lancelot kneeled down before the door. He knew well enough that the Holy Grail was contained within that chamber. "If ever I have deserved pity," he prayed, "oh, sweet Jesus, grant my plea that I may be permitted to see what is behind this door."

The door began to open, little by little, and there issued a light that blazed more brilliantly than the brightness of the sun and all the stars. Lancelot stood up, and would have entered; but once more he heard the voice. "Lancelot, Lancelot, go no nearer. It is not permitted to you." So he stepped back. Yet at the same time he peered into the room. He saw an altar of silver, with the Holy Grail covered in a cloth of red silk threaded with gold; angels were gathered about it, praising God. One of them held a burning candle, while another carried a crucifix. A priest stood before the holy vessel, holding up a young man towards it as if in consecration or sacrifice. But it seemed to Lancelot that the priest would fall to the ground, bearing such a weight. So he went forward to help. "Jesus, my Saviour," he called out, "surely it is no sin to help a good man in need?"

He came into the room and advanced towards the altar. But he was surrounded by a wind that burned like fire; he believed that he was being consumed in flame. He fell to the floor, and could not rise from it. He lost all powers of speech, of sight, and of hearing. He felt many hands lifting him up, and taking him out of the holy chamber.

The next morning he was found, stretched out before the door. One of the servants in the castle felt his pulse, and found the semblance of life still within him. Yet he could not stir. He was carried into a chamber, and placed gently in a bed. He lay there for four days.

Some said that he still lived, and others believed him to be already dead. One old man, wiser than most, was sure that he lived. "He has as much strength as any of you," he said. "Make sure that he is well tended until he is fully restored to health."

So Lancelot lay, still and silent, for twenty-four days and nights. On the twenty-fifth day, just after dawn, he opened his eyes. When he saw the servants standing around his bed, he cried for sorrow. "Why did you wake me? I was more at ease when I was asleep. I have seen such sights, by the grace of Lord Jesus! I have been given access to secrets."

"What did you see?" they asked him.

"I have seen marvels that no tongue may tell. If I had not been such a sinner, I would have witnessed more."

They told him that he had lain for twenty-four days and nights. "That is my punishment," he said, "for twenty-four years of guilt and sin. My name is Lancelot du Lake. I sought the Grail." They asked him how he was. "I am whole and healthy, thanks be to God. But tell me this. Where am I?"

They told him that he lay in the Castle of Corbenic. "This castle," they said, "marks the end of your quest. You have seen the Holy Grail. You will see it no more."

The Miracle of Galahad

Sir Galahad rode many miles, and many ways, without meeting an adventure. One morning he followed a path that led deep into a forest. In a grove there he found a well where the water boiled and bubbled. As soon as Galahad put his hand in the water, however, all became calm and cool. The heat was the sign of lust and lechery, but the power of his chastity proved too strong. Ever since, in that country, the well has been known as Galahad's Well.

He rode on until he came to the land of Gore. He found there an abbey where many kings were buried. It was known as the Abbey of the High Dead. He was told that one of the tombs in the crypt was surrounded by perpetual flame. "What is this fire?" he asked the monk who spoke to him.

"Sir, this is a marvel that can be removed by one man only. He must be the most virtuous, and most valiant, of all the knights in the world."

"Take me to the crypt," Galahad replied.

They led him down a flight of stone steps, and he walked towards the fiery sepulchre. As he approached it, the flames flickered and then went out. A voice could be heard, coming from the tomb. "I thank God that you have come to me. I am your kinsman. I have lain in this fire for three hundred and fifty years, in recompense for a sin I committed against Joseph of Arimathea. Now I can leave my purgation, and rise into paradise. I will be a soul in bliss!" At that moment a body was to be seen lying on top of the tomb, still fully formed. Galahad took it in his arms and carried it to the high altar of the abbey. He lay in the abbey all night in prayer, and then in the morning buried the body before the altar. He commended the monks to God, and then departed. He rode for five days until he came to the castle of the Maimed King. He was obeying the voice that had called to him.

Following in his steps, five days behind him, rode Sir Percival. He learned of the marvels of Galahad on the way, and he rejoiced. It so happened that, on leaving a great forest, he encountered Sir Bors. They saluted, and kissed one another; they retold the stories of their adventures. "For more than a year and a half," Bors said, "I have been riding alone in desert places, among mountains and wilderness."

"For more than a year and a half," Sir Percival said, "I have been lost in mists and marshes."

They went on together to the castle of King Pelles, called Corbenic, where Lancelot had seen the Holy Grail. Galahad had preceded them, having been welcomed five days before. The king was delighted to receive them because he knew that their quest, too, was coming to an end. They were shown the spear that had wounded the Maimed King; it was broken in three parts. Bors put his hands upon it, but then he flinched and drew back. Sir Percival had no power to touch it. So he turned to Galahad. "You are the only one who can achieve this feat," he said. "Take the spear."

Galahad took it up and, putting the pieces together, transformed it into a whole and shining spear. It was as flawless as when it was first forged. A little before twilight, as they sat in the hall, the spear began to glow. It rose into the air, burning more brightly at every moment, and then there came a voice. "All those who are not fit to sit at the table of Our Lord Jesus Christ must now leave. Only his knights may be fed."

So the whole company departed, with the exception of King Pelles, who stayed in the company of Bors, Percival and Galahad. There was also a young girl with them, the niece of the king. At that moment some other knights, in full armour, joined them. One of them addressed Galahad. "Sir, we have travelled far to be with you. We long to sit at the table where the holy meat will be granted to us."

"You are welcome, sirs," Galahad replied. "But from what country have you come?" He was informed that three of the knights came from Gaul, three from Ireland, and three from Denmark.

After they were seated together four gentlewomen brought into the hall a wooden bed; upon this bed lay a sick man, with a crown of gold upon his head. The women set him down in the middle of the hall, and then departed. The sick man lifted up his head, and spoke. "Sir Galahad, you are very welcome. I have desired your presence for a long time. I have been in such woe and suffering that no other man could have endured it. I trust now that death will soon release me and that I will pass out of this world. So I was promised long ago. I am the Maimed King."

A voice was heard in the hall. "There are two of you here that are not in quest of the Holy Grail. You must depart now." King Pelles and his niece left the chamber.

The knights were now outside time. An old man, in the company of four angels, came down from heaven. The man was dressed in the robes of a bishop, and he held in his hand a silver cross. The angels bore him up in a throne, hovering above the ground, from which he now spoke. "I am Joseph, the first bishop of Christendom, whom God rescued in the island of Sarras." The knights marvelled at this, because the bishop had been dead for three hundred years. "Do not be afraid," he said. "I, too, was once a mortal man."

Then the knights saw the doors of the hall open to admit a company of angels. Two of them carried wax candles before them, while a third bore a cloth. The fourth of them carried a spear which bled profusely; he captured the drops of blood in an enamelled box he held in his other hand. All at once the Holy Grail came down among them, its rays so bright that the knights were dazzled and fearful. The two angels placed the candles before it, and the third covered it with the cloth; the fourth angel stood the spear beside it. The bishop began to celebrate the communion of the mass, but the wafer he held in his hands became the image of a burning babe. He placed it within the holy vessel, and said the prayers of consecration. After the mass was over the bishop kissed Galahad on the cheek, and told him to greet his fellows in the same way. "Now," he said, "you have become the servants of Jesus Christ. You will be fed at this table with sweet spiritual meat that no knight has ever tasted."

After saying these words, he vanished out of sight. The knights sat at the table in sacred fear, praying silently, when suddenly Christ Himself rose from the vessel of the Holy Grail; he bore all the bloody marks of his Passion, and the wounds were still open. "My knights," he said, "you are also my servants. You are my children who have passed from the life of the world to the life of the spirit. I will stand forth in glory before you. I will grant you the revelation of high and secret things." He took up the Holy Grail, and offered it to Galahad; the knight kneeled, and received communion. In turn the other knights took the Eucharist, which tasted to them sweeter than any other thing on earth. "Son," Christ asked Galahad, "what is it that I am holding?" Galahad shook his head in wonder. He could say nothing. "This is the dish in which I eat the Lamb on Easter Day. Now you have seen the one thing you most desired. But you have not seen it as clearly as you will see it in the sacred island of Sarras. The Grail must leave this realm because the people here have sinned. So depart from this place. Go down to the sea, with Sir Bors and Sir Percival, where you will find your ship ready. Carry with you the Sword with the Strong Strokes that you won by your virtue. I must tell you one more thing. Take the blood from this spear, and anoint the legs and body of the Maimed King who lies here before you."

"What else can you tell us, Lord?"

"Only this. Two of you will die in my service. One of you will survive and will tell the story." He gave them His blessing and vanished from the hall.

So Galahad went over to the spear, and touched the blood with his fingers; with it he anointed the body of the Maimed King. The man was made whole, and rose from the bed rejoicing. The old books tell us that he joined a monastery of white monks, where he led a life of holiness.

At midnight, as they still sat in prayer, a voice came down to them. "My sons. My friends. Go from this place, in obedience to my words. Go towards the sea."

"Thank you, Lord," Galahad cried, "for calling us your sons!" The three knights armed themselves, and rode for three days until they came to the shore, where a ship was waiting for them. When they boarded the vessel they found the Holy Grail itself, covered with the red cloth of samite; so they knew that they were still blessed.

Sir Galahad fell on to his knees, and prayed for a long time to Our Lord. He asked Him on what day he might be able to leave this world. A voice then replied to him, "Whenever you wish to die, Galahad, on that day your wish will be granted."

Sir Percival had heard him praying. "Tell me, Galahad, for the fellowship I bear you, the reason you asked this question."

294

"When we saw the Holy Grail, in the hall of the Maimed King, I felt such glory in my heart that I was almost transported from the earth. I trust, and believe, that I will find joy with Jesus. My body will perish, but my soul will live for ever."

Sir Bors came up to him. "This is the bed, Galahad, in which you are supposed to lie."

Sir Galahad lay down, and slept for a long time. When he awoke their ship was coming close to the island of Sarras. Sir Percival saw the boat in which he had placed the body of his sister. "She has kept faith with us!" he cried.

They took from her ship an altar of silver, and carried it to the gates of the city. As they stood there, they saw an old man, crippled and infirm. "Can you help us, sir?" they called to him. "This altar is a heavy burden."

"For the last ten years," the old man replied, "I have relied on these crutches."

"Cast them off," Galahad said. "Trust in Christ."

The old man threw away his crutches, and found himself as whole and as healthy as he had ever been in his life. He joined the knights, and helped them to hold up the altar.

A rumour then passed through the city that a cripple had, by miracle, been cured by three knights. The knights returned to the boat where Sir Percival's sister lay, and brought her body into the palace, where she was prepared for royal burial. They were summoned into the presence of the king, Estorause by name, who asked them for an account of their wanderings. "Why," he asked them, "did you carry a silver altar into my city?" They told him the tale of the Holy Grail, and of the grace it had given to them.

This king was a tyrant, one of a long line of pagans who had ruled in Sarras. So he had no compunction in seizing them, and throwing them into a dark dungeon. But as soon as they were imprisoned, Our Lord sent them sight of the Holy Grail that kept them from all harm.

The king himself was wasted by long sickness and, when he believed that his end was near, he called for them to be brought to him. He confessed his fault, and begged them to forgive him for his trespass against them. They forgave him and, at the moment of repentance, his soul left his body. The people of Sarras were dismayed by the news of his death, and debated among themselves who should be the next king. As they sat in council a voice was heard above them, saying, "Choose the youngest of the three knights, who will rule you wisely."

So they made Sir Galahad their king. After he was crowned he ordered that a chest of gold and precious stones be built to hold, and to keep safe, the Holy Grail. The three knights kneeled before it, at dawn, and joined their voices in prayer. At the end of the year, one Sunday morning, they found a man in the robes of a bishop kneeling before the Grail. There stood around him a band of angels, who kneeled and prayed with him at the moment of consecration. After the host had been raised and lowered, the bishop turned to the knights. He called out to Sir Galahad. "Come forth, true servant of the Lord. See what you have always desired to see. He is before you."

Galahad began to tremble. He could feel the force of the spiritual world all around him and, as he kneeled upon the floor, he saw a vision of Jesus Our Saviour. He held up his hands towards heaven. "Lord, I thank You for the great gift You have vouchsafed to me. Now, blessed Lord, I beg to be taken from my body. I wish to leave this wretched world."

The bishop gave him holy communion. "Take this," he said to him. "It is the body of Jesus Christ." He looked down at Galahad. "Now do you know who I am?"

"No, sir."

"I am Joseph, the son of Joseph of Arimathea. Our Lord has sent me to you. I am with you for two reasons. Like me, you have seen the Holy Grail. And, like me, you have remained a virgin. Your time has come."

Galahad turned back, and walked over to Sir Bors and Sir Percival. He kissed both knights on the cheek, and commended them to God. "Fair lords," he said to them, "send my greetings and my love to Sir Lancelot, my father. Remind him that life on earth is very brief."

He kneeled down again before the silver altar, and prayed. As he prayed his fellows saw a host of angels come down, and carry his soul into heaven. Then they saw a hand reach down and take up the Grail and the spear. No man has seen them since.

When Sir Bors and Sir Percival approached the body of Galahad, they were overwhelmed with sudden weeping. There never has been such sorrow. If they had not been good men, they would have yielded to despair. But, as it was, they did their knightly duty. As soon as Galahad was buried, Sir Percival put on a simple robe and retired to a hermitage. Sir Bors stayed with him, but he did not become a hermit. He wished to bring the tidings of Galahad to Camelot. Within a year Sir Percival was dead, and Sir Bors buried him beside his sister in the precincts of the sacred temple upon the island of Sarras.

Sir Bors took ship and sailed away. He was sure of his destination and, after many months, he returned to the court of Camelot. He was greeted with great joy; he had been away for so long that King Arthur had believed him to be dead. The king held a high feast, and the drink flowed in honour of Sir Bors. Then Arthur summoned two scribes, and ordered them to write down the story that Sir Bors was about to tell. The knight spoke of the quest for the Holy Grail, and of Galahad's last days. He spoke of the despair, and the joy, that had marked their long journey. All marvelled at the miracles Galahad had performed. All wept when Bors described his death. The scribes completed their work, and the *Book of the Holy Grail* was placed in the library at Winchester.

Sir Bors turned to Sir Lancelot after he had finished his recitation. "Fair sir, I buried your son. With my own hands. But before he died he sent you his greetings. He asked me to remind you that life on earth is very brief. We have no certain city."

"I know this to be true," Lancelot replied. "I put my trust only in God." He took Sir Bors in his arms. "Cousin, you are welcome here. I promise to pray for you, and help you in any way I can. While the spirit is still in my body, I will support you. And I tell you this, dear cousin. In this life we will never again be divided."

"As you will, so I will."

LANCELOT AND GUINEVERE

The Poisoned Apple

After the quest of the Holy Grail was completed, the knights that were left alive made their way back to Camelot. King Arthur and Queen Guinevere rejoiced when they returned to the Round Table. They were most pleased by their reunion with Sir Bors and Sir Lancelot, because they had been away so long.

Then, as the old books tell us, Sir Lancelot began to keep company once more with the queen. He forgot the promise of perfection that he had made on his quest. He had indeed fixed his mind upon the queen even as he pursued the Holy Grail, and as a result he had failed of his purpose. Now that he had returned to Camelot, the two of them were more ardent than ever before. They were lovers again, and the whole court spoke of their affair. Sir Gawain's brother, Agravain, was, as usual, foul-mouthed.

So it transpired that Lancelot sought the company of other ladies to avoid suspicion; he became their champion, and once more he renewed his commitment to Christ. He tried to avoid the presence of the queen, so he might quell the scandal. Guinevere became angry with him as a result, and one day she summoned him to her chamber. "Sir Lancelot," she said to him, "I see and feel daily that your love for me is beginning to fade. You take no pleasure in my company. You are always out of court. And you champion the cause of other ladies more than you ever did before."

"Ah, madam, my queen," he replied, "you must excuse me. I have a multitude of reasons for my conduct. I was only recently in quest of the Holy Grail, and in that pursuit I saw as many sacred sights as a sinner is allowed to see. If my thoughts had not persistently turned to you, my queen, I would have been vouchsafed the visions permitted to Sir Bors, Sir Percival and Sir Galahad. So do not judge me unkindly. I cannot forget my high service so soon.

"Also, my lady, you must know well enough that many men of this court speak of our love. Sir Agravain and Sir Mordred, in particular, are waiting for our fall from grace. I fear them more for your sake than for mine. I can ride out and escape the court. You must remain here even when the rumours fly around you. If you stand in peril or disgrace, only I can rescue you. Be clear about this, my lady. Our boldness will bring us shame and dishonour. That is not a fate I wish for you. That is why I serve in the cause of other ladies and noblewomen, to show that I do not favour you."

The queen stood quite still as he spoke to her. When he had finished, she broke out in tears, crying and sobbing until all her grief was spent. "Now," she said, "I know you for what you are. You are a false lying knight, a coward and a lecher. You keep your distance from me, and seek the company of other women. I forsake you. I renounce you. I command you never to come into my presence again. And I order you to leave this court!"

Sir Lancelot left her, in deep dismay. He summoned his relatives — Sir Bors, Sir Ector de Maris and Sir Lionel — and told them what had transpired.

"You should not leave this court," Sir Bors told him. "You are needed here. Remember who you are. You are one of the noblest knights in the world, and you will perform many more great deeds. Women, in any case, are fickle and inconstant. The queen will repent her words. Wait and see. My advice to you is this. Ride out to a hermitage near Windsor, where a good knight now pays his devotions. His name is Sir Brastias. Stay there until you hear from me. I promise you that there will be better news in time."

"You know well enough, brother," Lancelot replied, "that I am reluctant to leave this country. But the queen has given me such a stern command —"

"She will change her mind. Has she not been angry with you before? And then forgiven you?"

"True enough. Well, I will take your advice. I will ride out to Sir Brastias. I will stay in the hermitage until I receive word from you that I can return. I beg this of you, brother. Help me, as far as you can, to regain the love of Guinevere."

"You may rely on me, brother, to do my best."

So Lancelot left the court that day, and no one knew where he had gone — except, of course, his kinsmen. The queen herself showed no outward sign of sorrow. But, as the old books tell us, she suffered much grief in secret. In public, she was resolute. That is why she arranged a dinner in London for twenty-four knights of the Round Table. She wanted to prove that she loved and honoured them all equally with Sir Lancelot. So there was a great feast.

Sir Gawain loved fruit, and in particular he favoured apples and pears. Wherever he dined, he was given them. The queen knew this, and ordered that a basket of fruit be brought to him at table. But he had an enemy at court, by the name of Sir Pionell. Pionell had by secret means managed to poison some of the apples sent up to Gawain towards the end of the meal. But, as fortune would have it, another knight picked up one of the poisoned apples and proceeded to eat it. This knight, Sir Patrise by name, fell dead in the throes of agony.

The knights leaped up from the table, enraged at this desperate crime. Their eyes turned to the queen. It was she, after all, who had arranged this feast and who had sent up the apples to Sir Gawain. "Madam," Gawain said, "you know well enough that this dinner was intended for me and my fellows. Everyone knows, too, that I love fruit. Now I see that I was close to being killed. What do you have to say?"

Guinevere was so alarmed and abashed that she simply stood there and said nothing.

"This cannot end here," said Sir Mador. "I have lost one of my kin. Sir Patrise was my cousin."

They were all silent, looking at the queen. She simply wept and sighed, still unable to speak. Then she fell into a swoon. King Arthur was informed, and came at once into the chamber where the meal was held.

Sir Mador saluted him. "My lord," he said, "I hereby appeal Queen Guinevere for treason." In those ancient days, many crimes were comprised under the name of treason, for which the punishment was death at the stake.

The king was dismayed. "Fair lords, I am distressed at the news of this fresh trouble. Yet I must be a rightful judge. I must not take sides. I cannot do battle for my wife, therefore, although I do not believe her to be guilty of this crime. I trust that some good knight will come forward on her behalf. I do not want to see her burned without cause. Therefore, Sir Mador, be not so hasty. I do not believe my queen to be without friends. Name some day of battle. We will see who will champion her cause."

"My gracious lord," Sir Mador replied, "you must excuse my words. But we are all bound by the rules of knighthood. You are a king, but you are also a knight. At the risk of incurring your displeasure I must tell you that not one of the knights here will defend her. They all suspect her." He turned to the company. "What do you say, my lords?"

They all agreed that there seemed to be no excuse for the queen. Either she, or one of her servants, must have poisoned the fruit. Guinevere had by now revived, and wept when they condemned her. "In the name of Jesus," she said, "I swear that I arranged this feast with no evil intent. I have done nothing wrong."

"My lord king," Mador said, "I require you, as a righteous ruler, to set the day when I may find justice."

"Be ready then, Sir Mador, in fifteen days' time. Ride to the great meadow beside Winchester, fully armed for battle, and there wait for the knight who will confront you in the queen's name. God will grant you justice. If no knight is ready to meet you, then my queen must be burned at the stake. There is no more to say."

"You have spoken well, sire."

When the king and queen were alone together, he asked her what she knew of the poisoned apple. "Nothing at all. As God is my witness, my lord, I played no part in it."

"If only Lancelot were at court," Arthur said. "He would do battle on your behalf."

"I do not know where he has gone," Guinevere replied. "But his kinsmen say that he has ridden out of this realm."

"Then we have lost our most loyal knight. I advise you, therefore, to approach Sir Bors and ask him to be your champion in the place of Lancelot. He cannot refuse. I know well enough that the other knights who attended your dinner will not fight for you." Guinevere set up a lament for Lancelot. "Why has Lancelot left us?" he asked her. She could not say. "It is a matter of regret," he said. "With Lancelot on our side, we would fear no harm. Hurry now, my queen, to Sir Bors. Beg him to help you."

So Guinevere went to Sir Bors, and asked him to do battle for her. "What would you have me do, sovereign lady?" he replied. "I was also at the dinner where Sir Patrise was killed. If I fight on your behalf, I will incur dishonour. My fellows may believe that I colluded with you in that crime. Do you see now how much you miss Sir Lancelot? He never failed you, and he rescued you from many dangers. You have driven him out of the kingdom, and reduced the honour of our court. How can you ask me now for a favour?"

"Alas, good knight," she replied, "I know my fault. I beg your forgiveness. I will perform any penance you ask of me." She fell down on her knees. "Have mercy on me, Sir Bors. Otherwise I will die a shameful death."

The king came into the chamber at this moment, and found his wife kneeling before the knight. Sir Bors gently lifted her up. "Alas, my queen," he said, "you do me grave dishonour."

"Ah, gentle knight," Arthur exclaimed, "have mercy on my queen! She has been defamed. I am certain of it. So I ask you on her behalf. Do battle for her. For the love you owe to Sir Lancelot, stay loyal to her."

"My lord," Sir Bors replied, "no greater request could be made of me. If I fight for the queen, I will forfeit the love and respect of the Round Table. Nevertheless, for the sake of Sir Lancelot and yourself, I will take up the challenge on that day." Then he paused. "Unless a greater knight than I decides to do battle for her."

"Will you promise me this on your faith?"

"Yes, sir. I will not fail you. But if a better knight comes to the field, he will take my place."

The king and queen were of course delighted. But Sir Bors was pleased for another reason. On the next day he rode out to the hermitage where Sir Lancelot was hiding, and told him what had occurred.

"Jesus be praised," Lancelot replied. "This has turned out better than I expected. Make yourself ready for battle, Sir Bors. Then wait on the field until you see me approach. Try to arrange a delay. Sir Mador is an impatient man. The longer you postpone the combat, the more headstrong he will become."

"Let me deal with him," Bors replied. "All will fall out as you wish."

Sir Bors returned to Camelot, where the whole court soon learned that he was ready to do battle for the queen. The other knights were displeased with him, as he had predicted, because they believed in her guilt. In all humility he approached them. "Fair lords," he said, "it would reflect on us all if Queen Guinevere was to suffer shame. Consider who she is. Consider the noble king to whom she is married."

One of them replied for them all. "We all love and respect our king. Of course we do. But we do not love or honour the queen. She has long been known as a destroyer of knights."

"Oh? This is the first time I have ever heard her described in that way. She has always been known to maintain good knights. She has been generous and bounteous in her gifts to us. She has always been gracious. So I say it again. It would shame us all if she were to suffer a shameful death. I will not allow it. I tell you that she had no part in the death of Sir Patrise. She had no reason to destroy him, or the rest of us who came to her dinner. She invited us out of good will, not

310

out of wickedness. I do not doubt that this will soon be proved, and that the real murderer will be revealed." Some were reassured by his words; others remained hostile to the queen.

On the evening before the battle, Queen Guinevere summoned Sir Bors. "Are you still well disposed towards me?" she asked him. "Will you still be my champion?"

"Of course. As I said to you before, sovereign lady, I will do battle on your behalf. I will decline only if a better knight takes your part."

The rescue of Guinevere

On the following morning the king and queen, together with the entire court, assembled on the great meadow outside Winchester. The queen was taken into the charge of a constable, and a great fire started around an iron stake; if Sir Mador was the victor, that was the place of her burning. It was the custom. No rank, not even that of royalty, could escape it.

Sir Mador and Sir Bors walked together up to the throne and presented themselves to the king.

"I am here to accuse the queen of treason," Sir Mador told him. "I will prove it in combat against anyone who says the contrary."

"I am here to fight for the innocence of the queen," Sir Bors said. "I will prove it in battle."

"Then make yourself ready," Mador told him. "Let us put it to the proof."

"I know you to be a good and brave knight," Sir Bors replied. "I do not fear you. But I have made a promise to my sovereign lord that I will remove myself from battle if a better knight comes forward."

"Is that all you have to say, sir? No more words. Let the battle begin."

"Take your horse on to the field then. I will follow you shortly." So they both made their way back to their tents, and armed themselves. Sir Mador rode out first. "Tell your champion to come forth!" he cried out to Arthur. "That is, if he dares to meet me."

Sir Bors felt shame at this taunt, and so he rode towards the lists. But at that moment he saw a knight riding on a white horse from the wood beside the meadow. This knight galloped up to him, and called out so that everyone might hear. "Fair knight, do not be displeased. I am the better knight, and I have come a long way to fight this battle on behalf of the queen."

Sir Bors went over to the king. "Did you hear him, sir?"

"I did. Who is he?"

"I have no knowledge of him," he replied. "But he claims this battle by right. I cannot refuse him."

The king called over the unknown knight. "You will fight for the queen?"

"That is why I have come, my lord. And I can wait no longer. It is a great dishonour to you and your court that so noble a lady as Queen Guinevere should be slandered and defamed. You must permit me to depart once the contest is over. I must fight many more battles elsewhere."

312

Sir Mador addressed the king. "It is time to begin, sir. I wish to see what mettle this knight is made of."

So they withdrew to the lists, couched their spears and rode against each other at great speed. The spear of Sir Mador was broken, but that of his opponent held; Mador was unhorsed and fell to the earth. He took up his shield, and drew his sword, challenging his opponent to join him in hand-to-hand battle. The knight dismounted, and showed his sword. They clashed at once, and for an hour they exchanged blow for blow. They fought, and bellowed, like wild boars. Sir Mador was a strong knight, proven in many battles. But he fell in the end, buffeted and beaten beyond endurance. He tried to rise, and struck at his challenger's thigh with his sword. The blood flowed, but then the unknown knight gave him such a blow on his helmet that he tasted the dust. Sir Mador then begged for mercy. "I have been overcome," he said. "I realize that the queen is innocent."

"I will grant your life," the knight replied, "on condition that you freely release the queen for ever from the taint of treason."

"Willingly," Sir Mador said. "I withdraw all charges."

The knights of the court took Sir Mador to his tent, while the king and queen embraced one another. Arthur and Guinevere went over to the unknown knight, and thanked him. "Take off your helmet, sir," the king told him. "Drink some wine." The knight complied and, when he removed his helmet, everyone saw that it was Lancelot standing before them. Arthur took Guinevere by the hand. "Sir Lancelot, I thank

God that you came back to us. You have saved my queen's life."

"My lord," Lancelot replied, "I am here by right and duty. Your battles are my battles. You, sir, were the one who gave me the Order of Knighthood. And you, my lady, have always honoured and favoured me. How could I do otherwise than fight on your behalf?"

"I thank God again for you," the king said. "And I will reward you."

Guinevere was now weeping for joy and for sorrow. She had treated him harshly but, in return, he had risked his life for her. He had paid unkindness with kindness. The other knights now came over to Lancelot and welcomed him with great warmth and affection. Sir Mador recovered from his wounds, and sat once more at the Round Table with Lancelot.

It so happened that the Lady of the Lake came to court soon afterwards. She was a great sorceress who had cast many spells for King Arthur. When she heard that the queen had been accused of killing Sir Patrise, she declared Guinevere to be innocent. By means of her magic she revealed that the killer was in fact Sir Pionell. He was the one who had poisoned the apple, with the intention of destroying Sir Gawain. Pionell fled the court at once, and retired to his own country. Guinevere rejoiced at the return of her good name.

Sir Patrise was then buried in Westminster Abbey, and upon his tomb was inscribed an account of the whole affair. Sir Mador eventually found favour with the queen once more. All was forgiven.

The Fair Maid of Astolat

In the middle of summer, on the feast day of the Assumption of Our Lady, Arthur proclaimed that there would be a tournament at Camelot where he and the King of Scotland would challenge all comers. As a result, many noble knights rode to the court. The king himself was ready to depart from London for Winchester, the English name of Camelot, and called for his wife to accompany him. She sent him word that she was sick, and could not ride with him.

Many in the court believed that she remained behind so that she could be with Lancelot. He had already refused the challenge, on the grounds that he was still recovering from his wounds after the battle with Sir Mador. The king himself was very angry, but he travelled on with his company of knights. On his way he lodged at Astolat, known in English as Guildford, in the castle of Sir Bernard.

After he had left, Guinevere called Lancelot to her chamber. "Sir," she said, "what are you doing here? Do you know what people are saying? They are convinced that we have planned this so that we can be together. You will bring shame upon me."

"Madam, I do not doubt you. You are wiser than me, and I will be ruled by your words. I will remain here tonight, but tomorrow I will make my way to Camelot. For the sport of it, I will fight in disguise against the king and all his fellowship."

"That is your decision," she replied, "but do not forget that the knights of the Round Table are fierce and resolute."

"What will be, will be."

On the following morning he heard mass, and then took his leave of the queen. He rode hard and soon reached Guildford, where he also found lodgings at the castle. Arthur glimpsed Lancelot as he walked in the gardens there. "Ah," the king said, "I see a knight who will take part in the tournament."

"Who is that?" one of his knights asked him.

"You will soon see well enough." The king smiled at him. "Be prepared."

When Sir Lancelot was alone in his chamber, his host, Sir Bernard, came to him. He did not know Lancelot by sight. After Bernard had welcomed him, Lancelot asked for a favour. "Fair sir," he said, "will you lend me a shield? I do not wish to carry my own. I hope to remain unknown."

"Willingly," Sir Bernard replied. "You seem to me to be one of the best knights in the field, and I will honour your friendship. I have two sons, and the eldest of them was just dubbed a knight. His name is Sir Tirry and, on the day he was knighted, he suffered a wound that prevents him from taking part in the tournament. You can use his shield. It will not be recognized. My younger son is Sir Lavane. Will you allow him to ride with you to the joust? He is young and strong. He will prove to be a good knight. But tell me this, sir. What is your name?"

"I cannot tell you at this time. But if God give me strength at the tournament, then I will let you know. In the meantime I am happy to take Sir Lavane with me. Thank you, also, for the loan of the shield."

Sir Bernard's daughter, Elaine, known at that time as the Fair Maid of Astolat, had been listening at the door. As soon as she saw Lancelot, she fell in love with him. She was so enamoured of him that she begged him to wear her token when he rode out to the tournament.

"If I grant you that, young lady," he said, "I will be performing a greater service than I have ever given to any other woman." Then he remembered that he wished to ride unrecognized. If he wore this girl's token, no one would suspect that he was Lancelot. So he smiled upon her. "Fair lady, I give in. I will wear your token on my helmet. What is it?"

"It is a red scarf of mine," she said. "It is scarlet, and it is embroidered with rich pearls." She brought it to him, and spent the whole day in serving him. She could not be long out of his sight.

The wounding of Lancelot

On the following morning Arthur and all his knights left Astolat. Sir Lancelot and Sir Lavane were among them. Both of them carried white shields, and Lancelot wore the scarlet token. They made their way to Winchester, where Sir Lavane made sure that they were lodged in secret with a rich merchant of the town. Lancelot did not wish to be seen.

The day of the joust soon came. Sir Lancelot was foremost in the fight, but he was wounded so badly that it took all of his strength to continue. The spear of Sir Bors had gone through his shield and entered his side. He would not surrender, however, and soon overcame his opponents. "God have mercy on us," Gawain said to the king. "Who is that knight with the red scarf? I would say from his bearing that this is Lancelot. But he would never wear another woman's token."

"Sir," Arthur replied, "I am sure that he will become known to you before we leave this place." The king blew the horn to signal the end of the tournament, and the heralds proclaimed that the victor was the knight with the red scarf. The King of North Wales came up to him. "Fair knight, God bless you. You have worked wonders today. Come with us now, so that we can properly honour you."

"Lord king," Lancelot replied, "if I have won the victory, I have been badly wounded in the fight for it. I must find someone who can heal me. So, fair lords, allow me to leave you. I do not need honour. I need my life." He rode off, groaning all the while, until he came to the wood where he had arranged to meet Sir Lavane. "Sir Lavane!" he cried out. "Sir Lavane! Help me to take this spear from my side."

"Sir," he replied, "I will do whatever you wish. But this might kill you."

"If you love me, draw it out."

Lavane did so, and as the spear came out Lancelot gave a great shriek. The blood burst from the wound, and Lancelot lay on the ground groaning. For a while he fainted with the pain. "What shall I do?" Lavane cried aloud. He turned Lancelot's head into the cool breeze, and then waited for any sign of recovery. Eventually Lancelot opened his eyes. "Help me on to my horse," he whispered. "Within a mile or two there lives a hermit who is a good healer. He was once a knight, Sir Baudwin of Britain by name, but he left his worldly possessions for the sake of God. He is my cousin. He is the one man who may be able to assist me."

Sir Lavane helped Lancelot on to his horse, and they rode on together; all the while Lancelot's blood ran down the flanks of his horse on to the earth. The hermitage was within a wood, close beside a steep cliff and a stream. Lavane beat on the door with the butt of his spear. "Let us in, for God's sake." A young boy came to the door and asked them what they wanted. "Fair son," Lavane replied, "go to your lord, the hermit, and tell him that there is a knight here who is badly wounded and who needs his help. Tell him this also. The knight has done more valiant deeds today than anyone before."

The hermit, a handsome and stalwart man, heard his words and came out. "What knight is he?" he asked. "Is he from the court of King Arthur?"

"I do not know his name, sir. Or from what court he comes. But today he has performed marvellous feats of arms."

"For whose sake did he fight?"

"I know only that he fought against the knights of King Arthur."

"There was a time," Sir Baudwin said, "when I would have thought the worse of him for that. I was once of their fellowship. Still, those times are long gone. I thank God that I am now otherwise disposed. Where is he? Let me see him."

Lavane brought the hermit to Lancelot. The knight was leaning over his saddle, bleeding and in pain. The hermit thought for a moment that he recognized him, but the knight was so pale and drawn that he could not tell. "What knight are you?" the hermit asked him. "Where were you born?"

"My fair lord," Lancelot replied, "I am a stranger to this realm. I have ridden through many countries to win honour."

Sir Baudwin noticed a scar on his cheek, and knew at once who it was. "Oh, my lord," he said, "why did you try to hide your name from me? I know you very well. You are Lancelot, the noblest knight in the world."

"Since you know me," Lancelot replied, "then help me. I do not care if I live or die, as long as I can be free of pain."

"You will live. No doubt about it." Sir Baudwin called two of his servants, and they took Lancelot into the hermitage; he was laid gently upon a bed, and was given some wine to drink. In those days hermits were nobly born, and were able to dispense food and drink to those who came to them.

Lancelot is discovered

The king and his court were feasting together, after the great tournament, and Arthur asked about the knight who wore the red scarf on his helmet. "Bring him before us," he said. "We should praise and reward him for his valour."

"He is badly wounded," the King of North Wales told him. "He is not likely to live."

"Is he so badly hurt? Does anyone know his name?"

"No one, sire. We do not know from where he came or where he has gone to."

The king was troubled by this. "If he were to die, it would be the greatest sorrow I have suffered. He is such a noble knight."

"Do you know anything about him?" the King of North Wales asked.

"I believe that I know something. I will tell you more when I have received some word of him."

Sir Gawain stood up. "In the name of Jesus, I will go in search of him. We cannot let the noble knight lie wounded in this realm. It would be a grave dishonour to us all."

"Well said, Sir Gawain," the king replied. "I hope that your search is successful, and that you find the knight alive."

Gawain called for his squire, and together they rode in the woods and forests some six or seven miles from the court. But they found no trace of Lancelot. Two days later the court removed from Camelot and slowly returned to London. Gawain himself was lodged at Astolat on the way back, in the same chamber that Lancelot had used. He was resting there when the lord of the castle, Sir Bernard, came in to greet him. He had with him his daughter, Elaine, the Fair Maid of Astolat. "Tell me," Sir Bernard asked him, "who did best at the tournament? Who was the victor?"

"There was only one champion that day," Gawain told him. "I do not know his name, but he bore a white shield and on his helmet he wore a red scarf. He beat down forty knights of the Round Table."

Elaine smiled and clapped her hands. "God be praised. He is the perfect knight. He is my first and only love. I will never have another."

"Oh, fair lady," Gawain asked her. "Is he really your love?"

"Certainly, sir."

"So do you know his name?"

"No. Nor do I know from where he comes. But, as God is my witness, I truly love him."

"How did you first meet him?" Elaine then told him the story of how Lancelot borrowed the shield of her brother so that he might not be recognized at the tournament. "I still have his shield," she said. "He gave it to me."

"May I see it?"

"It is in my chamber, sir, kept in a wooden case. Come with me. I will take you to it."

322

"No, daughter," Sir Bernard said, "that would not be proper. Call for it to be brought to you." So the wooden case was carried to her. She opened it, and showed Gawain the shield.

He knew at once to whom it belonged. "Ah, good Jesus. Now my heart is heavier than it ever was before."

"Give me the reason, sir."

"I have my reasons. Is he really your love?"

"I love him. But I am not sure that he loves me."

"You are right to love him, lady. He is the most valiant, and the most noble, knight in the world."

"I knew that as soon as I saw him."

"His name is Lancelot. I know his shield. You are blessed. In all the last twenty-four years I have never known him to wear the token of any lady. Yet I fear for you. It may be that you will never see him again in this world."

Elaine almost swooned. "Is he dead?"

"Perhaps not. But I believe that he has been wounded so badly that he may not recover."

"How may this be? How was he hurt?"

"The spear of Sir Bors pierced his side."

Elaine turned to her father in her distress. "Father, will you give me permission to ride after Sir Lancelot? I must reach him. Otherwise I will go out of my mind with grief."

"Go, good daughter. Rescue him, if you can."

So she made herself ready for the journey, weeping all the time. Gawain himself rode back to the court of the king in London, where he told Arthur that he had found Lancelot's shield in the safe keeping of the Fair Maid of Astolat.

"I suspected this," the king replied. "I saw Lancelot in the garden of Sir Bernard's castle. That is why I would not let you go after him at the tournament. Yet one thing still puzzles me. I have never known him to wear the token of any lady before. So why did he carry the red scarf?"

"I only know, sir, that the Fair Maid of Astolat loves him very much. She has now ridden out to find him."

When Guinevere heard from her husband that Lancelot had carried the token of another lady, she went almost insane with wrath. She called Sir Bors to her. "Have you heard," she demanded, "how Lancelot has betrayed me? I do not care if he dies now. He is a false traitor."

"You must not speak of him so, madam."

"And why not, Sir Bors? He is a traitor. Did he not wear a red scarf at the tournament?"

"Madam, I am sorry that he wore that token. But I am sure that he meant no ill towards you. He wore it so that no one would recognize him. That is all."

"The more shame on him," the queen replied. "For all his pride, Sir Bors, you proved yourself to be the better knight."

"No, madam. That is not right. He beat me and my fellows. He was better than any of us. He could have killed us if he wished. I am only sorry that I wounded him so badly."

"I hate him. I despise him. Sir Gawain tells the king that there is some great love between him and the Fair Maid of Astolat."

"Sir Gawain may say what he pleases. But I know that Sir Lancelot extends no favours to any lady, or gentlewoman, or maiden. He treats them all equally. I trust him. And now I will myself go forth to find him. God send me good news."

Lancelot and the Fair Maid

The Fair Maid of Astolat had ridden to Camelot in order to find the knight she loved best in the world, and by good fortune she came upon her brother. Sir Lavane was exercising his horse. She called out to him, and he rode over to her. "Where is Sir Lancelot?" she asked him as soon as he came close.

"How do you know, sister, that the knight I serve is Lancelot?"

"Sir Gawain told me. He recognized the shield that he left with me."

Together they made their way to the hermitage. Sir Lavane led her into the chamber where Lancelot lay, and when she saw him so pale and so sick she fell to the ground in a swoon. When she had recovered herself she could scarcely rise. "What is this, my lord? Why are you in such a woeful state?"

Sir Lancelot asked her brother to take her up and bring her to his bedside. "What is the matter with you, fair lady?" he asked her. "Your distress only increases my pain. Be cheerful. If you have come to comfort me, you are welcome. If God is gracious, I shall soon be healed of this small hurt I have suffered. But who told you my name?"

"Sir Gawain knew your shield."

"If my name is known, I may be harmed." He feared that Gawain would tell Guinevere about the red scarf, and that he would therefore incur the deadly anger of the queen.

Elaine never left his side, but watched over him day and night. Lancelot then asked Lavane to ride to London and find Sir Bors. "You will know him by the scar on his forehead," he told him. "He will be looking for me, since it was he who hurt me. Bring him to me."

Sir Lavane rode to the court, and made inquiries for Sir Bors. Eventually he found him, and explained his mission. "You are welcome," Bors said to him. "Of all men, I wish to see Sir Lancelot." Together they rode to the hermitage.

When Sir Bors saw Sir Lancelot lying, pale and disconsolate, he wept for a long time. He was at last able to speak. "Oh, my lord Sir Lancelot, God bless you and send you a speedy recovery. I am in despair at the wound I gave you. I might have killed the noblest knight in the world. I am nothing but a coward. God will hold me in His greatest displeasure, I know that. I am filled with shame. Will you ever be able to forgive me?"

Lancelot held out his hand. "Good cousin, you are welcome here. Do not feel grief. It was my own fault. It was my own pride that made me hide my shield. If I had told you my name, I would not have been wounded. There is an old saying that kinsmen should never do battle against one another. I ignored that. So say no more. What is done cannot be undone. I will soon be cured, I am sure of it. Let us talk of other things."

Sir Bors then sat on the bed, and whispered to him that Guinevere was very angry with him for wearing the token of another woman. "Why is she so angry?" Lancelot asked him. "I only wore it so that I would not be recognized."

"I have told her that. But she will not listen." Then he whispered even lower. "This young lady ministering to you. Is she the one known as the Fair Maid of Astolat?"

"Yes. I can find no way of getting rid of her."

"Why should you? She is pretty enough. I wish to God that you took her rather than Guinevere. And I can see that she loves you."

"I am sorry for it."

"She is not the first to have fallen for you."

"What am I supposed to do?" So they conversed.

Within three or four days Sir Lancelot began to grow stronger. Sir Bors told him of a tournament to be held at Camelot between King Arthur and the King of North Wales. It was to take place on the feast of All Hallows. Lancelot raised himself from his bed. "Is that so? Stay with me a little longer until I am whole again. I hope that I might take part." They were together for almost a month, while Elaine continued her ministrations. No mother could have taken better care of a child than the Fair Maid of Astolat cared for her charge.

Lancelot is healed

One day Sir Lancelot asked Elaine and the hermit to search for certain healing herbs in the wood. As soon as they were gone he put on his armour and mounted his horse; he wanted to see if he was fit for combat. But his horse was frisky; it had not been ridden for a month, and now wished to prove its mettle. It leaped up when it felt the spurs in its side, and Lancelot was forced out of the saddle. As he fell forward his wound burst open, and the blood poured out. "Help!" he cried to Sir Bors. "Help me! I fear that my end has come!" He fell to the ground.

Sir Bors and Sir Lavane rushed to his side, and cried out in their distress. Elaine heard their cries in the wood, and ran from among the trees. When she saw Lancelot lying on the ground, in his armour, she screamed aloud. She came over to him and, kissing him, tried to wake him. "You are false traitors!" she shouted at Sir Bors and her brother. "How could you allow him to leave his bed? If he dies, I will blame you both. I will see that you come to trial!"

The hermit now emerged from the wood. He spoke little, but it was clear that he was very angry with Bors and Lavane. "Help me bring him in," was all he would say. They laid him in his bed, and the hermit placed some herbs to his nose and put some water in his mouth. Still he did not stir. Eventually the hermit was able to stop the bleeding. After an hour or so, Lancelot opened his eyes. The hermit asked him why he had been so rash. "Sir," he replied, "I wanted to test my strength. Sir Bors has told me of a tournament. I wanted to see if I was ready for it."

"Ah, dear sir," the hermit replied, "your courage will be your undoing. You must not allow your heart to rule your head. Listen to me. Let Sir Bors go on to the tournament. You must remain here with me. When he returns, he will find you to be fit and well again."

What else could Lancelot do but agree? "Go forth to the tournament," he told his friend. "Do your best. I am sure that you will beat all challengers. I will remain here, at the mercy of God, and wait for your return."

Sir Bors rode off, but first he went back to the court at London where he told them all of Sir Lancelot's plight. "I am sorry for it," the king said, "but I thank God that he will recover."

Sir Bors told Guinevere of the dangers Lancelot had faced in the tournament. "He did all for love of you, my lady."

"Oh yes? I still spurn him. For all I care, he might as well die."

"Madam," Bors replied, "he will not die. If anyone else had spoken in this way, his kinsmen would have avenged him. And consider this. You have in the past condemned him, only to confess your fault later. You have always found him to be a true knight to you." Sir Bors left her, and joined the tournament. Here he performed splendid feats of arms, but all the time he was eager to return to Lancelot. He hurried back to the hermitage after three days, and rejoiced to find his friend on his feet. "I am recovered," Lancelot told him. "I am whole again."

The death of the Fair Maid

On the following morning they took their horses and rode on to Astolat, where they wished to say farewell to Sir Bernard. Elaine came into the chamber where he was lodged. "My lord," she said, "now I see that you are about to leave me. Have mercy on me. Do not let me die."

"What do you wish me to do, lady?"

"I wish you to marry me."

"Marry? That is not my fate. I will never be a husband."

"But can you be a lover?"

"Jesus defend me. What reward would that be to your father and your brother?"

"In that case, I must die for love."

"You will not, dear lady. You must understand that I will never be married. But I promise you this. Whenever you do marry, I will give you and your husband the sum of a thousand pounds each year."

"That is not for me, sir. You must either marry me or become my lover. Otherwise my good days are gone."

"Dear lady, these are two things I cannot do."

When she heard him, she screamed and fell into a faint. Her ladies carried her into her chamber, where she wept continually.

Sir Lancelot prepared himself for his departure, and he asked Sir Lavane what he proposed to do. "I wish for nothing except to follow you," Lavane said to him. "Unless of course you drive me away or command me to leave you."

"Then ride with me."

Sir Bernard now came to him. "My daughter," he said, "will die for love of you."

"I am sorry for it, sir. But what can I do? I bitterly regret that she loves me, but I did nothing to encourage her. I never made promises to her. I never proposed to her. I declare to you now that I did nothing to dishonour her. She is still innocent in word and deed. I am cast down by her distress, but I have no remedy for it."

"Father," Lavane said, "I know that Sir Lancelot is telling the truth. Yet I have sympathy for my sister. I share some of her feeling for this knight. That is why I will follow him to the ends of the earth."

Lancelot and Lavane took their leave of Sir Bernard, and rode to the court at London. When the king heard that his knight had returned, whole and healthy, he rejoiced. So did the other knights, except for Sir Mordred and Sir Agravain. Guinevere would not speak to Lancelot, and kept him at a distance from her. He tried to speak to her, but she turned away.

On his departure the Fair Maid of Astolat was so sorrowful that she could not eat or drink. All she could do was sigh for Lancelot. After ten days she was close to death. She made her confession, and received communion. Yet still she spoke only of Lancelot. Her priest asked her to leave behind such thoughts. "Why should I leave them?" she inquired. "Am I not an earthly woman? Lancelot is an earthly man. We were formed for love and, while the breath is still in my body, I will bewail my fate. Love itself comes from

God. And, as God is my witness, I declare that I will die a virgin. I beseech You, High Lord of Heaven, to take mercy upon me and upon my soul. My only offence was to love Sir Lancelot. I willingly face death rather than be deprived of him. May the pain I suffer purge my soul."

She called her father to her chamber. She asked him to write a letter for her, which she then dictated word for word. "When my body is still warm," she told him, "put this letter in my right hand. It will remain there when I am cold. Let me be laid upon a bed, dressed in my richest robes. Take me in a carriage to the bank of the Thames, and there place me in a barge. One man may steer me. Be sure, father, that the barge is covered in black cloth. Let all this be done in memory of me." And then she died.

The body in the barge

All was done as she had wished. Her body was taken to the bank of the Thames and laid in a barge. One man sailed the vessel down the river towards Westminster, where it rocked back and forth on the tides. Arthur and Guinevere were talking by a window, overlooking the Thames, when the king suddenly caught sight of it. "Do you see the boat out there, covered in black cloth?" He called over Sir Kay. "What do you make of it?"

"Sir," Kay replied, "it is a token of some sad event. I am sure of it."

"Go down to the shore," the king told him. "Find out more."

Sir Kay rode down to the Thames, and there saw the Fair Maid laid out on a bed. The steersman sat at the stern of the barge, but he would say nothing. The lady seemed to be smiling. Kay came back, and told the king.

"I will see this body," Arthur said. "Is it so beautiful?"

He went down to the water with Guinevere, and the royal couple marvelled at the fairness of the corpse. The queen saw the letter in her hand. "This will tell us who she is, and from where she has come," she said. So the king took the letter. They went back to their chambers where, in the presence of many knights, the missive was unsealed. A clerk then read it out to the assembled company. The words were as follows. "Most noble knight, my lord Lancelot, death has taken me into his dominion. But I die as your lover, the Fair Maid of Astolat. All ladies, grieve with me. Pray for my soul. Bury me decently. I die as a virgin, so help me God, and one so devoted to Sir Lancelot that I chose to leave life rather than live without him."

When the queen heard this she wept. The king called for Sir Lancelot, and the letter was read out to him. "My lord king," he said, "the death of this lady is a great grief to me. But God knows that I was not the willing cause of her death. Her brother, who is with me here at court, will testify to the truth of this. She was fair and good. But she loved me beyond all measure."

"Sir," the queen said, "you might have shown her some clemency. Some generosity of spirit."

"My lady, she wanted to be my wife or my lover. How could I allow her to be either? Love must spring from a loving heart. It cannot come from compulsion."

"That is true," Arthur said. "No one is bound to love another. But you, sir, must arrange her burial."

"It will be done as best I can, sire."

On the following morning a high mass was said for the Fair Maid of Astolat and, after the service was over, she was buried in the abbey with great circumstance.

The queen then called for Lancelot, and asked him for his forgiveness. "I have been angry with you without cause," she told him. "I called you false. I misjudged you."

"Madam," he replied, "it is not the first time that you have slandered me. I endure all for your sake, although you have little regard for my suffering." And so the winter passed.

The Knight of the Cart

Winter gave way to spring. It was already the month of May, when every loving heart begins to blossom. Just as the trees and flowers bud and burst forth, so do lovers now bloom. They recall moments of passion and tenderness from the past, and they prepare themselves for a renewal of gentleness and affection. So does the green spring erase the white blasts of winter. We walk in the garden of May.

The wise man reserves his true love for God, but then, after that, for the worship of good women. There is no earthly honour higher than that of service to a maiden. I call such love virtuous. There is no spot of vice in courtliness and chivalry.

Yet in these sad days no man can love for seven nights without wanting his way with the woman. All is brittle and untrue, worthless and unstable. Love is soon hot, and sooner cold. Summer gives way unseasonably to winter. In the old days a man and a woman could keep one another company for seven years without any hint of licentiousness. In the days of Camelot lovers could be true and faithful. I take as my example Guinevere, the flower of that court, who proved herself to be a loyal lover and therefore had a good end.

So it befell that in the month of May she called together ten knights of the Round Table, and told them that early the next morning she would ride out. "I warn you now," she said, "that you must be well horsed and that you must wear green silk or green cloth. We will go a-Maying together. I will bring with me ten ladies, so that each knight will have a companion. Every knight must also bring a squire and two yeomen."

The ten knights prepared themselves for this joyful expedition. On the following morning they set forth, and took great pleasure in the fields and meadows filled with flowers. It was usual for the queen to be accompanied by a force of knights, known as the queen's knights, who were armed and always carried plain white shields. But on this May morning she had dispensed with them. Sir Lancelot was also away from court on this day, and so he did not ride with her.

Treason against the queen

One knight, Sir Meliagaunt, had a castle a few miles from Westminster. The old books tell us that he had loved the queen for a long time, but that he would not come near her while Lancelot was by her side. He feared him too much. Now he saw that Guinevere was without her bodyguard, and of course without Lancelot. This was his opportunity. He summoned twenty armed men, and one hundred archers, and laid his plan to surround the queen.

The royal party had just ridden into a glade, when Meliagaunt and his men came out from their cover. He confronted the queen, and told her to stop where she was.

"Traitor knight!" she cried. "What do you think you are doing? Do you want to bring shame upon yourself? You are a knight of the Round Table. Are you about to dishonour the king who made you? You shame the whole Order of Knighthood by your conduct. And, as for me, I would rather cut my own throat than let you touch me."

"Your insults are wasted on me, madam," he replied. "I have loved you for many years, but I could never get close to you. Now I will take you as I find you."

The ten knights in the queen's retinue spoke out. "Sir Meliagaunt," they said, "you are about to bring dishonour on yourself and your men. You are also risking your life. We may be armed only with swords, but we will fight to the death to defend the queen."

"So be it," he told them. "Prepare for battle."

The ten knights drew their swords, and at first proved themselves to be more than a match for the spears and swords raised against them. But the numbers were too great for them. Seven of them were eventually struck to the ground, sorely wounded, while the three others fought on and cut down forty of their enemies. But they were now becoming desperate. Guinevere, seeing the carnage among her knights, called out to Sir Meliagaunt. "Do not kill my noble knights, I beg you. Let them live. I will come to an agreement with you. I will go wherever you ask me, as long as I can take them with me. I will not be parted from them."

"Madam," he replied, "I will agree to your terms for your sake. They shall all be taken with you to my castle."

The queen asked the three remaining knights to lay down their swords. "We will do whatever you require of us," one of them, Sir Pelleas, said. "We will suffer life or death as you command."

They put down their weapons, and helped the wounded knights on to their horses; some sat in their saddles, while some were too weak to hold themselves up. Sir Meliagaunt told them that they must all remain together, since he feared that a report of his deed might reach Sir Lancelot. The queen knew this, and secretly drew aside a page of the court. "Take this ring," she told the boy, "and carry it to Sir Lancelot. Tell him to ride to my rescue as soon as he can. Go now. Ride quickly."

The young boy took horse and fled from the scene like the wind. Some of Sir Meliagaunt's men saw him, and attempted to pursue him; they shot arrows at him, but he escaped unharmed into the woods. "Madam," Meliagaunt said to the queen, "I see that you wish to betray me. But I shall make sure that Lancelot does not reach you." He laid a plot, whereby thirty of his men would wait in ambush for Lancelot. "He will come on a white horse," he told them. "Kill the horse, by all means. But be careful before you come to close quarters with him. He will be difficult to defeat." Having left his men there, concealed, he went on with the queen and her company to his castle. He did not dare to violate her, despite his intentions, for fear of Lancelot.

The page came back safely to Westminster where, before long, he found the knight. He delivered Guinevere's ring, and told him what had happened. "I will be shamed for ever," Lancelot said, "unless I can save the queen from dishonour. Nor can I allow her to be killed. I would give all of France to have been there." He called for his arms, and quickly prepared himself for battle. Then he ordered the page to inform his squire, Sir Lavane, of his sudden departure. "Tell him that, if he loves me, he will follow me and ride on until he reaches the castle of Meliagaunt. There, if I am still alive, he will hear news of me." He rode out of Westminster, and then he made his way with his horse across the river to the bank known as Lamb-eth, or the House of the Lamb. Within a short time he came to the spot where the queen had been surrounded and taken. He followed the track made by the numerous horses, until he came to that part of the path where the ambush had been laid for him.

Lancelot rides in the cart

The thirty men, the force of Meliagaunt, now came out of hiding and barred his way. "What authority do you have," Lancelot asked them, "to stop a knight of the Round Table?"

"We have orders to shoot your horse. Either turn back, or make your way on foot."

"Little courage in that, my friend! Even if my horse is killed, I have no fear of any of you."

They fired their arrows, and badly wounded the horse. Lancelot leaped off and would have chased the men, but they made off. There were so many ditches and hedges in his path that he could not have caught them. "Shame on you," he called out, "to betray another knight! There is an old saying. 'A good man is in danger only when he meddles with a coward!' "

So he began to walk, weighed down as he was by spear, shield and armour. He was not in the best of tempers, but he did not want to abandon any of his weapons in case he might soon meet Sir Meliagaunt. Then by chance a carter came by him. "Good carter," he said, "how much money will you need to take me to a castle a mile or two away?"

"You cannot use my cart, sir," he replied. "I have been sent to fetch wood."

"Sent by whom?"

"By my lord. Sir Meliagaunt."

"That is the man I wish to see."

"You shall not go with me."

Lancelot leaped on to the cart, and gave the man such a blow with his gauntlet that he fell dead to the ground.

The carter had a churl with him, who kneeled down before Lancelot. "Save my life, sir, and I will take you wherever you wish to go."

"I charge you, then, to drive me to the gate of the castle where Meliagaunt is to be found." The churl took up his whip, and with the sound of "Hi!" rode on to the castle. Lancelot's horse, wounded with arrows, still managed to follow.

One of Guinevere's ladies was standing by a window of the castle, an hour or so later, when she saw an armed knight standing in a cart. "This is the strangest sight I have ever seen," she said.

"What?" the queen asked her. "Where?"

"Down there. I presume that the knight is about to hang."

Guinevere looked out, and saw at once by the knight's shield that he was Lancelot. "He is not riding to his death. Shame on you for suggesting it. You behold Lancelot himself. I see what has happened. His faithful horse has been wounded in some fight with Meliagaunt's men. He has been obliged to ride here in a cart. Jesus defend him!"

By this time Lancelot had come up to the gate of the castle. He jumped down from his horse and, in a voice that made the stones and rafters ring, he called out, "Where are you, false traitor Meliagaunt? Where are you, polluter of the Round Table? Come out with all your men. I, Lancelot, am here to fight you!" He burst open the gate and, with one blow, broke the porter's neck.

When Sir Meliagaunt heard that Lancelot had delivered his challenge, he ran at once in fear to the queen, and kneeled down before her. "Ah, madam," he said, "have mercy on me. I put myself under your protection."

"What is the matter with you, man? Did you not realize that some good knight would come here to avenge me?"

"I will do whatever you wish."

"What would you have me do in return?"

"I wish that you would go to Lancelot, and tell him to desist. Tell him that I give up my lands and castle. I will escort you to Westminster tomorrow, and there I will surrender."

"Is it so?" She paused for a moment. "Well, peace is always preferable to war." She went down to the gate with her ladies, where Lancelot was waiting impatiently.

"Where is that traitor?" he asked her.

"Why all this passion and anger, sir?"

"Why do you pose such a question? You are the one who has suffered shame and dishonour. I have come here to rescue you."

"And for that I thank you. But I will be a queen of peace. I will quell discord. The knight of this castle has apologized. He is sorry for his actions against me."

"If I had known, madam, that you would so easily forgive him I would not have hurried here. Clearly there was no need for haste."

"Why do you use such words, sir? Do you think I am reconciled with him out of love or respect for him? Of course not. I wish to avoid unseemly reports of battle and discord."

"I accept what you say, madam. Yet I tell you this. Only you, and my lord, the king, could persuade me to spare Sir Meliagaunt."

"I am grateful to you, Sir Lancelot. Now come with me to my chamber, where my ladies will look after you." They all went into the castle and, when Lancelot had taken off his armour, he asked after the ten knights who had been captured. The queen brought them to him, and all rejoiced in his company. They also wanted revenge on Meliagaunt but, for the sake of the queen, they stayed silent. Those who had been wounded were now tended by Guinevere and her ladies; she would not let them return to their chambers, but insisted that they lie down on beds and pallets in her own chamber so that she might minister to them.

Lancelot lies with Guinevere

But Lancelot had also arranged a tryst with the queen. He had agreed to go to a window in the garden, where Guinevere would speak to him secretly. He took his sword with him, in case he was surprised by Sir Meliagaunt. He entered the garden, and went up to the window that was encased in iron bars. Guinevere was waiting for him, and they spoke together of many things. "Ah, madam," he said after a while, "I wish I could enter this room and be with you."

"I wish for it, too," she replied.

"Do you tell me truly that you want me to be with you?"

"Yes. Truly."

"Then I shall prove how strong is my love for you." He put his hands around the iron bars and pulled them out of the stone wall, but one of the bars cut his hand to the bone. Lancelot entered through the window, and there was blood everywhere. "Make no noise," the queen told him. "My knights lie sleeping here."

Quietly they climbed into her bed, where Lancelot lay with her until dawn. When the time came to depart he left through the window and, as best he might, put back the iron bars in the same place as they were before. He returned to his own chamber, and showed Sir Lavane his injured hand; the young man dressed the wound, and then concealed it with a glove.

Meanwhile Sir Meliagaunt had gone to the queen's chamber. He had found her ladies already dressed, but the queen still lay sleeping. "What ails you, madam," he said, "to sleep so late?" He pulled back the curtains of the bed, and was horrified by what he saw. The top sheet, the bottom sheet and the pillow were all covered in Lancelot's blood. When he saw this he believed that one of the wounded knights had lain with Guinevere. "Ah, madam," he said to her, "now I understand that you are a false traitor to your husband, the king. You brought these knights to your chamber for a purpose. One of them, at least, has lain beside you in the darkness."

"You speak foully, sir. Not one of these knights has been near my bed."

The ten knights had heard his words, and they all spoke out at once. "You accuse the queen falsely," they said. "We will prove your falsehood when we are recovered from our wounds. Choose any one of us to take up the challenge."

344

"Oh yes? Look for yourselves. Do you not see blood upon the sheets?" They did not know what to say, and stayed silent, while Sir Meliagaunt was exultant. He hoped in this way to conceal his own treason against the queen.

At this point Lancelot entered the chamber. "What is the matter?" he asked them. "What is happening here?" Sir Meliagaunt said that he suspected the queen of infidelity. "It was shameful of you," Lancelot told him, "to pull back the curtains of the bed when the queen still lay in it. Not even my lord Arthur would be guilty of such discourtesy. You have brought still more disgrace upon yourself."

"I do not know what you mean by that, sir. But I do know that one of these knights has lain beside her, leaving all the marks of his blood. I will prove her treason by the force of my arms."

"Beware what you say, Meliagaunt. There may be someone who will take up your challenge."

"But you, my lord, must also be careful. Even the best knight cannot triumph in a bad cause. God will play a part in any contest."

"As to that, I will take my chance. God is always to be feared. But I tell you this plainly. Not one of these ten knights slept in the queen's bed last night. I will prove it with my sword and spear. Are you willing to make a contest of it?"

"Yes. Here is my gauntlet."

"I will take it up. On what day do you wish to do battle?"

"In a week's time. In the field beside Westminster."

"Very well. I will be waiting for you there."

"In the meantime we must both swear to behave fairly and honourably to one another. There must be no false practices. Do you so swear?"

"Of course. I have never yet been guilty of falsehood."

"Then let us go into dinner," Meliagaunt said. "After that, if you wish, you and the queen may ride back to Westminster." Lancelot gave his assent. "May I take you now, sir, on a tour of my castle?"

"I would be delighted."

They walked together from room to room. Lancelot did not fear a trap, because honest men trust their fellows. But a false man will always prove treacherous to a true one. As they went down one corridor Lancelot was lured to walk upon a trapdoor; it suddenly opened beneath his feet, and he fell some thirty feet into a cave filled with straw. Sir Meliagaunt went back to the others, and told them that Lancelot had suddenly departed — he did not know where — and that he had taken Sir Lavane's horse. The queen and her knights were astonished by this, but spoke no more about it. After dinner they returned to Westminster, with the wounded carried on litters, and Guinevere told the king about Lancelot's challenge on her behalf.

"I am afraid," Arthur said, "that Sir Meliagaunt may well be overmatched. But where is Lancelot?"

"We suppose," one of the knights told him, "that he has ridden to some adventure. That is his way. He took Sir Lavane's horse, because his own was badly wounded."

346

"Let him be," the king replied. "He will return on the proper day. Unless he has been captured by some act of treachery."

Meanwhile Lancelot lay in the cave, suffering great pain. A lady brought him meat and drink every day. She offered to help him escape if he became her lover. But he refused.

"That is not wise of you," she said. "You will never get out of this place without my help. And if you do not arrive on the field of battle, the queen will be burned at the stake."

"God forbid that she should be burned because of my default. But the king will know, as will the others, that I must be dead, sick or in prison. Otherwise nothing would prevent me from coming to her defence. Some good knight will take my place, I am sure of it. If you were the only woman left in the land, I would still have nothing to do with you."

"Then you will be shamed before your king. You will die here."

"Whatever God sends me, I will endure."

Lancelot rescues Guinevere

The day of battle came. The lady brought him food and drink as before. "Sir Lancelot," she said, "you are being too hard-hearted. I will make a pact with you. If you give me just one kiss, I will free you from this place and provide you with the best horse in the castle stable."

"There is no disgrace in giving you one kiss," he said. So he kissed her. She was as good as her word. She brought him armour and took him to the stables, where twelve fine horses were kept. He chose the one he liked best. With great joy he took up his sword and spear. "Lady," he said, "thank you for your good deed. If ever I can do you service, call upon me."

On the field beside Westminster, a fire was being prepared for the queen. Sir Meliagaunt was sure that Lancelot would not arrive, and so he cried out to the king to do him justice. The court were all ashamed that, in the absence of Lancelot, the queen would be burned to death.

"My lord king," Sir Lavane said, "we all know that something has happened to Lancelot. He is either dead or gravely ill. Otherwise he would have kept his promise to be here. I have never yet heard that he failed to do his duty. Let me take his place, sir. Let me do battle with Meliagaunt."

"Thank you, Sir Lavane," Arthur replied. "You are fighting for the right cause. I have spoken to the ten wounded knights, and they have sworn to me that they never lay with Guinevere. If they were well again, any one of them would be willing to defend her name."

"And so shall I, sir, if you give me leave."

"I do. And I wish you good fortune. I believe that some treason has been attempted against Lancelot."

Lavane prepared himself for battle and, just as the heralds cried out for the contest to commence, Lancelot himself galloped on to the field. The king saw him, and cried out, "Hold! Wait!"

Lancelot rode in haste to the king, and told him what had happened at the castle of Meliagaunt and how he had been cruelly imprisoned. The queen was freed from the stake at once, and brought back to the king. She had complete faith in her champion.

Lancelot and Meliagaunt rode against one another. Lancelot's spear carried Meliagaunt over the tail of his horse; he fell heavily to the ground. Lancelot leaped down from his saddle and took up his sword. They exchanged many hard blows, but one of them knocked Meliagaunt to his knees. "Most noble knight, Lancelot," the traitor cried out, "spare my life! I surrender. By the rules of the Round Table, you must let me live. I put my trust in you and the king!"

Lancelot was not sure what to do. He wanted to kill this man, more than anything else in the world. He looked up at the queen, to see if by any sign she would tell him what to do. She nodded her head, as if to say "slay him". She wanted him dead as much as he did.

"Get up," he said, "for God's sake. Have you not shamed yourself enough? Do battle with me once more."

"I have surrendered. I am now your prisoner. You cannot force me to fight."

"I will make you an offer. I will disarm myself, on my left side, and have my left hand tied behind my back. Will you then fight me?"

Sir Meliagaunt leaped to his feet. "Did you hear his offer, lord king?" he called out. "I accept it."

"Take heed, Lancelot," the king said. "Will you abide by this?"

"What I have said, sir, I will do."

The knights on the field took off the left part of Lancelot's armour, and then bound his left hand behind his back. Once more the challengers rode down on one another. Sir Meliagaunt raised his sword, hoping to strike Lancelot on his undefended side, but Lancelot parried the blow by twisting his body and then brought his sword down upon his opponent's helmet. The blow was so powerful that Meliagaunt's head was crushed. His body was then taken from the field, and buried without any further ceremony. The manner of his death was then carved on his tombstone.

Lancelot found favour with the king and queen more than ever, and he continued to live at court.

THE DEATH OF ARTHUR

The Strife Begins

A year had passed since Lancelot rescued Guinevere from the stake. Once more it is the season of May, when every heart is bursting with life and joy. It is the season of fruitfulness and lustiness, when the fields are filled with flowers and all folk keenly await the coming of summer. In winter, the season of snows and tempests, we can do nothing but cower in corners or hold our hands in front of the fire.

Yet this particular spring was different. In the merry month of May there descended upon the world anger and strife that did not end until the flower of chivalry was lost or destroyed. All this misfortune was the work of two knights, Sir Agravain and Sir Mordred, who were kinsmen of Sir Gawain. These knights harboured a secret hatred for their queen, Guinevere, and for Sir Lancelot; they watched Lancelot day and night, hoping to do him an evil turn.

It so happened that, by mischance, Sir Gawain and his kinsmen were sitting together in the privy chamber of King Arthur. It was here that Sir Agravain spoke out openly in front of the other knights, although they were not in any formal council.

"I marvel," he said, "that we are afraid to speak the truth. We all know that Lancelot sleeps with the queen, but none of us says a word. You can all attest to the truth of this. Is it not a disgrace to us that we allow the king to be shamed in this way?"

Then Gawain replied to him, "Agravain, my brother, I pray you — I charge you — not to mention these things. I tell you this. I will not join with you in laying these accusations against Lancelot."

The two knights, Gaheris and Gareth, spoke in agreement with Gawain. "So help me God," Gareth said, "I will not meddle with any such matters."

Mordred stood up. "But I will!"

"Then you are hastening towards misfortune," Gawain told him. "The snare is set. Listen to me. Leave these affairs alone. Otherwise I know what will happen."

"Let the dice fall as they may," Agravain replied. "I am going to tell the king!"

"Don't be a fool," Gawain said. "If enmity arises between Lancelot and ourselves, there will be powerful knights and great lords who will take the side of Lancelot. And don't forget this. There have been many times when Lancelot has ridden to the rescue of the king and queen. If he had not been their champion, the greater number of us would still be in a state of fear and mourning. He has proved himself time and time again. Do you recall the fate of Sir Meliagaunt last spring? For my part I will never take up arms against that brave knight. Once he rescued me from King Caradoc and helped me escape from the Tower of

Sorrow. He slew Caradoc and saved my life. And is it not true that Lancelot saved you, Agravain, and you, Mordred, from the snares of Sir Tarquin? He rescued many other knights, too, on that occasion. Do you not think that such noble deeds should be remembered? Do you think that such kindness and valour should be forgotten?"

"Do as you please," Agravain replied. "I can endure it no longer."

As he was speaking, King Arthur entered the chamber.

"Now, brother," Gawain warned him, "stop this talk."

Agravain and Mordred looked him full in the face. "We will do no such thing."

"Will you not? Well I, for one, am leaving. I am not going to sit here and listen to your tales. I want nothing to do with your conspiracy."

"No more will I," said Gaheris.

"Me neither," returned Gareth. "I will never speak evil of another knight."

So the three companions made ready to leave the chamber, in great grief of mind. "Alas," Gawain murmured, "this realm will now be destroyed. The noble fellowship of the Round Table will be torn apart. We are entering a world of woe."

So he and his two companions departed. King Arthur was astonished and asked Agravain the meaning of all the noise and confusion.

"My lord king," he replied, "I shall tell you. I can keep it secret no longer. Mordred and I have had a disagreement with the three noble knights. I will keep it brief. We all know that Sir Lancelot is the queen's lover. There is no doubt about it. We are your sister's sons. We can endure it no longer. We are all keenly aware that your rank is higher than that of Lancelot, and that you made him your knight. So we will prove that he is a traitor to your person."

"If all this is true, then he has committed treason against me. But I would be unwilling to proceed against him until I have sure and certain proof of his guilt. Sir Lancelot is a brave knight, as you both know. I would go so far as to say that he is the best and boldest of all knights, and he will fight against any man who lays this charge against him. Therefore, if you speak the truth, you must catch him in the deed itself."

Arthur was in fact most unwilling to entertain these rumours about Lancelot and Guinevere. The king already had his suspicions about the matter, but he stopped his ears against any gossip. Sir Lancelot had performed so many services for him, and for his queen. In truth, Arthur loved him more than any other man.

"My lord king," Sir Agravain declared, "when you go out hunting tomorrow morning, I doubt very much that Sir Lancelot will ride with you. When twilight falls send a message to the queen that you will lie in the fields all that night and that you need the service of your cooks. Then, under cover of darkness, we will surprise him in bed with the queen. We will bring him to you, dead or alive."

"I hear you," the king replied. "But I advise you to be careful. Take with you some loyal companions."

"Sir," Agravain declared, "we will take with us twelve knights of the Round Table."

"Beware. I warn you. You will find him doughty and strong."

"We will deal with him, sir. Come. We must prepare."

On the following morning Arthur rode out to hunt, and then sent word to the queen that he would be resting in the pavilions that night. Sir Agravain and Sir Mordred chose twelve knights and rode with them to the castle at Carlisle, where the queen was staying.

That night, Sir Lancelot informed Sir Bors that he wished to speak with the queen in private.

"Sir," Bors replied, "I advise you not to go to her tonight."

"Why?"

"I dread the presence and influence of Sir Agravain. He plots against you continually. I implore you not to see the queen. I beg you to avoid her. I suspect that the king has gone from the castle for some reason. He may have set a watch upon her chamber. I am afraid that there is a plot hatched against you."

"Have no fear, good nephew," Lancelot replied. "I shall not stay with the queen. I will be with her for an instant."

"That does not comfort me. I dread the fact of your being with her at all. This night may undo us."

"Fair nephew, I marvel at you. You know very well that the queen has sent for me. Who am I to disobey her? Do you think me a coward? Should I flee her grace?"

"Then God protect you. Return safe and well."

Sir Lancelot left him and, taking his sword with him under his cloak, he walked towards the queen's chamber. Now was a time of danger. He knocked softly on the door, and he was admitted. Lancelot and Guinevere were together again. Whether they engaged in any of the sports of love, I cannot say. I do not like to mention such matters. I can assure you of one thing. Love in those days was quite a different game.

When the queen and Lancelot were enjoying each other's company, there was suddenly a great clattering of swords and shields. Mordred, Agravain and the twelve knights gathered outside the door of the queen's chamber, exclaiming in unison, "You traitor, Lancelot! Now you are taken!" They were savage and exultant, shouting so loudly that the whole court could hear them. They were armed and dangerous, as if they were about to charge into a battle.

Guinevere cried out in alarm, "Alas! We will both be killed!"

"Madam," Lancelot said to her, "is there any armour here that I can put on? I have only my sword with me. If there is a shield or spear in this chamber, give it to me now. I will soon put an end to their malice."

"Truly I have no weapons here. I believed that I had no need of shields and helmets, of swords and spears, in my private chamber. Do you hear them? I am sure now that our love will end in ruin. By the noise outside the door, I know that there are many noble knights well armed and well protected. You will not be able to defend yourself against them. You are likely to be killed while I — I will be burned alive. If you could escape them, only then would I be rescued from such a fate."

"Oh God!" Lancelot was desolate. "Never have I more needed a suit of armour than this moment!"

At the same time Sir Agravain and Sir Mordred were hammering on the door and shouting out, "Traitor knight, come out of the queen's chamber! You are surrounded. You know well enough that you cannot escape!"

"Jesus have mercy," Lancelot whispered. "I cannot endure this shameful noise and riot. It would be better to die than to endure the dishonour." Then he took the queen in his arms and kissed her. "Most noble Christian queen," he said, "I beseech you to listen to me. You have always been the special lady of my heart, and I have always served you faithfully as a true knight. I have never failed you since the first day I was made a knight by King Arthur. Will you pray for my soul if I am slain here? As for your own fate, rest assured. My nephew, Sir Bors, and all my kinsmen, will not fail to rescue you from the fire. Comfort yourself, sweet lady. Sir Bors and the other knights will do homage to you and serve you. You will live as a queen upon my lands."

"No. Don't talk so," the queen replied. "You know well enough that I cannot live after you are gone. Once you are slain, I will accept my own death as meekly as any martyr who died for Christ Our Saviour."

"Well, madam, since this is the day when our love may be undone for ever, I assure you that these knights will purchase my death at a very high price. I am more sorry for you than for myself. Oh, how I wish for a suit of armour! It would be dearer to me than the lordship of all Christendom. Then, with breastplate and halberd, my deeds would be remembered in the mouths of men."

"I wish that these men would take me and kill me here, so that you might escape."

"That will never be, dear queen. God defend me from such dishonour. Christ will be my shield. Christ will be my armour."

He took his sword in his right hand, and his cloak in his left. Sir Agravain and Sir Mordred had taken up a great wooden bench, with the help of the other knights, and began to pound it against the door. "Fair lords," Lancelot called out, "leave off your bellowing! I will open the door for you. Then you can do what you like with me."

"Do so!" Sir Agravain shouted back. "Open it. It will do you no good to fight against us. If you let us into the chamber, we will not kill you. We will wait to bring you into the presence of the king."

Lancelot unbarred the door very cautiously and opened it a fraction. Only one man could come through at a time. So one of the knights thrust himself into the space. He was a good and mighty knight, Sir Collgrevaunce of Gore by name. As soon as he came forward, he struck at Lancelot. But the noble knight deflected the blow and with his own sword he attacked his opponent. Collgrevaunce fell instantly, killed with one blow upon his helmet. Lancelot then dragged the dead knight into the chamber, barred the door once more, and with the help of the queen donned the armour of the fallen man.

Meanwhile, on the other side of the door, Sir Agravain and Sir Mordred were shouting abuse. "Traitor knight, traitor warrior, leave the queen's chamber now!"

"Sirs," Lancelot said calmly, "please stop all this noise. I tell you this, Sir Agravain. I will not be your prisoner tonight. I suggest that you all turn around and leave quietly. Slander me no more. I promise you, on my word of honour as a knight, that if you now depart in peace I will appear before you all tomorrow morning. I will stand before the king, too, and then let us see which of you will call me a traitor to my face. I will answer for myself, as truthfully as a knight should, and I will swear that I came to the queen with no manner of mischief in mind. I will prove this, if necessary, in trial by combat."

"Shame upon you, traitor!" Sir Mordred called out. "We will slay you, if we please. Do you not know that King Arthur has given us the choice of killing you or arresting you?"

"Ah, sir knights, is there no graciousness or generosity among you? In that case, stand guard and defend yourselves." With that he flung open the chamber door, and strode among them with his sword raised high. With his first stroke he killed Sir Agravain, and then proceeded to dispatch the others with the greatest ease. Within a short time they lay dead upon the floor, since not one of them could withstand the prowess and strength of Lancelot. Sir Mordred alone escaped. He had been wounded, and had fled from the scene in great haste.

Sir Lancelot returned to the queen. "Madam," he said, sighing, "you must know that our true love is now in mortal jeopardy. King Arthur will always be my foe. But if you wish I will take you under my protection and save you from any dangers that threaten you."

"That is not the best course, sir. Enough, and more than enough, harm has already been done. Be still. Venture no more. I have only one request. If you learn that I have been sentenced to death tomorrow, I ask you to rescue me by any means in your power."

"Have no fear, lady. While I am alive I will be your saviour. Do not doubt it." And with that he kissed her, and the two of them exchanged rings. He left the queen and returned to his lodgings.

Wherein Lancelot gathers his knights

When Sir Bors and his kinsmen saw Sir Lancelot return safely, they were overjoyed. "Jesus mercy!" Lancelot exclaimed. "You are all armed to the teeth. What is the meaning of this?"

"Sir," Bors replied, "when you set off to see the queen all of us that share your blood — and all those who support you — were so afraid of treachery that we leaped out of bed naked and ran for arms. Some of us even dreamed that we were already fighting, sword in hand. We all believed that some great strife was about to break upon us, and so we prepared ourselves. As you can see, we are ready for anything."

"My dear nephew," Lancelot replied, "I must tell you that I have this night been harder pressed than at any other time in my life. God be thanked that I managed to escape imminent danger." Then he told them the story of the night's adventures, as I have already related to you. "Therefore, my comrades," he concluded, "be of good heart and spirit. I hope that you will assist me in any way you can. For believe me. Great war is now upon us."

"Sir," Bors replied, "we will accept any fate that Almighty God bestows upon us. In your company we have received much reward and honour. Now we are willing to face with you the pain as well as the prosperity."

The other knights took up the same refrain. "Look," one of them said to Lancelot, "do not be disconsolate, sir. There is no company of knights in the world who can defeat us. We will match blow for blow, and strike for strike. We will call for all those whom we love, and who love us; together we will achieve victory. Have no fear. Joy follows jeopardy."

"God thank you all," Lancelot replied. "You have comforted me in my distress. And you, Sir Bors, dear nephew, have reassured me. I ask you now to act before it grows late. I wish you to go among the knights that attend the king, and find out who are friends and who are foes. I need to know the measure of my support."

"I will go at once, sir. I will return before seven o'clock, and let you know who is with you."

Sir Bors called to him all the knights who supported Lancelot's cause, some twenty-two of them; when they were armed and on horseback, they all pledged allegiance to Lancelot. These in turn were joined by one hundred and forty other knights, from North Wales and from Cornwall. When they were gathered together, Lancelot rode in front of them and addressed them.

"I must tell you in earnest truth that I have always been a supporter of King Arthur and Queen Guinevere. When the queen sent for me to speak with her, I feared treachery. Not that I suspect the lady herself. Far from it. But I suspected that there would be an attempt on my life. God be thanked, I prevailed." Then he told them the story of the events in the queen's chamber. "Therefore I know well, my fair lords, that open warfare will be declared against me. I have slain Sir Agravain, the brother of Sir Gawain, and twelve of his kinsmen. I am sure that King Arthur sent these knights against me. In his malice and anger he is certain to condemn the queen to burning at the stake. I cannot permit that to happen. She will not die for my sake. It may be that I will be taken in battle, but I intend to fight for Queen Guinevere and to prove by combat that she is a true and faithful wife."

"My lord Lancelot," Sir Bors replied, "I advise you to take the good with the bad. Since events have fallen out in this way, I believe that you must defend yourself forcefully. Surely there is no band of Christian knights who can defeat you? I will also counsel you, my lord, to protect the queen. If she is in distress, and about to suffer for your sake, it is your duty to rescue her. Otherwise the shame of your name will stretch to the ends of the world. Since you were surprised in her company, it is your responsibility to take her part and ensure that she is not put to death. I do not know whether you were with her rightfully or wrongfully, but I do know this. If she should die, the shame would lie upon your head for ever."

"Jesus defend me from all shame," Lancelot said. "I call upon the blessed Saviour, too, to protect the life and good name of our sovereign lady. She cannot be condemned for my sake. So, my lords, friends and kinsmen all of you, what will you do?"

They called out in one voice. "We will do as you do!"

"Then let me put the case to you. I believe that King Arthur, our lord, will in the heat of anger consign his wife to the fire. His evil counsellors will urge him on. So what, lords, is it best for me to do?"

Sir Bors stepped forward. "You must rescue the queen. If she is burned, it will be for your sake. If you are caught, then you are likely to suffer the same fate or perhaps an even more shameful one. You must be resolute. Save her."

Lancelot listened to them very gravely. "My fair lords," he replied, "you know well that I will never do anything to dishonour you or my own blood. You also know that I am determined to save the queen from a cruel death. If you now counsel me to rescue her at all costs, you must also be aware that I will wreak much harm in the process. I am likely to destroy some of my best friends. There are other knights who, in loyalty to me, will desert their sovereign. These are not outcomes I seek or desire.

And tell me this. Once I have rescued Queen Guinevere, where will I take her?"

"That is the least of the problems," Sir Bors told him. "How did Sir Tristram behave in a similar plight? Did he not follow your advice and keep Isolde for almost three years in your own castle of Joyous Garde? Since that castle belongs to you, why not use it for the preservation and safety of the queen? If the king condemns her to death by burning, you have every right to ride to her protection. You can keep her in Joyous Garde until the wrath of the king has passed. Then you may lead her back to him, and earn the gratitude of both of them."

"I am not sure that the example of Sir Tristram is a good one," Lancelot replied to him. "Do you not recall that when he brought Isolde back to King Mark, that false king slew him with a sharp spear? The lance pierced his heart even as he played the harp before the queen. It grieves me still to speak of his death, because he was one of the finest knights in the world."

"All that is true enough," Bors said. "But remain steadfast. Surely you know that there is no comparison between King Arthur and King Mark? Arthur has always kept his word. He is honourable."

They discussed the matter for a long time, until they all agreed that for better or worse they would rescue the queen. If she were condemned to death, she would be kept safe in Lancelot's castle. They rode out to a wood close to Carlisle, and awaited the judgement of the king.

Sir Mordred had escaped, severely wounded, from Lancelot; weak from the loss of blood, he was still able to mount his horse and make his way to the king. He explained what had happened to his sovereign, and described how all the other knights had been killed.

"God have mercy on us!" cried the king. "How can this be? Do you say that you found him in the queen's chamber?"

"Yes, sir, in God's name it is the truth. He was not armed but, having dispatched Sir Collgrevaunce, he donned that trusty knight's armour. Then he fell upon us."

The king was disturbed by this news. "Sir Lancelot is a mighty warrior. He has no rival. I bitterly regret that he has now turned against me, for in becoming my foe he will surely break up the fellowship of the Round Table. He has so many noble kinsmen that our unity will be gone for ever. There is something else. To save my honour, I must also consign my wife to the flames." Arthur bowed his head in sorrow.

A short time later, the proclamation was made about the trial of the queen. The verdict itself was not in doubt. She was led to the Stone of Judgement, in the field of the fifty footsteps, where the evidence was pronounced against her. She stood in silence, with her head bowed, before the great lords of the court.

Just as the trial ended, Sir Gawain stood up and addressed the king. "My lord Arthur," he said, "I would advise you not to be too hasty in pronouncing death upon Queen Guinevere. Can you not declare a delay in judgement? There are many reasons for urging this. One of them is simple. It may be that, when Lancelot was found in the lady's chamber, he was there with no malicious intent. You know from your own experience that the Lady Guinevere has many reasons for showing gratitude to Sir Lancelot. He has saved her life on several occasions, and has done battle for her when no other knight was willing to do so. It may well be that she sent for him out of the goodness of her heart, in the wish to reward him for all his generous deeds. If she sent for him secretly, that was because she knows that there are many scandalmongers and gossips at the court who would love to sow mischief. She may have made the wrong decision, but things we do for the best often turn out to be for the worst. That is a law of life. I am sure, sir, that Queen Guinevere is a true and faithful wife. As for Sir Lancelot, I know that he will challenge to the duel any knight who dares to impugn the modesty of the queen or the honour of his own conduct."

"That may well be true. Lancelot trusts so much in his own strength that he fears no man. But I refuse to take your advice, Sir Gawain. The law is the law. The queen must go to the stake and, if I catch Lancelot, I will condemn him also to a shameful death."

"God forbid, sir king, that I should live to see such a thing!"

"Why do you say that? You have no reason to love him. He has just slaughtered your brother, Sir Agravain, and he almost killed Mordred. Has he not also murdered two of your sons, Sir Florens and Sir Lovell?"

"I know that. I bitterly regret the death of my two sons. But I warned them all — brothers and sons alike — about the outcome of any struggle with Lancelot. They refused my advice. So I will not meddle with him or try to take revenge upon him. They put themselves in the path of perils. They are the cause of their own deaths."

King Arthur listened to him gravely. "Prepare yourself, Sir Gawain. Put on your finest armour and then, with your brothers Gaheris and Gareth, attend upon the queen. Bring her to the place of judgement and consign her to the fire."

"No, my most noble king. I cannot do it. I will never escort my lady, the queen, to a miserable and dishonourable death. I could not endure to see her tied to the stake, and I will play no part in her death."

"Then see to it that your brothers take your place."

"My lord, they know well enough what shame will fall upon them. But they are too young and inexperienced to refuse you."

Gaheris and Gareth stepped forward from the company of knights, and addressed the king. "Sir, you may command us to be there," Gareth said. "That is your right. But we will attend against our wishes. Will you not excuse us?" The king shook his head.

"Very well," Gaheris said. "But we will not wear armour or bear arms. We will give the queen the kiss of peace."

"In the name of God, then, prepare yourselves." The king was very stern. "She shall be brought to judgement very soon."

Gawain cried out in sorrow. "Alas that I should live to see this unhappy day!" He turned away, weeping, and rushed out of the hall.

Very shortly after, Queen Guinevere was commanded to put on a plain smock, and was escorted from the castle to the place of execution. She made full confession of her sins to the priest in attendance, even as the assembled lords and ladies grieved for her.

Sir Lancelot had placed one of his men among the courtiers to give him good warning of the event. As soon as this man saw the queen being led forward, he leaped on to his horse and rode to the wood in order to inform Lancelot. The knights broke from their cover and, with Lancelot in the front rank, they galloped across the field towards the queen. The assault was a fierce one, and Lancelot himself killed a score of worthy knights. By ill fortune he also killed Gawain's two young brothers, Gareth and Gaheris, who were in fact unarmed. In the alarm and heat of battle, he had failed to recognize them. The French books tell us that he dealt them mighty blows about their heads, so that they fell to the ground with their brains spilling out. Yet Lancelot never saw them. They were found lying in a pile of corpses.

When Lancelot had killed or put to flight all of his opponents, he rode up to Guinevere. He gave her a gown and girdle, to put over her plain smock; he asked her to sit behind him on his horse and, when she was safely seated, he told her to be of good cheer. All would be well. As they rode off together, she praised God for her deliverance from death. And, of course, she also thanked her rescuer.

They made their way to Lancelot's castle, Joyous Garde, where he entertained her in knightly fashion. Many great lords, and other knights of his affinity, assembled there to pledge their allegiance to the queen. When it was clear that King Arthur and Sir Lancelot had become enemies, there were some who welcomed the news. There were others, however, who prophesied more woe and warfare. They were right.

The Vengeance of Gawain

When King Arthur was told about Sir Lancelot's daring rescue of the queen, and of the death in battle of many knights, he was distraught. When he was informed of the deaths of Sir Gaheris and Sir Gareth, he fainted from the sorrow he felt. When he was roused from his swoon, he spoke to those around him. "I curse the day that I was crowned! I have lost the fairest fellowship of noble knights that ever served a Christian king. Forty knights have been killed within the last two days. Sir Lancelot and his kin will never ride by my side again. Such is the outcome of this war. I have lost my lordship over the bravest warriors in the world." He stood up, and remained very still before his throne. "My lords, I solemnly charge you to keep silent. You must not inform Sir Gawain of the fate of his two young brothers. If he hears of this, he will go out of his mind." He put his hand to his mouth in a gesture of fear or of fury. "How could Lancelot do such a thing? He knew well enough that Gareth loved him better than any other man alive."

"That is true, sire," one of the knights told him. "But they were slain in the raging torrent of battle, when Lancelot was surrounded by spears and swords. He struck out at them without knowing who they were."

"Well, it matters little how or why they were killed. Their deaths will cause a mighty and miserable war. Gawain will never rest until Sir Lancelot and his kin are all overthrown. He will insist that I destroy them — or else he will destroy me. My heart has never been so heavy as it is now. It is strange that I feel the loss of my knights more than the loss of my queen. Queens can be replaced. But how can I find again such a noble company as that of the Round Table? It should not have come to this. I blame Agravain and Mordred for stirring up such a sea of trouble. Their evil will against Lancelot will bring doom or discredit upon us all." And, at that, the knights in the hall set up loud cries of lamentation.

Wherein Gawain learns the truth

In another part of the castle, one courtier had made his way to Sir Gawain. "Lancelot has taken away the queen," he said. "In the contest around her, he slew some twenty-four of our company."

"Is it so? Well, it is not unexpected. I knew well enough that Lancelot would either rescue her or die in the attempt. No man of worship would behave differently. If I had been in his situation, I would have acted in the same way. Twenty-four knights dead? Jesus

373

keep my brothers safe! But where are they? I do not see them. Surely they would have sought me out?"

"Truly, sir," the man said, "Gaheris and Gareth are dead."

"What are you saying to me?" Gawain's face lost all of its colour, and he took a step backwards. "That is the worst news in the world. I loved them both. I loved Gareth more than life itself!" He stared ahead. "Who killed him?"

"Sir Lancelot slew them both."

"I cannot believe that to be true. Gareth loved Lancelot better than he loved me or any of my brothers. Gareth reverenced him above the king himself. If Lancelot had asked him to take his part against Arthur, he would have done so willingly. He would have fought against me for Lancelot's sake. No. Lancelot could not have killed Gareth."

"I am afraid, sir, it is known by all that he slaughtered both of them."

"So now," Sir Gawain said, "all joy is gone for ever." He lay upon the floor in a stupor of sorrow. When eventually he roused himself, he began a long low moan of pain. Then he went to the presence chamber of the king, weeping, and fell down in front of him. "My uncle, my sovereign, two of your noblest knights — two of my dearest brothers — have been piteously slain." The king wept with him, and together they sent up many cries and lamentations. "Sir lord," Gawain said, "I must see the body of Gareth."

"You cannot see him," Arthur replied. "I have ensured that he and Gaheris are already buried. I knew

374

well enough that your sorrow would be hard to bear and that the sight of your brothers would only increase your anguish."

"But can you tell me this, my lord? In what manner did Lancelot kill them both? They were unarmed. No knight would kill a man without shield or sword."

"I am not sure. But I am told that Sir Lancelot swung at them while in the heat of battle, and that in his fury he did not recognize either of them. No more questions, Sir Gawain. We must now form a plan to take revenge."

"My king, my lord, my uncle, by all the ties that bind us I swear to you that from this day forward I shall not rest until I have wreaked vengeance upon him. I will kill him, or he will kill me. That is the sum of it. So I ask you, sir, to prepare yourself and your knights for war. You know what I have promised. If you wish to have my service and my love, assist me in my task. Even if I must seek Sir Lancelot through the realms of seven kings, I will find him and avenge my brothers."

"You will not need to seek him so far," Arthur said. "Sir Lancelot is waiting for us in his castle of Joyous Garde. Many of his allies have joined him there."

"I can well believe it. Sir, prepare your friends for battle. I will prepare mine."

"So be it. We will assemble so large a force that we will break down the best-defended tower in the greatest castle."

Arthur sent letters and writs throughout the kingdom of England, summoning all of his warriors to his side. In response there came riding to him many knights, dukes and earls. He told them all the causes of this conflict, and outlined his plans to lay siege to Joyous Garde.

In the meantime Lancelot had also assembled many knights, some of them in his service and some of them in the queen's service. Both sides were well armed and well prepared with all the instruments of war. The army of King Arthur, however, was much larger than that of Lancelot. The knight declined to give battle against his opponent, and instead he drew his forces within the castle.

The great host, brought together by Arthur and Gawain, surrounded the castle and lay siege to it. For fifteen weeks they battled earnestly to dislodge the defenders, but to no avail. Lancelot refused to ride out into the open fields beyond the protection of the walls, and ordered all of his knights to stay within.

Wherein Gawain taunts Lancelot

One morning in harvest time, Lancelot went out on the battlements and called down to Arthur and Gawain. "My lords, you know that this siege will fail. It will bring only contempt and dishonour upon your heads. If I were to come out at the head of my company of knights, I would defeat you soon enough."

"Then come," Arthur said to him. "If you dare, that is. Prove your mettle. I promise that I shall meet you in the middle of this field."

"God forbid," Lancelot replied, "that I should engage in battle with the noble king who made me a knight."

"Fair words are worthless now. Remember this, Lancelot. I am your mortal enemy, and will be so until the day of my death. You have slain too many of my best knights. You have killed my noble kinsmen. But you have dishonoured me more closely. For too long you have consorted with my queen, Guinevere. Now, like a traitor, you have taken her away from me by force."

"My most noble lord and king. Say what you will. I will never take up arms against you. You are angered that I have destroyed some of your best knights. I admit the fault, and I bitterly regret it. But I was forced to do battle with them in order to save my life. Would you wish me to have surrendered and been killed? You have spoken about your wife, the dear lady queen. There is no knight alive who would dare to charge me with any crime or treason against you in that regard. I swear that Guinevere is as loyal to you as any wife to her husband. I will fight in judicial combat to prove it so. It is true that she has been gracious enough to show me her favour over the years, and has cherished me more than any other knight."

"I know it, Lancelot."

"Let me continue, sir. In all modesty I believe that I have deserved her trust. I have done battle on her behalf, when she has been falsely accused; on each occasion I have defeated her adversary and rescued her from burning. Do you not recall when in the heat of her anger you condemned her, only to thank me in the end for saving her good name? You promised me then that you would be my good lord for ever. But now you have rewarded me only with evil. Do you imagine that I could stand by and see her burned for my sake? I would have been branded with perpetual shame. I have fought for her before. It was all the more important to fight for her on this occasion. And therefore, my good and gracious lord, I beg you to take her back into your favour. I swear that she is both true and good."

"Shame on you!" cried out Gawain. "I tell you this, false perjured knight, that the king will have both you and his queen at his mercy. He will save you, or slay you, as he wishes."

"That may be so," Lancelot replied. "But remember one thing, Gawain. If I come from the shelter of these walls, and engage you in battle, I promise you the hardest struggle of your life."

"Proud words prove nothing, Lancelot! As for my lady, the queen, you know that I will never speak disrespectfully of her. But tell me this, traitor and coward, why did you strike down Gareth? My brother loved you more than he loved his own family. You dubbed him a knight with your own hands. Why did you kill one you cared for?"

"I will not excuse myself. It can do no good now. But I swear, in the name of Jesus and by the faith I owe to the high Order of Knighthood, I did not intend to kill him. I would rather have slaughtered my own nephew, Sir Bors. In the mêlée around me, I did not see him. I bitterly regret it, but it is the truth."

378

"You are lying, Lancelot," Gawain replied. "The real truth is that you killed him to spite me. There was malice in your heart. That is why you will be my enemy to the end of time."

"I am sorry for it, Gawain. But I realize that there can be no concord between us while you harbour such angry thoughts against me. The king himself will not be able to pacify you, even though I am sure that he would bring me back into his favour."

"Believe what you like. For many long days you have tried to gain the mastery over me. You have slaughtered many bold and brave knights."

"Speak on, Gawain."

"I will say only this. I will never leave you until you are in my hands."

"I trust you in that, at least. I would gain no mercy from you."

It has been said that King Arthur would willingly have forgiven Guinevere, and brought her back into favour, but Sir Gawain would not hear of it. That is why he delivered so many insults to Lancelot, calling him coward and traitor, and why he encouraged his knights to do the same. He wanted to strengthen the king's resolve.

When they heard Gawain, the knights of Sir Lancelot, among them Sir Bors and Sir Lionel, came up to him as he stood on the battlements. "My lord," Sir Lionel said to him, "you can hear their insults, can't you? How can you tolerate such crude abuse? Let me and my fellows now ride out of the castle and engage these fools in battle. If you want us to remain in your service, grant us our wish. You are behaving, sir, as if you lived in fear of the enemy. Gawain will never allow you and King Arthur to be reconciled. So fight for your life. Fight for your rights."

"I do not wish to meet them on the field, where I might slay them, but if you and the others are adamant —" Lancelot called down again to Arthur and Gawain. "I am required by my men to ride into battle against you," he said, "so on your lives I conjure you both to stay away from the fighting!"

"What are you talking about?" Sir Gawain replied. "Have I not enlisted in the king's quarrel with you? I am here to avenge the death of my two brothers."

"So be it. But I warn you both that you will bitterly repent your decision to fight me."

Wherein the fortunes of battle turn

The battle lines were drawn up, the knights armed and their mounts made ready. Sir Gawain ordered a body of knights to watch for Lancelot, to pursue him and slay him.

On a pre-arranged signal the fellowship of Sir Lancelot galloped towards them from the three gates of the castle; Sir Lionel came out of the first gate, Sir Lancelot from the central gate, and Sir Bors from the third. They were the flower of chivalry in that land. But Lancelot had ordered his men to spare the lives of Arthur and Gawain at all costs.

Gawain himself rode out from the king's host, and challenged any of his opponents to joust with him. Sir

Lionel took up the challenge gladly, but Gawain struck him with his lance; Lionel fell to the ground as if he were dead. He was taken into the castle by two or three of his comrades-in-arms.

There followed a general battle in which many combatants were slain, although Sir Lancelot did his best to protect those around Arthur and Gawain. The king eagerly sought Lancelot's death, but the knight would not retaliate against him. He had too much respect for his crown. But Sir Bors attacked Arthur with his lance and short sword, thrusting the king from his horse. He cried out to Lancelot, "Sir, shall I make an end of this war with one blow?"

"No. On your life, I forbid you to touch him. I will never see the king, who made me a knight, slain or dishonoured." Lancelot rode up to Arthur, and courteously helped him back on to his horse. "Ah, sir king," he said, "make an end to this strife. You will win no plaudits here. I have asked my knights to spare you and Gawain, but you urge your men to pursue me to the death. I pray you, my lord, to remember all the services I have performed for you in the past. Do you not think that I have been poorly rewarded?"

The king had now regained his saddle and rode away. But he turned to look once more at Lancelot, and he wept at the courtesy and gentleness of this most virtuous knight. "I wish to God," he muttered to himself, "that this war had never begun."

As twilight fell, the battle subsided. The opposing parties buried their dead and conducted the wounded to safety. They passed the night in prayer, or sleep, before preparing for war in the morning. Once more they were ready for battle.

Sir Gawain came out from the king's host, bearing a great spear in his hand. Sir Bors saw him at once, and resolved that now was the time to avenge Gawain's treatment of Sir Lionel. Both men confronted one another; they lowered their spears, held their swords and shields tightly, and galloped towards each other. Such was the collision between them that they were both thrown to the ground, where they lay dazed and badly wounded.

This was the signal for general battle, and once more there was great slaughter on both sides. In the middle of the conflict, however, Lancelot was able to rescue Sir Bors and send him into the safety of the castle. Still he would not strike at Arthur or at Gawain. "We see that you are sparing our two greatest enemies," Sir Lavane and Sir Palomides cried out to him. "This is injuring our cause. Do you see how they aim their spears against you? Return the compliment. Strike them down."

"I do not have the heart to fight against my king," Lancelot replied to them. "I know I do wrong but, still, I cannot do it."

"My lord," Palomides said, "you may spare them, but they will never thank you for it. If they capture you, you will be a dead man."

Lancelot knew that Palomides was speaking the truth. So he revived his efforts, and showed his strength against his enemies. His anger was all the greater because he knew that Sir Bors, his nephew, had been badly injured. During the course of that day Lancelot's party got the better of the engagement; the very fetlocks of the horses were covered in blood. Then, out of consideration for the king, Lancelot allowed the forces of the enemy to return to their camp while he led his men back to the castle.

Yet something else had happened. Sir Gawain had been badly wounded. The king's commanders were not so eager for battle as before, and they withdrew from the field.

Wherein a truce is agreed

The news of this war soon spread throughout Christendom, until it reached the ears of the pope. The holy father knew of Arthur's reputation as a wise king, and of Lancelot's fame as the noblest knight in all the world. He called the Bishop of Rochester into his presence, and charged him to deliver a papal bull to the king in which he was commanded to take back his queen and to be reconciled with Lancelot.

The bishop travelled from Rome to Carlisle, where he attended Arthur's court. Here he presented the king with the pope's decree, with its seal of lead; Arthur read the document in private, but was unsure how to proceed. He would have been happy to reconcile himself with Lancelot, but Sir Gawain would not permit it. Gawain would allow the queen to return to the court but on no account, he said, could Lancelot be admitted to the king's good grace.

So Arthur summoned the Bishop of Rochester, and told him that the queen would not be accused of any wrongdoing and that Lancelot himself would be given safe passage in delivering her.

The bishop rode at once to the castle of Joyous Garde, where he acquainted Lancelot with all these matters. He showed him the king's writ and the mark of his great seal. He also reminded him of the dangers in withholding the queen from her husband. "Sir bishop," Lancelot said, "it was never my intention to keep Queen Guinevere from King Arthur. I wished only to save her from the fire. That is all. So I thank God that the pope has intervened on her behalf. It will give me more pleasure to bring her back than it ever did to take her away. As long as I am given safe passage, and as long as the queen enjoys her liberty as before, then I am content. If the queen is ever placed in peril again, then hard misfortune will befall the king."

"That will not happen," the bishop told him. "You must know that the pope will be obeyed. Arthur will follow his commandment for his own soul's sake."

"Yes. I see from the king's own words that he has granted me safety. So tell him this. Within eight days I will return the queen to him. And tell him this as well. I will always defend that gracious lady against any knight."

The bishop returned to Carlisle and informed the king of Lancelot's response; hearing of his loyalty and fidelity, Arthur wept. On the following day Lancelot summoned one hundred of his best knights. He dressed them in a livery of green velvet, and draped their horses in the same cloth; he asked each one of them to hold a branch of olive in his hands as a token of peaceful intent. The queen had twenty-four ladies-in-waiting riding with her, and Lancelot himself was accompanied by twelve pages; they all wore white velvet trimmed with precious jewels and cloth of gold, and the trappings of their horses were also fashioned out of gold. Never was so much brightness seen upon the earth.

In this array they rode from Joyous Garde to the royal castle at Carlisle, and those watching the procession wept with joy at the queen's homecoming. When they entered the gates of the castle Sir Lancelot dismounted, and helped Guinevere from her horse. He led her into the royal court where King Arthur sat upon his throne, with Sir Gawain and other great lords assembled around him. Lancelot and Guinevere came towards the king, and both of them kneeled humbly before him. There were many tears shed, among Arthur's knights, at the spectacle. But the king sat still and said not a word. After a moment Lancelot stood up and, raising Guinevere also, he spoke aloud.

"Most honoured king, by the pope's commandment and by your own royal command, I have brought to you my lady, the queen. It is only right and proper that I should do so. If there be any knight in this company who dares to lay any blame upon this lady, then I will fight him in judicial combat and thereby prove her purity and faithfulness. But, sir lord, you have been listening to liars and scandalmongers. As a result there has been enmity between us. There was a time when you were greatly pleased with me, especially on those occasions when I did battle on behalf of the queen. So

385

why should I not save her when she was threatened with death for my sake?

"Those who lied about her were malicious men, and their malice fell back upon their own heads. Only by the grace of God was I able to defeat the knights who came with Mordred and Agravain to the queen's chamber; they were armed and ready, whereas I was unarmed and unprepared. I had been summoned to the queen unexpectedly, but no sooner was I in her presence than they called me traitor and coward."

"They were right!" shouted Gawain.

Lancelot turned to him. "My lord Gawain," he said quietly, "their defeat and death suggest otherwise."

"Well, well, Sir Lancelot," the king replied, "I have given you no cause to treat me in this fashion. I have honoured you above any other of my knights."

"In turn, sir," Lancelot replied, "you know that I and my company have performed more services for you than anyone else in the court. Where you have been in peril, I have rescued you. On horseback and on foot, I have saved you from manifold dangers. In jousts, in tournaments, and in set battles, I have defended you. I have protected you also, Sir Gawain, against many hazards." Lancelot was silent for a moment, and looked at Gawain. "If you reflect on these things, sir, you will grant me your good will. When I have that, I trust to God that I will be given the king's grace."

"The king may do as he wishes," Gawain replied. "But, as for me, I tell you that there never can and never will be friendship between us. You have killed three of my brothers, two of them unarmed."

"I wish to God they had been armed," Lancelot told him. "Then they would still be alive. I loved no knight better than Sir Gareth. I loved him for the love he bore towards me. I loved him for his gallantry and faithfulness. I dubbed him knight, and now I bitterly regret his death. There is another reason for my sorrow. As soon as I heard that he was dead, I knew that you would be my enemy for ever and that you would turn King Arthur against me. But I swear, on the name of the Almighty, that I did not kill your brothers willingly or knowingly. It was an unhappy day when they came unarmed on to the field." He stepped forward. "I offer you this, Sir Gawain. If it pleases you and the king, I will set out from Sandwich wearing a smock and hood like any ploughman. I will then walk from Sandwich to Carlisle. Every ten miles along the road I will found a house of monks or nuns who will offer perpetual prayer for the souls of Gareth and Gaheris. Their chapels will be stocked with candles and incense. Their voices will rise in unison for the sake of your brothers. Will this not be more beneficial for their souls than everlasting warfare between us? What will enmity solve?" On hearing his words, the ladies and the knights of the court wept with King Arthur.

Sir Gawain shook his head. "I hear your fine words and fine promises. But I tell you this. The king can do as he wishes. But I will never forgive you. If the king is reconciled with you, I will leave his service. You have proved false to me and to him."

"Then I will prove myself in combat against you. The lance will be my answer."

"No. The pope has decreed that you will pass safely through this court. So must it be. You will ride away unharmed. But the king and I have agreed that, once you have left this place, a sentence of banishment will be pronounced against you. You will be given fifteen days to leave the kingdom. If the pope had not spoken, I would have fought you today and furnished proof of your falseness. Wherever and whenever I find you, in the future, I will wreak my vengeance upon you."

Sir Lancelot, dismayed, bowed his head and looked down upon the ground. "I love this noble and most Christian land more than life itself. Here I have won honour and glory. Am I to leave it now, innocent of any crime? I wish that I had never come here, if I am to be expelled in shame and dishonour. Well, the old sayings are true. Fortune is fickle. The wheel always turns. There is no abiding city. Fortune favours no man for long. So it is with me. I have increased the renown of the Round Table more than any other knight. I have given it more glory than any of you. Yet now you wish to banish me. But think of this, Sir Gawain. I am allowed to dwell upon my own land in peace. And if you, most high king, and you, Gawain, trespass upon my domain I will defend it. As for you, Gawain, if you repeat your charges of treason and felony against me I will answer you in battle."

"Do as you choose," Gawain replied. "But you must be gone as quickly as possible. And understand this. We will follow you, and tear apart the strongest castle that you possess. Its stones will fall around you."

"That will not be necessary, Sir Gawain. I will meet you in open combat."

"Enough words then. Return the queen to us, and leave this court. I hope you have a swift horse."

"If I had known how you would receive me, I would have thought twice before coming here with the queen. If I had been a traitor, as you taunt me, I would have kept her in Joyous Garde." Sir Lancelot turned to Guinevere. "Madam, now I must depart from you for ever. I must also leave the noblest band of knights in the world. Pray for me as I will pray for you. If anyone should slander you or accuse you of any crime, send me word of it. I will come back to defend you as I have done before." In front of the court he kissed the queen, and turned to the assembly. "If anyone wishes to swear that the queen is unfaithful to the king, then do so now."

There was silence. Lancelot took her hand, and led her to her lord. All of the company watched this, and wept; only Gawain was unmoved. When Lancelot mounted on his horse and rode from Carlisle, there was general lamentation. He made his way in sorrow to Joyous Garde that, from this time forward, he named Dolorous Garde. So Lancelot departed from Arthur's court for ever. He and his brave company of knights returned to his ancestral lands in France, in the territory known as Pays du Soleil, or Land of the Sun.

Lancelot and Gawain

When King Arthur heard that Lancelot had departed for Pays du Soleil, he summoned a great host of sixty thousand men. He had called together these warriors to follow Lancelot across the sea and to make war upon his dominions. Arthur had decided to make Mordred, his son, the governor of Britain in his absence; he also gave him the custody of Guinevere. What is more natural than the father trusting the son? Mordred had been begotten in an act of incest, with Arthur's half-sister, but he had proved himself to be a valiant knight.

Arthur and his army set sail from the firth near Carlisle and, when they landed on the shore of France, the king gave orders that his men should waste and ravage the countryside in revenge for the crimes committed by Lancelot. Sir Gawain urged him on, delighting in vengeance for its own sake.

Lancelot was advised by his men to ride out and fight the invaders at once. "You know your worth as a knight," Bagdemagus told him. "You know our worth as your companions. Come. Let us meet our enemies in the field, and cut them down."

"That can be easily done," Lancelot told them. "But I am reluctant to go to war. I pray you all, my lords, to be ruled by me for the time being. I will not confront the king until our lives are in danger. Only then can we with honour take up arms against our liege lord."

They said no more, and took their rest that night. When they awoke at dawn, they discovered that Lancelot's words were answered sooner than they expected. Arthur's army had marched up to their castle, and had already set up ladders against the walls. Lancelot's knights took up their defences and beat the soldiers back, thrusting the ladders to the ground. Then Gawain rode out and, with his spear in his hand, stopped before the main gate.

"Where are you, Lancelot?" he called out. "Where are you, you false coward and traitor? Why do you cower behind these walls? Show some courage. Come out and defend yourself. Let me take my revenge for the death of my three brothers!"

Sir Lancelot heard every word of Gawain's taunt. "Sir," his knights said to him, "it is time. You must defend yourself, or else be dishonoured for ever. You have slept for too long. Now you must awake and arm yourself for battle."

"Now that Gawain has accused me of treason," Lancelot replied, "I have no other course. I will not be convicted of cowardice."

Lancelot ordered that his strongest horse be saddled and that his armour be brought to him. He climbed the tower of the gate, and addressed Arthur himself. "My lord king," he said, "it grieves me to go against one of your knights. In the past I have been patient, and declined to do battle with you. Otherwise you would have found your knights slain or subdued on the field. But I cannot, and will not, endure the charge of treason. I must fight for my honour. I must defend myself."

"Leave off your babbling!" Gawain called out. "It is time for battle. Let us ease our hearts!"

Sir Lancelot rode out, with his lance in his hand, and led his army from the castle. When Arthur saw the number of his troops, he was dismayed. "I curse the moment I quarrelled with Lancelot. Now I see the end of my days coming."

When Sir Gawain and Sir Lancelot faced one another, it was agreed that no other warrior should assist or attack them until one of the two contestants had been slain. The two knights drew apart, waiting their moment. Then suddenly they began galloping down on one another with extreme speed and fury. With a cry they met and clashed, the spears smashing down on the middle of the shields; the knights were so strong, and their spears so large, that the horses could not bear their force. The animals fell to the earth in despair. Lancelot and Gawain sprang from their saddles, and their shields clashed; they fell to fighting with their swords and spears, inflicting serious wounds on one another. Sir Gawain had a secret. A holy man had given him a special grace, so that between nine in the morning and high noon his strength increased threefold. As a result he won great renown. That is why Arthur insisted that all of Gawain's battles be fought at nine, so that he might have the mastery. Only these two men knew the source of such supernatural strength.

So Lancelot, blooded and wearied, wondered how his opponent was able to withstand all of his blows. When Gawain's strength was redoubled, after two hours of combat, Lancelot doubted whether he was fighting a knight or a fiend. He began to feint and parry, conserving his breath and his strength as best he could. He covered himself with his shield, as blow after blow buffeted him. The knights, witnessing this fight, did not believe that Lancelot could bear it for much longer.

But then the hour of noon came, and all of Gawain's secret strength was gone. When Lancelot sensed that the force was fading from his foe, he stood his ground. "I feel now that you have done your worst," he said to him. "And now, my lord Gawain, I must play my part. I have endured many great and grievous strokes this day, and suffered pain. It is time to teach you a lesson." Lancelot redoubled his blows, and gave Gawain such a blow on the side of his helmet that he fell down upon the ground. But Lancelot sheathed his weapon, and watched him.

"Why do you pause now?" Gawain asked him. "Why not kill me, false traitor? If you let me live, then surely I will come after you again."

"By God's grace, I am sure that I will survive. But you know, Gawain, that I will never kill a knight that cannot fight back. Rise to your feet and return to your army." Then he turned to Arthur, who had watched the whole combat. "Good day to you, lord king! You see now that you will win no worship at my walls. If I were to lead my men into battle with you, many noble warriors would die. Remember me with kindness, and at all times follow the will of Our Lord Jesus."

"I regret," Arthur replied, "that this unhappy war was ever begun. Lancelot has been courteous and correct in all his dealings with me. He has never attacked me or my kin. And see how kind he has been to Gawain himself!"

Lancelot turned away and with his men marched back into the castle. Sir Gawain was carried into Arthur's pavilion, where the doctors tried to heal him with salves and sweet ointments. The king himself fell sick with sorrow for Gawain's great hurt, and for the grievous war between the two noble knights. In the following days, there was little appetite for warfare on either side.

For three weeks Gawain lay low in his tent, where he was slowly restored to health by all manner of medicines and herbal remedies. But as soon as he felt able to fight once more, he armed himself as before and rode out on his charger. He stopped before the main gate of the castle and called out, "Where are you, Lancelot? Come out and face me, you false and cowardly knight. Gawain is here, ready to prove that you are a traitor!"

Lancelot heard him clearly enough, and replied from the battlements, "Gawain, it grieves me that you use such foul, insulting language. Why boast about your prowess? I know the limits of your strength, and I know that you cannot greatly hurt me."

"Come out then, and prove it. I have come this day to make amends for my misadventure at your hands. I will lay you as low as you laid me."

"Jesus defend me from that fate. If you were able to match me, then I would indeed be at the door of death. But that will not happen. Yes. I will come out from the gate. You have accused me of treason once more, and I will answer with my lance."

The armies of both knights were assembled to watch the contest. Lancelot and Gawain were prepared for the battle, their lances at the ready; they rode towards each other, their horses galloping furiously, and such was the shock of the encounter that Gawain's horse reared in fright. He was thrown sideways, and scrambled to unseat himself; he dismounted and quickly raised his shield in defence. "Alight, traitor knight," he said, threatening Lancelot with his sword, "and meet me in combat. My horse has failed me. But I am of royal blood. I will not rest until I kill you."

Lancelot dismounted and, with sword in hand, fell upon his enemy. They fought hard and bloodily. But of course Lancelot now knew Gawain's secret. While the strength of his opponent increased he held himself back for those three hours, covering his body with his shield and trading stroke for stroke. He dodged and dived, diverting Gawain wherever he could; he preserved his strength for all that time and, when at last the might of Gawain began to fade, he called out to him. "You have proved twice," he said, "that you are a valiant and resourceful warrior. You have shown yourself to be strong, deceiving other knights with your boldness. But those deeds are done. I will now show you my power."

Lancelot attacked Gawain with redoubled strokes of his sword, until one blow caught Gawain's helmet at that point where the first wound had been inflicted. With a groan Gawain fell to the earth, and for a moment lost consciousness. When he revived, he waved his sword and tried to lift himself from the ground. "Traitor knight," he said. "You see that I am not dead. Come close to me now and fight to the finish."

"I will do no more than I have already done. I will do battle with you when you can stand on your feet. Not before. God defend me from the shame of smiting a wounded man."

He turned away, and went back into the castle. Gawain called after him, "Traitor knight! Traitor knight!" But Lancelot did not pause. "I will return!" Gawain shouted. "I will return and kill you. I shall never leave you until I see you lying at my feet!"

So the siege went on. Gawain lay wounded for a month but, when he recovered from his injuries, he was ready once more to challenge Lancelot. Before that battle could take place, however, King Arthur received news from England that sent him and his army home.

The Day of Destiny

While Sir Mordred ruled all England at the behest of his father, King Arthur, he forged letters to the effect that the king had been killed in battle with Lancelot. He summoned a parliament and persuaded the lords and prelates to crown him as the new king. There was a coronation ceremony at Canterbury, and the feasting lasted for fifteen days.

He then rode in state to Winchester, where he informed Queen Guinevere that he intended to marry her, despite the fact that she was already his stepmother. He named a day for the wedding, and made preparations for the celebration that would follow. Guinevere herself lamented her fate in secret, but did not reveal her sorrow to the world. Instead she spoke fair words, and seemed to accept Mordred's wish.

But then, one morning, she appeared before him and requested leave to travel to London; there, she said, she might buy a bridal gown and train. Trusting her, he granted her request. As soon as she arrived in the city, however, she went to the Tower of London and turned it into her fortress. She provided it with men and arms and all manner of supplies.

When Mordred was informed of this, he grew angry beyond measure. He summoned his army at once, marched upon London, and laid siege to the Tower. But Guinevere had done her work well. She was more than a match for his guns and his siege engines. She discounted his threats as well as his promises, knowing what would happen if she fell into his hands.

The Archbishop of Canterbury, a most holy man, eventually sought an audience with Mordred. "Sir," he asked him, "what are you doing? Will you displease God? Will you bring shame upon yourself and the entire class of knights? Did not your father, Arthur, beget you on his half-sister in horrible incest? How can you now propose to marry your father's wife? Abandon this course, sire. Otherwise I will have no choice but to excommunicate you. By bell, book and candle you will be damned to eternal fire."

"Do your worst, bishop. I defy you."

"Think. Turn aside from the path of damnation. I tell you this. I will not hesitate to do my duty. And there is one other thing. I do not believe that Arthur is dead. You lied to the parliament and people."

Mordred was roused to fierce anger. "Silence, false priest! One more word, and I will take off your head!"

So the archbishop departed and in due state pronounced the words of excommunication upon the false king. Mordred then sought him out, in all haste, but the holy man had fled from Canterbury and had taken refuge at Glastonbury. Here he found a hermit's cell, beside a chapel, where he lived in poverty and prayer. He prayed for the realm of England because he knew that danger was rushing upon it.

Mordred, meanwhile, sent many letters to Guinevere imploring her to leave the safety of the Tower and entrust herself to his care. She was not persuaded. She told him, shortly and decisively, that she would rather kill herself than marry him.

Then the news came that Arthur and his host had abandoned the siege of Lancelot, and were about to return home in order to wreak vengeance on Mordred. At once Mordred summoned all the magnates of the land. Many of them supported him, saying that Arthur had given them nothing but bloodshed and battle whereas Mordred promised peace and prosperity. So was Arthur slandered and his good deeds slighted. He had rewarded many lords with land and treasure, only to be betrayed by those whom he had benefited.

Do you not see, all you Englishmen, what evil had come among us? Here was the noblest king and worthiest knight in the world. Here was the sovereign who had most loved the fellowship of his warriors of the Round Table. Yet the lords of our country were disloyal to him and lacking in reverence. What was the reason? The English are forever unstable and untrue, seeking novelty in new guises. Nothing satisfies us for long.

And so it happened this time. The people were better pleased with the false Mordred than the noble Arthur; they saluted him, and promised their support. Mordred thereupon marched with his army to Dover, where Arthur was supposed to disembark, with the firm intention of depriving his own father of his lands. The fleet of Arthur approached, complete with galleys and carracks, while Mordred waited for him on shore. Those on land tried to thwart the arrival of those at sea, but they could not withstand their might. Many knights fought in hand-to-hand combat, and were laid low. King Arthur himself made his way on to the beach, and made short work of his assailants. His courage inspired his followers, and they poured on to the land. Mordred fled with the remains of his army.

After the battle was over Arthur ordered that the dead and the dying should be taken up and cared for. Sir Gawain was discovered, lying half-dead on the deck of a great ship. When Arthur was informed he hurried over to him, and took the knight in his arms. He cradled his injured companion, and cried out in sorrow. "Alas, good Gawain," he said, "you are the son of my sister and the man I loved most in all the world. Now you lie dying. All my joy is gone. Let me tell you this. You and Lancelot were the two knights I revered and cherished. Now I have lost you both. What is left for me but woe?"

"My dear uncle," Gawain replied, "you and I know that the day of my death has come. My fate is entirely my own fault. I was injured today in the head, where Lancelot wounded me. I will be dead before noon. There is no escape. And I blame myself for all this warfare. My pride has been the cause of your shame and sorrow. If I had not quarrelled with Lancelot, this war would not have been fought. If Lancelot had been at your side, he would have kept all your enemies in fear and subjection. Now you will be deprived of his company for ever! My conceit has caused you nothing but grief. Please, uncle, bring me pen, paper and ink. I wish to write a letter to Lancelot before it is too late."

The materials were quickly brought to him and, after being confessed by a priest, Gawain took up his pen and began to write. "To you, Sir Lancelot, flower of all chivalry, I, Sir Gawain, send greetings. I wish to tell you that on this day, the tenth of May, I received a deep wound where you wounded me before. That wound will now be the cause of my death. Outside the walls of your castle you delivered a perilous stroke to me. But I tell the world that you are not responsible for my death. I caused it through arrogance and self-seeking. I have slain myself. Wherefore I beseech you, Lancelot, to return to this realm of England and come to my tomb; I beg you to pray there for the salvation of my soul. I will sign this letter now with my own blood, just two and a half hours before my death. I beseech you once more, Lancelot, to make your way to my tomb."

He wept, with Arthur, and was so frail that he fainted away. When he recovered he was given the last rites and, at noon of that day, he died. The king buried him in the chapel of the castle at Dover. His skull, with the mark of the wound that Lancelot gave him, may still be seen there.

The civil war continued. Mordred had marched his army to Canterbury, and there offered battle. The king encountered him on the following morning and, after a long and bloody fight, claimed the victory. Other warriors now joined Arthur, volunteering for his cause as a just one. So he took his army west, to the neighbourhood of Wells, and a day was fixed for combat between the forces of Arthur and Mordred. It was to be held, in a field close to the coast, on the Monday after Trinity Sunday. Whereupon Mordred raised more troops in London and in the counties of Kent, Sussex, Surrey, Essex, Suffolk and Norfolk; these were the shires that had always favoured the usurper. The army of Arthur came from other parts of the kingdom. The supporters of Lancelot, however, followed Mordred.

On the night of Trinity Sunday, Arthur dreamed a wonderful dream. In this dream he sat in cloth of gold upon his throne, raised high on a wooden platform; but the throne was fastened to a wheel. Beneath him he could see a deep pool of black water, horrible to behold, filled with serpents and snakes and other writhing things. Suddenly it seemed to him that the wheel turned and he was toppled from his throne, falling into the dark water where the fangs of the creatures fastened upon him. He cried aloud for help. His courtiers ran to his side and woke him, but he was so disturbed by the dream that at first he did not know where he was. He could not sleep, and lay awake until it was almost day. Just before dawn he fell into a light slumber that was neither sleep nor waking. In this state he saw, or seemed to see, Sir Gawain come towards him with a number of fair ladies. "Welcome, son of my sister," the king said. "I thought you were dead. Now I see you in life. Jesus be praised! But tell me, fair nephew, who are these ladies walking by your side?"

402

"Sir," Gawain replied, "these are all ladies for whom I fought when I was among the living. I did battle for them in righteous quarrels, and God has granted their prayer that they should be allowed to bring me to you. God has also given me leave to foretell your death. If you fight with Mordred tomorrow, gracious king, you will fall. So will many of your bravest knights. Out of pity for you and your men, Almighty God has by His especial grace granted me this chance to give you warning. Do not engage in battle with Mordred tomorrow morning. Sign a treaty with him that will last a month. Lancelot will then come to these shores and assist you. He will slay Mordred and all his men."

When he had finished speaking, Gawain, and the attendant ladies, melted into a mist. All at once Arthur awoke and called for his courtiers. He told them to summon the magnates and prelates of the realm. When they arrived the king informed them of his vision and of Gawain's warning to him. He instructed Sir Lucan and Sir Bedevere the Bold, together with two bishops, to visit the camp of Mordred and there arrange a treaty with him. "Spare nothing to persuade him," he told them. "Give him lands and treasure."

So they departed and rode to Sir Mordred, who was settled in the fields with one hundred thousand soldiers. They bargained with him for a long time, eventually promising him the territories of Kent and Cornwall. It was also agreed that, after Arthur's death, Mordred would rule over all England. The two men were to meet, before their armies, with fourteen of their noblest followers; they would there exchange the kiss of peace.

"This is well done," Arthur said on hearing of the treaty. But then he turned to his knights. "If you see any one of Mordred's men raise his sword from its scabbard, then fall upon Mordred himself. I do not trust him. He is wily. He is treacherous."

In turn Mordred told his supporters that, if any one of Arthur's men should unleash his weapon, they were to massacre as many of the enemy as they could. "I do not trust this treaty," he said. "I know well enough that my father wishes to be revenged on me."

The two men met at the appointed time, and made their agreement. Wine was fetched, and they drank together. At that moment of assent, an adder came from the cover of a heath bush and stung one of Mordred's knights on the foot. The warrior unsheathed his sword to slay the snake, and was of course seen by Arthur's men. They feared the worst and, with drums and trumpets sounding, they fell upon the enemy. The two armies rushed at each other, their swords and lances raised. Arthur rode forth, whispering, "This day will not bring me good fortune."

There never was, or will be, such a dreadful battle in any Christian land. There was nothing but blood and slaughter, savagery and sorrow. King Arthur led his troops into battle, swinging his sword from side to side, while Mordred fought him back with stroke and counterstroke. They exchanged bloody blows all that long day, until the knights were brought low on the cold earth. They fought until nightfall, when one hundred thousand warriors lay dead upon the field. Arthur was almost mad from grief, with all his men gone from his side. He looked about him, and could see only two knights of his allegiance. Yet these two — Sir Lucan and his brother, Sir Bedevere — were badly injured.

"Have mercy on us, Jesus Our Saviour!" the king cried out. "What has happened to all of my noble knights? I should not have lived to see this doleful day. Now I have come near to my end! Yet I pray to God that I may yet see my son, Mordred, and slay him. He is the maker of all this mischief." He looked over the field of battle and found him; Mordred was leaning on his sword among a heap of dead men. "Give me my spear," Arthur said to Sir Lucan. "I have seen the traitor who has wrought all this woe."

"Let him be, sire," Lucan replied. "Can you not see he is in despair? If you survive this day, then you will be sufficiently revenged. Do you not recall your dream? Do you not heed the words of Gawain concerning your fate? God has protected you so far. You have won the victory. The three of us are still alive, whereas Mordred is alone. He has lost all his men. So leave off now, sir king, and this dreadful day of destiny will pass."

"Whether I live or die, I will have my revenge upon him. What better time than now?"

"Then God go with you," Sir Bedevere told him.

Arthur took up his spear and ran towards Mordred, crying, "Traitor! Your death day has come!"

When Sir Mordred saw Arthur rushing upon him he took up his sword, ready to defend himself. Arthur caught his son in the body below the shield, and his spear went through the flesh; Mordred, knowing that he had received his death wound, forced himself along the length of the spear in terrible agony. Then with his sword he struck a great blow against the side of the king's head, breaking his helmet and cracking his skull open so that the brain could be seen. After that stroke, Mordred fell dead to the earth.

Arthur collapsed in a faint to the ground. Sir Lucan and Sir Bedevere supported him, and with great effort they carried him to a little chapel on the seashore where he might rest.

While they remained there, they heard the shouts and screams of people coming from the field of battle. "What noise is that?" Arthur asked. "Sir Lucan, can you return there and report to me?" So Lucan, grievously wounded though he was, made his way back to the site of the struggle. By the light of the moon he could see clearly enough that robbers and rioters were looting the bodies of the dead and the dying. They stripped the armour and the jewels from the corpses; they took the rings from their fingers, and the saddles from their horses; they finished off those who were wounded, and fell upon them. When Lucan understood that this had become a place of pillage, he went back to Arthur and informed him of what he had seen.

"In my judgement," he said, "it is best that we take you to some town close by. You will be safer there."

"I am of the same opinion. But look at me. I cannot stand upright. My head is . . ." Arthur seemed to waver. "Ah, Lancelot! I have missed you this day! Why was I ever against you? Now I am close to my death, as Gawain warned me in a dream."

Sir Lucan and Sir Bedevere tried to lift up the king, but the effort was too great for Lucan. He fell in a swoon upon the ground, and his guts spilled from his body; then he died.

When the king saw that his follower had fallen, he set up a great lament. "Nothing but death and despair all around! He was so intent upon serving me that he did not save himself. He never complained, or cried out. Now Jesus have mercy on his soul." Bedevere was bowed over in grief, weeping at the death of his brother. "We must leave aside our mourning," the king told him quietly. "Weep no more, gentle knight. Tears will not help us. If I were going to live, I would cry for ever at the fate of Sir Lucan. But my time on earth passes quickly. I cannot stay. Therefore I beseech you to take my good sword, Excalibur. Here. Lift it up. I charge you to carry this sword to the lake that lies just beyond the edge of the forest. When you arrive at the lake, you must throw the sword into the water. Then come back and tell me what you saw and heard."

"My lord, I will obey your command and bring you word of what happens." So Sir Bedevere departed. On his way to the lake, however, he looked more carefully at Excalibur; he noted how richly it was decorated with precious stones on the pommel and upper guard. "If I throw this costly sword into the water of the lake," he said to himself, "it will be a great loss to the kingdom." So he hid the sword under a bush and returned to

Arthur. "I have fulfilled your order," he said. "I have dispatched Excalibur into the lake."

"Then what did you see?" the king asked him.

"Sir, I saw nothing but wind and water."

"You are lying to me. Go back to the forest and the lake. Take the sword and toss it into the water as I commanded you."

Bedevere returned to the forest and retrieved the sword. Yet he still believed it to be a sin, and an indignity, to throw away such an expensive and noble weapon. So he hid it within a hollow tree, and once again lied to Arthur. "So what did you see?" the king asked him again.

"I saw nothing, sire. Just the long lake beneath the sky."

Arthur rose up from his bed of suffering. "You are a false traitor to me, Bedevere. You have betrayed me twice. Who would believe that so dearly loved and cherished a knight would covet my sword? Will you deceive me for the sake of some jewels? Now return as quickly as you can. Take up the sword and throw it into the lake. Your long delay has brought me closer to death. I feel the cold coming upon me. If you disobey me again, I will kill you with my own hands."

Bedevere returned to the forest, took up the sword, and went with it to the water's edge. He wrapped the girdle around the sheath and hurled Excalibur into the lake as far as he might. Then a hand and arm rose from the water, took up the sword and brandished it; the hand waved the sword three times in the air, and then disappeared with it beneath the surface of the lake.

Sir Bedevere returned to the king, and told him what he had witnessed.

"Help me now," Arthur replied. "You must take me to the lake. My time has come."

Bedevere lifted the king upon his back, and carried him to the side of the lake. As they stood there a dark barge crept over the waters towards them; Bedevere saw that this barge held many fair ladies, three sovereign queens among them, all of them wearing black hoods.

"Now put me into the barge," Arthur told him.

Very gently he lowered the king into the craft, and the ladies received him with great mourning. The king lay down and set his head softly in the lap of one queen. "Ah, my dear brother," she whispered, "why have you waited so long to see me? The wound on your head is wide and cold." It was Morgan le Fay, his sister.

Thereupon they rowed the barge away from the land. Bedevere watched them depart, and cried out in grief, "Ah, my lord Arthur, what shall become of me? I am alone now among all my enemies."

"Comfort yourself," Arthur replied to him. "Trust in your own strength. Look not to me, for I can no longer help you. I must hurry to Avalon and be healed of my wound. If you never hear of me again, pray for my immortal soul."

The ladies wept and wailed as they bore Arthur away on his last journey. Bedevere, standing alone on the shore, cried bitterly at this parting. He took himself into the forest, and roamed among its trees all night.

In the morning he saw, half-hidden in some rocks, a small chapel and hermitage. He walked into the chapel, where he saw a hermit kneeling on the ground and weeping beside a freshly dug grave. He knew him at once to be the Archbishop of Canterbury, whom Mordred in his pride and anger had banished so many months before. "Tell me, father," he asked him, "what man is buried here? For whom do you pray?"

"Fair son, I do not know. I can only imagine. Last night, at midnight, some ladies came here bearing a body. They begged me to bury him, offering me a hundred candles and a thousand gold coins."

"You have interred your king. My lord Arthur is buried here." In his grief Bedevere fell down upon the floor. When he had recovered himself, he begged the hermit to let him stay as his companion. "I will never leave this place. I will kneel by the tomb in everlasting prayer."

"Welcome, sir. I know you already. I know you very well. You are Sir Bedevere the Bold, brother of the noble duke Sir Lucan." Then Bedevere told the good priest the story of Arthur's death and departing. He put on the clothes of a poor hermit, and from that time forward began a life of prayer and penance.

I have learned no more of the death of Arthur. The hermit himself did not know for certain that the tomb contained his body. Nothing is written in the old books of England, except for the fact that the king was carried across the lake in the company of three queens. One was the sister of Arthur, known as Morgan le Fay; the second was the queen of North Wales; and the third was the queen of the Waste Lands. Some say that the Lady of the Lake, Dame Nineve, was also with them;

but I have no sure proof of this. I have only the tale that Sir Bedevere has caused to be written. So I will leave him and the hermit, mourning by the sepulchre.

When Queen Guinevere learned that the king was dead, and that all his knights were killed, she rose up and with five ladies made her way to the abbey at Amesbury. She was professed, and took on the nun's habit of black and white; her life was spent in penance for her sins. And the people marvelled at her devotion.

Some men also say that Arthur is not dead, but by the will of Jesus Christ he will come to us again when we need him. I do not know. I will only say that here in this world he changed his life and that on his tomb at Glastonbury was written: HIC IACET ARTHURUS, REX QUONDAM REXQUE FUTURUS. That is to say: Here lies Arthur, the once and future king.

The Dolorous Death and Departing out of This World of Sir Lancelot and Queen Guinevere

Sir Lancelot had received the letter written by Gawain, and had learned of the treachery of Mordred. He was told, also, of Mordred's pursuit of Guinevere to the walls of the Tower. He summoned his knights, and angrily addressed them. "Now I know of the double treachery of Mordred. He has brought woe and wickedness into Arthur's land. This letter from Gawain — on whose soul God have mercy — tells me that the king is hard pressed on all sides. He has been betrayed by his own subjects. In this letter, too, Gawain begs me to visit his tomb. His sad words will never leave my heart. He was the noblest knight on earth. In an unhappy hour I was born, destined to slay Sir Gaheris, Sir Gareth and

412

now Sir Gawain. Why cannot I kill Mordred, who deserves to die?"

"Leave off your complaints," Sir Bors told him. "Your first task is to avenge the death of Gawain. You must visit his tomb, as he asks you. Then you must march against Mordred and fight for Arthur's sake as well as for the honour of Queen Guinevere."

"Your advice is sound and strong, Sir Bors. Let us make haste."

He marshalled his forces, and sailed with them over the sea to the shores of England. He had with him seven kings, and the sight of their armies was astounding. The people of Dover, however, cried out to him that he had come too late. They told him that both Arthur and Mordred were dead, having fought hand to hand, and that one hundred thousand warriors were slain on the field of battle. Sir Lancelot bowed his head. "This is the heaviest news that I have ever heard," he said to them. "It touches my heart. Grant me this favour, good people. Take me to the tomb of Sir Gawain."

So they brought him to Dover Castle, where the body of Gawain was buried. Lancelot kneeled in front of the sepulchre, weeping, and prayed for the soul of the noble knight. That night he proclaimed a great gift-giving. All those who came to the town would be granted fish and flesh, wine and ale, together with twelve pence. Dressed in a cloak of mourning, Lancelot himself distributed the pennies to the people. He wept, and urged them all to pray for the repose of Gawain.

On the next morning the priests and canons of the region assembled together for a solemn requiem. Lancelot paid one hundred pounds for perpetual masses to be performed in memory of the dead man; the seven kings each offered forty pounds, and a thousand knights each pledged one pound. So the soul of Gawain was secured.

Lancelot lay on the sepulchre for two nights, sighing and sorrowful. Then on the third day he summoned the leaders of his host. "My fair lords," he said, "I thank you all for accompanying me here. As you know very well, we have arrived too late. I will regret this all my life, but who can rebel against death? It must be so. But I will do this. I will ride to my good lady, Queen Guinevere, and try to comfort her. I have heard that she is in great distress, and that she has fled somewhere to the west. I will follow her. I ask all of you to wait here for my return; if I do not come back within fifteen days, then board your ships and unfurl your sails. Return to your own lands."

Sir Bors stepped forward. "It is not wise, sir," he said, "to ride alone through this realm. You will find few friends here."

"I know that. But I forbid you, or anyone else, to follow me. I must make my own way."

Lancelot would listen to no arguments. He mounted his horse, and for seven or eight days he rode westward. Then by chance he arrived at the nunnery of Amesbury, where Guinevere had been appointed as abbess. She was walking in the cloister when she saw him and, in her amazement, she fainted into the arms of the gentlewomen who attended her; they found it hard to keep her from falling on to the earth. When she had recovered from her swoon, she addressed them. "You may marvel, fair ladies, at my fainting fit. I have been surprised by the sight of the knight over there. Call him to me."

When he came into the cloister, she pointed to him. "Through the deeds of myself and this man, all the wars have risen in England. We are responsible for the deaths of the noblest knights in the world. Because of the love that this man and I shared, my most noble king and lord has been slain. Therefore, Sir Lancelot, know this. I have come to this place to do penance and prepare my soul. I trust through the grace of God to climb into heaven and see the face of Christ Our Saviour; on the day of doom, I hope to be seated on His right side. Sinners such as I have become saints in heaven. So, Sir Lancelot, I command you now to leave my company. I forbid you to see my face on this earth. Turn again and go back to your kingdom. Keep it safe from woe and warfare. I loved you well, in former times, but now I can no longer serve you. Both of us have been the ruin of knights and kings. I beg you now to return home, and take a wife who will live with you in bliss. Pray for me, Lancelot, and plead with God to forgive my sins."

"So, sweet madam, you would like me to go home and get myself a wife? No. It cannot be. I will never be false to you in this life. Instead I will pursue the same course as you have done, and put on the habit of a monk or hermit. I will pray for you day and night."

"Keep that promise, sir. Can it be true that you will never turn towards the world again?"

"Do you not trust my word? Have I not kept all my promises to you in the past? If you can forsake and forget the world, then so can I. In the days when I sought the Holy Grail, my sole weakness was my love for you. Otherwise, with clean heart and will, I would have passed all other knights in the quest. So, fair lady, I will follow you now in search of holiness. If you had retained any joy in earthly things, I would have taken you back to my kingdom. But I find you changed. I promise you, therefore, that I will dedicate my life to prayers and devotions. I will seek out a friar, and become his fellow. I will live in poverty, and do penance. Yet before I go, good queen, give me one kiss."

"No, sir. I will not do that. I ask you to leave aside such thoughts."

So they left one another, but with such long lamentations that all those around them began to weep. Lancelot cried aloud, as if he had been pierced by a lance. Guinevere swooned. And the good nuns carried the queen to her chamber.

Sir Lancelot rode away and, weeping, roamed through the wood all that day and night. By chance he came upon a chapel and hermitage, half-hidden between two great cliffs of rock, where he heard the mass bell ringing. He rode up, tied his horse to the wooden gate, and entered the chapel. And who did he find there but the holy hermit, once Archbishop of Canterbury, and Sir Bedevere? After the mass was over the two knights talked over the events of the time.

When Bedevere had told his story of Arthur's death and departing, Lancelot lay down upon the earth and wept. "Alas," he said, "who can trust this world?"

He kneeled before the archbishop, and begged to be confessed and to receive Holy Communion. He asked to become his brother in Christ. "I bid you welcome," the archbishop said. "You may serve with Sir Bedevere." He blessed him and clothed him in the habit of a hermit. So Lancelot served God, day and night, with prayer and fasting.

The great host of Lancelot's army remained at Dover for fifteen days before sailing back across the Channel. But Sir Bors and some other knights stayed in England, with the sole purpose of locating Lancelot. Then by good fortune Sir Bors rode the same way as Lancelot, and found the chapel between the rocks. He heard the mass bell, too, and after the service was over he begged the archbishop to enrol him in the same habit as Lancelot and Bedevere. He was joined here by seven other knights, who for six years lived in prayer and penitence.

After the years were over, Lancelot was ordained as a priest by the archbishop. He recited the mass each morning, with the other knights around him as his servers with bells and candles. They no longer considered themselves to be knights, and let their horses wander away in the wood at will. They had no regard for worldly riches, but reverenced only the kingdom of God. They grew thin and pale, but they were willing to endure pain for the sake of spiritual reward.

One night Lancelot was vouchsafed a vision. He was told to hasten to the abbey at Amesbury, where he would be granted full remission of his sins. "By the time you arrive there," the messenger told him, "Queen Guinevere will be dead. Take your fellows with you, and find a bier for her. You must then carry her body back with you here, to Glastonbury, and bury her beside her husband, Arthur." Lancelot was granted this vision three times that night and, in the morning, he rose up and told the archbishop.

"You must obey this summons," the archbishop said. "You must journey to Amesbury."

Lancelot took his companions with him, and they made their way on foot to the abbey. It was some thirty miles distant, but they were so weak and weary that it took them two days.

When they arrived at the abbey, they were told that Guinevere had died just half an hour before. The ladies informed them that she had prophesied their coming, and that she knew they were prepared to take her corpse to the tomb of her husband. The queen had said, in hearing of them all, "I beseech Almighty God that I may die before I see Lancelot again."

"And this," one of the ladies told them, "was her incessant prayer for two days before her death."

Sir Lancelot was taken to her bedside; he wept only a little, but he sighed very deeply. He performed the rites of the dead, and in the morning said mass for the sake of her soul. A horse-bier was brought to the abbey, and Guinevere was placed upon it. A hundred candles were lit around her, and the holy men offered up incense and

418

prayer as they carried the queen to Glastonbury. They sang hymns, and beat their breasts, as they made their slow way.

When they came to the chapel they were met by the archbishop and Bedevere singing "Dirige" with great devotion. On the following morning the archbishop, now hermit, performed a requiem mass in memory of her. After the service was over the queen was wrapped in thirty layers of waxed cloth; she was encased in a sheet of lead, and consigned to a marble coffin. When she was lowered into the earth, Lancelot lay still upon the ground.

The archbishop bowed over him and whispered in his ear, "This is unseemly. You displease God with so much excess of sorrow."

"I mean no dishonour," Lancelot replied. "I trust that God knows my intent. My sorrow was not, and is not, for earthly things that have passed. Yet when I saw Arthur and Guinevere lying here together, in death as they once were in life, my poor heart could not bear the burden of pity. I know too well that my own pride and anger have brought them to this place. They had no peers in Christendom, but my unkindness towards them has undone them. I cannot live. I have no right to life."

From that time forward Lancelot ate frugally of bread and wished only for a little water; he grew thin and frail, and so weak that few recognized him as the knight he once was. He slept fitfully, praying day and night; he would lie upon the tomb of King Arthur and

Queen Guinevere, calling out to Jesus Our Saviour. He could not be comforted.

Within six weeks he was sick unto death. His fellows brought him to bed, where he begged to be given the last rites. "Archbishop," he said, "I pray that you give me the grace owed to all Christian men."

"There is no need," the archbishop replied. "Your blood is sluggish. Nothing more. Once you have rest and nourishment, you will be well again."

"My fair lord," he said, "my time is past. My body longs for the earth. I have seen signs of the end. I will not live till the morning. So I ask you again. Grant me the gift of extreme unction." So Lancelot was confessed and anointed. He raised himself at the end of the ceremony and, calling the others to him, he spoke his last words. "Once I made an oath," he said, "that I would be buried at the castle of Joyous Garde. I do not wish to break my oath. So, I beg you, carry me to that place."

They all went to their beds heavy of heart that night, and lay themselves down in a single chamber. About midnight they were all awoken by the sound of laughter. The archbishop was laughing in his sleep. They woke him, and he sat up with a start. "Why did you wake me?" he said to them. "I was never so happy in my life." They asked him what he meant. "Sir Lancelot was here with me, but there were more angels around him than I could count. Suddenly I saw them lifting him into heaven, and the gates of the eternal kingdom were opened to welcome him."

"This is the delusion of a dream," Sir Bors said. "I am sure that, as we speak, Lancelot is on his way to recovery."

"It may be so," the archbishop replied. "Go to his bedside and see."

But when Sir Bors and the other hermits hastened to his side, they found him already lying dead. He was smiling, as if he had been surprised by joy, and there arose from his body the sweetest savour they had ever sensed. As dawn broke they were still kneeling in the chamber, their rough cloaks wet with their tears.

The archbishop celebrated a solemn requiem that morning, and the body of Lancelot was reverently placed in the same horse-bier that had borne Guinevere on her last journey. They made their way slowly towards Joyous Garde, with the body surrounded by a hundred burning torches, and after fifteen days they reached the castle. They laid Lancelot's corpse in the choir of the church there, singing psalms and prayers about the bier. According to custom his face was displayed to the people, as they came to say their devotions. And all who saw him wept. Sir Bors stood before the body, and spoke aloud. His voice rang through the church.

"Oh, Lancelot, you were the leader of all Christian knights! You were the most courteous knight who ever carried a shield into battle. No one was your match in might or mercy. You were the truest friend, and the most faithful lover, in all the world. You were the most devout of all warriors, and the most courageous. You were meek and gentle as a lamb with the ladies of the court; you were as stern and unyielding as a lion with the enemies of your kingdom!" There was deep wailing out of measure.

The corpse of Lancelot was displayed for fifteen days before it was prepared for burial beneath the floor of the choir. The archbishop then returned to Glastonbury with his followers.

Sir Constantine, son of Sir Cador of Cornwall, was chosen to be king of England. On his accession he sent for the archbishop, and returned him to his office. The knights who had remained at the hermitage with Lancelot dispersed into their own countries. King Constantine wished them to remain with him in his realm, but they were not willing to stay. They longed to be gone and, when they returned to their own lands, they lived as holy men.

Sir Bors and Sir Hector, however, rode out to the Holy Land where Our Saviour lived and died. They fought against the infidels, and won many victories over their foes. This is what Lancelot, before his death, had begged them to do. Both men died in the same battle, on Good Friday, in the service of Our Lord.